Praise for *White*

"... as in *White Tombs*, Valen writes well about St. Paul and surrounding areas. He gives just enough sense of place to make you feel like you're there, but he never loses track of his story's fast pacing. And he does a super job of keeping the suspense going as the action reaches a crescendo ... "
—*St. Paul Pioneer Press*

"... John Santana was introduced in Christopher Valen's first book *White Tombs*. This second book is just as exciting as the first and one that keeps the reader guessing right up to the final page. Either book can be read as a stand-alone, but I hope Valen brings us more stories involving Detective Santana."
—*Buried Under Books*

"The second John Santana St. Paul police procedural is a terrific thriller ... Christopher Valen provides the audience with his second straight winning whodunit."
—*Midwest Book Review*

Praise for *Bad Weeds Never Die*

Named Best Mystery of 2011 by Reader Views and Rebecca's Reads

"... *Bad Weeds Never Die*, the third of the John Santana novels, delivered on all fronts. Once again I enjoyed Mr. Valen's well-plotted and intriguing mystery for all the obvious reasons: flowing and well paced storyline, great dialogue, multi-layered and vivid characters, a great sense of place and time, relevant issues and believable events ..."
—*Reader Views*

"... This is the first of Valen's books that I have read in the John Santana series and surely will not be the last ... Valen's novel is gripping, fast-paced and will have you guessing until the end.

The characters are intriguing and there are many plot twists and turns. It is a true page turner in every sense of the word . . ."

" . . . The latest John Santana police procedural is an excellent investigative thriller as the two detectives methodically work a case that spins out of control with homicides. Readers will enjoy accompanying Santana and Hawkins as they follow twisted leads in Minnesota while John learns you can't go home in world filled with violent predators."

—Midwest Book Review

"Christopher Valen's third novel, Bad Weeds Never Die, continues the story of John Santana, a homicide detective in St. Paul, Minn., who was introduced in White Tombs, and whose story was continued in The Black Minute. The three novels are all great police procedural stories with a policeman who must follow the law, rely on his partner and collect evidence to solve the case . . . I have thoroughly enjoyed reading Christopher Valen's novels based on Detective John Santana, a character who lives by his wits and trusts his instincts, which serve him well in his dealings with the public, his department and the criminals he brings to justice."

—Bismarck Tribune

Also by Christopher Valen

White Tombs

The Black Minute

Bad Weeds Never Die

BONE
SHADOWS

A John Santana Novel

Christopher Valen

Conquill Press
St. Paul, MN

BONE SHADOWS

Conquill Press
387 Bluebird Alcove
St. Paul, MN 55125
www.conquillpress.com

Cover Design: Jeff Holmes

Library of Congress Control Number: 2012939830

Valen, Christopher

Bone Shadows: a novel / by Christopher Valen – 1st edition

ISBN: 978-0-9800017-5-4

Conquill Press/October 2012

Printed in the United States of America

10 9 8 7 6 5 4 3 2 1

For My Sister,

Judy

Chapter 1

A COOL MARCH WIND HELD THE SCENT of decayed leaves, moist earth, and the pungent odor of a decomposing body that had been pulled from the Mississippi River. Forensic techs had wrapped it in an unzipped body bag to retain any trace evidence. Then they had carried the body ten yards up a steep, stony riverbank to a level patch of brown grass, where they had placed it on a clean, white sheet under a crime scene tent.

St. Paul Homicide Detective John Santana could see that the man's ears had been partially chewed away by fish and crustaceans. White foam spilling out of the mouth had formed spongy, cloud-like puffs of mucus on his lips and nostrils. Santana noted the travel abrasions on the forehead, nose, and backs of the hands. The abrasions were consistent with a body that had sunk and drifted along the river bottom in the strong current, remaining submerged until bacteria in the stomach and chest cavity produced enough gas to float it toward the surface. He figured heavy clothing might have delayed but hadn't prevented the body from rising.

Reiko Tanabe, the Ramsey County Medical Examiner, knelt near the body bag and looked up at Santana through the water-spotted lenses of her round, wire-rimmed glasses. She was clothed in white coveralls detectives called a "bunny suit." SPPD was printed in large black letters on the back.

"Lividity is fixed," she said, pointing toward the pooling of blood in the head and neck. "The cyanotic color is due to the cold temperature of the water."

Santana knew that lividity would be most prominent on the head, neck, and anterior chest because of the semi-fetal position in the water. But the reddish violet marks on the skin appeared blotchy and were irregularly distributed, reflecting movement of the body in the currents.

When Tanabe opened one of the dead man's lids, the eye glistened, a sign that the vic had died in the water and not beforehand, on land.

She lifted each of the hands and examined them. The skin of the fingers, palms, and backs of the hands was blanched, swollen, and wrinkled, and had started to separate and peel off like a thin glove.

"All of the nails are either broken or torn," she said. "Probably broke them on the rocks trying to save himself."

Santana wondered what had happened before the man drowned. Had he somehow fallen into the river and been swept away by the current? Had he decided to take his own life and then changed his mind at the last moment? Had he been conscious when he went into the river, and if so, what had he been thinking in the final desperate seconds of his life as he clawed at the rocks and debris in the river? What thoughts had been racing through his mind as he sank beneath the surface, struggling to hold his breath?

"If he jumped from a bridge into water," Tanabe said, "I'll find fractures of the ribs, sternum, and thoracic spine, and lacerations of the heart and lungs when I open him up."

Santana had seen enough suicides by drowning to know that it was usually an orderly scene, with clothing removed and neatly folded.

"You want to hazard a guess as to how long the vic's been in the water, Reiko?"

She gazed at the river as though the answers to the puzzle of this man's death could be found in the swiftly moving current.

Sunlight had fallen victim to dark clouds that rolled across the late morning sky. It was only mid-March, but unseasonably warm weather had melted most of the winter snowfall, leaving flat, lifeless grass the color of a calcified bone.

Fifty yards to the west near a small parking lot, media vans sat behind temporary roadblocks on Shepard Road, while reporters and cameramen swarmed around broadcast equipment. Two news helicopters were circling over the downtown skyline and crime scene, the downdrafts of their blades sounding like scythes cutting through the air.

"Everything slows down in water-immersed bodies, especially when the water is this cold," Tanabe said. She felt the body and then looked up again. "No rigor. But in his struggle to stay afloat, he probably exhausted the supply of ATP in his muscles. That affects the TOD estimate."

She was referring to the amount of adenosine triphosphate in the muscles at the time of death. Without a supply of fresh oxygen, the muscles quit producing ATP, which caused the stiffening effect of rigor mortis.

"It's hard to tell how fat he was because of the bloating," she said. "And alcohol consumption and meals high in carbs can cause a quicker refloat." She paused. "Taking everything into consideration, including the decomposition, I'd say the body has been in the water ten days to two weeks. But it's only an estimate."

Tanabe removed her glasses and wiped the lenses on her sleeve, a sudden gust of wind snapping the canvas tent above her head as she glanced at the river.

Santana could see a foundry on the opposite riverbank, a tugboat towing a long barge, and the heavy concrete piers holding the Robert Street Bridge high above him. He heard the whine of a corporate jet flying low as it crossed the river and prepared to land at nearby Holman Field, the jet engines momentarily drowning out the buzz and chatter of police radios.

Tanabe looked at Santana again. "Someone could spot the body from the walking path if they were looking toward the water."

If the vic had not accidentally fallen or chosen to enter the water, he thought, there should be physical evidence proving that he had been forcibly drowned or killed before he was dragged or thrown into the river. But Santana doubted the forensic techs searching the area would find any evidence or witnesses.

"I believe he went into the water somewhere else, Reiko." He pointed to a rusted cable in the water used to anchor barges along the riverbank. It was hooked to a heavy chain that was fastened to a rusted post encircled with automobile tires. "The cable snagged the body, probably while it was floating down river in the strong current."

"How'd you know there was a body floating in the river?"

"I received an anonymous tip on my cell."

"Isn't that unusual?"

"Very," he said.

"The caller give you a name?"

Santana shook his head. "Sounded like he'd had quite a bit to drink and hung up when I asked. The ID came up unknown caller."

A small group of curiosity seekers stood behind a border of yellow crime scene tape strung between the lampposts along a wide asphalt path. Most were dressed in a light jackets and jeans, while others wore jogging outfits and had iPod buds in their ears. One man standing beside a blue metal sculpture of a *pez vela*, or sailfish—a gift from Manzanillo, Colima, St. Paul's sister city in Mexico—wore a long, wrinkled raincoat and a fedora, the kind seen in the old Hollywood movies. Santana remembered how popular the hats were in Colombia when he was growing up. The fedora appeared to be making a comeback with some of the younger generation seeking to be different, but the older man standing with the onlookers didn't appear to be a fashion trendsetter.

Tanabe pulled a water-soaked wallet out of the dead man's zippered jacket pocket and opened it. "His driver's license IDs him as Scott Rafferty. Twenty-three years old. St. Paul address." She handed the wallet to Santana.

The wallet contained twenty-seven dollars in cash, a debit card from Wells Fargo, a VISA credit card, and an auto insurance card from State Farm.

"Hey, John," she said. "Isn't there a detective in Narco/ Vice named Hank Rafferty?"

Santana peered at the driver's license for a long time, though he knew that staring at it wouldn't change the facts or lessen the shock. "Yeah," he said. "I think the vic is his son."

Death—Santana's constant companion—brought him abruptly, uninvited, into the lives of others. Two SPPD detectives, preferably one male and one female, were usually assigned to deliver the news of a death to the victim's family. Like soldiers assigned to a Casualty Notification Team, Santana never knew how the victim's parents or guardians would react.

But his mission remained clear. His job was to seek justice and to offer the grieving relatives the possibility—if not a guarantee—of a resolution. He was acutely aware that whatever he found in the course of his investigation might lead to further pain and grief, that others might be hurt by things he would learn. But nothing would deter him from seeking the perpetrator, no matter where the evidence led.

Kacie Hawkins, Santana's partner, had gone to Chicago to tend to her ailing mother, and the seven-member Homicide

Unit was stretched thin. So Santana called Rita Gamboni, the SPPD's Homicide Commander. She agreed to set up a meeting in her office that afternoon with Scott's parents, Hank Rafferty and Rachel Hardin.

Gamboni was waiting alone when Santana arrived. She had arranged four chairs in a small circle in front of her uncluttered desk, the arrangement designed to eliminate any power positions and encourage communication.

"I'm glad you got here before Hank and Rachel," she said.

"That was the idea."

"Would you like me to break the news?"

"Thanks, but I'll do it, Rita."

Like almost everyone Santana knew inside or outside the department, Hank Rafferty was not a close friend. But Santana remembered that Hank had been single for years after his first wife's death and had raised his son, Scott, alone. Then one year ago, after a brief courtship, Hank had married Rachel Hardin, a well-respected Ramsey County judge who was at least a decade younger. Six months after their marriage, Rachel had lost the child she was carrying.

Santana was about to select a seat when Hank appeared, his wide frame nearly covering the open doorway.

"You wanted to see me, Commander?"

Gamboni gestured for Rafferty to enter.

He stepped quickly into the office and then hesitated when he saw Santana, his dusty brown eyes suddenly wary, his hand clutching the doorknob. "What's going on?"

"Close the door behind you, Hank," Gamboni said.

He shut the door very slowly and then rested his back against it as if for support. "Has something happened to Rachel?"

Santana shook his head. "Not Rachel."

The blood drained from Hank's face, and he staggered toward Gamboni. "Oh, Jesus. Not Scott."

Gamboni stepped out from behind her desk, brushed a strand of white blonde hair off her forehead, and gave Hank a hug. In her one-inch heels, she was the same height as his five feet ten inches. As she rested her chin on Hank's shoulder, she squeezed her blue eyes closed in sympathy, as though absorbing his pain.

Hank broke the embrace and made his way to a chair, his upper body bent forward as though he were leaning into a stiff March wind. Gamboni sat beside him and directly across from Santana.

Hank placed his forearms on his thighs, his stomach sagging over his belt, and looked at Santana. "Are you sure it's Scott?"

"We're pretty sure, Hank. We found his driver's license in a wallet."

Hank's eyes looked at the floor and then back at Santana. "How did he die, John?"

Gamboni gently touched the sleeve of Hank's sport coat. "I think we should wait for your wife. That way John only has to go through it once."

Santana offered a sympathetic nod. He felt guilty for not responding to Hank's request and was grateful for Gamboni's intervention.

Hank loosened his tie, unbuttoned the top button of his white shirt, and sat back stiffly in his chair, his handsome face a mask of grief, his mouth a tight knot. He seemed to have grown suddenly older in the past year, as if his body was fighting a lingering disease. Gray streaks feathered his short, curly hair, and the lines at the edges of his eyes and around his wide mouth had grown more pronounced. His once muscular body seemed to have slackened and appeared as soft as an overripe fruit.

There was a knock on the door. Gamboni said, "Come in," and Rachel Hardin entered, carrying her 5' 5" frame with confidence and purpose, projecting an aura of unassailability and determination that many men found attractive.

Santana thought her chestnut hair was her best feature. It was thick and expertly cut along her firm jawline and never seemed to be mussed or out of place. Her fingernails were carefully manicured and polished, the light shade of pink matching the color of her lips. The makeup on her heart-shaped face was understated, and the expensive tweed suit she wore accentuated her shapely figure.

She acknowledged Gamboni and Santana with a brief, "Commander, Detective."

Santana recalled that she preferred to be called "Judge Hardin," both in and out of the courtroom, although most detectives and attorneys privately referred to her as "Hardcase," a nickname that applied to her demeanor in court, as well as the length of sentences she routinely doled out to convicted criminals.

She grasped her husband's big hand in hers as she sat down. "What's this meeting about?" she asked, the concern in her voice betraying her self-confident appearance.

Gamboni gave Santana a nod as a signal to begin.

"I'm afraid we've found your stepson's body this morning."

Rachel let out a gasp and covered her mouth with a hand.

"We're very sorry for your loss."

"What happened?" she said.

"Initial indications are that he drowned in the Mississippi River."

Hank shook his head in puzzlement. "That doesn't make any sense. Scott never liked being around water after he saw his mother drown."

Santana recalled reading an article in which near-drowning victims reported that their last thought before unconsciousness was imagining other people's reaction and feeling embarrassed

8

and ashamed for being so stupid, believing that smart people would be able to prevent their own drownings.

Hank looked at Santana steadily. "No marks on the body?"

"None that were visible. But that could change once the body dries."

Santana operated under the theory that all death scenes should be treated as homicides until the medical examiner declared otherwise. But he had no evidence yet supporting his theory, so he had to remain cautious while still open to the possibility. "Right now, I'm just trying to cover all the bases."

Hank nodded as if Santana's answer confirmed whatever suspicions he harbored in his mind.

Santana saw no point in debating the circumstances of Scott Rafferty's death, at least until he had the autopsy report in hand. But he needed to ask the next set of questions he had worked out in his head. So he pushed aside his concerns and hoped Hank wouldn't resent the bluntness of his questions. "Did your son drink, Hank?"

"Sure. But I've never seen him drink to excess."

Most parents Santana had met, like Hank Rafferty, had an unrealistic view of their children's habits. But Santana sensed that questioning his use of the word "never" would serve no purpose other than to provoke a needless confrontation. Still, he thought, his next question might do exactly that. "Was your son depressed?"

"I know what you're getting at, John. But no, Scott wouldn't commit suicide."

"But Scott *was* depressed, Hank," Rachel said.

"He was *not* depressed, Rachel." Hank's voice was tight in an obvious effort to control it, and he spoke with conviction and in a tone meant to remove any doubt.

Rachel Hardin removed her hand from her husband's and fixed her steely gray eyes on Santana, as she might a defendant in her courtroom. "Scott was seeing a psychiatrist," she said,

9

apparently unconcerned that her admission might further upset her husband.

Hank let out a short breath that was not quite a laugh. "So are you, Rachel. Does that mean you're depressed?"

Her jaw dropped, as though she were stunned by Hank's revelation and breach of trust. Her cheeks flamed, and for a second Santana thought she might slap her husband. As she glared at him, his gaze faltered, and he lowered his head in submission like a scolded dog.

"Your son was seeing a psychiatrist for depression?" Gamboni said, trying to redirect the conversation and defuse the sudden tension in the room.

Hank focused his eyes on Gamboni. "Scott was being treated for PTSD."

"At the VA?"

"No. In order to be treated there, he had to make a formal request. The whole process would have taken several months, and there was never any guarantee that his request would have been granted. And even if it were approved, there's a huge backlog at the VA." Hank shook his head in frustration. "Applying to the VA was far too complicated and stressful. We decided to help him pay for private counseling with a psychiatrist."

"And let's be honest," Rachel said. "Scott didn't want his psych reports made part of his military record."

Hank stared at her. "Who would?"

Santana wondered if Hank was making a thinly veiled reference about his wife's visits to a psychiatrist.

But before he could change the subject, Rachel said, "I believe Scott never got over his mother's death."

"That's not true," Hank said, only his voice was softer and lacking in conviction. He looked at Santana. "Scott served two tours in Iraq. He saw more than a young kid should see. More than any of us should ever see. That's why he sought help from a psychiatrist."

10

"Had anything else in his life changed recently?" Santana asked.

"He dropped out of the University of Minnesota," Rachel said.

"Do you know why?"

Rachel shifted her gaze to her husband. "Hank?"

He looked at his wife, but his eyes seemed unfocused.

"Detective Santana just asked you why Scott dropped out of school."

Hank's eyes drifted to Santana. They were as cloudy as the muddy Mississippi. "I don't know. I hadn't seen or spoken with Scott for a while."

Santana wanted to ask why, but he saw Hank's body suddenly stiffen as an undercurrent of reluctance formed in his eyes. Santana let him continue.

"Scott's a bright kid with a near genius IQ. He can do anything he wants."

Santana noted that Hank continued to speak about his son in the present tense, as if he were still alive.

Rachel shifted her gaze to Santana. "But he'd become more of a loner since he came back from Iraq."

"He had a lot to deal with, Rachel, a lot to work through."

"Maybe Kimberly has some answers," she said.

Santana took out his notebook and a pen. "Who's Kimberly?"

"Kimberly Dalton. She's Scott's girlfriend. She called a few nights ago and spoke with my husband."

Santana looked at Hank.

"She told me that she hadn't seen Scott for more than a week and was worried. I told her to file a missing person's report. I should've taken her call more seriously."

Given the condition of Scott Rafferty's body, Santana figured that no matter what Hank had done, it would have been too little, too late. But he wondered why Hank had taken the

11

call so casually, wondered if Hank and his son were estranged, and if so, why? "Do you have Kimberly's address?"

Rachel recited it to Santana, and he wrote it down. "What about Scott's friends?"

Rachel peered at Hank, who shrugged. "I don't know that he really had any close friends," she said.

"Somebody killed him," Hank said.

Rachel jerked as though startled by a sudden noise.

Santana stopped writing in his notebook. "What makes you think your son was murdered, Hank?"

"He had a job and was getting his life together. He told me his psychiatrist thought he was making good progress. He had no reason to commit suicide."

Santana suspected that nothing written in the autopsy report would change Hank's mind. Believing that his son was murdered allowed him to avoid any consideration of the unpleasant alternatives. Accidents and suicides were usually preventable, which meant the blame would be placed on the victim, or, as often was the case in suicide, the victim's family. By focusing his thoughts and anger on an unnamed predator, Hank had someone other than himself to blame, someone who could be held accountable for taking his son's life.

"When did you last speak to him?" Santana asked.

Hank thought about it. "I believe it was about ten days ago."

That fits with Tanabe's TOD estimate, Santana thought. "Do you have any idea why someone might want to harm your son?"

"Of course not," Rachel said. "He was a likeable kid."

Hank wrinkled his brow and looked at her. Santana could sense waves of anger emanating from Hank like heat off tar pavement. "That doesn't mean squat, Rachel. Likeable young men get killed all the time. You know that."

"So maybe it was a random killing," Gamboni said.

Santana figured neither speculation nor recriminations would get them anywhere. And at this point, he wasn't even sure it was a murder. "What psychiatrist was your son seeing?"

"Benjamin Roth," Rachel said. "His office is in Galtier Plaza."

"How long had he been seeing him?"

"For the past three months."

"Where was Scott working?"

"He drove a hearse for a mortuary," Rachel said, her tone suggesting it was the lowest rung of the occupational ladder.

Hank held his eyes on hers until she looked away. "It was temporary work," he said. "Scott was planning to return to school fall semester."

Santana thought it strange that a soldier who had recently been in combat and had experienced the sight of the dead first-hand would decide to drive a hearse for a mortuary. But everyone dealt with demons in his or her own way.

"You have the name of the mortuary?" he asked.

"It's the Lessard Mortuary."

"Had Scott expressed any concerns about someone following or harassing him?"

Hank shook his head. "If he was in any danger, he would have let me know." He gathered his thoughts for a moment and then continued. "My son was a tough kid, John. He never picked fights or looked for trouble, but he could handle himself."

Santana could see Hank's eyes beginning to fill with tears.

"He got along with everyone," Hank said.

Maybe not everyone, Santana thought.

13

Chapter 2

THAT AFTERNOON, SANTANA PARKED in the lot directly underneath the now-vacant Adult Detention Center and headed across the street to the Ramsey County Courthouse with its Art Deco, wedding cake design. He badged his way past security at the main entrance and walked to the elevators in Memorial Hall, near a thirty-six-foot-tall onyx statue. The Vision of Peace statue—depicting five Native Americans sitting around a fire smoking their peace pipes—was dedicated to Minnesota veterans. The names of the state's war dead from WWI through Grenada were inscribed in the black marble walls near the statue. The dead from Iraq and Afghanistan had not yet been added.

The recessed lighting, bronze railings and light fixtures, and gold-mirrored ceiling left him feeling as if he had stepped back in time. But metal detectors and security installed at each of the first floor entrances created small traffic jams and considerable noise in the hall—and reminded him of how times had changed under a threat of terrorism.

He rode an elevator to the tenth floor courtrooms, which were modeled after the British system. Attorneys representing each side—along with the plaintiff and defendant—all sat at one long, rectangular table.

Santana had to wait fifteen minutes until the duty judge assigned to criminal warrants was off the phone. Once he had a signature on the search warrant he had prepared for Scott Rafferty's apartment, he drove to the Macalester-Groveland neighborhood of St. Paul, known as "Tangletown." A sudden rain that drummed on the roof of the car and slithered like snakes on the windshield slowed him down.

Small Craftsman-style single and two-story bungalows with sloping roofs and dormer windows were interspersed with Tudor, Prairie Style, and Colonial Revival homes built prior to 1940. Several colleges and universities were located in the area, along with the St. Paul Seminary and numerous private high schools. This meant that many of the residents were students, professors, and working professionals.

The cedar-shingled carriage house Scott Rafferty had lived in consisted of a two-car garage on ground level and an apartment above it. Wooden stairs beside the garage led up to the door.

The rain lightened up as Santana got out of the Crown Vic and checked Rafferty's mailbox near the alley. The box was filled with junk mail except for two bills addressed to him from Citibank and Comcast cable.

"May I help you?"

Santana looked at a middle-aged woman standing under an umbrella. She had curious brown eyes, graying hair, and light skin freckled with age spots. "I'm Detective John Santana from the St. Paul Police Department." He showed her his badge and ID. "I'm investigating Scott Rafferty's death."

"Yes. I saw it on the news."

"Do you own the carriage house?"

She nodded toward the Tudor-style home in front of the carriage house. "My husband and I live in the main house. My name is Elaine Moore." She offered a small hand.

Santana was surprised by the firmness of her grip. "I have a warrant to search Mr. Rafferty's residence." He removed the warrant from an inner pocket of his sport coat, unfolded it, and handed it to her. She took it and looked it over.

"I'll need your signature," he said.

She lifted her eyes. "Do I get a copy?"

"Absolutely. And I'll also leave you an inventory of anything I seize from Mr. Rafferty's apartment."

She closed her umbrella and slipped it under an arm. "Do you have a pen?"

He handed her one.

"A young man drowning in the river like he did is a real tragedy," she said as she signed the warrant and returned it along with the pen.

Santana gave her a copy, but offered no comment. "When was the last time you saw Scott Rafferty?"

"Can't say as I remember exactly."

"Was it within the last week to ten days?"

"I don't think so. Mr. Rafferty kept pretty much to himself. Seemed like a nice young man, though. Always paid his rent on time."

"Did he have many visitors?"

"You mean outside of his girlfriend?"

"Yes. Outside of her."

"Well, I do remember seeing an odd-looking pickup truck parked in the alley a week or two ago. But I didn't see the driver."

"What do you mean by odd?"

She took some time before replying. "The truck was painted strange colors, like those clothes that hunters wear in the woods."

"You mean camouflage?"

"Yes. I don't think I've ever seen a truck or car painted that way before."

"Do you remember what time it was when you saw the truck?"

"I remember it was after dark because it was parked under the streetlight in the alley."

Santana gave her a business card. "If you remember any-thing else, Mrs. Moore, please give me a call."

"All right. I'll do that." She peered at the card. "You're a homicide detective? Was Mr. Rafferty murdered?"

"It's standard procedure to investigate any unusual death."

"Oh." She put his business card in a jacket pocket.

"I'd like to look at the apartment and then the garage. Did you share the garage with Mr. Rafferty?"

"My husband and I did. But he's gone for the day."

"That's okay. I'll start with the apartment first. I just need to get my briefcase out of the car."

Santana collected his briefcase and followed Elaine Moore up the wooden steps to the main door of the carriage house. Before she unlocked the door, he looked quickly for tool marks or a broken lock but saw no sign of forced entry. Then he knocked on the door to announce his presence.

"Why knock?" she asked.

"It's the law."

"Oh," she said, inserting a key into the lock when no one responded. "Is someone going to clean out the apartment?"

"Once I'm finished here, Mrs. Moore, I'm sure Mr. Raffer-ty's family will move everything. Can you make sure the side door in the garage is unlocked as well?"

"I will."

Santana thanked her and stepped into the large studio apartment.

He could not be certain that Scott Rafferty's death was an accident, nor could he assume that Rafferty had been killed near the river rather than here. So he treated the apartment as a possible crime scene. At first glance, it appeared clean and orderly. He saw no evidence that a struggle had occurred and no bloodspatter on the floors, walls, or ceiling. No shoe prints were visible on the floor, and he hadn't noticed any in the area immediately outside the apartment.

He detected the odor of cigarette smoke and fried food as he set his briefcase on the dark wood floor, which was mostly covered with area rugs. He could see a sleeping area at the far end of the living and dining area, an L-shaped kitchen with a full complement of appliances, and an open door that led to the bathroom. An old roll-top desk sat in one corner of the living room, which also contained a worn fabric couch, an easy chair, and a marred, rectangular coffee table. A movie poster from *A Few Good Men* featuring Tom Cruise, Jack Nicholson, and Demi Moore hung on a living room wall.

Santana opened his briefcase, slipped on a pair of latex gloves he kept inside, and checked the windows first, making sure all of them were closed and locked. Then he went through the desk drawers.

From the number of Garth Brooks, Brad Paisley, and Kenny Chesney CDs Santana found in one of the drawers, he figured Scott Rafferty was a country music fan. Rafferty's checkbook showed a balance of $500.18, with the last check written to Comcast Cable twenty-seven days ago. Inside a manila folder, he located Rafferty's AT&T mobile phone records. Over the last two years, Santana had noted that many people, especially those involved in suspicious or criminal activity, had requested that their phone company no longer include call details on the phone bills. He was glad to see Rafferty hadn't made that request.

There were four detailed pages contained in the most recent bill, and Rafferty had used nearly all of his 550 minutes. Santana had no way of knowing to whom the numbers belonged since only the city was recorded. One phone number consistently appeared on the list as both an outgoing and incoming call, and he wondered if it belonged to Rafferty's girlfriend, Kimberly Dalton. He wrote the number in his notebook and placed the phone logs in an evidence envelope. Then he searched the remaining drawers but found nothing else he deemed of evidentiary value in or on the desk.

Rafferty's queen-sized bed was neatly made, the wool blanket tucked so tightly under the mattress that Santana could have bounced a quarter on it. A set of dog tags was draped over the corner of the headboard, and a wood-bladed ceiling fan hung above the bed. An oak dresser with an attached mirror rested against one wall, a matching bookshelf against the opposite wall. A nineteen-inch flat screen television was centered atop the mostly empty bookshelf. A lone 5x7 gold frame without a picture sat on the dresser.

Santana found Scott Rafferty's Marine dress blue uniform and a tan battle dress uniform hanging in the closet over a pair of tan combat boots. Besides the uniforms, a white peaked service cap, and shiny black shoes, there were few clothes hanging in the closet and fewer still in the dresser drawers. Rafferty's socks were carefully rolled beside a pair of white gloves, and the few shirts he owned were neatly folded and arranged by color.

A clock on the nightstand showed the correct time. An ashtray next to the clock was filled with Camel cigarettes. He saw no lipstick marks on the butts.

Inside the nightstand drawer beside the bed Santana found a 5x7 photo of Scott Rafferty and a thin young woman he assumed was Rafferty's girlfriend, Kimberly Dalton. He wondered why Rafferty had put the photo in the drawer. He wrote the question in his notebook.

Next to a dollar bill rolled into the shape of a tube, he saw a piece of scratch paper with a phone number and the name *Devante* written on it. When Santana unfolded the dollar bill, he detected traces of a white, powdery substance he suspected was cocaine. He confirmed his suspicion by rubbing his index finger on the bill and then placing his finger on the tip of his tongue.

Santana knew it was not unusual to find traces of cocaine on US currency since it was easily bound to the green dye in money. Ninety percent of paper money circulating in cities contained traces of it. In the course of its average twenty months in circulation, currency could be contaminated with cocaine during drug deals or if a user snorted with a bill, which Santana believed Scott Rafferty had done.

He wrote the name *Devante* and the phone number from the scratch paper in his notebook and placed the contaminated dollar bill and the scratch paper in separate evidence envelopes.

Santana was well aware that the presence of a suicide note might or might not indicate an actual suicide because it only occurred in about twenty-five percent of the cases. Still, he kept his eyes open for one, though his intuition and Scott Rafferty's broken nails gave him the sense that his death was not intentional.

The trashcan in the bedroom was empty, so he moved on to the kitchen. There were no dirty dishes in the white porcelain sink. All flatware, cups, glasses and silverware were neatly stored in cabinets and drawers. The countertop was wiped clean. Underneath the sink, he located a box of garbage bags. He pulled one out of the box and unfolded it on the kitchen table. Then he carefully emptied the contents of a wastebasket onto the plastic, one item at a time.

There were used paper towels and Kleenexes, a coffee filter, and two empty cans of Budweiser. Underneath the cans in the wastebasket, he found what appeared to be a time-release capsule that had been broken open. He placed the beer cans and the broken capsule into separate evidence envelopes he retrieved from his briefcase and moved on to the dishwasher. Inside it, he found two wine glasses, one with a red lipstick stain along its edge.

After removing it from the dishwasher, he placed the glass carefully in an evidence envelope and went into the bathroom, searching for any evidence that someone had attempted to clean up after a crime. But the towels were dry and the bathroom neat. He opened the medicine cabinet above the sink, looking for a vial that might have held the empty capsule, but found nothing besides a toothbrush and toothpaste, shaving gear, cologne, and a box of Band-aids.

He made sure the door was shut on his way out before he went down the stairs and into the garage through the unlocked side door. A dusty brown Land Rover with rusted rocker panels was parked in one of the stalls. Santana opened the passenger side door and then the glove compartment, where he found a vehicle registration card listing Scott Rafferty as the owner.

He wondered if Rafferty had met someone here prior to his death. Given the lipstick stain on the wine glass, perhaps it was his girlfriend Kimberly. He searched the rest of the SUV but found nothing of evidentiary value.

Before leaving the premises, Santana used his cell phone to dial the number he had found on the scratch paper in the nightstand. He knew whoever answered the phone would only see UNKNOWN on the caller ID.

The phone on the other end of the line rang three times before a male voice answered, "Talk to me."

"Devante?"

There was a long pause before the voice spoke again. "You got the wrong number, bro."

The line went dead. But Santana recognized the voice of Devante Carter—a known drug dealer.

21

Chapter 3

SANTANA TOOK THE EVIDENCE ENVELOPES to the SPPD lab and, following the chain of custody, signed them over to Tony Novak, the SPPD's chief forensic analyst.

As Novak bent over a microscope on a long lab table in a room that looked like a high school chemistry classroom, Santana could see the perfectly round bald spot on the crown of his head, which was the source of Novak's nickname, "Monk." Novak looked up at Santana, pushing the dark frames of his thick glasses up the bridge of his wide, flat nose, a nose that had been busted more than once during his Golden Glove days. Under his open lab coat he wore a black T-shirt with the slogan YOU'RE NEVER TOO OLD TO LEARN SOMETHING STUPID printed in white block letters across the front of it.

"Hey, John. You see the Pacquiao and Clottey welterweight championship fight the other night?"

"I did."

"Pacquiao has seven titles in seven different weight divisions. No one has ever done that before. He has to be the best pound-for-pound fighter in the world."

"Floyd Mayweather may have something to say about that."

"Yeah. If he ever agrees to fight Pacquiao, we have to get tickets."

Novak was Santana's closest if still somewhat distant friend in the department. They shared an interest in boxing, a skill Santana had learned under the tutelage of Phil O'Toole, a SPPD homicide detective who had taken him in after he fled Colombia and the Cali cartel at the age of sixteen. Phil was retired now and lived in Santa Fe with his wife, Dorothy. Santana would always be grateful for their love, for the skills Phil had taught him, and for the encouragement both of them had given him. Channeling the anger he felt over his mother's murder into a physical sport like boxing and eventually into a career as a homicide detective had quieted the vengeful demon inside him and given him a purpose, a mission in life.

Novak had surprised him with tickets to the Manny Pacquiao/Miguel Cotto fight last November. They had flown to Las Vegas on Friday afternoon for the Saturday fight and had returned home Sunday evening without missing a day of work. Santana was not an avid gambler, but Novak had convinced him to try his hand at blackjack. Santana had won a hundred and twenty-five dollars, which he had promptly spent on dinner for the two of them.

Now, Santana set the evidence envelopes on a lab table. "See if you can collect some DNA samples from the lipstick on the wine glass and beer cans in these envelopes, Tony."

"Even if I'm able to extract a good DNA sample, John, I'm going to need an exemplar of the lipstick to make a comparison."

"I know. We'll worry about that later."

Novak nodded and peered at the remaining envelope in Santana's hand. "That all?"

Santana handed it to him. "There might be some latent prints on the broken capsule in this envelope. And I'd like to know what might've been in it. Though both tasks could be difficult."

"Since when have you ever asked me to do anything easy?"

"Good point," Santana said.

Kimberly Dalton was seated on the edge of a worn print couch in the living room of her apartment, her waif-like body barely making a dent in the cushion. Her long brunette hair hung like dark curtains along the side of her narrow, pretty face. She seemed to Santana a shorter version of a runway model. She wore no lipstick, but that didn't mean she *never* wore it.

"I'm sorry about Scott," he said.

She nodded and dabbed her large, doe-like eyes with the wad of Kleenex she clutched in the palm of one small hand. "I'm a bit confused, Detective Santana. I thought his death was accidental." She peered at the business card he had placed on the coffee table directly in front of her. "It says on the card that you're a homicide detective."

"That's correct."

"Do the police believe someone killed Scott?"

"I don't know, Ms. Dalton. My job is to make sure I have all the facts, all the details, so I can make a clear determination."

She sat quietly with her knees pressed together, her hands folded in her lap, the sleeves of her black cotton sweater pushed up on her forearms. A small silver locket shone on a thin chain against her chest where the neckline of her sweater formed a V. "I can't believe someone would murder Scott. I mean, why would they want to do that?" Her midnight blue eyes were like tiny puddles, and her voice was choked.

"You're getting ahead of yourself," he said. "Let's talk about what you specifically know first before jumping to any conclusions."

"All right."

Santana took out his notebook and pen. "How long had you known Scott Rafferty?"

Soft afternoon light filled the room. She gazed out the window, as though the memories and the possibilities she and Scott had shared were already fading like the daylight. "About five years."

"You were dating all that time?"

Her eyes returned to his. "Steadily for the last nine months," she said with surprising force.

Santana recalled the empty gold frame on Scott Rafferty's dresser and the photo of Rafferty and Kimberly Dalton he had found in Rafferty's nightstand. He wondered why Rafferty would take the photo out of the frame if he and Kimberly were still dating.

"How did you two meet, Ms. Dalton?"

She cocked her head. "Is that important?"

"The more I know about Scott, the better chance I have of understanding exactly what happened to him."

She looked at him silently.

Santana had spent hours of his life waiting while witnesses and suspects either tried to answer his questions to the best of their ability, or tried to avoid answering them altogether. But he never considered waiting a waste of his time. Good detective work required patience.

"I first met Scott when our fathers became partners," she said.

"Your father works for the police department?"

"Yes. David Dalton. Do you know him? He works in the Gang Unit."

"I've met him." Santana hadn't made the connection when he first heard Kimberly Dalton's name. Now he wondered why Hank Rafferty had failed to mention that his son was dating his former partner's daughter.

She glanced at the 8x10 photo on an end table of Scott Rafferty in his Marine dress blue uniform.

"Tell me about the last time you saw Scott."

She inhaled and then let the air out slowly. "It was ten days ago. We were having drinks at Billy's Tavern on Grand Avenue."

"Just the two of you?"

"No. Jeff Tate was with us."

He could tell by the frustrated tone of her voice that she seemed unhappy Tate was there. "How do you know Mr. Tate?"

"Scott introduced us. Jeff works as a bartender at Billy's."

"Was Tate working that evening?"

"No. He was drinking with Scott."

"Did you go to Rafferty's place before you went to Billy's?"

"No. I met him there."

"Do you know if he drove to Billy's?"

"I assume he did."

"What happened the last night you saw him?"

"Nothing unusual. At least while I was there. I had to work, so I left at nine-thirty."

"You didn't go to Scott's apartment later that night?"

She shook her head.

"Where do you work?"

She sat quietly, her eyes distant and unfocused. Finally she said, "I'm an RN at Regions Hospital. And I was drinking Diet Coke that night, not alcohol."

Santana gave her an understanding nod. Outside the living room windows he could hear the scream of a distant siren. "What about Scott?"

"He and Jeff ordered a pitcher of beer."

"Was Scott drunk?"

"No. He wasn't a heavy drinker."

"And after you left the bar that night, you never heard from Scott again?"

She shook her head.

"Did you notify the SPPD that he was missing?"

"Not right away. I was working a rotating shift and had to work again at three that afternoon. Scott usually worked from eight to four or nine to five. Sometimes we didn't see each other for a week or more."

Santana detected a trace of anger in her voice. "So not seeing each other for a while was not unusual."

She nodded. "Scott's boss left a message on my voice mail asking if I knew where he was. I tried calling and left messages on Scott's cell phone but got no reply."

Santana recited the cell phone number he had written in his notebook. "Is that your cell number?"

"Yes," she said. "How did you know?"

"Rafferty's AT&T bill."

"Of course. You would be looking at that."

Santana remembered that she had called Scott Rafferty at least twenty or more times. "What did you do when you didn't hear back from Scott?"

"When I didn't hear anything, I phoned Scott's father. He said he hadn't seen Scott and advised me to file a missing person's report."

Santana wondered why Hank hadn't been more concerned about his son. "Did you do that?"

"Yes. But nothing came of it."

Santana wrote the information in his notebook while she wiped her eyes with a fresh Kleenex. "Are you all right?"

"No," she said.

"Would you like me to come back another time?"

She inhaled deeply and let out a breath. "I'm fine. Just give me a minute." She wiped her eyes again and said, "Okay."

"I understand Scott drove a hearse for the mortuary."

"You've spoken with Hank and Rachel."

"Yes."

She closed her eyes for a long moment, as if she were reading something on the back of her eyelids. Santana had wit-

27

nessed habitual eye closing before when conducting an interview or interrogation, or when he was merely having a conversation with someone. It could mean that Kimberly Dalton was trying to shut out the world and the terrible tragedy that had recently befallen her boyfriend. She could be a visual thinker who closed her eyes sometimes when talking so she could better see internal images without external distraction. But it could also mean she was avoiding eye contact for some specific reason.

"Did your parents disapprove of your relationship with Scott Rafferty?"

"My mother was fine with it," she said.

"Why not your father?"

She shrugged her shoulders. "You'll have to ask him."

"How did Scott's father feel about your relationship with Scott?"

"Same scenario."

"So both fathers disapproved of the relationship."

"I guess," she said.

"And you don't know why?"

She closed her eyes briefly before she replied, "I don't."

"What about Rachel Hardin, Scott's stepmother?"

"I really don't know her well. But if she cared, she never said anything."

Santana had one more question before he moved to another subject. "How does your father get along with Hank Rafferty?"

"I don't think they do. Not anymore."

"Do you know why?"

She shook her head.

Santana recalled that Hank Rafferty and David Dalton had been partners when they worked in the Gang Unit, before Hank transferred to Narcotics and Vice. He had heard of no animosity between the two detectives. If they had been at odds with one another, rumors would have spread like a virus through the ranks of the SPPD. If something personal had caused their breakup, maybe both detectives had a strong motive for keeping it quiet. Santana made a note to check and moved on.

"Had you noticed any change in Scott's behavior recently?"

"Oh, no," she said much too quickly.

Santana had found no suicide note in Rafferty's apartment, though he had sensed from the very beginning of the case that the young man had not taken his own life. Still, he had to ask the question.

"Did Scott ever talk with you about suicide?"

The flicker of recognition in her eyes was like a match lit in a darkened room. She lowered her gaze. "I don't believe Scott killed himself."

"But he did talk about it."

Her eyes shifted back to his face. "Because he talked about it doesn't mean he would do it. Besides, he had a reason to live."

"What was that?"

Her cheeks colored. "We were in love and planning to marry." Tears welled up in her eyes and she wiped them with the Kleenex.

"Can I get you a glass of water?"

She shook her head.

Santana let some time pass before proceeding with his questions. "Did Scott ever speak with you about his mother's death?"

Kimberly Dalton inhaled several times and let each breath out slowly, like a diver about to enter deep water. "No. But I was aware he was seeing a psychiatrist."

"About his experiences in Iraq?"

"Yes. He had nightmares."

"Often?"

She nodded. "Sometimes they were really bad."

Santana knew all about nightmares and the terror they could cause. "Did therapy help him?"

"He seemed to be happier and not so depressed all the time."

"Was he taking any prescription medication?"

"Yes, he was. But then he stopped."

"Do you remember what medication?"

"Inderal."

"Why would he stop taking it?"

She shrugged. "I don't know."

Santana wanted to catch her off guard with his next series of questions so he could watch her reactions. "Were you aware that Scott was using cocaine?"

Her pale cheeks colored again, and she averted her eyes. "Why do you think that?" Her voice was weaker now.

Santana answered her question with one of his own. "Do you know a man named Devante Carter?"

"No."

"Did Scott ever mention his name?"

"He may have."

Santana fixed his eyes on hers. "Do you use cocaine, Ms. Dalton?"

"What has that got to do with Scott's death?"

"Maybe nothing," he said. "Or maybe something."

"I've tried it."

"Were either of you addicted?"

She looked directly into his eyes. "Absolutely not."

The Preliminary Report regarding Scott Rafferty's death wasn't intended to be a complete record, and since Santana knew little about the manner of death at this early stage of the investigation, most of what he wrote was guesswork. No witnesses had come forward, but he hadn't expected any. He believed that if there had been a crime, it had occurred in a location other than where Scott Rafferty's body had been found.

After completing the report, he drove to the renovated brick house he called home. It sat on two heavily wooded acres of birch and pine on a secluded bluff overlooking the St. Croix River, which formed the boundary between Minnesota and Wisconsin. He had purchased the house for a song from a gourmet chef who was involved in an ugly paternity suit. The price of the house had doubled during the housing boom, and then had lost a third of its inflated value when the economy tanked. Still, Santana knew he had gotten a good deal—or at least a better deal than the chef.

Most of all he appreciated the privacy, the fieldstone fireplace, the vaulted beam ceiling, and the deck off the master bedroom upstairs that offered a clear view of the river. He didn't mind the twenty-five minute drive into St. Paul, except in winter, when the travel time often doubled.

He changed into a pair of Nike shoes and a blue jogging suit with zippers at the ankles and an orange Day-Glo stripe down the leg. Before leaving, he armed the security system, and then he took his golden retriever, Gitana, or "Gypsy" in Spanish, out for a run. Because he was often at work for extended periods, he had installed an electronic doggy-door in a wall and a computer chip in her collar, which gave her access to the dog run he had built in the back yard. But she still looked forward to the time with him.

They ran together along the flat tar road that paralleled the river, Santana's Glock 27 comfortably resting in the Kydex kidney holster strapped to his waist. He never left the house without his compact Glock or the slightly larger SPPD standard issue Glock 23. He wasn't paranoid by nature, nor did he feel that carrying a gun enhanced his masculinity. The Cali cartel had tried to kill him on more than one occasion, and he knew they would never stop trying until they succeeded. He believed in being prepared.

It was six o'clock in the evening, and darkness was already settling slowly over the landscape, as though a heavy shroud were being pulled across the sky. The sharp edge of winter still cooled the air.

After the first mile, sweat had loosened his muscles, and Santana picked up the pace. As he ran, he recalled the strained conversation he'd had with Hank Rafferty and his wife, Rachel Hardin. Because both Santana's parents had been killed while he was in his teens, he understood how devastating the unexpected loss of a loved one could be. Still, he wondered if the tension he had sensed between the two of them was due to a marriage based on necessity and appearance rather than love, or if the tension was based on something else.

When he returned to his house, Santana went to a main floor bedroom, which he had converted into a workout room. He did one hundred sit-ups followed quickly by three sets of bench presses and curls. Then he put on a pair of Everlast bag gloves and hammered the heavy bag with combinations of jabs, straight rights, and hooks. Thoughts of his own near drowning experience during a previous investigation bubbled to the surface of his mind as he shuffled around the bag, turning his shoulders, getting his whole body behind each punch, keeping his feet the same distance apart and his weight balanced.

He remembered struggling to hold his breath in the confined space of a water pipe, feeling as though his lungs were expanding to the point where they would explode, wondering if the calming vision he saw of his sister's face would be his last thought before his mouth burst open in a futile search for air. As with Scott Rafferty, loss of consciousness and death would have occurred within two to three minutes. Santana knew it would have been a helpless, terrifying way to die.

22222222222222222

He moved to the speed bag, hitting it rapidly with the front of one fist, then the side, then the front of the other fist, then the side, left and right, making the bag dance against the backboard, varying the rhythm, trying to shake the dark images and thoughts clouding his mind, until he was drenched in sweat. His workouts were as much about mental health as exercise. He had learned in his years in homicide that by focusing his mind on the precise details of his exercise routine, he was often able to break through the dam of decomposing bodies and faces that blocked the flow of ideas and prevented him from solving the case. But he also knew that intense physical exertion helped keep the demon at bay. It had reared its ugly head when he was sixteen, murdered his soul, and haunted his dreams for years.

He finished off his workout with ten minutes of jumping rope. Then he took a long, hot shower, followed by a burst of cold water. As he toweled off he looked at his reflection in the mirror above the bathroom sink. The chest wound he had received in a previous case had healed, leaving a circular, pinkish scar. Occasionally, he felt a burning sensation when he exercised, as though the hot bullet was again coring through the soft tissue surrounding his heart. The dark whiskers that shadowed his face even after a close morning shave were more evident now, but his ice blue eyes were clear and full of energy. He rubbed a towel through his black, wavy hair, which he preferred to keep a little longer in the cooler months.

He put on a pair of Levi's, deck shoes, and a sweatshirt and went downstairs to the kitchen, where he opened a package of *Moros y Cristianos*. As he poured the contents of black beans and rice into a cooker and added water and olive oil, he wondered in this age of political correctness if the Nueva Cocina Company in Miami had ever considered changing the name of their black beans and rice product to something other than Moors and Christians.

While the rice cooked, he poured an inch of vegetable oil into a deep fryer on the counter and waited until it was hot. Then he fried the *patacones* he had purchased the previous day at the El Burrito market on St. Paul's West Side until they were golden brown on both sides. He removed them from the fryer, let them drain on a paper-towel-covered-plate, and sprinkled them with salt. His remembered that his sister, Natalia, used to eat *patacones* with a thin slice of *queso blanco* on top, but he preferred to eat them without the salty white cheese.

He fixed a cup of hot chocolate using a portion of the sugarless dark chocolate he had brought back to the States with him during a recent visit to Colombia, a visit that had nearly cost him his life. Santana enjoyed the chocolate here, but nothing he had found could match the taste of the chocolate made by the Luker Company in his city of birth, Manizales, Colombia.

After dinner, he read a few more chapters of an interesting and well-written biography about Colombian writer Gabriel García Márquez, before the stress of the long day and the exertion of his workout forced him to bed. But he slept fitfully, his dreams punctuated by thoughts of his mother's murder, and the night he had fought for his life in a rainy forest in the mountains of Colombia, a forearm pinned against his throat, the blade of a knife glinting in a flash of lightning that veined across a black sky.

He awoke in a cold sweat to the ringing of his landline. It was after midnight. He took two deep breaths to calm his racing heart before picking up the phone. "Hello?"

"Detective John Santana?" The male voice was low and raspy, as though the speaker had a mild case of laryngitis—and it sounded very much like the voice that had told him where to find Scott Rafferty's body.

"Yes."

"I wanna talk to you."

The words were slurred. It was obvious that the man had been drinking or was heavily medicated. "Go ahead."

"Not on the phone."

"And why should I take the time to meet with you?"

"Because I can tell you who killed Scott Rafferty."

There was a loud crash as if the phone had been dropped —and the line went dead.

Chapter 4

THE FOLLOWING MORNING SANTANA attended
Scott Rafferty's autopsy. Then he called
Devante Carter's parole officer to find out where Carter lived.
He was surprised to learn that the parolee worked as a custo-
dian at the Lessard mortuary, Scott Rafferty's former place of
employment. But the more Santana thought about it, the more
he realized it made sense. While they were working at the mortuary, Scott Rafferty could easily have acquired cocaine from a
known drug dealer like Carter.

A gray blanket of clouds covered the city as Santana drove
to the mortuary located in a large, two-story, Romanesque mansion with deeply recessed windows, two gabled dormers in the
hipped roof, and a tall tower with a conical roof. Santana parked
his Crown Vic beside a black van under a porte cochere supported by thick piers. Written in large white letters on the sides
of the van were the words VAIL BIOMEDICAL RESEARCH
and a phone number with a St. Paul area code. The March wind
was swirling out of the north, the dry leaves blowing across the
dead grass and dancing on the hard pavement.

He went into the building through a heavy wooden door
that set off an entry chime. The open double doors to his right
led to a chapel. Straight ahead was a long center hallway covered with wine-colored carpet. There were French provincial
couches and chairs on each side of the hallway, expensive-
looking oil paintings on the walls, Tiffany lamps on end tables,

and vases filled with flowers sitting on coffee tables. Hidden speakers pumped soft, relaxing music into the incense-scented air. *Business must be good*, Santana thought.

He held up his badge wallet as a lean man of medium height approached. The man wore an expensive-looking, black, pinstriped suit, white shirt and burgundy tie with a perfect Windsor knot. He had thick black hair and exceptionally smooth white skin that was tight against the bone, as if he had a mask pulled over his face. Although the man looked to be in his early thirties, Santana wondered if plastic surgery had knocked at least ten years off his appearance.

"Can I help you?" He smiled faintly, a suggestion that he really wasn't all that thrilled to help Santana after all.

"I'm looking for Devante Carter."

"Is there a problem, Detective . . ." He leaned his head forward and squinted at the badge wallet ". . . Santana?"

"And you are?"

"William Lessard."

Santana slipped the badge wallet into the side pocket of his sport coat. "Is Carter here?"

"Yes, he is. Can you tell me what this is about?"

"I'm afraid I can't."

Lessard nodded slowly and considered Santana's response. Then he said, "Some of my employees are ex-cons. I give them a second chance. Most of them take advantage of it. Some, unfortunately, don't." He spoke rather slowly and precisely, enunciating the consonants at the beginning and end of each word, in a voice that was soft and breathy.

"Scott Rafferty worked here as well."

"Is that what this is all about? Scott Rafferty's unfortunate death?"

Santana said nothing.

Lessard made a come-along gesture with a long-fingered, feminine hand with buffed fingernails. "Why don't you wait in the arrangement room, Detective Santana, while I summon Devante?"

He led Santana to a room in the back of the building where there was an oval table with a shiny black finish and six dining chairs upholstered with a striped chenille fabric. The glass shelves on the walls were filled with examples of guest books, photos of expensive-looking coffins, decorative cremation urns, and elaborately carved boxes.

The room reminded Santana of a similar one in Aparicio's Funeral Home in Manizales, Colombia, where he and his mother had gone to make arrangements for his father's burial. The pointless death at the hands of a drunken driver when Santana was fourteen had loosened the bond that held him to his Catholic faith; his mother's death two years later had severed it completely.

Devante Carter shuffled into the room, his baggy jeans low on his waist, his Twins cap crooked on his head. He lowered himself into a chair opposite Santana and rested his forearms on the table, his skin nearly as black as the tabletop, the white T-shirt with the cut-off sleeves revealing well-defined arms typically found in ex-cons who had spent most of their hard time lifting weights.

"Long time no see, Santana." Carter emphasized each of the three syllables in Santana's name.

Carter had supposedly cut his drug-dealing ties with the East Side Boys and had served as an informant in a previous homicide Santana had investigated. But Santana had never really trusted him, despite Carter's pleas that he had changed his ways.

"I understand you've been working here since you were paroled, Devante."

He gave Santana a wide grin, his bright white teeth shining like polished bone. "Been a year now."

"You work days?"

"Nights mostly. I just workin' the day shift this week while a man's on vacation."

"You enjoy the work?"

"Everything all good, my man. I straight."

"Really?"

He nodded enthusiastically. "Ax me anything. I got nothin' to hide."

"Tell me about Scott Rafferty."

His one-hundred-watt grin dimmed to fifty. "I seen the ghetto bird flyin' around the river yesterday and figured somethin' was up."

"What about Rafferty?"

"What's to tell, man? Other than he dead."

"Let's start with why he had your cell number in his apartment."

Carter's dark eyes—barely visible through heavy, lowered eyelids—darted like bugs seeking light. "You found my number in Rafferty's apartment?"

Santana pushed the scratch paper with the phone number across the table. "That your cell number, Devante?"

He glanced at it. "Must've been you that called earlier, huh?"

"Must've been you that hung up on me."

"Lotta telemarketers tryin' to sell me shit. Know what I mean?"

"But you're not selling anything."

"You got that right. I get caught sellin', I goin' down for the count."

Carter was practiced enough in lying that he knew how to disguise his tells and mannerisms. But Santana noted that he hadn't given a direct answer to the question. He decided to squeeze Carter some more and see what came out.

"Why would Scott Rafferty have your cell number?"

"We work together."

"So you were close friends."

"I seen him around here. That's it. 'Sides, lots of peeps got my number. It don't mean jack."

"Oh, I think it does mean something, Devante. And if Rafferty's autopsy report shows there was cocaine in his system, you can bet I'll be paying you another visit."

Carter waved his hands. "Hey, don't get all twisted on me, Santana. Maybe Rafferty be in the wrong place at the wrong time and got assed out. That ain't my fault."

"Why would anyone want to kill him?"

Carter's eyes slid away. "Got me, man. But leave me your digits. I hear anything, I call you. I gotta bail now."

Santana handed Carter a business card. "Stay in touch, Devante."

Carter stood and slipped the card into a front jeans pocket. "No problem."

"Tell Lessard I want to see him."

"You got it, man."

Carter shuffled out of the room and closed the door behind him.

Two minutes later, William Lessard came into the room and sat in the same chair where Carter had been sitting. "You wanted to see me?"

"Tell me what you know about Scott Rafferty."

Lessard set his elbows on the table and tapped his pursed lips with an index finger, as though he were contemplating. Engraved on the head of a ring he wore on the third finger of his right hand was the image of a serpent eating its tail.

"I received a phone call some months ago from Hank Rafferty," Lessard said. "Hank told me his son was having trouble finding work and wondered if I had any jobs available."

"How do you know Detective Rafferty?"

"As I told you, I often hire ex-cons. A few of them have had dealings with Detective Rafferty."

"And that's how you two met?"

"Yes."

"How well did you get to know Scott Rafferty?"

Lessard leaned forward and clasped his hands on the table. "He was a quiet individual. He came to work on time and did what was asked of him. I certainly had no problems with him."

"Did he perform any duties besides driving the hearse?"

Lessard shook his head. "That was pretty much the extent of it."

"What did he do when he wasn't driving?"

"Well, as we say in the business, death never takes a holiday. Working as you do in homicide, Detective Santana, I'm sure you understand that unfortunate reality." He smiled, revealing teeth that were small and rather sharp. He added a wink, as though sharing a secret between friends.

Santana looked at him without expression.

Lessard's manner quickly turned serious again. "We keep very busy here, Detective. When Scott wasn't driving bodies to funerals, he was picking them up from hospitals, nursing homes, and from the medical examiner's office."

"You provide burial and cremation services?"

"We do. But along with the traditional form of cremation, we're one of the few mortuaries that uses the newest process called alkaline hydrolysis."

"What's that?"

"Bodies are placed in a stainless-steel cylinder similar to a pressure cooker. Lye is added and water heated to three hundred degrees and sixty pounds of pressure per square inch."

"You're using lye to cremate people?"

"I know it sounds unusual. But it's legal in Minnesota and very environmentally friendly. More and more families are opting for this method of cremation once we explain the pollution-free benefits." Lessard gazed at the photos of coffins on the glass wall and then turned his face to Santana again. "If you have some time, Detective, I could show you the cylinder."

Santana wanted to take a look around, so he agreed.

Lessard led the way out of the office and down a set of stairs to the basement. As they walked down a long corridor with a cement floor, Santana saw a tall man using a key card to open a wide door marked EMPLOYEES ONLY. The man wore a green splatter gown over khaki pants and a blue denim shirt with the sleeves rolled up over his elbows. Directly below the large lettering on the door was a square red sign with black lettering warning that protective clothing had to be worn inside the room.

"This is Ronald Getz," Lessard said, gesturing toward the man.

Getz offered a nod instead of a handshake. At 6' 4" he was a good two inches taller than Santana. He had the same color of black hair, but he had a widow's peak with the hair receding substantially on either side of the peak, a dark mustache and goatee, a hawk nose, and a hard, bony face. Santana remembered his mother calling men with hard faces *caraconcha*, or shell face.

"What is it you do here, Mr. Getz?" Santana asked, recognizing the sharp odor of embalming fluid that clung to Ronald Getz like cheap cologne.

Getz's right eye roamed over Santana's face, but his left never made eye contact. Santana suspected it was made of glass.

"Ronald works part time for us and for Vail Biomedical," Lessard said before Getz could respond.

"Been working here long?"

"Not long," Getz said in a deep, resonant voice.

Santana noted the spider web tattoo on Getz's left forearm, a tattoo commonly found on ex cons and white supremacists. On the opposite arm, Getz wore what appeared to be a medical bracelet.

"I'm sure Ronald has much to do," Lessard said.

As if taking a cue, Getz went inside and closed the door behind him.

"Big man," Santana said to Lessard.

"Yes, he is," Lessard said, signaling Santana to follow. They walked to the wide door of a white-walled room that smelled strongly of ammonia. It was bare except for a long, stainless steel cylinder with a hatch at one end that allowed a body to be slid into it. The cylinder sat directly over a large drain grate in the tile floor.

"The odor you smell is from the residue," Lessard said.

"Residue?"

"Once the cremation process is completed, there is a brownish, syrupy residue with the consistency of motor oil that's flushed down the drain."

"Everyone okay with that?"

Lessard shook his head. "Some believe that flushing a portion of human remains down a drain is undignified and a sin. But the idea is gaining acceptance with each passing year. The Mayo Clinic in Rochester has used alkaline hydrolysis to dispose of cadavers for the last five years. Veterinary schools, universities, pharmaceutical companies, and the US government also have been using the process."

"Are the costs the same?"

"An alkaline hydrolysis operation is more expensive to set up than a traditional crematorium, but we charge customers about the same. What we end up with in both processes are some bone shadows."

"Bone shadows?" Santana said.

"Calcium phosphate, which makes up about seventy percent of the mass of bones and teeth. It's soft and easily crushed into powder and given to the family."

Santana nodded.

Lessard reflected a moment. "It's always good to plan ahead, to make the necessary arrangements. Too many people fail to plan for their death even though we all know that it's inevitable. Have you made arrangements for the disposal of your remains, Detective Santana?"

"I have."

Lessard smiled without much pleasure, his dark eyes as vacuous as a shadow. "It's good to be prepared. I mean, a man in your line of work. You never know when something tragic might happen."

Chapter 5

WHEN HE LEFT THE MORTUARY, Santana ran a check on Ronald Getz using the Crown Vic's mobile computer system. The computer was connected to the statewide Law Enforcement Message Switch, which was connected to the FBI's National Crime Information Center HotFiles. Santana wasn't surprised to learn that Getz had done a three-year stretch in Stillwater prison for second-degree assault. The criminal sentence had been discharged once he had served his time and completed his parole. Santana wrote down the information in his notebook. Then he drove to Billy's Tavern on Grand Avenue.

Jeff Tate had been drinking with Scott Rafferty the last time Rafferty had been seen alive, and Santana wanted to know how much Tate remembered about that evening. But Tate wasn't working. The only relevant information Santana acquired from the manager was Jeff Tate's home address, and the fact that he often volunteered at a homeless shelter on University Avenue. Santana gave the staff business cards and requested a phone call if they remembered something. Then he climbed back into the Crown Vic, entered Tate's address into the GPS, and headed for the city of Stillwater, a thirty-minute drive from St. Paul.

Just north of Stillwater, Santana turned off a two-lane blacktop and followed a narrow dirt road a quarter mile till he came to a NO TRESPASSING sign attached to a barbed wire fence. He ignored the sign and continued through an open gate and along a road that was pitted with potholes and flanked by a black mass of trees whose branches scraped at the sides of the Crown Vic.

In the middle of a clearing at the end of the road was a small, A-frame log cabin built of rounded pine logs. A large, black Doberman pinscher with cropped ears stood beside a Ford F-150 pickup truck near the front door of the cabin. The Ford had a camo vinyl wrap finish like the truck Scott Rafferty's landlord had seen the night Rafferty disappeared.

Jeff Tate was closing a horizontal steel hatch that was twenty yards to the left of the cabin as Santana drove up. From the outside, the cover looked like a small bush and was the same color as the ground around it, making it difficult for anyone to know it was there—or what was beneath it. Santana was unable to spot any ventilation pipes, but he suspected that Tate had built himself a bomb shelter.

Tate picked up a bolt-action Kimber 84M rifle that was leaning against a woodpile at the corner of the cabin. He turned his big, muscular frame toward the Crown Vic and held the gun in a military patrol ready position across his body, the dog now standing watchfully by his side.

Santana held his badge wallet out the Crown Vic's open driver's side window. "My name is John Santana. I'm a St. Paul homicide detective."

"You didn't see the sign on the gate?" Tate spoke with a slight southern accent.

"I did."

"So why are we talking?"

Tate was dressed in a bright green flannel shirt, blue jeans, and scuffed work boots. His thin blond beard matched the blond hair on his head that was cut so short Santana could see his scalp.

"I need a few minutes of your time, Mr. Tate."

"For what?"

"I'd like to ask you some questions about Scott Rafferty."

"Go ahead."

"Mind if I get out of the car?"

Tate hesitated. "I don't know anything about Rafferty's death, if that's what you're here about."

"Maybe you do, maybe you don't. But why not give me a few minutes of your time? I'd hate to inconvenience you further by requesting your presence downtown."

"Rafferty drowned."

"No one said he didn't."

Tate stood quiet and unmoving.

Santana could smell the heavy, clean scent of pine and see bands of sunlight boring through the clouds, melting the patches of dirty snow that lay in the shaded areas at the edges of the property.

"What about it, Mr. Tate? Do we talk here or downtown?"

He set the rifle with the walnut stock against the woodpile. "Okay. I'm not going to harm you."

"And the dog?"

He glanced down and gently shoved the dog with his knee. The dog didn't budge. "Brando won't do you any harm either. Unless I tell him to."

As Santana got out of his sedan and closed the door, the dog came to him and sniffed his pants legs. "Brando, huh?"

"I named him after the actor."

"I figured that."

"Probably how you got that detective shield, huh? Able to take a clue and make something out of it." He had no smile on his face or humor in his eyes.

"I wish it were that easy, Mr. Tate."

Tate stood silently for a while with his arms folded across his chest before he spoke again.

"So what about Scott?"

Santana leaned against the driver's side door, took out a pen and his notebook, and flipped it open to the page he was looking for. "You and Kimberly Dalton were with him at Billy's the last night he was seen alive."

"She told you that?"

"Uh-huh. She also told me you were still with Rafferty when she left the bar to go to work."

"I didn't stay long."

"What time did you leave?"

"I can't say for sure. Ten maybe."

Santana could see no hint of a lie in Tate's eyes or face. "Can anyone verify that?"

"Lots of people know me at Billy's."

"How long have you worked there?"

"Two years now."

"But you were off that night."

"Yeah."

"Did you stop anywhere after you left Billy's?"

"I drove straight home."

"You didn't give Rafferty a ride home?"

"No."

"Was Rafferty alone when you left?"

"Far as I know."

Santana wrote the information in his notebook. "How long had you known him?"

"A couple of months."

"How did you meet?"

"He started coming into Billy's regularly."

"What's regularly?"

"Couple times a week."

"Was Rafferty a heavy drinker?"

"I never saw him drunk."

"You remember how much he drank the last night you saw him?"

"We had a few beers. That's all."

Santana looked at the rifle leaning against the building. "You serve in the military, Mr. Tate?"

He nodded but offered no details.

"You serve with Scott Rafferty?"

"Nope."

"You know of anyone who might want to harm Scott Rafferty?"

"No. But that doesn't mean a whole hell of a lot considering how completely fucked up the country is."

"What did you talk about with Scott that night?"

"The usual."

"What's the usual?"

"Sports, women. The things guys usually talk about."

"You ever talk about Rafferty's military service?"

"We might've on occasion."

"What did he have to say about it?"

Tate shook his head as though the answer were obvious. "He thought the war was a mistake, that guys were dying for nothing in Iraq. We should've been chasing down that asshole Bin Laden in Afghanistan." He gave short laugh. "Or in Pakistan where the SEALS finally found him."

"What was Rafferty's emotional state when he returned from the war?"

"Depressed. But, hell, who wouldn't be?"

"Did Rafferty ever talk about suicide?"

"Not to me."

"Did you know he was seeing a psychiatrist?"

"No crime in that."

"No, there isn't. You seeing one?"

"None of your business," he said.

"I understand you volunteer at a homeless shelter."

"Lots of vets need help."

"What kind of help?"

49

Tate continued to look at Santana but remained silent.

"What were you doing at Scott Rafferty's house the night you two were at Billy's?"

"I wasn't doing anything 'cause I wasn't there."

Santana gestured toward the Ford pickup. "I have a very reliable witness who can place your truck there. Not too many trucks around town have the camo wrap like yours, Mr. Tate." Santana knew he might be stretching the truth, since Elaine Moore hadn't been able to pinpoint the exact date when she saw the pickup, but Tate didn't know that.

His gaze slid off Santana's face. Before it did, Santana saw the apprehension in his eyes.

"All right. I stopped by Scott's place and picked him up earlier that evening. He said his Range Rover had ignition problems."

"Why lie about being at his house that night, Mr. Tate, if you have nothing to hide?"

His gaze returned to Santana. "I know how cops operate."

"Really?"

"Yeah. It's easy to put words in someone's mouth. Make it seem like things mean something they don't."

"You drive Rafferty home?"

"I already told you I left the bar around ten and drove straight home."

Santana made a show of looking at his notes, as though he hadn't remembered. "So you did." He peered at his notes a moment longer and said, "I understand Rafferty and Kimberly Dalton were going to get married."

Tate laughed. "Yeah, right."

"You don't believe that."

"No way. He dumped her."

"When?"

"Maybe a few weeks ago. I don't remember for sure."

50

Santana recalled the empty picture frame in Rafferty's apartment and the photo of Rafferty and Kimberly Dalton in the nightstand drawer. "How come?"

"Lots of reasons. But mostly because she's a control freak."

"How do you know that?"

"Scott told me she was constantly calling him, wanting to know where he was and when he could see her. She was driving him nuts."

Santana remembered the numerous incoming calls from Kimberly Dalton he had seen on Scott Rafferty's cell phone bill.

"So how come she was with him at Billy's that night if they'd broken up?" he asked.

"She wasn't *with* him," Tate said. "She just showed up."

"How did Rafferty react?"

"He was upset. It got ugly."

"How ugly?"

"Kimberly accused Scott of seeing someone else. Said she was gonna fix him good."

"Is that exactly how Ms. Dalton phrased it?"

Tate nodded. "More or less."

Santana wrote it down. "You ever see Scott or Kimberly use cocaine?"

Tate looked at Santana for a long moment. "That's another reason why Scott wanted out of the relationship."

"Because she used drugs?"

"Yeah."

"What about Scott?"

"He was getting his head together. Drugs would've only messed him up."

"You know a man named Devante Carter?"

Tate shook his head.

"Was Scott Rafferty seeing someone else?"

"I don't know. If he was, he never mentioned it to me. I think it was mostly in Kimberly's head."

51

"Anyone else notice the argument they had?"

He shrugged. "It was real noisy and busy that night. But someone could've heard."

Santana pointed toward the bomb shelter in the ground. "Getting prepared for the coming apocalypse, Mr. Tate?"

His wary brown eyes narrowed. "You think I'm crazy?"

"I never said that."

He dismissed Santana's response with a wave. "It doesn't matter. You can live like some Pollyanna and be unprepared. But the shit storm is coming real soon. Believe me. We're gonna be hit with an NBC attack sooner or later."

"You mean a nuclear, biological, or chemical attack."

"Damn right. Terrorists are real committed. They believe that bullshit about seventy-two virgins waiting for them in heaven. They're going to get their hands on nuclear or biological weapons one of these days. That's if those con artists and money manipulators running Wall Street and the banks don't cause a complete economic collapse and the EOTW first."

"EOTW?"

"Where the hell you been, Detective? EOTW. End of the world. At least the end of the world as we know it. You better get yourself a BOL. That's a bug out location." Tate pointed with his index finger toward the shelter. "I got everything I need. And I got my GOOD kit in my pickup."

"What's that?"

He let out a frustrated breath and shook his head. "Man, you really are out of the loop. That's my get-out-of-Dodge kit. I'll be completely self-sufficient here. If you can't do anything else, Detective, at least load up on ammo. Another Dark Age is coming. It's only a matter of time."

After leaving Jeff Tate's cabin, Santana drove to Vail Biomedical Research to interview Ronald Getz. The tall ex-con with the widow's peak had given him an uneasy feeling. The company was housed in a small one-story building near a Metro Transit park-and-ride site on an open stretch of land, directly across the highway from a sprawling, low-rise shopping center. Santana parked his Crown Vic in a paved lot near a free-standing company sign facing the highway. A foyer led into the stark white lobby of the building. He showed his badge wallet to the middle-aged woman with platinum blond hair seated at a desk behind a high counter. "I'd like to see Ronald Getz."

She looked down at what appeared to be a schedule and then at Santana again. "I'm afraid he's out right now. But Mr. Vail is here if you'd like to speak to him."

"All right."

The receptionist made a quick phone call and then directed Santana to an office in a short, narrow corridor to his left.

A heavy-set man dressed in a worn sport coat and button-down striped shirt open at the collar came to the office door with his hand outstretched. The remaining strands of his blond hair were parted just above his left ear and swooped thinly over his shiny balding head. "Pleasure to meet you, Detective Santana. I'm Kenneth Vail." He gripped Santana's hand tightly and offered a big, friendly smile. "Please, come in."

Santana followed him into a gray-walled room and sat in a white ribbed leather chair with a chrome steel frame. It had a lower backrest than the average chair, and the cushion felt stiff and uncomfortable.

Kenneth Vail lowered his large frame into a much more comfortable-looking leather chair behind his very sleek and modern glass-topped desk. The remaining furniture in the office—two file cabinets with chrome steel handles, a bookshelf with a chrome steel base, and a mushroomed-shaped stool—were all made of high gloss black lacquer. The cool, bare environment reminded Santana of an autopsy suite.

"My receptionist said you wanted to speak with Ronald Getz."

"That's right."

"Concerning?"

"Scott Rafferty."

Vail cocked his head. "Where have I heard that name before? Oh, yes. I read about him in the *Pioneer Press*. I believe his body was found in the Mississippi River. An unfortunate tragedy—very sad," he said, shaking his head. "But why would you want to talk with Ronald about a drowning victim?"

"Mr. Getz works at the Lessard Mortuary. Scott Rafferty worked there. I was wondering if they'd had any recent conversations."

Vail nodded as if Santana's response made sense.

"What does Getz do here?"

"He's mostly a gofer. He also does some janitorial work."

Santana took out his notebook and pen. "You're the sole owner of Biomedical Research?"

"My wife and I own the company."

"I couldn't find a website."

"No. I employ a couple of research assistants, but it's pretty much a bare bones operation right now."

"What kind of research are you doing?"

"Drug research."

"What kind of drug?"

"One that can help those suffering from PTSD."

"Tell me more."

Vail hesitated before answering. "I'd rather not."

"And why is that?"

"I'm in a race to get the drug on the market, Detective Santana. The less my competitors know about my research, the better."

Without some information he could use to pressure Kenneth Vail, Santana knew he would learn nothing more about

Vail's research. He moved on. "How well do you know William Lessard?"

"I've met him on occasion."

"How did you happen to hire Ronald Getz?"

"Mr. Lessard recommended him."

"So you took a job recommendation of a man you hardly knew?"

Vail shrugged. "It's not unusual, Detective Santana. In business, as in most fields, you often have to rely on the judgment of others."

"Do you have many ex-cons working for you, Mr. Vail?"

Vail's forearms were resting on the desktop, his head tilted slightly, as though he found Santana's question curious. "Ronald is my first hire. But if he continues to do well, I may hire more ex-cons. Everyone deserves a second chance, don't you think, Detective Santana?"

Santana offered no reply. Instead, his eyes were drawn to the silver-framed 5 x 7 photo on Vail's desk of a much younger-looking woman. She had high cheekbones, flawless white skin, and straight yellow blonde hair cut short with bangs, like a young boy. Her nose was perfectly shaped, her lips full, and her large eyes blue.

"That's Monica," Vail said. His gunmetal eyes focused briefly on the picture and then returned to Santana's face. "She's beautiful, isn't she?"

"She's a very attractive woman."

"Fortunately, she's my wife."

Santana detected a not-so-subtle threat in the man's voice, as if Vail inexplicably viewed him as a potential suitor. But Santana had been threatened before and in more menacing ways. If Vail was trying to intimidate him, it wasn't working.

He took a business card out of his wallet and pushed it across the desktop. "Please have Mr. Getz call me as soon as he returns."

Santana spotted the black Chevy Tahoe with the dark tinted glass shortly after he signed in his Crown Vic and drove his Ford Explorer out of the SPPD parking lot. Like most experienced cops, his eyes were always on the move, looking for something or someone out of the ordinary, regardless of his environment or activity. But being aware of his surroundings was not just a matter of habit; it was a matter of life and death.

At sixteen, Santana had killed the twin sons of Alejandro Estrada, the head of the Cali cartel, after they had murdered his mother. Estrada was dead now, but Santana knew that neither time nor Estrada's death would stop the assassins from coming. Killing him was a matter of pride and honor for the remaining members of the Estrada family and for the cartel—and a matter of revenge. It was a concept deeply ingrained in Colombian culture, a concept many Americans did not fully understand.

The Tahoe slid in behind him, its headlights tunneling the early evening darkness and glaring in his rearview mirror. Part of his brain told him to turn around and head back to the station, where he would have protection and reinforcements. But another part told him that if there were assassins behind him, he would have to deal with them sooner or later. Instead of heading east toward Interstate 94, which would take him to his house along the St. Croix River, he headed west toward downtown.

Santana crossed Wall Street, a narrow patch of road flanked by brick buildings, which looked nothing like the street in New York City. As he turned north at the next intersection, the Tahoe swung quickly in behind him. There was no doubt now that he was being followed. He fingered the Glock in the Kydex holster on his hip and stepped on the gas pedal, adrenaline surging through his body.

He increased his speed to ten miles over the limit as he passed Regions Hospital and crossed busy University Avenue, a major east/west thoroughfare connecting St. Paul and Minneapolis. He needed to widen the distance between his SUV and

56

the Tahoe behind him, but not so much that he would lose the tail. Santana wanted the confrontation to happen in a place where citizens would not be hurt.

Traffic quickly thinned along the bumpy road that led past a railroad yard and into the blue-collar North End neighborhood of Craftsman houses. There were no signal lights ahead and no major intersections where he could get trapped between cars and blocked in.

The street he was on dead-ended at the main gate to the Oakland Cemetery. In order to continue driving north, he would have to turn right and then make a quick left turn again. But that would take him deeper into residential neighborhoods. Santana was hoping the gate to the hundred-acre cemetery was open. If he had to make a stand, he would make it among the already dead in the cemetery.

The new moon was a scar on the black face of night as Santana drove through the open cemetery gate. The Explorer's headlight beams scythed the darkness and illuminated a metal sign indicating that the gate was open until eight p.m. On the dead grass to the right of the gate, a granite sign listed the grave decoration regulations. Wall crypts holding cremated remains sat on a hill above the sign, and mausoleums the size of small cottages flanked the tar road directly ahead.

Turning left at the first road inside the gate, Santana drove through night shadows cast by tall trees. A large cluster of closely grouped headstones stood in the brown grass to his left. Having attended funerals in the cemetery before, he knew that the names on the headstones were all Hmong, the mountain people from Laos who had fought on the side of the US during the Vietnam War. Many had come to the States after years of living in refugee camps in Thailand. A small chapel made of granite stones sat on a rise directly to his right. In his rearview mirror he saw the Tahoe slow as it passed through the cemetery gate.

Santana followed the narrow road as it curved to the right and drove into a circular drive behind the chapel. He killed the headlights and ignition and was out of the SUV and into the darkness in a matter of seconds, his Glock held securely in his right hand.

He ran up a slope to his left and along the south side of the chapel and knelt near the front of the building. He peered around the corner just as the Tahoe turned onto the road leading past the Hmong headstones. Again he made his way along the side of the chapel and knelt at the back corner of the building. He had a clear view of the road and the circular drive, where he had left his SUV.

The Tahoe came slowly around the curve and stopped just before the circular drive. It sat still for a moment, its headlights piercing the darkness like tracers of rifle fire. Santana could hear the low hum of the Tahoe's engine and the sound of his own breathing. Tiny clouds of carbon dioxide misted in the cool air as he exhaled.

Then the driver's side door opened and a man emerged and stood in the pool of light cast by the Tahoe's interior lights. Santana could not see his features clearly, but he could see that the man was wearing a raincoat and fedora. He stood with his hands on his hips and gazed at his surroundings. Then he approached Santana's SUV and opened the driver's side door, the interior light spilling over his face.

Santana moved quickly down the slope and came in behind him and pressed the barrel of the Glock against the back of the man's skull. "Lean forward, put your hands against the SUV, and spread your legs."

"Take it easy."

"Do it!"

The heavy-set man followed the directive. He was a couple of inches shorter, and Santana had to hold his gun at a slight angle as he patted him down.

"My name is Jack Brody. I'm not carrying. My ID is in my left side pocket." He spoke in a gravelly voice Santana recognized.

Santana found a wallet in the man's side pocket and flipped it open. In the light he could see the name on the driver's license and that he was from New York.

"Mind if I turn around?"

Santana backed away and held his aim steady at chest level. "Do it slowly. And keep your hands where I can see them."

Brody turned around. "Can I lower my hands?"

"Easy."

He lowered his hands to his side.

"You're the guy that called me last night. Said you knew that Scott Rafferty was murdered."

Brody nodded. "Yeah. Sorry. I was a little under the weather."

"And a lot under the influence of alcohol."

Brody shrugged.

"Why were you following me?"

"I wanted to talk."

"Poor way to go about it."

"I can see that."

"Why not just come down to the station?"

"I've got my reasons," Brody said.

"How about a phone call?"

"I damaged my cell when I dropped it the other night. I need to buy another."

"So what do you have to tell me?"

"I'd rather not discuss it standing here in a cemetery. How about we go somewhere and have a drink?"

"Maybe you should've made that offer in the first place."

"Live and learn," he said.

Chapter 6

THEY EACH DROVE TO ALARY'S, a downtown sports bar not far from the Law Enforcement Center and a popular hangout for off-duty police officers, firefighters, attorneys, and city and state workers. The bar featured thirty, fifty-inch flat-screen plasma TVs; police, fire and sports memorabilia; and young, pretty waitresses in tight T-shirts and short skirts.

They found a table and ordered two bottles of Sam Adams.

"You were standing in the crowd when Scott Rafferty's body was recovered," Santana said.

"I was."

A network of blue veins ran under the skin of Brody's wide nose and florid cheeks, which were slightly pitted with acne scars.

"Why call me and not 911 when you first found the body?"

"I'm aware of your reputation."

"And what reputation is that?"

"You're the best detective in town."

"Says who?"

"People who should know."

Santana felt uncomfortable receiving praise. "I work with a lot of good detectives, Brody."

"I'm sure you do. In my career, I've met many of 'em. But only a few I'd consider better than all the rest."

"You're a cop?"

He took a business card out of his soiled shirt pocket and slid it across the table. "I'm an investigative reporter."

"For what paper?"

"Right now I'm freelancing."

Santana figured "freelancing" was a euphemism for unemployed. "Your business card and driver's license have a New York address. What are you doing in St. Paul?"

"You get right to the point."

"I'm a busy man."

"Understood."

A waitress arrived with two bottles of Sam Adams. After she left, Brody swallowed some beer. Then he pulled out an 11 x 17 map from a side pocket in his raincoat and unfolded it on the tabletop. Interstate 94 through Minnesota and Wisconsin was highlighted in red. Various cities in the Midwest were circled in the same color. Black numbers were written beside all the circled cities.

Brody made a sweeping gesture over the map. "Let me summarize the scenario I heard in all the circled cities, and what I suspect I'll hear in St. Paul about the death of Scott Rafferty. A twenty-something college student is having drinks with his friends on a Friday or Saturday evening at a local restaurant or bar. Later in the evening he decides to walk home alone to his apartment or dorm room. That's the last time anyone ever sees him alive. The kid is usually pretty responsible and wouldn't leave town without telling someone, so a search is organized. But no one can find a trace of him. It's like he just disappeared into thin air. Then one day, his body is recovered in a river or lake close to where he was last seen alive. The ME determines that the death is an accident. The police put out a story to the media that the kid was drunk and apparently wandered into the river and drowned."

"Okay," Santana said. "So Scott Rafferty drank too much and made a fatal mistake. It happens."

"Of course it does. And had Rafferty's death been one of a few similar cases, I'd chalk it up as an unfortunate accident. Hey, I was in college once. I know how kids like to drink and party and how stupid they act. But I've discovered a whole string of student drowning deaths, the majority of them involving young men who attended colleges along the Interstate Ninety-four corridor in the Midwest. I figure at least forty college-age men have drowned under these circumstances. That's more than a coincidence. That's a pattern."

Santana's interest piqued as he mentally added the numbers written on the map until he arrived at forty.

"All the victims have nearly the same physical description and are around the same age," Brody said. "They were popular, athletic, and mostly good students."

"That description doesn't fit Scott Rafferty's profile."

"Let me finish. The majority of these young men either became separated from friends or disappeared after drinking in a bar or at a party. And all the deaths occurred during the school year when college was in session."

"That would make sense, Brody. There would be fewer parties and students on campus during the summer and less drinking. Sounds like the common thread connecting all these deaths is alcohol."

Brody tapped an ink-stained index finger on the map. "Nearly all of the deaths have occurred along Interstate Ninety-four. So if your conclusion is correct, Detective, then I guess only Midwest college students have a problem with alcohol and fall into rivers, ponds, and lakes."

Santana could hear the sarcasm in Brody's voice, but he wasn't convinced.

Brody must have seen the doubt on Santana's face because he quickly spoke again. "And it would be a real stretch if you're thinking that all these kids committed suicide, Detective."

Santana knew Brody was correct. People rarely committed suicide by drowning. Hanging and gunshots were much quicker ways to die, and males generally chose one of them, unlike females, who tended to slit their wrists or overdose on drugs, often in a cry for help rather than in a real attempt to end their lives.

"Has the FBI looked into the drownings, Brody?"

"A few. But they found no evidence of foul play."

"And you think you know more than the FBI."

"The feds ever make a mistake, Santana?"

"Sure. Investigators are human."

"That includes the feds," he said, coughing into his hand.

"What about local departments?"

Brody drank some beer before replying. "I've tried convincing them that the drownings are related. But they label me and anyone else who talks about a serial killer as just another crazy conspiracy theorist."

"Can you blame them?"

Brody turned his head away from the table and coughed again. "I need a smoke."

Santana thought maybe Brody needed a lung transplant, but he kept his suspicions to himself.

"When you receive the autopsy report on Scott Rafferty," Brody said, "you won't find a whole lot of alcohol in the kid's system. And whoever was last with him will tell you he wasn't drunk."

"So if all these young men weren't drunk and the drownings aren't purely accidental, how do you think they're being killed?"

"I believe they were drugged and then their bodies were tossed into the water to make it appear as if they'd accidentally drowned. The water washes away fingerprints and trace evidence so the killer can't be identified."

"Was evidence of a drug found in any of the previous autopsies?"

"Not that I'm aware of. But if the coroner or ME doesn't know what drug to look for, they won't necessarily find it."

"So what makes you think the young men were drugged?"

"These young guys wouldn't willingly go into a river in winter. And if they were forced into the water, there would've been a struggle and physical or trace evidence would've been found. No," he said with a shake of his large head. "They were given something that weakened them and that couldn't be detected by an autopsy unless an ME was specifically testing for it."

"Bad things can happen when you drink, Brody."

He nodded as if he'd had some bad experiences of his own with alcohol.

"Maybe they got disoriented and found themselves in an unfamiliar environment near a riverbank," Santana said.

"You're not listening to what I'm saying, Detective. It just doesn't stand to reason that all of these guys were so drunk and disoriented that they wouldn't recognize a river and understand what they were doing."

"You've looked at some of the autopsy reports."

"I have."

Santana knew that under Minnesota law, basic demographic information and the cause and manner of death were matters of public record. All other information was confidential and treated like a medical record. The information was available only to immediate next-of-kin, legal representatives of the decedent's estate, and treating physicians. In cases of homicide, medical examiner information and autopsy reports could only be provided to law enforcement agencies investigating the death and to the county attorney until the matter had made its way through the courts.

"How's that possible, Brody?"

"Friends," he said with a crooked smile. "But for the sake of discussion, let's suppose the majority of young men *were* really drunk when they left the bar or party. If that were the case, then they would be vulnerable to a predator. It would be very easy for someone to push a drunken college kid into the water without leaving any trace evidence indicating foul play. Would you agree?"

Santana didn't respond.

"Well, you wouldn't disagree. So it's possible some of these students may have been drinking heavily. They may have stumbled away from friends unnoticed or said they were going home. They may even have wandered near the water's edge and accidentally fallen in and drowned, especially in a strong current. But here's the problem with that theory. How did they get to the river in the first place? How could all these kids get completely disoriented on the streets in a town where many of them had been attending college for years? Why would they head for a river blocks away from where they were last seen? I've been to these sites, Detective. In many cases, it's nearly impossible to fall into the river even if you are drunk and disoriented. And if the blood alcohol levels in these students were so high they didn't know what they were doing, they'd be in a stupor and would barely be able to stand. So how could they walk for a mile or more and end up in a river? No, I believe these guys were specifically targeted and drugged."

Santana considered the information before he spoke again. "How is it that you just happened to discover Scott Rafferty's body?"

Brody's smile showed off his yellow teeth. "I was wondering when you'd ask me that." He pointed to the map again. "I've been studying these cases for a year using a computer program I've developed to map out the crimes."

He removed a small spiral notepad from an inner pocket and showed Santana what he had written. "Eighty percent of

65

the deaths happened on the first day of the new moon. The victims usually vanished between ten p.m. on Friday and four a.m. Sunday. The majority of the victims were attending college within fifty miles of I-Ninety-four. The timeline of the drownings moves in a consistent pattern up and then down the I-Ninety-four corridor. Last month, they found the body of a college kid in the river in St. Cloud. I figured the killer would follow his pattern and head south again, which meant a return to the Twin Cities."

"You think he's killed here before."

"I believe at least three times." Brody turned the page with a stubby index finger and pointed to three names written in pencil. "Go back and take a look at these deaths, Detective, and then tell me you don't see a pattern." He tore out the page and slid it toward Santana.

"Even if your theory is correct, Brody, it's still hard to believe you'd be the one person that found Scott Rafferty's body."

"There was a new moon on March fourth. I figured a body would surface around the middle of the month. I drove and walked along the shoreline from Minneapolis to St. Paul. The body wasn't hard to spot if you were looking for it."

He seemed sincere, but Santana still had doubts. "I investigate based on facts, Brody, not hope."

"There's one other thing that should convince you that I'm on the right track," he said. "A symbol was found painted on trees and other surfaces near the water's edge at some of the crime scenes."

"What kind of symbol?"

Brody leaned over and drew a radial pattern comprised of eight arrows in his notebook.

"Any idea what it means?" Santana asked.

"It's generally recognized as a symbol for chaos. I think the killer left it. I think he's taunting the police."

"Has this drawing been found near every drowning victim?"

Brody shook his head. "Not all of them. Still, it tweaks your curiosity, doesn't it?"

Santana could see a twinkle in Brody's eyes. "Maybe. But the drawings and everything else you've told me hasn't convinced the FBI or local police that there's a serial killer on the loose. So why do you think it should convince me?"

"Just keep an open mind, Santana. Take a look at the autopsy and police reports on the three names I gave you. See if you can come up with something that other investigators may have missed. See if those cases aren't similar to Scott Rafferty's death. I'm convinced there's a serial killer on the loose and he's preying on college students. I want to stop him. Is that so difficult to understand?"

"If you're right, it would be a very big story."

Brody smiled crookedly again. "Yeah, it would be. But it would also be a big story for you."

"I don't need or want publicity."

"You think that's what this is all about?"

"You're giving me far too much credit."

"I don't believe so. And you won't walk away without taking a closer look."

"You think I'm that curious?"

"I'm counting on it, Detective."

Later that night, Santana sat down at his computer and opened a private e-mail account that his uncle, Arturo Gutiérrez Restrepo, in Bogotá, Colombia, had set up. Only Arturo, Santana, and Santana's sister Natalia, who lived in Barcelona, Spain, knew the password to the account. Santana could not risk sending a direct e-mail to her given that it might be intercepted, thus revealing her whereabouts to the Cali cartel that wanted her dead. And so he and Natalia had worked out a system in which they would write each other e-mails but never send them. As long as each of them had the password to open the account, they could read the e-mails.

After finishing his latest e-mail, Santana opened the dream journal he kept on his nightstand and crawled into bed. Whether at home or traveling, he wrote in the journal immediately upon waking from a vivid dream. This habit had helped him recall more dreams and the elements and signs that were common to many of them.

When he had first begun studying and practicing lucid dreaming, he was only vaguely aware that he was asleep and dealing with an altered state of reality. His dream recognition had improved considerably, though he hadn't yet reached the stage in which he could have complete control over his thoughts and actions within the dream state. And he still saw events in certain dreams as threats. But lucid dreaming gave him some power over the nightmares that had haunted his soul ever since his deadly encounter with the Estrada brothers in the mountains of Colombia.

The most difficult part of lucid dreaming was remembering to stay calm during stressful, vivid nightmares. Excitement during a lucid dream often caused him to wake up suddenly. He also needed to remain still when he woke from any dream because moving would activate muscle neurons, making it more difficult for him to access the parts of his brain that allowed him to recall his dream.

He had learned over time that many of his lucid dreams were about the future or a particular case he was working. But the nightmares he experienced often dredged up dark memories of his past. Drowning inside a narrow pipe filled with water was a nightmare he had experienced before, though he had never been fully aware that he was dreaming. But tonight, when he finally fell asleep and dreamt again that he was in a narrow pipe, fighting to keep his head above water, instead of continuing to struggle, he let himself sink below the surface.

Now, as he floats quietly underneath the surface of the water, he sees something large and dark about ten yards away drifting just below the water's surface. He cannot distinguish the shape because it is surrounded by a school of fish. As he paddles slowly toward it, the fish swim away, and he sees a decomposing body. The eyes are tightly closed and the face partially eaten away, but Santana recognizes Scott Rafferty.

Suddenly Rafferty's eyelids fly open, revealing nothing but empty dark sockets. "Help me!" he screams as a large black snake swims out from his mouth toward Santana's face.

Santana awoke with a start and sat up in bed, the dream quickly slipping away from him, like a shark vanishing into deep water.

Chapter 7

THE FOLLOWING MORNING, SANTANA SAT at his desk in the SPPD's Homicide Unit on the second floor of the six-story Griffin Building, just northeast of downtown St. Paul. A skyway connected it to the Ramsey County Sheriff's Department. The two buildings were referred to as the Law Enforcement Center, or LEC.

He poured himself a cup of hot chocolate from his thermos and peered at the covers of the case files he had pulled—Michael Johnson, Matthew Miller, and Thomas Hunter, the names Jack Brody had provided. He had also pulled a fourth file of an unidentified man who had recently drowned in the Mississippi.

He opened Michael Johnson's file first. The case had been assigned to Pete Romano, the Homicide Unit's most senior detective. The reports Romano had filed were in chronological order beginning with the Preliminary Report. Santana glanced quickly through it and then looked at the Death Investigation Report.

Reiko Tanabe had pronounced Michael Johnson dead at the scene and had listed the date and then the time of death at approximately 1:00 a.m. that same morning, based on witnesses who had seen Johnson leaving a bar an hour earlier and on how much undigested food was found in his stomach. In the narrative section of the report labeled WHO, WHAT, WHERE, and WHEN, Romano had written that an ice fisherman had spotted

Michael Johnson's body floating face up in the Mississippi River at 7:30 a.m. on January 21. The body had snagged on a drainpipe near the Ford Motor Company power plant in St. Paul. Tanabe had noted that Johnson's hands and arms appeared to be very stiff when he was recovered from the river. He had been fully clothed and his down jacket zipped. His wallet had been found with him, and he had been quickly identified.

Santana considered what he had just read. If the TOD estimate was correct, Johnson hadn't been dead long enough for rigor to form. Cadaveric spasm resulting from his violent struggle at the time of drowning was no doubt responsible for the stiffness in his hands and arms. It occurred virtually instantly and only in voluntary muscles, unlike rigor mortis, which progressed evenly throughout the body at a steady rate. It indicated Johnson must have panicked and been under extreme physical stress at the time of his death.

Santana did a quick Google search on his office desktop computer for the January lunar cycle and verified that the moon had been in a new phase that weekend. Then he returned to the Death Investigation Report.

Three-fourths of the way down the page, underneath Romano's narrative, was a section labeled FUNERAL HOME. Directly underneath that was a section that read BODY TAKEN TO. A YES box had been checked following the question, Was Autopsy Requested? A similar box below it had been checked following the phrase, Was Toxicology Requested? Michael Johnson's body had been taken to the Ramsey County morgue at Regions Hospital and then to a funeral home in Minnetonka.

The last section on the Death Investigation Report contained a brief medical history, which included the name of Johnson's physician and the date, location, and the reason Johnson was last seen. Santana noted that Johnson had gone in for a routine physical. Reiko Tanabe had signed off on the last line of the report.

71

The next report in Johnson's case file was the Evidence Inventory listing the items recovered from the body. Besides Johnson's clothing and wallet, a gold watch and a gold chain had been recovered. Those items had all been returned to Johnson's parents after the death was ruled an accidental drowning and the case closed.

Santana moved on to the Summary Reports on the interviews conducted during the investigation. There were no eyewitness accounts. Pete Romano had interviewed Johnson's parents and a University of St. Thomas student, Joseph Krause, who was the last witness to see Michael Johnson alive. He had been drinking beers with Johnson at Dixie's on Grand Avenue in St. Paul the night before Johnson's body had been found in the Mississippi River. Krause claimed that when he drove back to campus around 11:00 p.m. Johnson had remained at the bar talking with a dark-haired woman. Krause did not remember the young woman's name. Witnesses had confirmed that Krause had indeed returned to his dorm at approximately 11:15 p.m. Romano had noted that the witnesses and Krause were cooperative and credible. Romano had attempted to locate the dark-haired woman Johnson had last been seen with, but had turned up nothing.

Santana paused and drank more hot chocolate. Scott Rafferty and Michael Johnson had both been drinking in bars on Grand Avenue the last time they were seen. Both had lived within walking distance of the Mississippi River. He wrote the information in his notebook and returned to the last section of the case file containing Johnson's autopsy report.

He skimmed the information on the top half of the first page, noting that Johnson's father, James, had identified his son's body and had requested a copy of the ME's autopsy report, which Tanabe had mailed to him. Santana found nothing unusual in the report.

He spent another hour reading through the other case files, finding all the reports and autopsy results remarkably similar.

Drowning was listed as the cause of death for Johnson, Miller, Hunter, and the unidentified man, though their blood alcohol levels gave no indication they were drunk when they entered the water. Johnson had been a student at the University of St. Thomas, and Miller and Hunter had attended Macalester College. Both schools were near Grand Avenue and the Mississippi River. An Air Force ring had been found on a finger of the unidentified man.

Santana saw that the case of the unidentified man had been referred to Katherine Bailey, a forensic anthropologist at the University of Minnesota. She made casts of cranial remains to recreate three-dimensional facial reconstructions. Santana was familiar with her excellent work, but had never had an opportunity to work with her.

When she answered her phone, he told her who he was and what he was working on. She promised to notify him as soon as she had completed the facial reconstruction.

Santana then located the home addresses and phone numbers for the family members of the three identified young men. James Johnson seemed eager to talk about his son's death, so Santana scheduled a meeting for later that morning. Thomas Hunter's parents lived out of state, and their number had been disconnected.

Irene Miller was listed on the autopsy report as the person who had identified Matthew Miller's body. Santana wondered if there was a Mr. Miller or if she was a single mother. She answered on the third ring.

"Ms. Miller?"

"Yes?"

"My name is Detective John Santana. I'm with the St. Paul Police Department." He could hear her breathing softly into the phone as he waited for a response. "Ms. Miller?" he said again when she failed to reply.

"Why are you calling?"

"First of all, let me express my condolences for your loss."

"But that isn't why you called, is it?"

"Not specifically. I'd like to talk with you about Matthew's death." He decided not to mention that he was a homicide detective since it might create a false impression before the conversation even began.

"I've already spoken with a Detective Romano from your department."

Santana wanted a face-to-face meeting. It would allow him to probe more deeply and to see Irene Miller's body language and reactions to his questions. "Perhaps, if we could meet, you'll recall something now that you didn't recall when you spoke with Detective Romano. I won't take much of your time."

There was a long pause. He could hear what sounded like a small dog barking in the far background.

"Are you God, Detective Santana?"

"Excuse me?"

"Are you God?"

"I'm a detective, Ms. Miller. That's all."

"Then you can't bring my son back."

"No, I'm afraid I can't."

"So what's the point of endlessly discussing Matthew's death? Every time you people call, I have to relive that awful memory."

He could hear the anguish and frustration in her voice. The dog continued barking, but now it seemed to be very close to the phone.

"Shut up, Daisy!" she screamed.

The loud scream startled Santana, and he held the phone away from his ear until the dog went quiet. He could hear nothing, not even Irene Miller's breathing. He wondered if she had broken off the connection. Then he heard a small sob. "Ms. Miller?"

She stayed silent.

"I'm sorry if I upset you."

She took a deep breath. "Then why did you call in the first place? I don't know anything about my son's death other than what the police have told me."

Santana wanted to let her know that he was investigating the deaths of other young men who had drowned in a similar fashion in the Mississippi River. She might be able to tell him something important, something she probably didn't even realize was important, something that might help him decide if her son had been murdered. But he had to weigh the emotional costs of questioning her, especially when he had no hard evidence indicating that her son's death had been anything but an accident. And he had to ask the right questions, though he wasn't sure yet what those specific questions were.

"Please accept my condolences, Ms. Miller." He was always very careful about making promises he couldn't keep, so he said, "I'll try not to bother you again."

She hung up the phone in reply.

Santana signed out a Crown Vic and drove out of the SPPD lot. The morning was cloudy and dark. People in long raincoats were carrying black umbrellas as they crossed glistening asphalt streets. The rain was good for the lakes, whose water levels had dropped considerably over the last few years, but it would make flood control along the Mississippi River significantly more difficult.

The big sedan jumped as Santana stepped on the accelerator and headed west on Interstate 94. Since Ford had quit making the Crown Vic, he wondered what make of vehicle the department would purchase in the future. Enough Crown

Vics had been purchased to replace what they currently had, so everyone still drove the Fords for now. Santana appreciated the Crown Vic's size and speed as well as the power it had to run the computers, GPS, and communications system, and the space it had to transport prisoners and store tactical weapons, first aid and forensic kits, and stop sticks. Whatever vehicle the department chose, he would miss the Crown Victoria.

He was on his way to the Johnsons' house on Lake Minnetonka, fifteen miles west of Minneapolis and home to some of Minnesota's most affluent families. Many of the houses and estates had been built in the early 20th century and were priced in the millions of dollars, even after the recession.

The Johnsons' cottage-style house overlooking a bay sat on a lifeless March lawn surrounded by a low fieldstone wall with short fieldstone pillars on each side of the entrance. Oak, maple, and birch trees were scattered across the two-acre property, their bare branches black and shiny in the rain. A long driveway made of brick led to a three-stall garage.

Santana stood by his car for a moment, looking out at the water. Fingernail-sized zebra mussels had been discovered in the lake. They would soon proliferate by the millions, consuming food needed by fish, clogging water intake pipes, ruining fish spawning beds, and littering beaches and shallow areas with razor-sharp shells. There was no way to kill the mussels without killing the fish. Santana wondered what the expensive homes would be worth once the predators and invasive species completely infected the lake.

A thin, attractive woman wearing an aqua blouse with navy blue pants and shoes answered the door and introduced herself as Mary Johnson. She had a dark complexion, hollow cheeks, and thinning brunette hair. Her eyebrows were narrow and dark, and her heavy, powder blue eye shadow matched her eyes.

She led Santana into the living room, where he shook hands with James Johnson. Then he sat on a comfortable beige cushioned chair across from the man and admired the tastefully decorated living room with its hardwood maple floor, wool silk rug, and marble, gas-burning fireplace surrounding a recessed plasma screen television. Linen curtains allowed natural light to filter into the room through a sliding glass door, which offered an expansive view of the lake. Family photos were strategically placed on end tables and on the mantel. One of the photos was of a young woman who appeared to be in her twenties and was probably a daughter. The framed art on the walls featured ocean views and landscapes, which added to the relaxed, but elegant feel of the room.

"I'm really glad you came," James Johnson said.

He was a large, fair-skinned man with a round, friendly face. His sport coat was draped over the back of a chair, and the sleeves of his white shirt were rolled up to his elbows.

"Would you like some coffee, Detective?" Mary Johnson asked in a voice that seemed to come from somewhere far off. She had a fixed smile on her face and a glazed, distant look in her eyes, as though she were heavily medicated.

"Water would be fine," Santana said.

When she exited the room, her husband said, "We've been wanting to talk to your department again about Michael's death for some time, but we couldn't get anyone to listen."

"Let's wait a minute until your wife returns, Mr. Johnson."

"Oh, sure."

"What is it you do for living?"

James Johnson explained that he and his wife sold real estate, though the recession had wreaked havoc on their business.

"I've seen a number of foreclosure signs on houses in St. Paul," Santana said. "And one in the neighborhood where I live."

Johnson shook his head in empathy. "It's best if those properties are bought by banks and then put up for sale quickly. Otherwise, it can negatively affect the housing prices in the whole neighborhood."

His wife came into the room carrying a silver serving tray filled with a pot of coffee, a silver cream pitcher, sugar bowl, three bone-china cups, saucers, spoons, and three neatly folded white linen napkins, as well as a small plate of chocolate chip cookies. She set the tray on the glass-topped coffee table and sat stiffly beside her husband on the couch.

"I hope you like the coffee," she said.

Her husband looked at her. "The detective asked for water."

"It's no problem," Santana said.

Mary Johnson's forehead wrinkled in thought. "Oh, I'm so sorry. I must not have heard you, Detective."

"It's okay, honey," her husband said. "I'll get him some water."

"Don't worry about it," Santana said.

James Johnson waved as if it were no bother. "Bottle or glass?"

"Bottle is fine."

"I'll be right back." He stood and hurried out of the room.

"Please help yourself to the cookies, Detective," Mary Johnson said.

Always a sucker for chocolate, Santana thanked her and did. The cookies were soft and warm, as though they had just come out of the oven.

"They're delicious," he said.

Mary Johnson's eyes were focused on the tray in front of her, and she appeared not to have heard his response. Her concentration was nearly palpable as she poured two cups of coffee without spilling a drop despite the tremor in her hand. Picking up a sugar cube with a pair of tongs proved to be too difficult for her, however.

"Allow me to do that," Santana said with a smile. He took the tongs gently out of her hand, picked up a cube, and dropped it into a cup.

"One for my husband, too, please," she said.

Santana repeated the motion. Then he set the tongs on the serving tray and smiled at her as though nothing was amiss.

"I'm a little surprised you're investigating Michael's death," James Johnson said as he returned to the living room. "Though I'm happy to hear it." He handed Santana a cold bottle of water. "We've always believed his death wasn't accidental. Isn't that right, Mary?"

She gave no indication that she had heard him as she picked up a cup with a shaky hand, the sugar cube bobbing on the coffee's surface like a small life raft on a wavy sea.

Santana finished the cookie and wiped his mouth with a napkin. "Actually, I'm not investigating your son's death. I'm looking into the death of Scott Rafferty."

He could see the immediate disappointment register in James Johnson's face. But Mary Johnson's expression remained emotionless and unchanged.

James Johnson recovered quickly from his disappointment. "When I read about Scott Rafferty's death in the newspaper, I told Mary that his death sounded eerily similar to Michael's, similar to a number of drowning deaths over the past few years." He leaned forward and rested his elbows on his knees. "I don't want to speak negatively about one of your colleagues, Detective Santana, but I believe Detective Romano thought all along that Michael had gotten drunk and drowned. I think his investigation reached a foregone conclusion. But we believed Michael's case matched the cases of other young men

79

who'd gone missing in the Midwest. So we hired a private detective."

"What's the name of the private investigator you hired?"

"Jordan Parrish. She has an office in Minneapolis."

"Was she helpful?"

"Absolutely. When Michael's body was found in the river, he was floating on his back. Jordan explained to us that drowning victims are usually found floating face down. And Michael grew up on the lake. He was a good athlete and a strong swimmer. Hell, he was on the swim team in high school."

Mary Johnson looked at her husband as if she wanted to say something but couldn't quite form the thought.

"Sorry," he said, patting her on the thigh. "I get a little worked up when I start talking about the evidence."

"It's all right, Mrs. Johnson," Santana said. "Just take your time."

She took a moment to compose her thoughts before she spoke. "Michael had nightmares from the war."

"Your son was a vet?"

Mary Johnson looked at her husband, who nodded. "Iraq. The war was pretty rough on him. But he was tough kid. When he returned, he enrolled in college."

"Did your son seek any help?" Santana asked.

"He said he had sought help. But he wouldn't talk to us about it. He was doing pretty well until . . ."

"Until what?" Santana asked.

James Johnson sipped some coffee and set the cup in a saucer on the table, his brown eyes direct and steady as he looked at Santana. "Michael was having difficulty remembering things. Simple things that shouldn't have been difficult."

"He hadn't had a problem like that before?"

"No. He had an excellent memory."

"And you noticed his forgetfulness just prior to his death?"

"Yes. Michael noticed it, too. And his nightmares had gotten much worse."

Santana was wondering if Michael Johnson's PTSD and subsequent nightmares had caused him to commit suicide. But he kept his suppositions to himself.

"The current was strong and the water obviously very cold the night he drowned," James Johnson said. "But Michael was fully clothed." He paused as his eyes looked inward, perhaps imagining the struggle his son had gone through in trying to survive. "My son wasn't a big drinker, Detective Santana. For the life of me, I can't understand how he could've possibly ended up in the middle of the river in winter unless someone drugged him and forced him into the water."

Mary Johnson's blank eyes teared and she dabbed them with a napkin.

"I read the autopsy report," Santana said. "No drugs other than alcohol were found."

"But we all know there are drugs that disappear quickly from the system. And unless the medical examiner knew exactly what drug to look for, she wouldn't find it."

Johnson had echoed the same thoughts as Jack Brody. Santana knew Johnson was correct. But he had no evidence to support the contention that Michael Johnson had been drugged and then murdered, and no desire to encourage speculation and the possibility of a resolution supporting that conclusion.

"Is there anything else you can tell me?" Santana asked.

James Johnson finished his coffee and stared at the empty cup a moment. "Well, when I went to Michael's apartment to retrieve his belongings, it was a mess, like someone had gone through the drawers and closets, looking for something."

"Was the lock damaged?"

"Yes," he said. "I believe someone broke in."

"What would they be looking for?"

"I have no idea. But you ought to talk to Mark Conroy."

"Who's Conroy?"

"A young man who survived."

"There's someone who fell in the river and lived to tell about it?"

"He didn't fall in," Johnson said with a slight edge in his voice.

"Where does Conroy live?"

"I don't know. You'll have to ask Jordan Parrish. But are you going to reopen the investigation into my son's death?"

"I can't promise that, Mr. Johnson."

"I'm not interested in promises, Detective Santana. I'm interested in results." His voice was louder now and more demanding. He turned to his wife. The skin below her eyes was streaked with blue eye shadow and damp with tears, though she was crying soundlessly. He slipped an arm around her shoulder and drew her to him. "Someone took our son from us," he said, his eyes suddenly gleaming with intensity. "And we want that someone to pay for what he did. Isn't that right, honey?"

The fixed smile returned to Mary Johnson's face as she stared at Santana, but her eyes held no hope.

Chapter 8

AFTER LEAVING THE JOHNSONS, Santana called Jordan Parrish and set up a meeting for early that evening. Then he drove to the Ramsey County Medical Examiner's Office on Plato Boulevard to see Reiko Tanabe. The concrete building, set back from the road, had a two-story wing attached to a dark brick and tinted glass atrium with another four-story wing to the west. In front were a large asphalt lot and two flagpoles closer to the entrance, one flying an American flag, the other a flag with the Ramsey County logo and name.

Drowning cases represented a unique challenge because the circumstances often complicated efforts to determine the exact cause of death. Santana needed to know if Scott Rafferty had been alive when he entered the water. And he needed to know why Rafferty had entered the water. But he might never know the circumstances surrounding Rafferty's death, unless he could prove it was a homicide.

When Santana walked into Tanabe's dark green, windowless office, she was sitting at an angle, working at her computer. Whitewashed furniture and light gray carpet brightened the room. The lampshades over the brass lamps on the end tables flanking the couch matched the walls, as did the wicker basket that held a tall silk plant standing in one corner. A large anatomy chart hung opposite a bookshelf filled with medical texts. Because Tanabe often met with the victim's family to discuss autopsy results, she had made a conscious effort to make her office warm and inviting. The office reminded Santana of a relaxing study.

"Am I interrupting, Reiko?"

As she shifted her head toward him, her long black ponytail swung across the back of the white medical coat she wore over a blue shirt. "Of course. But that's never bothered you before." She smiled and shook her head in resignation.

Santana noted that as usual Tanabe wore no makeup, and her only jewelry was a thin gold band on her left hand. Despite the trauma of viewing and cutting open dead bodies on a daily basis, her face was youthful. Most people would think she was in her twenties. But the graduation dates on her bachelor's and medical degrees from the University of Minnesota and her license from the American Board of Pathology hanging in frames proved she was actually in her forties. Santana saw no photos of any kind in her office, though he knew she was married and had two children.

"Let me guess," she said as he sat in a straight back chair opposite her desk. "You're here about the autopsy report on Scott Rafferty."

"You're so insightful."

She laughed and unconsciously touched the small café au lait mark on her neck. Then she swiveled her chair toward Santana, lifted a manila folder off the desktop, and handed it to him, her dark brown eyes shining behind the lenses of her wire-rimmed glasses. "I figured you'd be stopping by, so I printed a copy of this for you. Take a look at it and let me know if you have questions."

Santana opened the folder labeled SCOTT RAFFERTY. The first page of the autopsy report began with the date and time Tanabe had conducted the complete autopsy on Rafferty. Rafferty's full name, date of birth, age, race, and sex, along with the approximate date of death, and a case number followed this information. The SPPD was listed as the investigative agency.

The results of the external examination began halfway down the page with a description of the body after the clothes had been removed. Tanabe had indicated that hemorrhaging was present in the conjunctival surfaces of the eyes. Santana knew that exertion had probably caused the hemorrhaging. He skipped to the second page of the report and Tanabe's internal examination of the body.

She had noted the weight of the lungs and their ballooned appearance, which was caused by the active inhalation of air and water, something that could not be reproduced by passive flooding of the lungs with water. Both lungs had felt doughy and pitted when pressure was applied. On sectioning she had observed a flow of watery material. Bruising could be seen in the lower lobes. Tears in the alveolar walls had produced hemorrhages. Aspiration of large quantities of water had resulted in "over-distension of the pulmonary alveoli, which were thinned and stretched with narrowing and compression of the capillaries."

Santana wanted to know what it meant.

"It suggests that Rafferty came to the surface several times to inhale air and probably drowned over a relatively long period of time."

"Which means his death was likely not a suicide."

She nodded and Santana went back to the report.

Scott Rafferty's heart had a normal size, weight and configuration. Tanabe had found no evidence of atherosclerosis. Stomach contents had been saved. Routine toxicologic studies had been ordered. Samples of blood type had been collected, along with bile and tissue samples from the heart, lung, brain, kidney, liver, and spleen. Evidence collected included Rafferty's clothes, eleven autopsy photographs, one postmortem CT scan, and a postmortem MRI.

Toxicological tests revealed that Rafferty had had a low level of alcohol in his system. Tanabe had listed the cause of death as heart failure combined with blood volume expansion from the absorption of fresh water, as reflected in engorgement of the right side of the heart and large veins. Drowning was listed as the manner of death.

"So Rafferty drowned."

"That's my conclusion, John, but there are no universally accepted diagnostic laboratory tests for drowning. The diagnosis is largely one of exclusion. However, I did identify some pathological findings that indicate Scott Rafferty was alive when he went into the water."

"Such as?"

"You recall the foam exuding from the mouth and nostrils when the body was carried from the river."

"I do."

"The foam is a mixture of water, air, mucus, and probably a surfactant whipped up by respiratory efforts. The color was caused by blood. I've seen similar-looking foam with severe pulmonary edema in drug overdoses, congestive cardiac failure, and head injuries. But I found no such injuries when I autopsied Rafferty. I found the foam in the trachea and main bronchi. It's an indicator that Rafferty was alive at the time of submersion."

"Anything else?"

"Rafferty had water in his lungs."

"And if there was an absence of water in the lungs?"

"That could be an indication of death before submersion, or a very rapid death by drowning."

"Is that enough evidence to make a clear determination?"

She shook her head. "I found traces of silt and weeds in the airways. Also, diatoms taken from the lungs and circulatory organs matched the aquatic flora where the body was recovered. There was vomit in the esophagus and airways and large quantities of water and debris in the stomach, which again strongly suggests immersion during life. I also found hemorrhages in the boney middle ears that are commonly seen in drowning cases."

"Any evidence of ante mortem injuries?"

"Well, it's difficult to distinguish ante mortem from post mortem injuries because water immersion leaches the blood out of ante mortem wounds. On the other hand, post mortem wounds tend to bleed more readily than usual due to the fluidity of the blood, particularly in areas of dependent lividity, such as the face."

"And according to the toxicology tests, his blood alcohol level was low."

She leaned back in her chair again and looked at him. "Scott Rafferty weighed one hundred and seventy-two pounds and had a blood alcohol level of point zero seven."

"That's not high."

"No. That would be three or four drinks for a kid approximately his size."

"Any cocaine in Rafferty's system?"

"A trace."

"So you're saying that Rafferty was definitely alive when he entered the water."

She glanced at her computer screen and then shifted her gaze to Santana once again. "Yes. I'm basing this on the evidence I mentioned. Plus, victims struggling violently to survive in water bruise or rupture muscles. I found bilateral hemorrhages of the shoulder girdle, neck, and the scalene and pectoralis major muscles of the chest. They are strong indicators that Scott Rafferty was alive in the water."

Darkness was settling against the windows of the White Castle restaurant on Rice Street in St. Paul. The air was filled with the smell of steam-grilled beef patties, fried onions, and cheese. Santana sat down across a table from David Dalton, who wore a black leather jacket over a gray sweatshirt and a navy blue watch cap over his long brown hair. Dalton had a day-old growth of whiskers covering his cheeks and chin, and the same narrow face as his daughter, Kimberly.

Four black teenagers wearing blue shirts with matching shoelaces were seated at a table in the opposite corner of the restaurant talking loudly while warily eyeing the two detectives. Their jeans were two sizes too large for their skinny waists, and their baseball caps were cocked sideways on their heads. The blue colors and the belts with the ESB buckles indicated they belonged to the Eastside Boys, one of the most troublesome gangs in the city.

Dalton appeared to pay no attention to them as he finished a hamburger. "I was expecting you a half hour ago, Santana."

"Traffic is being diverted because of the rising river. Downtown is like a parking lot."

He nodded as if it were yesterday's news. "You're investigating Scott Rafferty's death."

"That's right. I understand he was your daughter's boyfriend. And you weren't real happy she was seeing him."

"I imagine Kimberly told you that."

"She did."

Dalton drank some coffee from a Styrofoam cup and gazed in the general direction of the four gangbangers. "You have any children?"

"I don't."

His eyes came back to Santana. They were the same color as the dark coffee in his cup. "If you had a daughter, then you'd know why I wasn't real happy about the relationship."

"Since I don't, maybe you can enlighten me."

Dalton set the cup on the table and wiped his mouth with a napkin. "She could do better than Scott Rafferty."

"Why is that?"

"Rafferty had all sorts of mental health issues. The war fucked him up good."

"Wouldn't be the first emotional casualty."

"No," Dalton said with a shake of his head. "It wouldn't. But I think he had a problem with the sugar booger as well."

Santana thought it might be Dalton's daughter that had the problem with cocaine, but he let it go. "Did Kimberly talk much about Scott?"

Dalton reached for his cup and then seemed to change his mind. "She wouldn't because she knew how I felt."

"But you knew about Scott Rafferty's problems because your partner was Hank Rafferty."

"Yeah. Hank used to tell me about his kid."

"Is that why you decided you wanted another partner?"

Dalton shrugged. "Partnerships get old, Santana. Sometimes you need a change."

"Nothing more than that?"

He shook his head again.

"You think Hank would say the same thing?"

"I don't know. Why don't you ask him?"

"What if I already have?"

A half smile curled his lip. "Don't play head games with me."

"Okay, Dalton. If you say there's nothing more to it."

His eyes flamed with anger. "Since when did it become any of your business, Santana?"

The four teenagers stood and shuffled noisily out of the restaurant, their gaze never settling on the two detectives.

"I've got nothing more to tell you," Dalton said. "Except I don't want you hassling my daughter."

"So interviewing her is out of bounds?"

He pointed his index finger. "You know what I mean."

"You ever have any dealings with an ex-con named Devante Carter?"

Dalton's gaze slid away. "Name doesn't ring a bell."

Santana sensed David Dalton was lying. He wanted to know why.

Santana drove over to O'Gara's after leaving the White Castle. As he parked his Crown Vic in the lot behind the restaurant on Snelling Avenue in St. Paul, his eyes settled on a gray, late model Dodge van with tinted windows. It was larger than a family van and had rear doors instead of the more common side door. Most vans its size belonged to companies, with the company name lettered on the sides. He was sure he would have noticed it regardless of the circumstance, because it was a surveillance vehicle. But he wasn't surprised to see it in the lot considering he was about to meet private investigator Jordan Parrish.

The bar was dark and warm and full of the dull gleam of bottles, mahogany, and brass. Santana stood still for a moment till his eyes caught those of a woman sitting alone in a booth. Her dark blond, medium-length hair was layered so that it appeared slightly tousled. He had heard the style referred to as a bed haircut, because women could comb and style it with their fingers when they got out of bed.

She stood and offered a slim hand as he approached. Her grip was firm and warm. "Nice to meet you, Detective Santana." Her white, even teeth gleamed in the soft light as she smiled, and tiny smile lines appeared at the corners of her mouth.

"Thanks for agreeing to see me on such short notice," he said. "Sorry I'm late."

"No problem. I just got here myself." She unbuttoned her navy blue blazer, revealing a red crewneck cotton sweater.

"That your surveillance van in the lot?"

She nodded. "My most recent purchase."

He caught the hint of lavender and jasmine in her floral perfume as they sat down in the cushioned booth. She was tan, and he wondered if she had recently vacationed in Mexico or the Caribbean. He wasn't sure why, but he thought he would like her better if her color had been acquired naturally rather than in a tanning bed.

"Can I order you a drink?"

"You most certainly can," she said. "I'll have a glass of Cabernet."

Santana called the waitress over and ordered a glass of wine and a bottle of Sam Adams. "So has the economic downturn hurt the private investigating business?"

She shook her head. "I'm busier than ever."

"Any idea why?"

"A significant portion of my business involves cheating spouses. When the economy is bad, men and women struggle financially. That struggle often leads to problems in the marriage, which leads to cheating. At least that's my theory."

"Might be some truth in it," he said. "How long have you been a private investigator?"

"Nearly eight years."

"Kind of an unusual choice of a profession."

"My dad was a Minneapolis cop, my mom a public defender."

"Ever any conflicts representing both sides of the law?"

She smiled. "Occasionally. My mother tended to be more liberal than my father. She still has photos of herself marching against the war in Vietnam. But they loved and respected each other enough to put aside their political differences. I think it helped that my father retired early and did some security consulting."

"How did you get into the business?"

"I spent three years with the MPD."

"Not very long."

"Too long, really. I like a job where I can set my own hours. I also had some difficulty taking orders," she said with another smile. "After I left the department, I worked with my father in security consulting for two years and then started this business."

The waitress returned with the glass of Cabernet and a bottle of beer.

Jordan Parrish's pretty hazel eyes moved around the room until the waitress left and then settled on his face again. "You think what I do is kind of sleazy, Detective?"

Santana shook his head. "Not in the least. You work homicide cases, you become a little jaded about the behavior of the human race."

"Not a real optimist, huh?"

"Let's just say the future of society appears rather bleak."

"Then why do it? Why not look for another line of work?"

"I find satisfaction in putting criminals behind bars. And I'm good at what I do."

"Nice to meet a man with confidence," she said and sipped her wine.

She looked at him without speaking for a time, her eyes glittering with amusement and intelligence. They focused briefly on the long, jagged scar on the back of his right hand and then moved back to his face. Finally, she said, "I've read about you in the papers."

"Have you."

"You've had some high profile cases."

"That's true," he said.

"And you were nearly killed."

"That's true as well."

"The possibility of death doesn't bother you?"

"You mean my death or the perp's death?"

"Both, I guess."

He looked at the bottle of Sam Adams and then at her again. "I'm not in any hurry to die."

She nodded and drank more wine, her lips leaving a small red crescent on the edge of the glass. "I've never killed anyone. Haven't even fired my gun."

"It's better if you don't."

"I imagine taking a life would be difficult to live with." She seemed to be waiting for him to reply. When he didn't, she said, "How come you're interviewing Michael Johnson's parents? I thought the SPPD closed that case."

"We did. I'm actually investigating the drowning death of Scott Rafferty."

"The young man whose body was found a few days ago in the river."

"Uh-huh. Do you know anything about him?"

Her eyes were direct and unwavering as she looked at him. "No. Why would you think I would?"

"You've had dealings with Michael Johnson's parents. And with Mark Conroy."

"Only because Johnson's parents hired me."

"So what can you tell me about Conroy?"

She opened the large purse resting on the leather cushion beside her. As she rummaged through it, Santana saw a hot pink can of mace pepper spray and a black polymer G-27 Glock, the same type and caliber backup weapon he carried while he was off-duty.

She found the spiral notebook she was searching for and flipped open the pages, scanning her handwritten notes before her eyes focused on Santana again. "Conroy claimed he was drinking with friends in a St. Paul bar until one in the morning and then somehow ended up in the middle of the Mississippi."

"What bar?"

"Billy's on Grand Avenue."

"That's the same bar where Scott Rafferty was last seen."

"Remarkable coincidence, huh?"

Santana nodded but said nothing.

"Anyway, Conroy fought the strong current that carried him downstream till he was able to grab onto an overhanging branch and pull himself to shore, where he passed out. Later that morning he showed up at a Regions Hospital, confused and missing his shirt and shoes."

"And he had no idea how he ended up in the river?"

She shook her head. "He recalled leaving the bar and walking toward his dorm on the St. Thomas campus. Next thing he remembered, he was in the river."

"Did he meet anyone new that night?"

"He remembered talking with one woman."

"What did she look like?"

"Black hair. Attractive."

Santana thought of Kimberly Dalton. "Long hair or short?"

"Shoulder length."

"Tall or short?"

"She was medium height. Kind of thin."

"Anything distinctive about her?"

"That was all Conroy remembered about her," she said.

"Did he recall talking with anyone else?"

"Outside of the bartender, no."

"What was the bartender's name?"

Jordan checked her notes. "Jeff. Conroy didn't know his last name. But he's been a bartender there for quite awhile."

"This happened when?"

"Middle of January."

"And the river wasn't frozen over?"

"There was ice but also open water."

"If he was drunk and confused, he could easily have fallen through the ice or into open water," Santana said.

"Conroy told me he only had two beers. He needed to complete an essay, so he made sure he wasn't drunk."

"You think he was telling the truth?"

"I do. His friends supported his contention that he was sober."

"And none of them saw anything or anyone suspicious or unusual."

"No."

"What do you think happened?"

She paused and drank some wine, holding the glass in her right hand, her pretty eyes flickering up and to the right as she accessed her visual memory.

Santana had learned to read people and to determine if they were telling the truth by watching for shifts in breathing, body posture, gestures, eye movement, and language patterns. It was second nature to him now, though he wished sometimes that he could step out of his cop persona on occasion and just have a normal conversation.

"I believe someone drugged Conroy in the bar," she said. "Then they followed him when he left and waited for the drug to take effect."

"You believe the same thing happened to Michael Johnson?"

"The situations sound awfully similar."

"Which means what? There's a serial killer on the loose targeting college age young men?"

"You sound skeptical."

"It's my nature."

"Well, I'd say there's a definite pattern," she said. "It's always in the back of my mind. Whenever I have time, I find myself coming back to it."

"Was Conroy a vet?"

She shook her head. "Why do you ask?"

"No reason," he said.

Her eyes searched his face, as if she might find the meaning of his question there.

95

"Do you have an address and phone number for Conroy?" he asked.

She held her gaze for a moment longer before she peered at her notes again. Then she wrote down an address and phone number on a clean sheet of paper, tore the page out of her spiral notebook, and pushed it across the table.

"I don't think he'll talk to you, Detective."

"Why not?"

"He's afraid."

"Of what?"

"He thinks someone's stalking him."

"He has no idea who it is?"

"No. But I recall he had slight tremor in his hands, and there were dark circles under his eyes, as if he lacked sleep. He had dropped out of college. He was a mess."

"Why did he agree to talk to you?"

Jordan Parrish smiled coyly and lifted her wine glass and held it close to her lips. "I can be very persuasive."

Santana had absolutely no doubt about that. "How did you find out about Conroy when no one else did?"

"Actually, I didn't. He contacted the Johnsons to ask about their son's death. I just tracked him down."

"Why didn't Conroy go to the police?"

"Apparently, he did. But the detective assigned to the case didn't believe his story."

"Pete Romano?"

"That's right."

"Did Conroy tell Detective Romano about the dark-haired woman he talked to?"

"He said that he did."

"Has Conroy told the police he thinks he's being stalked?"

She shook her head. "The SPPD didn't believe his story the last time. He figures they won't believe him now."

Santana drank some beer. He hadn't eaten since breakfast and could feel the heat of the alcohol in his bloodstream. He had noted that Jordan Parrish wore no wedding ring, so he took a chance.

"You in a big hurry, Ms. Parrish?"

She cocked her head and let the seconds stretch before responding. "Why do you ask?"

"I wondered if you would join me for dinner?"

"I'm sorry. I do have another appointment."

Santana shrugged. "Perhaps another time, then."

"No one at home to cook for you, Detective?" she said with a wry smile.

"Just me."

"That's a shame."

"Maybe," he said. "Then again, maybe not."

Santana was waiting for the waitress to bring his dinner when a man slid into the booth opposite him. He had a bottle of Budweiser in his right hand and bags under his brown eyes. The streaks of gray in his brown crewcut hair, and the crow's feet and lines at the corners of his mouth, told Santana he was middle-aged. Along with his blue suit, black tie, and hi-gloss oxford dress shoes with thick soles, he might just as well have worn a sandwich board that read "federal agent."

"Ed Kincaid, FBI," he said, holding up his wallet.

"I would never have guessed."

"Who's the babe you were talking to?"

Santana looked at him without answering. "What do you want, Kincaid?"

"We need to discuss your current case."

"I don't think so."

"Look, Santana, I'm doing you a favor. I could be talking to your commander right now instead of you."

"Is that supposed to frighten me?"

"Why don't you cut the wiseass routine and listen to what I have to say?"

"Fine. I'll listen until my dinner is served."

Kincaid shrugged and leaned forward, the bottle of beer standing between his two thick hands. "We know all about you, Santana."

"Really?"

"Yeah. How you came to the States from Colombia at sixteen. How you changed your name from Juan Carlos Gutiérrez Arángo to John Santana."

Santana felt a current of concern shoot through his body. He feared the FBI knew that he had killed the Estrada brothers, knew about his sister, Natalia, which could put her life in danger.

"You were in Colombia recently," Kincaid said.

"So?"

"So you hadn't been there for over twenty years."

"And that's a crime?"

"No. But maybe you can tell me why you changed your name?"

Santana stared at him, relieved the feds didn't know as much about him as he'd feared. But he offered no response.

"Well," Kincaid said after a long pause, "women change their names when they get married. Hell, some men do it, too." He had a smile on his face but none in his eyes. "If my background info is correct, you're not married."

Santana waited.

Kincaid drank slowly from his bottle of beer and then wiped his mouth with a napkin as a drop of condensation slid down the side of the brown bottle. "I get the whole Gutiérrez Arángo thing. That's your Latino culture. But I never understood the idea behind the hyphenated name crap we see with women in this country. Where's the tradition? When a woman marries a man, she takes his name. That's the way it's supposed to be."

"You married, Kincaid?"

"Divorced."

"I'm not surprised."

Kincaid gave a joyless laugh. "Spoken like a guy who's never been married."

The waitress came with Santana's dinner. "Can I get you both another beer?"

"He'll be leaving soon," Santana said with a nod at the FBI agent. "And I'm fine." When she left, he said, "Why don't you get to the point, Kincaid, before my food gets cold?"

He smiled again without warmth. "Okay. Here's the point. Scott Rafferty drowned. He wasn't murdered."

"How do you know?"

"Because I looked at the same autopsy results you did. There was no murder."

"Maybe not."

Kincaid's posture straightened and he spread his hands. "Well, then. We've got no problem." He drank some beer.

"Why does the FBI care if I'm investigating Scott Rafferty's death?"

"That's not your concern."

Santana looked straight at him. "I think it is."

"Wrong again."

"First you threaten to talk to my boss. Now you're telling me to back off and won't give me a reason. All this lame ass intimidation makes me curious, Kincaid."

"I wouldn't call this discussion intimidation."

"What would you call it?"

"Good advice."

"Thanks. But I don't like being told what I can and can't do when it comes to an investigation."

"That fits with your history, Santana. It's why I'm giving you fair warning before you step in some deep shit that won't rub off easily."

"Gee, Kincaid. You're the first fed who's ever genuinely cared about me."

"Don't fuck up your career by wasting your time investigating the kid's death. He drowned. And don't waste time listening to Jack Brody. The guy's a lush."

"You know Brody?"

"Yeah. And I know about the bullshit he's been slinging."

"What bullshit is that?"

"There's a serial killer drowning scores of college kids. Brody's been peddling that story for years, ever since he drank himself out of a job."

"Scott Rafferty wasn't the first to drown."

"And Rafferty probably won't be the last college kid to drown," Kincaid said.

"Scott Rafferty wasn't a kid, and he wasn't currently enrolled in college. He was an Iraq war vet who had a fear of water."

"Here's a news bulletin for you, Detective. Young guys get drunk and careless. That's what happened to Rafferty."

Santana shook his head. "I thought that at first. Rafferty got drunk and fell in the river. But for his family's sake and to satisfy my own curiosity, I wanted to do a thorough investigation."

"Any good cop would."

"But now you show up, Kincaid. That raises questions in my mind."

"Such as?"

"We wouldn't be talking if the FBI didn't suspect something else was going on."

"You're on the wrong track."

"Maybe. But I think I'll keep digging. See what turns up."

Kincaid finished his beer and stood up. "It's you
Santana. Don't say I didn't warn you."

*That night, Santana dreams he is seated on the deck c
powerboat docked in the Caribbean. Sunlight glistens off whi
bones floating on the surface of the water.*

*Off the bow, he spots a tanned Jordan Parrish in a small
drifting toward him.*

*He stands and waves to her, but she does not see him.
are locked on the water around her, and on the three shark fins
suddenly circling her small boat.*

*Along the horizon behind her, Santana can see dar
strung with curtains of rain. He calls to Jordan to toss him a
she is bound to the seat of the boat and unable to move.*

*Other small boats are floating toward him now, piloted
whose bodies have caught fire. Santana can hear their scream:
flames peeling away the flesh from their bones.*

*The sun is sinking fast in the western sky, creating long
that darken the shoreline and fall across the boats like smudge
prints. He watches helplessly as the men's bodies collapse like
ed buildings—and the flames turn their bones to dust.*

Chapter 9

EARLY THE NEXT MORNING, SANTANA spent an hour at his office desk reviewing the notes he had written during his investigation of Scott Rafferty's apparent drowning. He also updated the Investigating Officer's Chronological form. Then he found a Wikipedia link to Jack Brody on his office computer.

> Jack Brody was born on January 2, 1947, in Richmond, Virginia. He attended Columbia University, where he earned his bachelor's degree in 1969. After his graduation, he was drafted into the United States Army and served in the Vietnam War, where he was assigned as a correspondent for the military newspaper *Stars and Stripes*. Brody won several Army journalism awards for his work. After receiving an honorable discharge from the Army, he earned his master's degree at Columbia and took a job at the *Washington Post*. He later worked for the *New York Times*, where he won the Pulitzer Prize for investigative reporting that exposed corruption within a narcotics unit of the NYPD. A congressional investigation resulted in a review of several tainted criminal cases and the firing of three NYPD officers and two FBI agents. In 2008, Brody left the *New York Times*.

In the box to the right of the article, Santana could see that Brody had been married and divorced twice and that he had no children. Since Pulitzer Prizes were not handed out like candy, Santana drew the obvious conclusion that Brody had been a very good investigative reporter. Whether he was still a good reporter with a legitimate story to tell was an open question.

Santana called Brody and set up a lunch meeting. Then he found a number for the *New York Times* and dialed. He spoke briefly with three people before he was connected to an editor named Carl Costello who knew Brody.

"You say you work out of St. Paul homicide, Detective Santana."

"That's correct."

"Has something happened to Jack?"

"No. He's fine."

"What's he doing in St. Paul?"

"Let me explain." Santana summarized what Brody had told him about the numerous drowning deaths of college-age young men.

Costello said, "That sounds like something Jack would pursue."

"Are you familiar with the story?"

"I am. But, frankly, the *Times* never put much stock in it."

"I'm more interested in what you can tell me about Brody than the story."

"Well, I haven't seen or talked with Jack for a couple of years. But I do remember that he was one hell of a reporter."

"Was?"

"Hell, he probably still is."

"Why did he leave the *Times*?"

"I'm not at liberty to discuss that, Detective Santana. There was a confidentiality agreement."

"Would you consider Brody a violent man?"

"No. I don't believe Jack was ever an aggressive man. What he saw and experienced in Vietnam pretty much reinforced his non-violent nature."

"Did he tell you that, or is it your opinion?"

"Both."

"Do you think he's trustworthy?"

"I've known Jack for over twenty years. I've never known him to lie. In fact, he can be a little too honest. Some people might call him abrasive. I'd call him tenacious. That's a quality I think you need in a reporter. Probably the same in a detective."

"So it's unlikely that he would fabricate a story."

Costello paused before he answered. "I don't believe Jack would ever do that."

"Why the hesitation?"

"I think he would like to get his career on track again before he retires."

"Meaning he might be chasing ghosts?"

"You said that, Detective Santana, not me."

The seven detectives assigned to the Homicide Unit each had a separate desk. Six were located in a large common work area, which was separated from the rest of the floor by sound partitions. Only the most senior detective, Pete Romano, and the commander, Rita Gamboni, had separate offices.

Romano's office door was open. Santana walked over, leaned against the doorframe, and said, "Got a minute?"

Romano was seated behind his cluttered desk, his olive skin and jet-black hair a stark contrast to his white shirt. He waved Santana in.

Santana closed the door behind him and sat in a chair facing Romano. "I heard you applied for the Eastern Patrol District's senior commander position."

Romano nodded. "I think it's time for a move. Particularly when there are positions about to open."

"You mean besides the district position?"

Romano waved his thick hands in a defensive gesture. "I can't say anything more right now, John."

Like in any public or private business, promotions within the SPPD were based as much on ass kissing as on qualifications. Santana had no desire to be anything but a homicide detective. He had an excellent record and a medal of valor, and members of his department respected him. But Rita Gamboni had often run interference for him with the higher brass and protected him from those who viewed him more as a loner and renegade. He knew he had little chance for promotion if he ever desired one. That wasn't the case with Pete Romano. He was a good detective, but he was also a man who rarely made waves.

"Good luck," Santana said.

"I appreciate the support, John, but something else brought you in here."

"I've been looking into the drowning death of Scott Rafferty."

Romano nodded as though he had expected the response. "Yeah. That was a real kick in the balls for Hank. I don't know what I'd do if I lost one of my sons."

Romano had family pictures of his attractive wife, three sons, and two daughters, the gold-framed photos hanging on the walls and sitting on his desktop. He had come from a large Italian family and was always talking about family events. One kid was in college and another would soon enroll. Santana figured some of Romano's ambition was driven by the need for a higher salary.

Santana stared at one of the Romano family photos on the desk and reflected that the only photo of his own family he possessed was a faded, wrinkled one he kept in his wallet. It was of his deceased mother taken shortly before she was murdered.

"You worked the Michael Johnson case," he said.

Romano nodded. "That's right."

"And you found nothing unusual about his death."

Romano narrowed his dark eyes as though not understanding the question. "What are you getting at, John?"

"Maybe you had some thoughts about the case that weren't in your written report?"

"You read it?"

"I did."

"Then you know as much as I know."

Santana waited a few beats before speaking again. "I talked with Johnson's parents."

Romano sat back in his chair and let his eyes wander toward the ceiling and then back to Santana's face. "Yeah. I remember the mother was as fragile as cracked glass. And the father didn't like it much when I couldn't find any evidence supporting his contention his son was murdered."

"So you believe Michael Johnson's death was accidental."

Romano shrugged and laced his fingers over his burgeoning belly. "Unless it was suicide."

"You didn't suggest that in your report."

"I didn't suggest it because I had no concrete evidence it was. Just like I had no evidence suggesting he was murdered."

"What about Mark Conroy?"

Romano raised his heavy eyebrows in surprise, creating long horizontal wrinkles in his forehead. "You talked with Conroy?"

Santana shook his head. "Not yet."

"Don't waste your time. The kid can't tell you anything new."

"Maybe not."

"No maybes about it, John. Conroy got drunk and wandered into the river. He was damn lucky he didn't drown. Michael Johnson wasn't as fortunate."

Santana nodded but remained silent.

Romano regarded him a moment and said, "You know something about either of those cases that I don't?"

"No."

"So why the sudden interest?"

"I'm just making sure Scott Rafferty's death isn't something other than it appears."

Romano leaned forward, his hands gripping the armrests on the chair. "Don't go reading something into these deaths that isn't there."

Santana knew what Romano was getting at. If Michael Johnson was murdered rather than drowned, it wouldn't look good on Romano's record and might sink his chances for a promotion. Santana was only interested in the truth whatever the consequences, but there was no sense in alienating Romano. He might need his help later. Santana thought of a way he could smooth things over with his colleague.

"It's the least I can do for Hank," he said.

"Yeah. It's good you're doing it for Hank."

Santana caught the sarcasm in Romano's words, but he made no objection. He was continuing the investigation as much for himself as for anyone else, and apparently Romano understood that.

"You know Gamboni may not be around forever," Romano said.

"What's that supposed to mean?"

"Forget it. Was there something else?"

Yes, Santana thought. But he knew he wouldn't get anything more from Romano.

Later that morning, Santana rode a glass-sided elevator up twelve floors to Dr. Benjamin Roth's office. He checked in with the receptionist, then sat on a black leather couch and glanced around the waiting room. The modern paintings hanging on the walls looked like Rorschach inkblots. A large dieffenbachia crouched in a corner, and classical music played quietly in the background. Santana paged through copies of *The New Yorker* and *Forbes* magazine that were carefully arranged on the coffee table in front of him until the receptionist gestured toward Roth's office and said, "Dr. Roth will see you now."

Thick brown carpeting, light brown leather chairs, and mahogany paneling gave Roth's office an expensive appearance, while track lighting bathed it all in a soft glow. Bookshelves filled with heavy bound volumes covered two walls. On a third wall, a thin drape covered the floor-to-ceiling glass that offered a view of the downtown skyline and the cloudy western horizon. A narrow hallway along the fourth wall led to a private door that faced the tenth-floor corridor. Santana figured the door ensured that arriving patients wouldn't encounter departing ones.

"Nice to meet you, Detective." Roth smiled warmly as he came around his mahogany desk and put out his hand. His handshake was firm, and his eyes were filled with reassurance. They nearly matched the color of his steel gray hair. He wore a charcoal cashmere sweater over a white button-down shirt, gray slacks, and black loafers. Casual. Successful.

"Coffee, tea, or water?" he asked, walking with the tall grace of an athlete toward a serving cart near the window.

"I'm fine. Thanks."

"Please sit down," he said as he poured a cup of tea from the teapot on the serving cart. Santana lowered himself into a soft leather chair opposite the desk.

Roth carried a teacup and saucer to his desk and settled into a high-backed leather chair behind it. He took a sip of tea and then set the cup and saucer carefully on the desktop in front of him.

"I appreciate you taking the time to see me," Santana said.

"Fortunately, I had a cancellation. But I have another appointment in forty-five minutes."

"I'll make this as brief as I can."

Roth added a smile to his nod. "My receptionist indicated you're investigating Scott Rafferty's death."

"I am."

Roth rested his elbows on the arm of the chair, tented his hands, and placed his fingertips under his chin, contemplating. "Was Scott's death something other than an accidental drowning?"

"I don't know. And until I'm sure, I'll keep looking."

"I imagine persistence is an asset in your profession."

"I think it's an asset no matter what you do for a living."

Roth smiled again. "Well said, Detective. How I can help?"

"I understand you were treating Scott Rafferty for post-traumatic stress disorder."

"I'm sorry I can't give you specific information about a patient, Detective, even a dead one. But I'm guessing you already knew that."

Santana did. But he had taken a chance, hoping to save himself time. Now he tried another approach. "Have you treated a number of Iraq and Afghanistan veterans?"

"Unfortunately, I've seen far too many young men with PTSD as a result of their war experiences. Over half the Iraq and Afghanistan combat vets report readjustment problems. Many of them suffer from MTBI."

Santana was leafing through his notebook, looking for a clean page. He looked up. "Sorry?"

"Mild traumatic brain injury," Roth said. "You're probably more familiar with the term 'shell shock' or getting your bell rung. It's a physical injury to the brain caused by blows to the head. Boxers sometimes suffer from it. But it's the most common battlefield injury. Nearly twenty percent of the soldiers returning from Iraq and Afghanistan have had an MTBI. Most of those are what we call closed brain injuries caused by exposure to a blast from improvised explosive devices."

Santana had seen plenty of newsreel footage of heavily armored US vehicles being blown apart like tin cans while driving over IUDs on the dirt roads in Iraq and Afghanistan. He could only imagine what the explosions could do to the brains and bodies of the soldiers inside those vehicles.

"PTSD frequently co-occurs with MTBI in combat soldiers returning from Iraq and Afghanistan," Roth continued. "So much so that together we refer to them as signature injuries. Most vets recover from MTBI within a year, but up to one-third will have ongoing physical, cognitive, and emotional symptoms, often called post-concussion syndrome."

Roth paused for a moment and drank some tea before speaking again. "In previous wars, soldiers were less likely to survive blast injuries. But advances in body armor have resulted in more soldiers surviving. Kevlar helmets have reduced the frequency of penetrating head injuries. However, they can't completely protect the head and neck, nor prevent closed brain injuries."

"Is MTBI difficult to diagnose?" Santana asked.

Roth nodded. "It's also nearly impossible to visualize on magnetic resonance imaging or computerized tomography. And symptoms such as amnesia are common in both MTBI and PTSD. But it's difficult to determine if the amnesia is an organic symptom related to the brain injury or a psychological symptom associated with PTSD."

"It's my understanding that some veterans refuse to be treated, especially by the VA."

"Unfortunately, that's true. Mental health problems are still stigmatized in the military, more so than brain injury. Soldiers are often concerned that seeking psychiatric help will impede career advancement or their ability to obtain a security clearance. So they may purposely misattribute symptoms of PTSD to MTBI."

"Because MTBI is more acceptable?"

"Exactly. But accurate assessment and diagnosis of the two disorders is important."

"How so?"

"The two conditions are treated differently. PTSD is usually treated with counseling and anti-anxiety or antidepressant medications, whereas MTBI typically requires some combination of occupational, physical, and cognitive therapy. The military use screening instruments that can be helpful, but many aren't empirically sound. So diagnosis depends a great deal on a psychiatrist's ability to recognize symptoms of the two disorders."

Santana wrote some notes and then looked at Roth again. "Perhaps we could talk in general terms about the symptoms of post traumatic stress disorder."

"I believe we could do that," he said with a nod.

"What symptoms might a veteran like Scott Rafferty experience?"

"Many have flashbacks, nightmares, and difficulty falling or staying asleep. Memory complaints, headaches, dizziness, fatigue, and noise and light intolerance are not uncommon. Some suffer from depression, anxiety, irritability, increased aggression, and hypervigilance."

"I'm not sure what hypervigilance means."

"It's one of the classic symptoms of PTSD. A soldier is overly sensitive to sights and sounds in the environment and is constantly expecting danger. That leaves him—or her—feeling keyed up and on edge most of the time. It also leaves him exhausted. Many vets have difficulty returning to routine or daily activities."

"So just thinking about a traumatic event can trigger a flashback."

"Yes. The memory of it is inadequately processed in the brain and stored in an isolated memory network. Whenever this network is activated, the victim re-experiences aspects of the original event and often overreacts."

"I imagine many vets don't want to talk or think about the incident."

"That's correct. They often choose to avoid anything that might lead them to remember it. Some actually withdraw from life."

Although Santana had never experienced flashbacks, his vivid nightmares of his deadly encounter with the Estrada brothers were surely a symptom of PTSD. These nightmares had never debilitated him, nor had they affected his ability to function, so he had never sought therapy and had only shared his violent childhood history with Phil and Dorothy O'Toole—and with his former partner and now his homicide commander, Rita Gamboni.

"Could a traumatic childhood event also cause PTSD? For example, witnessing your mother's drowning?"

Roth sipped some tea before responding, his pinky finger pointed out as he drank. "Certainly. Some psychiatrists ascribe to the nurture model, which postulates that environmental stress can trigger the symptoms. Others believe that certain individuals are predisposed to abnormal behavior. The nature model."

"Where do you stand?"

"I believe certain disorders may result from a combination of one's genetics and early learning. But even if that's so, less than ten percent of the population develops full PTSD. A tragic childhood experience may contribute to PTSD. But war experiences and other violent encounters can lead to PTSD and to a depressed state."

Santana could still see his own mother's death vividly in his mind's eye, as though it had occurred yesterday. He couldn't help but wonder now if therapy could end the nightmares that so often disrupted his sleep.

But his nightmares and vivid dreams often gave him a direction to follow in cases where he saw nothing but darkness and dead ends. And memories of his past kept him focused on his purpose and on his mission in life. He would not be the man he was without his memories. Yet those same memories also fed the vengeful demon inside him that sometimes sought to push him over the edge and into the shadowy world of those murderers he pursued.

"So the majority of returning troops don't show symptoms of PTSD."

"No," Roth said. "But the behavioral manifestations of PTSD and MTBI may not become evident until weeks or months after the battlefield experience. Many vets frequently don't associate the problems with exposure to trauma or brain injury, or they underestimate their symptoms. Many engage in risky behaviors. Many also have anger issues."

Santana recalled Hank Rafferty's claim that his son was improving and was planning to enroll in college this fall. If true, it made Scott Rafferty's death all the more tragic.

"You're a licensed psychiatrist," he said.

"That's correct."

"So you can do what psychologists can't do in the US."

"You mean prescribe drugs."

Santana nodded.

"I believe that Louisiana and New Mexico allow psychologists to prescribe drugs after consulting with a psychiatrist, but you're essentially correct."

"Is that the main reason why a veteran like Scott Rafferty might choose to see you instead of a psychologist or clinical therapist?"

Roth sipped some tea and thought about it. "A common misconception about psychiatrists is that we only treat people with severe mental illness and diseases for which medication is the primary course of treatment, that we leave psychotherapy to psychologists and patients with less severe problems. In fact, many of my clients are not on medication."

113

"But you're more expensive."

Roth's pleasant smile indicated he was not the least bit offended. "That's true. And if a client participates in a health insurance plan, the plan's fee structure may discourage time spent on psychotherapy, which may last for months. So many seeking treatment choose a psychologist or clinical therapist rather than a psychiatrist, with the encouragement of their insurance provider."

"So why not concentrate less on therapy and more on prescribing medication?"

"Because I enjoy counseling and therapy," Roth said. "And often both are necessary."

Santana peered as his notebook and the questions he had written. "What can you tell me about a drug called Inderal?"

"It's the brand name for propranolol."

Santana shook his head. "I've never heard of it."

"Well, I'm sure you've experienced periods of adrenaline release, Detective Santana, especially in your profession."

"On occasion."

"Then you know that feelings of fear can cause the body to release large amounts of adrenaline into the bloodstream. While an adrenaline release may be useful when preparing for a fight or fleeing a dangerous situation, it can become inhibitory when one wishes to remain calm, such as when giving a presentation or taking a test. Musicians and actors sometimes take the drug to prevent stage fright. It's one of the banned substances in the Olympics. I recall that a North Korean pistol shooter who won two medals at the 2008 Olympic games was disqualified for using it. Propranolol is also often prescribed for migraines or for hypertension because it lowers blood pressure."

Santana wrote down the information. "So you prescribed propranolol for Scott."

Roth smiled again. "I can't tell you that."

"Well, then, what specifically does the drug do, Dr. Roth?"

"It's a beta-blocker, which means it prevents unnecessary cardiac stimulation by restricting adrenaline release during anxious moments. By blocking the trigger response of adrenaline, propranolol helps the patient to remain in control during stress-inducing situations."

"Such as a flashback."

"Yes, that would be one example."

"How is it taken?"

"Usually in sustained-release oral form."

Santana straightened in his chair. "Like a capsule?"

"Yes. That's how a patient would normally take it."

"What's a normal dose?"

"A single, forty milligram, fast-acting dose immediately after memory recall, with an additional sixty milligram, extended-release dose administered about two hours later."

"What would happen if the capsule was broken open?"

"Well, a broken capsule would cause too much of the drug to be released at one time."

"What if it was taken in conjunction with alcohol?"

"Drinking alcohol would increase blood levels of propranolol."

"What are the symptoms of an overdose?"

"Slow or uneven heartbeats, dizziness, weakness, fainting, nausea and vomiting. In severe cases an overdose could induce coma, convulsions, shock, or respiratory depression."

Santana flipped back his notebook pages to his interview with Kimberly Dalton and found what he was looking for. "What happens if a patient stops taking the drug?"

"A patient has to be gradually weaned off the drug. They can't just decide one day to quit taking it."

"Why is that?"

"Suddenly stopping a patient from taking propranolol could cause sharp chest pain, irregular heartbeat, and sometimes heart attack. The risk would be greater if the patient had heart disease. The best way is to slowly lower the dose over several weeks. I also advise my patients to limit their physical activity while the dose is lowered."

"And why would you take Scott off the drug?"

Roth smiled again and let out a small sigh. "Now Detective Santana, you recall we're talking in generalities and not about a specific patient like Scott Rafferty."

"My mistake."

"I doubt that it was a mistake." Roth was still smiling.

Santana ignored his response and re-phrased the question. "So why would you take a patient off the medication?"

Roth thought about it before replying. "In most cases we would be making progress using a therapeutic technique called Eye Movement Desensitization and Reprocessing."

"Like reading body language?"

"No. That's different. EMDR therapy uses right and left eye movement to activate the opposite sides of the brain. Remember I said earlier that traumatic memories are stored in the brain with all the sights, sounds, thoughts, and feelings that accompanied those memories. When soldiers suffering from PTSD get very upset, their brains are unable to process the experience as they normally would. The negative thoughts and feelings of the traumatic event are essentially trapped in the nervous system. Since the patient's brain can't adequately process these emotions, soldiers often suppress their war experiences from consciousness. But the distress lives on in the brain and nervous system and affects their ability to function emotionally. Traditional therapies such as cognitive behavioral therapy often focus on memories from the unconscious mind and then analyze their meaning to gain insight into the problem. EMDR therapy unlocks the negative memories and emotions stored in the nervous system and helps the brain successfully process the experience."

"Do you generally see results?"

"Absolutely. Whenever soldiers recall a traumatic event, we work together to re-direct the eye movements that accompany the recall of the experience, allowing the accompanying emotions to be released. I continue the patterns of eye movements until the emotions are neutralized and the event is re-associated with more positive thoughts and feelings." Roth ended the thought with a glance at the Rolex on his wrist.

"I know you have an appointment," Santana said. "I have just two more questions."

"All right."

"Would a patient have any extra capsules of propranolol?"

"Well, I monitor prescriptions very closely. But a patient could miss a dose."

"Did you see Scott Rafferty as suicidal?"

"Again, I can't provide a definitive answer to that question. I believe the circumstances surrounding Scott's death fall under your area of expertise, Detective Santana."

Chapter 10

SANTANA LEFT ROTH'S OFFICE and took the elevator to the parking ramp underneath the building. When he was settled inside his detective sedan, he called Reiko Tanabe.

"I want you to recheck Scott Rafferty's tissue samples for propranolol, Reiko. His psychiatrist was using it to treat him for PTSD."

"Okay," she said. "I'll let you know when the propranolol tests are complete."

Santana ended the call and dialed Tony Novak's number at the station. When Novak answered, he said, "Remember the time release capsule I found in Scott Rafferty's apartment, Tony?"

"Explicitly," he said. "I found a set of prints."

"Rafferty's?"

"No."

"Did you run the prints through IAFIS?"

"I did, John. But I got no match."

The Integrated Automated Fingerprint Identification System provided automated fingerprint search capabilities, latent search capability, electronic image storage, and electronic exchange of fingerprints and responses as well as corresponding criminal histories. The system also included fingerprints of individuals who'd served or were still serving in the US military or had been or were employed by the federal government. It

118

was likely that whoever had touched the time release capsule had no arrest or conviction record.

"Do one other favor for me, Tony. Check the capsule for traces of propranolol."

"You got it," he said.

That afternoon, the gray clouds that had hung like heavy drapes over the city all morning had drawn apart, and sunlight glistened in the puddled streets and sidewalks along Grand Avenue in St. Paul.

Santana was seated at a table with Jack Brody in Billy's Tavern. The room had a slate floor, a warm fire crackling in a stone fireplace, big screen TVs mounted in the corners, and neon beer signs attached to the walls.

Santana looked across the table at Brody. "Were you here the night Scott Rafferty disappeared?"

Brody finished the last bite of his Cajun burger and washed it down with a sip of black coffee. He had placed his raincoat and fedora on a vacant chair at the table, and for the first time Santana saw that Brody had thick silver hair slicked back on his head.

"I already told you I'd pinpointed the approximate date the killer would strike again. I was in a number of bars that night. I could've been here. I really don't remember."

"Maybe you saw Scott Rafferty."

He shrugged and wiped his mouth with a napkin. "I saw a lot of young guys that night. Rafferty might've been one of 'em. But I was more interested in looking for the perp than the next victim. And I didn't recognize Rafferty's photo in the paper."

Santana wondered if Brody had been drinking while in each of the bars, and if alcohol had dulled his memory of that night. "Maybe you followed Rafferty from Billy's."

Brody smiled and shook his head in amusement. "Yeah. Then I killed him, called you, and told you where to find his body after it surfaced. Now here we are, and you're accusing me of being the perp. My plan is working perfectly."

"Coincidences make me suspicious."

"Me, too, Santana, which is why I know these young men are being murdered and not falling accidentally into the river because they're drunk."

"Scott Rafferty lived a long way from the river."

"Exactly. So how did he end up in it?"

Santana had no answer.

"I'm closing in on the son-of-a-bitch responsible for the deaths," Brody said. "I can feel it. So it shouldn't be seen as a coincidence or a surprise if I happened to be in the same bar as one of the victims."

"You think the perp is from St. Paul?"

"You saw the map. He's operating primarily along the Interstate Ninety-four corridor. I believe he lives near, if not in, the Twin Cities."

Santana ate the last of his walleye sandwich and drank the last of the hot chocolate.

Brody raised his eyebrows. "How come you don't drink coffee?"

"Never acquired a taste for it."

"But you're Colombian."

"So everyone in the country drinks coffee?"

Brody smirked. "I bet they do if their name is Juan Valdez."

"That's stereotyping."

"So sue me."

Santana pushed the plate to the side and leaned his forearms on the table. "I spoke with Carl Costello yesterday."

Brody nodded. "I figured you would."

"How come?"

"Because he's one of the few editors I know who still works for the *Times*."

"He says you were a good reporter."

120

"Still am."

"You won a Pulitzer."

"Fame is fleeting, Santana. Maybe you heard."

"Why did you leave the *Times*?"

Brody drank some coffee. "Carl didn't tell you?"

Santana shook his head.

"Well, good for old Carl. He always was a standup guy. You can't say that about too many people these days."

"Costello said you and the paper signed a confidentiality agreement."

"He still wouldn't have told you why I left."

"Probably not. You willing to share the story with me?"

Brody set down his coffee cup, leaned back in the chair, and rubbed the gray stubbles on his heavy chin. Santana wondered if Brody's wrinkled white shirt was the same one he had worn the first time they had met.

"I wrote an investigative report about corruption in the NYPD and the FBI," Brody said. "It cost some cops and agents their jobs. I made some enemies. It comes with the territory. But they never forgot."

"The NYPD or the FBI?"

"Both. But it was the feds that gave me the hardest time. I was followed and harassed. Eventually, they planted some cocaine in my car and I was busted."

"I've heard that line before."

Brody pulled back the lapel on his checkered sport coat, revealing a thin plastic flask in the inner pocket. "This is my drug of choice, Detective. Not cocaine."

"So the feds planted the coke and got you fired?"

"The paper chose to let me go rather than fight the charge. But I knew they didn't want a scandal plastered above the fold, so they agreed to a confidentiality statement."

"You know an FBI agent named Ed Kincaid?"

"How do you know Kincaid?"

"He introduced himself last night. Said he knew you."

"Oh, yeah. We're real good friends. That's why I didn't want to come to the station to talk the other day when I followed you. I'd heard through my sources that Kincaid got transferred to the Minneapolis field office. I was hoping he didn't know I was here, too."

"How did you two become so close?"

"Kincaid's best friend in the FBI was involved in the corruption scandal in New York. He's spending his retirement years in the gray bar hotel. Kincaid blames me because I broke the story."

"You think Kincaid planted the drugs in your car?"

"If I had to put money on it, yeah. Even if he didn't actually plant the coke, he damn well knows who did."

"Must've been hard to leave the paper."

Brody shook his head. "Investigative reporting isn't what it once was. When I joined the profession, people thought newspapers were institutions that would never change, that they'd last forever. Nobody thinks that way anymore. I'm sure you've heard the sad stories."

"It's been in the papers."

"Is that your idea of a joke?"

"My attempt at irony."

"Well, whatever the hell it was, budgets have been cut to the bone." Brody looked like he still cared.

"What about those who say the future of investigative reporting isn't in newspapers at all?"

"Look, I'm the first to admit that bloggers have written some pretty good stories. They've also written a ton of crap. Imagine if your job was outsourced to a bunch of amateur detectives on the Internet." Brody drank some coffee and shook his head in frustration. "Media and politics are too intertwined now."

"I thought the media's job was to clarify the issues."

"Hell," Brody said. "The networks and journalists are petrified of being accused of bias, so they treat every argument equally. That just leads to sound bite journalism."

Santana wondered how that kind of thinking would play out in a courtroom. Every legal argument would carry the same weight and no decision could ever be made. In the end, there would be nothing but hung juries and criminals walking free.

"So what's the answer, Brody?"

"I don't know if there is one."

"I still enjoy reading the morning paper."

"Good to hear, Santana. But most people expect their news to be digested for them, and that hurts investigative reporting. They just don't care to think for themselves anymore. The majority of both the media industry and the political system are designed to dumb down the population."

"You ever consider teaching at a college or university?"

"I don't have the temperament for it. I'm more of a loner. That served me well in the past, but not so much anymore."

An attractive, young waitress wearing a red "Billy's" T-shirt came to the table, refilled Brody's coffee cup, and set a fresh cup of hot chocolate topped with whipped cream in front of Santana. "I thought you might like another," she said with a bright smile.

"Thank you."

"You're welcome."

When she went away, Brody said, "Is it always that easy?"

"What do you mean?"

"Don't play dumb, Santana. She was hitting on you."

"She was just being polite."

"Yeah, right." Brody looked around to see if anyone was watching. Then he removed the small flask from an inner pocket of his sport coat, poured a shot of alcohol into his coffee cup, and slipped the flask back into the pocket.

"A little early for that, isn't it?"

"Never too early." Brody drank some coffee. "I believe it was Bogart who said, 'The problem with the world is that everyone is three drinks behind.' I agree."

"It doesn't bother you that I'm a cop?"

"Should it?"

"Probably."

Brody took another sip of coffee and set the cup carefully on a saucer. "You know, Santana, you and I aren't that much different."

"We aren't?"

"Well, I'm not talking about in the looks department. I admit you got me there. Although when I was your age and thirty pounds lighter, I turned a few heads. No, I'm talking about our professions. Investigative journalism is really done by people who believe in the importance of the story and discovering the truth. That focus isn't much different than yours."

"I suspect it isn't."

Brody nodded. "Reporters like me work on stories whether we get paid a lot or not. My compensation is the story, just as your compensation is solving the homicide. Oh, newspapers still care about good stories, but they rarely support reporters with the travel money or time we need to do the research like they did twenty years ago. The last few years I was at the *Times*, the paper expected me to work more and more off the clock. That doesn't pay the bills."

"Why not write a book?"

"No doubt books are the new outlets for investigative reporting. I might write one after we solve this series of murders."

"We?"

"Yeah, Santana. Like it or not, we're in this together." He stood up and put on his coat and hat. "How 'bout you pick up the tab this time, and I'll get the next one."

"Okay."

Brody waved as he walked away. "I'll be in touch."

The waitress stopped by with a warm smile and the bill. Santana paid her and included a generous tip. As he was putting on his coat, the manager came up to him, clutching the business card Santana had given him when he first stopped by to see Jeff Tate.

"I wonder if I could have a word with you, Detective Santana," he said.

"Sure."

He looked around to see if anyone at the surrounding tables was paying attention to him. Not satisfied, he gestured for Santana to follow him. They walked toward the back of the restaurant and into a large room with pool tables and a bar. No one was in the room.

The manager, a short man with thinning blond hair, said, "Jeff Tate didn't show up for work today."

"He call and tell you why?"

"He never called. Never said anything. And that's not like Jeff. He hasn't missed a scheduled workday since I hired him."

"You try to contact him?"

"Of course. But there's no answer on his cell phone. Only his voice mail." The manager shrugged his narrow shoulders. "I just thought you should know."

The drive to Jeff Tate's cabin took Santana twice as long as it had on his first visit due to heavy late afternoon traffic. The metal gate across the dirt road leading to Tate's property was closed and padlocked. A set of tire tracks was impressed in the soft dirt that was puddled from the recent rains. Santana left the Crown Vic on the shoulder of the paved county road that ran perpendicular to the property and walked in.

The sky was still sunny above the forest of oak, pine, birch, and spruce bordering the dirt road leading to Tate's cabin. Trees blocked most of the cool, damp breeze that felt ten degrees colder than the fifty-degree temperature. Santana was glad he had worn his overcoat.

It took three minutes before he was out of the woods and standing in the clearing forty yards from the rustic log cabin. High above the cabin, Santana saw a hawk circling, its tail a cinnamon-red stain against the blue sky. He scanned the property and saw Tate's truck with the camo vinyl finish, but not his dog.

He crossed fifteen more yards of damp ground and called out, "Mr. Tate," but all he heard in response was a gust of wind. He stood still, listening and watching the cabin for a time until an uneasy feeling came over him.

He drew his Glock and advanced—slowly—his attention focused on the cabin, the weight of the Glock comfortable in his hand. Shades were drawn on the two square windows flanking the front door. Santana knocked hard and identified himself. Again, there was no response. He pulled down on the brass, lever-style handle, discovered it was unlocked, pushed open the thick pine door, and stepped cautiously inside the cabin.

In the right corner of the main room, Tate's Doberman pinscher, Brando, was lying motionless in a dried pool of blood.

Santana could feel no heat radiating from a wood-burning stove to his left. On the kitchen table he saw a half eaten plate of beans and a half-empty bottle of Budweiser. The cupboards above the stove and refrigerator on the back wall were open, and broken dishes were scattered on the floor. Tate's Kimber 84M rifle was resting in a gun rack on the wall. A door in the middle of the back wall was riddled with holes, and the wall around it was peppered and splintered from shotgun pellets.

Who, he thought, would shoot Tate's dog? And what were they searching for? And was Tate dead, too?

Santana kicked the door shut behind him and went up the staircase, where he checked the bathroom and bedroom and made sure the perpetrator had left the premises. The mattress and box spring were half off the double bed that faced a sliding glass door and the balcony, as though someone had looked underneath them. Dresser drawers had been removed and the contents dumped on the floor.

He returned to the main level and went to the dog. Its body was cold. The gaping wound in its side, and the scattered satellite pellet holes around it, told him the dog had been killed with a shotgun from at least four feet away. There was no trail of blood.

Santana walked out the back door and around the cabin, looking for Tate and any trace evidence—but he found nothing.

He located the camouflage steel hatch over the bomb shelter and yanked it open. The entryway was only four feet in diameter and was tilted at a sixty-degree angle. A steel ladder leading down to the shelter was tilted at the same angle. There was a removable lock hasp on the inside of the hatch. Santana listened for a moment, hoping to detect a noise or movement below, but all he could hear were birds chattering in the trees. He holstered his gun and climbed down the ladder.

It led to a tube-like structure made of corrugated steel seven feet high and eight feet wide. It was lit with fluorescent lights and was cool, but not cold. Twelve feet ahead, the tube angled ninety degrees to the right. He drew his Glock again and moved forward.

As part of his emergency training with the SPPD, Santana had participated in chemical, biological, and nuclear defense drills. He remembered that gamma radiation from a nuclear explosion was directional and did not corner well. Tate had obviously been aware of this when he constructed his bomb shelter and chose the narrow entrance, since a small hatch and ninety-degree turn would significantly reduce radiation.

Santana made a sharp turn into a longer tube that ran straight ahead for about fifty feet. Miniature twelve-volt lights were placed every eight feet along a ceiling beam in case the fluorescent lights failed. There were two sets of double-hinged bunks and two sets of single-hinged sitting bunks along the first section. Unlike the cabin, the shelter hadn't been ransacked.

But Santana had no clue what someone had been searching for in Tate's cabin, and thus, no idea what to look for.

He started with the storage spaces under each of the hinged bunk beds, but they contained nothing but extra blankets, bedding, and pillows. Then he moved forward into the next section of the shelter that was lined with long metal shelves on both walls. The shelves held neatly arranged personal hygiene products, disinfectants, canned goods, dry cereals, military Meals, Ready to Eat, or MREs, and potassium iodide tablets.

Santana knew from the coverage of the nuclear disaster in Japan that explosions and meltdowns produced considerable amounts of radioactive iodine that could be ingested or inhaled. Potassium iodide tablets taken just before or after expected contact with radiation reduced the likelihood of radioactivity being absorbed into the thyroid gland, which could cause deadly cancer to develop.

He held his Glock steady as he crept past a diesel-powered generator and a marine alcohol stove. Further along the narrow passageway he found two chemical toilets, a fire extinguisher, first aid kit, battery-operated radio, CB radio, two flashlights, and extra batteries.

Santana followed a second ninety-degree turn to a ladder leading to an emergency exit covered by a second hatch. He climbed up and came out in the woods just beyond the clearing, the blue sky above him, the red-tailed hawk circling lower now, as though homing in on its prey.

Santana called Tony Novak at home and asked him to drive out to Jeff Tate's cabin with his print kit. Since Tate was in the military, his prints would be in IAFIS. If someone besides

Tate had fired the shotgun and ransacked the cabin without wearing gloves—and if they had been in the military, worked for the government, or had a criminal record—their prints would also be in the database. Santana was hoping he would get lucky.

"My wife and I are on the way to Scott Rafferty's wake," Novak said. "And all you've got is a dead dog. For all you know Tate shot him."

"I need you, Tony. You can stop by the wake later."

He sighed into the phone. "You owe me, John."

"It wouldn't be the first time."

"Nor, I suspect, the last," he said.

After Novak arrived, Santana had him dust the cabin, bomb shelter, and shotgun for prints, while he called animal control and had the dead dog taken away.

"I'll run the prints tomorrow," Novak said when he finished.

"Apologize to your wife for me."

"You can apologize to her yourself when you come for dinner a week from Sunday. And don't give me a lame ass excuse that you have plans. I know better."

Santana thought he might ask Jordan Parrish out. "I might have a date."

Novak peered at him behind his thick lenses. "With who?"

"Just someone I met."

"Huh," Novak said, as though he were mystified.

"What does that mean?"

"It means huh."

On his way home Santana stopped by Scott Rafferty's wake. The Lessard Mortuary was jammed with SPPD cops, brass, and friends and family who knew or were related to Rachel Hardin and Hank Rafferty. After speaking briefly with Rachel and Hank, Santana saw Kimberly Dalton surrounded by mourners. He wanted to talk with her again, but he knew he would have to find a better time.

It was nearly nine in the evening when he arrived home. The night was clear and cool, so he took Gitana for a short run. Then he showered, changed, took his Glock-23 out of its Kydex holster, and sat down at the kitchen table.

The chief was on a mission to replace 400 of the 610 Glocks SPPD police officers carried, because they were nearly two decades old. Many of the rest of the Glocks were between one and ten years old. Santana had replaced his gun during the last year and was not concerned about its reliability. But the urgency to replace the majority of standard issue handguns with new ones had become a major concern after a patrol officer's gun had misfired during a struggle with a suspected carjacker.

Replacing the Glocks was part of the chief's public safety plan that included promoting six officers to sergeant, increasing the frequency of range training, and adding a commander to the FBI Safe Streets initiative, a cross-agency effort focusing on gangs and drug cartels. Santana was wondering if Rita Gamboni had applied for the new commander position as he field stripped, brushed out, oiled, and reassembled his department issue Glock-23 and his backup Glock-27. That might explain Pete Romero's insinuation that Gamboni wouldn't be around to watch Santana's back, and her reluctance to give Santana a straight answer when he asked if she was leaving the department.

After he finished cleaning his weapons, he put them aside and placed a spiral notebook, briefcase, and a yellow 8 1/2" x 11" legal pad on the kitchen table. He drew a vertical line down the middle of a blank page and labeled the left hand column "Possible Suspects" and the right hand column "Motives." He wrote the names "Kimberly Dalton" and "Jeff Tate" in the left hand column, the last two people to see Rafferty alive. Each of them had told a different story regarding Kimberly's relationship with Scott Rafferty. One of them was lying.

Santana wrote "jealousy" in the "Motives" column across from Kimberly Dalton's name. If Jeff Tate was telling the truth about Dalton's obsessive personality and Scott Rafferty's desire to end his relationship with her, then she would have had a possible motive to murder Rafferty. Santana believed she had a problem with cocaine. He also suspected she knew Devante Carter, a supplier. He wondered if Rafferty's death could be drug related. He made a note in the margin next to her name.

In the "Motives" column across from Jeff Tate's name, Santana wrote a question mark. Tate could have been lying about Kimberly Dalton. He could have deliberately implicated her in an effort to deflect suspicion from himself. The question was, why? What would Tate gain by killing Rafferty? And what had happened to Tate? Santana didn't believe he would shoot his own dog, unless he'd had a complete meltdown. Yet, given Tate's obvious paranoia about a coming apocalypse and his possible PTSD, Santana couldn't rule it out.

He examined the "Motives" column again. Impulse, jealousy, revenge, greed, ambition, self-protection, and blood lust were all possible motives for murder. If Jack Brody was correct, then a sociopath intent on satisfying a blood lust had murdered Scott Rafferty, Michael Johnson, Thomas Hunter, Matthew Miller, and a host of other young men across the Midwest.

Murders were also committed for social, political, and religious reasons, though Santana could see no connection to Scott Rafferty's death. He could have unintentionally drowned, but like Johnson, Miller, and Hunter, Rafferty had had very little alcohol in his system and had been apparently fearful of water. As for suicide, Rafferty appeared to have been making progress in therapy, which made it less likely.

The empty propranolol capsule Santana had found in Rafferty's apartment troubled him. If Roth had decided to discontinue the drug, what was the capsule doing there, and why had it been broken open? Rafferty could have had a capsule left over from his prescription, or—as with most drugs—it could have been stolen. Had he not asked Reiko Tanabe to do so, she wouldn't have been looking for propranolol in a typical autopsy blood screening.

Santana looked at all the empty space under the "Possible Suspects" column. Then he turned to a fresh page and wrote down Mark Conroy's name. Conroy had told Jordan Parrish that he had no memory of events from the time he left the bar until the time he woke up in the river. If he was telling the truth, then he might have been drugged with something like Rohypnol, gamma-hydroxybutyrate, or ketamine. All were common club drugs or date rape drugs, which Santana thought was a misnomer since many rape victims weren't dating the perpetrator at the time of the crime. The drugs were powerful and could take effect very quickly without the victims knowing they had been drugged. And alcohol increased their potency.

But Santana knew that trying to find any of the drugs in the tissues of the drowning victims now would be difficult, if not impossible. When ingested they usually remained in the system for only one or two days. And GHB was naturally produced in the body in small amounts, especially during the decomposition process.

He figured the best thing to do would be to meet Mark Conroy and get his own impression of the young man.

Chapter 11

THE WIND WAS SWIRLING out of the north the next morning, the rain driving hard on the Crown Vic's roof, as Santana parked in front of the two-story brownstone building on Marshall Avenue where Jordan Parrish had told him Mark Conroy lived. Santana was hoping Conroy, if given a chance, might remember a previously forgotten detail about the events leading up to his unintended plunge in the river.

The inner door to the apartment building near the University of St. Thomas campus was locked, so Santana stood in the small lobby and used his cell phone to dial the number Jordan Parrish had given him. Conway didn't answer.

A few moments later, a young woman came down the stairs and exited the building without giving him a second look. Careless, Santana thought as he slipped through the open inner door. He went up two sets of stairs to the second floor and knocked on Conroy's apartment door.

He waited a minute and then knocked again. "Mr. Conroy?"

Out of curiosity, he turned the doorknob and found it unlocked. The door opened into a small alcove.

"Mr. Conroy?"

Nothing.

Then, through the open door of the bedroom straight ahead, Santana could see a man dressed in socks, jeans, and a sweatshirt with a St. Thomas logo lying at the foot of the bed, blood leaking out of his head, a .22-caliber rifle on the floor beside him.

Santana came in low behind his Glock, his heartbeat accelerating, his eyes quickly scanning the small entryway and then the bedroom. Kneeling, he felt the carotid artery in the man's neck for a pulse but found none.

He slipped on a pair of latex gloves and dug a wallet out of the man's back jeans pocket. The driver's license identified him as Mark Conroy. Santana used his cell and called it in. Then he focused his eyes and thoughts on the scene in front of him.

He could see powder deposits and blood stippling on the roof of Conroy's open mouth, which confirmed contact with the end of the barrel. The inside of Conroy's right leg and sock were blood-spattered, as were the outside of his left sock and pant leg. He figured that Conroy had sat on the edge of the bed, placed the rifle between his legs—holding it with his knees to steady it—put the end of the barrel inside his mouth, and pulled the trigger. The image lingered in his mind for a time before he pushed it out of his thoughts.

He sketched the scene in his notebook and then went into the living room. It contained a battered couch that was leaking foam, a cushioned chair, a coffee table, and a small round dining table with two wooden chairs. In a photo on an end table, Conroy was standing with two other young men. He had been a short, stocky man with shaggy ash blond hair, long sideburns, and legs slightly bowed like a rodeo rider's.

What had Conroy been like before his near death experience in the river? Santana wondered. Why had he decided to take his own life? Santana unconsciously ran his fingertips over the long, jagged scar on the back of his right hand, caused by a *rienda*, or sharp spine on the trunk of a *guadua* tree, the scar a constant reminder of how close he had come to dying in the mountain forests of Colombia at the age of sixteen. That experience—and the murder of his mother—had profoundly changed his personality and outlook. He was far more cynical and distrustful than he had been in his early teens, far more aware of the tenuous hold he had on life. Mark Conroy also had looked into the dark, empty eyes of death, felt its cold touch. The experience would certainly have forever changed Conroy. But had it led to his suicide?

After the paramedics arrived, Santana searched for a suicide note, but Conroy had apparently not written one.

In a kitchen drawer Santana found an address book. Under the letter 'D' Mark Conroy had written the word 'Dad' and a phone number. Santana told Conroy's father what had happened and how sorry he was, and then explained to him what he would have to do to collect the body once the autopsy was completed.

As Santana ended the call, he glanced at the textbook on the small dining table to his right. Beside the textbook was an 8 1/2" x 11" spiral notebook and a syllabus for a course entitled "Social Psychology." The professor's name on the syllabus was Dr. Monica Vail.

Santana waited till forensics arrived and Mark Conroy's body was taken away to the morgue before heading for the University of St. Thomas. Parking spaces along Summit Avenue near the campus were non-existent, unless you had a student or faculty permit—or happened to be an SPPD detective. Santana parked along the curb facing two stone arches and joined a large wave of students entering the campus. The rain had let up, but the day remained overcast, and the wind that bit his face was as sharp as the teeth of a small animal. The psychology department, located in the lower level of the John Roach Center, was to his right.

He went in a double door, down the stairs, and along a wide, carpeted corridor. A helpful phone receptionist had given him Monica Vail's office hours and room number. He found Vail sitting in a chair behind her desk when he approached her open door.

A man Santana estimated to be in his late twenties was sitting in a chair in front of the desk. He had blond hair, cut very short, and wore running shoes, tight-fitting jeans, a cranberry turtleneck, and an expensive-looking black leather jacket over his muscular frame.

Monica Vail peered over his shoulder. "Can I help you?"

Santana introduced himself and held up his ID.

"Detective John Santana," she said, pursing her full lips. "You spoke with my husband Kenneth the other day."

"I did."

The man pushed back his chair and stood, his gaze casually roving over Santana as though he were taking the measure of him. He had slightly sunken cheeks, a cleft chin, and deep-set brown eyes that conveyed a sense of challenge. He struck Santana as neither a student nor a professor at the university.

"I have to go, Monica," he said.

"Sorry to interrupt," Santana said to her.

But it was the man who replied, "No problem, Detective."

He said goodbye to Monica Vail. Then his shoulder brushed against Santana's as he walked past him and out the door. Santana figured it was no accident.

"What can I do for you, Detective?" Monica Vail asked.

"I'm looking into the drowning death of a young man named Scott Rafferty. I wonder if I can have a few minutes of your time?"

She seemed inclined to say no, then relented and came around the desk and shook his hand.

She was dressed in a dark purple, long-sleeved, turtleneck sweater dress that hugged her curves, and black boots with two-inch heels. Santana could see why her husband might be jealous. She looked just as stunning as her photos. Maybe better. Monica Vail indicated a cushioned hardback chair facing the desk, and Santana settled into the seat.

Her small office was located in a pod containing four offices. It had no windows, but it was decorated with green plants and bookshelves. Santana saw no photo of her husband, but he recognized a painting by Belgian artist René Magritte on the wall directly behind her. It depicted a man looking at himself in a mirror that reflected the back of his head. Having studied and cultivated an interest in surrealism in his youth, Santana recalled that Magritte's mother had committed suicide by drowning herself in a river.

"Was Scott Rafferty a student here?" she asked.

Santana removed his notebook and pen from the inner pocket of his sport coat. "No, he wasn't."

She shook her head slightly and regarded him as though he were making a joke. "Then how can I help you?"

"I don't know that you can, Professor Vail. But let's give it try."

She sat back in her chair and nodded her head.

"Did you ever meet Mr. Rafferty?"

"You just said he wasn't a student here." She looked straight at Santana, her large blue eyes unblinking.

"I did. But Rafferty worked for the Lessard Mortuary that does business with your husband's company. I wondered if you might've met him at some point."

"I know very little about my husband's business activities or his associates." The large diamond in her gold wedding band sparkled in the light as her fingers played with her gold rope chain necklace.

"You and your husband live in the area?"

"In Lilydale."

"Lived there long?"

"Nearly five years."

Santana knew Lilydale was a mostly professional, well-educated, very small community near the city of St. Paul, close to the Mississippi River. It was made up primarily of people of German, Irish, and Scandinavian ancestry with above-average incomes.

"Any children?"

She shook her head.

"Do you know Mark Conroy?"

She looked at him for a time before responding. "I think you already know the answer to that question, Detective Santana. Did you ask it to test my truthfulness?"

Santana held her gaze and said nothing.

She hesitated a moment and then said, "Mark Conroy is doing an independent study to make up an incomplete in my class."

"I'm afraid he just committed suicide."

She gave a start, as if she had touched a live wire. "That's awful."

"Are you aware of why he dropped out of school?"

"I believe he nearly drowned last January."

"What can you tell me about him?"

Her gaze slipped from his as she rearranged some neatly stacked papers on her desk. "Not much, I'm afraid."

"How long have you taught at the university, Dr. Vail?"

"About five years."

"Do you teach anything besides introductory psychology?"

"Depending on the semester, I also teach courses in psychopathology, social psychology, and one on alcohol, drugs, and behavior."

"Tell me something about your psychopathology course."

"Are you planning to enroll, Detective Santana?" There was a hint of a smile on her full red lips.

"I've completed my academic education."

"But you continue to study."

"Every day."

"I assume you're speaking of the human race."

"I am."

"Well, the goal of the psychopathology course is to help students understand abnormal or maladaptive behaviors such as depression and schizophrenia. We also discuss causal factors and treatments."

"And your course in social psychology?"

She squared her shoulders and sat more straight. "Is this relevant?"

"I imagine I can find information about the courses on the university's website. But you could save me time." He gave her his best smile.

"Well," she said with a sigh. "Social psychology is primarily a survey of theories and research findings. We cover topics such as attitude change, love and liking, aggression, stereotypes, altruism, and conformity."

Santana peered at his previous notes. "What topics are discussed in your course on alcohol, drugs, and behavior?"

She paused again and looked past him and out into the hallway. "We discuss various classes of drugs and their use and misuse," she said, her eyes meeting his again. "We also discuss chemical dependency and its treatment."

"Anything else?"

"The course surveys some basic facts about drugs."

"Specifically," he said.

She sat silently, looking at nothing, before speaking again. "We discuss principles of administration, absorption, action, and elimination of drugs."

"What about the effects?"

"Of course we talk about how drugs affect mood, behavior, and consciousness."

"What kind of drugs do you discuss?"

"Primarily stimulants and depressants."

"Like cocaine and alcohol?"

She nodded. "Drugs that are commonly misused by society."

"Ever discuss propranolol, Professor Vail?"

"I'm afraid I'm not familiar with that drug, Detective Santana." She pushed herself away from the desk, stood up, and grabbed her coat. "And I have an appointment."

She had provided very few details unless prompted and had sometimes hesitated before replying. He had considered asking a few probing questions, but that would only reveal that he was suspicious of her answers. If she was lying, she could then adjust her behavior to appear more honest.

Santana had interviewed and interrogated enough liars to know that people who were hiding something often gave more details or information than was required when asked a simple question. Practiced liars, on the other hand, intuitively understood that it was better to offer few details when responding to questions. Still, his confidence in detecting deception could interfere with his ability to actually detect it. At this point in the investigation he had no reason to suspect Monica Vail had a reason to lie. But he sensed something was amiss in the same way he sensed a storm was coming.

Santana had just returned to his car and settled into the front seat when he spotted a red Porsche Boxster with a rear license plate that read MONICA pulling out of a St. Thomas parking lot just ahead of him. A gray Dodge van with no lettering on the side drove out of the lot and followed the Porsche. Santana fell in behind them and flicked the wiper switch on high and his lights on low beam. He was certain the van belonged to Jordan Parrish, but he ran the plate just to make sure. He figured she would be concentrating on the Porsche and wouldn't be looking for a tail—but why was she following Monica Vail?

The temperature was just above freezing, and rain was coming down hard. It sluiced on the windshield of the sedan and rattled on the hood. The dark sky gave the impression that it was much later in the day. Santana maintained a comfortable distance while keeping the vehicles in sight. He followed them to a Fern's Restaurant in the Cathedral Hill neighborhood of St. Paul, four blocks from the St. Paul Cathedral, where Monica Vail pulled into the restaurant parking lot. Santana made a U-turn and found a parking spot along the curb on the opposite side of the street from the restaurant, two cars behind where Jordan Parrish had parked her van. He wondered if the private investigator would follow Monica Vail into the restaurant, but she didn't. A few moments later, he saw a hostess escort Vail to a table beside a wall of windows that faced the street, and she sat down in one of the two chairs.

Raindrops collecting on the driver's side window of his sedan made it difficult to see clearly. Santana removed a pair of Bushnell binoculars from a briefcase in the Crown Vic. He hit the power button and opened the window just enough to see over the lip of it, but not enough to allow much rain to enter. From where he was parked, he couldn't see Jordan Parrish inside the van, and she couldn't see him. But he guessed she had a camera with a telephoto lens.

A waitress handed Monica Vail two menus and left the second place setting. It was clear that she was meeting someone. The question was, who? Ten minutes later a blond-headed man in a dark suit sat down opposite her.

There were a number of indicators that would lead someone to believe two people were attracted to one another. Physical touch was fairly obvious. Other indicators, such as eating in proportion and mirroring one another's body language, were subtler. Some studies Santana had read claimed that couples in love even had heart rates in perfect synchronization. He couldn't measure heart rates, but he didn't need to. What he saw now as he peered through the restaurant's water-streaked window glass at Monica Vail and the stranger—the way they touched and mirrored each other's body language—reinforced his belief that they were more than friends.

Santana poured a cup of hot chocolate from the thermos he kept in the sedan and looked at his watch. Twenty minutes had passed since the last time he checked. He figured neither of the parties could spend the whole afternoon in the restaurant, but maybe they had cancelled everything on their schedule.

He wondered if the stranger was married, if his wife suspected her husband was cheating and had hired Jordan Parrish, or if Kenneth Vail had enlisted the aid of the private investigator. It might explain some of the jealousy Santana had heard in Kenneth Vail's voice during the interview in his office. It might also explain his threatening manner.

A waitress brought the lunches. But as Santana continued to observe their body language, he noticed that all was not well in their relationship. Their bodies were now inclined away from each other, and there was no touching or physical contact. The man was gesturing excitedly with his hands, while Monica Vail fidgeted with her purse. He had eaten most of his meal, but she had eaten very little. Finally, she stood, tossed her cloth napkin on the table, and strode out of the restaurant.

Chapter 12

JORDAN PARRISH'S OFFICE WAS LOCATED in a shopping and office complex at St. Anthony on Main in Minneapolis. The complex sat along the east bank of the Mississippi River near a touristy area of parks, walking and bike trails, picnic areas, restaurants, and boutique shops that offered a scenic view of the Minneapolis skyline. In the summer months, the decks and patios of the cafes and restaurants were usually packed with customers dining and listening to live bands. But the decks and patios were barren and unusable in March.

The private investigator had a small suite on the third floor of the complex, which featured hardwood maple floors, wood beams, and open ceilings. Two large glass windows with blinds flanked a pair of glass doors leading into her office. A code had to be entered on a security keypad in order to open the door. Santana could see her hunched over her cherry wood desk, her hand poised with a pen above a sheet of paper. The city's skyline was visible through the three large arched windows in the stone wall behind her. He knocked lightly on the glass door.

She lifted her head, smiled when she saw him, and came around the desk to let him in. "Nice to see you again, Detective Santana." She shook his hand firmly. "Please, come in."

As he followed her to the desk, he could see that she was about 5' 10" in her two-inch heeled boots. She slid a wooden director's chair with a blue canvas cover away from a wall and gestured for him to sit. Along the opposite wall to his left was another desk with a laptop Apple computer on it. On a rectangular table to the right of the desk, Santana saw a wireless video interceptor used to scan an area for hidden wireless video bugs, a GPS tracker, and a digital spotting scope.

Jordan Parrish sat down behind her desk, straightened a sheaf of papers, and knitted her hands on the desktop. "What can I do for you?"

Although it was late afternoon, she looked and smelled as fresh as a March rain. Her makeup was expertly applied, including the light shade of pink lipstick. The black blazer she wore over a white turtleneck was without wrinkles, as though it had just come from the dry cleaner's.

Her tanned complexion reminded him of the dream he'd had in which he was seated on the deck chair of a powerboat docked in the Caribbean, gazing at glistening whitewashed bones floating on the surface of the water.

"Were you in the Caribbean recently?" he asked.

"As a matter of fact, I was. I took a week's vacation to St. Maarten."

Santana believed his subconscious was trying to tell him something through the dream, but he wasn't sure what it was.

"We stayed on the Dutch side," she said.

He was hoping she would explain if the "we" was a husband or significant other, but no further details were forthcoming. He pressed blindly ahead. "Been there before?"

"My first time. But I'd definitely go again."

He nodded, feeling like an idiot who had lost his way and walked into a dead end.

She tilted her head and said, "Was there something else you wanted to ask about besides my tan, Detective Santana?" She was smiling at him, but her smile and the tone of her voice both had a teasing quality now, as though she knew exactly what he really wanted to know.

He felt the heat in his face and immediately reached for the notebook and pen in his sport coat as a diversion. "There was something else, actually," he said, keeping his gaze glued to the notebook as he flipped it open to a blank page—not because he planned to write anything, but because it gave him something to do while the blood flushed out of his face.

"Have you been to St. Maarten, Detective?"

After he had regained his composure, he looked at her and said, "No, I haven't. But the island is near Colombia."

"And that's where you're from?"

"Yes," he said.

"Do you travel to Colombia often?"

"Not often. But I was there last year."

"Vacation?"

"For a case I was working."

"Oh, yes. I remember reading about that case in the paper."

He wanted to avoid discussing the case in detail and what had happened to him during the investigation, so he redirected the conversation. "I was wondering why you were tailing Monica Vail."

Jordan Parrish lost her smile, and it was *her* complexion that colored now. But her hazel eyes didn't blink or leave his face. He noted that they looked greener and less blue than they had been before. His mother, Elena, had had the same chameleon eyes, which seemed to change from green to blue depending on the color of clothes she wore or the light.

"How do you know I was following Monica Vail?"

He was relieved to detect curiosity in her voice rather than anger. "I happened to be leaving her office earlier today and saw you following her."

"And you followed us."

"I did."

She gave one nod and leaned back, her hands resting on the armrests.

"Did Kenneth Vail hire you?" he asked.

She appeared to consider the question, but offered no reply.

"So it was Kenneth Vail."

"Did I say that?"

"You don't have to, Ms. Parrish. Who's the guy Monica Vail met at Fern's?"

She took in a small breath and exhaled. "Does your interest in this particular matter have something to do with Scott Rafferty's death investigation?"

"It might. Then again, it might not. I'm not sure."

"Client privacy is important in my business," she said.

"No one has to know that we've talked."

She sat forward again and placed her forearms on the desktop. "If I'm going to share information with you, Detective, then I expect something in return."

"I have nothing concrete."

"That hardly seems fair. I'm sure if you thought about it, you could come up with something helpful." A smile lingered on her mouth. It was hard to resist the temptation to respond, but Santana did his best and waited.

Finally, she said, "Kenneth Vail hired me a few weeks ago because he suspected his wife was having an affair."

"Does Vail know who she's seeing?"

"No. I'm preparing a report to give to him."

"Who's Lyle Cady?"

"You ran his license number."

He nodded. "Any idea how long Cady and Monica Vail have been seeing each other?"

"Well, at least for a few weeks. But time isn't the most important factor here."

Santana thought how traumatic it would be to discover that the woman you loved was having an affair—and what some men would do if they found out.

"What can you tell me about Cady?" he asked.

"He runs a company called Venture Tech. They offer venture capital to scientists and entrepreneurs. They've been in business for a decade and appear to have a stellar reputation. From what I've been able to gather, Cady has provided capital to Monica's husband."

"Capital for what?"

"I don't know specifically. But I believe it's for some sort of research."

"What do you know about Kenneth Vail?"

Jordan Parrish opened a manila file folder on her desk and scanned the first page. "Kenneth Vail completed his undergraduate work in biochemistry at the University of California-San Diego in 1991. In 1997 he received his PhD in biochemistry, molecular and cell biology from the same university, where he conducted his thesis research on brain injury and memory loss."

"Memory loss?"

"Yes. Is that important?"

"Maybe. What else do you have?"

She looked at her notes again. "Vail later became an assistant professor of molecular and cellular neurobiology, and then taught at the University of Texas, Harvard University, the University of Wisconsin, and at the University of Minnesota as a professor in the department of neuroscience. He left the university two years ago to form his own company."

"Seems like he bounced around quite a bit."

"That's his MO. He's known as a brilliant scientist, but he has a reputation as a charismatic figure with a giant ego. Apparently, he often clashed with colleagues at the universities where he was employed. But he was also viewed as a cash cow because he could raise money—lots of it. His research has been published in numerous peer-reviewed journals. Though much of his early research was widely praised and well reviewed, some of his most recent work has been criticized for its unsub-

147

stantiated claims and substandard research. Vail, it seems, often wanted to move faster than many of his colleagues were comfortable with. So he branched out on his own, relying on private grants and venture capitalists that were more than willing to fund his research."

Kenneth Vail hadn't mentioned anything about his background or memory research when Santana had asked him about his company and his employee, Ronald Getz. That might have been unintentional since Santana's main focus had been on Getz. But now, Santana sensed it was important to learn more about Vail and his research.

"Do you have anything on Monica Vail?" he asked.

Jordan Parrish opened another manila folder. "Monica Vail grew up dirt poor on a small farm in North Dakota. She graduated high school at sixteen and received a full scholarship to the University of Wisconsin in Madison, graduating in three years with a degree in psychology. She then completed her graduate and post-graduate work at the same university, with a focus on social and personality psychology."

She closed the folder. "So now that you know what I know, how about sharing some information with me?"

Santana considered her request. "According to the DMV, Monica Vail has had two speeding tickets in the last three years, but has no outstanding warrants."

Jordan Parrish squinted her eyes and cocked her head. "That's it? That's all you have to share?"

"On Monica Vail."

"All right. What about Scott Rafferty?" She gave him a smile of encouragement.

"It's all based on instinct."

"Well, I often rely on instinct, too. And my instinct tells me that someone is murdering these young men found in the river, and that Michael Johnson's and Scott Rafferty's deaths were no accident."

"You have experience with serial killers?"

She smiled again and shook her head in amusement. "If you're trying to make me angry, Detective, you're going to have to try harder. I have a very long fuse."

"That isn't my intention, Ms. Parrish."

She stayed silent awhile. Then she said, "Why don't you call me Jordan? It'll make it easier while we're working together."

"Who said we're working together?"

"It appears that we have mutual interests and concerns. I'd say we're already working together."

"You're the second person who's told me that," Santana said, thinking of Jack Brody.

"Someone in your department?"

"No."

"Then who?"

Santana decided to tell her about Brody. But he didn't mention the propranolol and his suspicions that Scott Rafferty had been drugged. And he wouldn't say anything until he was sure it was relevant to the investigation.

"I knew it," she said when he had finished. "A serial killer is responsible for the murders."

"Brody's a reporter, not a detective."

"Pulitzer Prize-winning investigative reporter," she said.

"Still a reporter."

She looked at her watch and got up from her desk. "Would you care for some bottled water or something stronger, John? You don't mind if I call you that?"

"Not at all." He saw no point in debating the issue with her. Besides, he had a feeling he would lose the argument, or more likely, that he had already lost it.

Jordan Parrish walked across the room to a small cherry-wood cabinet standing beside the table filled with surveillance equipment. She bent over at the waist, her jeans tightly hugging her shapely backside, and opened the door. "Let me see what I can find." She slid a wine bottle out of the cabinet and peered at the label. "Oh, I have a lovely Don Amado Cabernet Sauvignon from Chile I think you'd like. Unless, of course, you'd prefer water." She held her pose and gave him a sidelong glance.

He quickly pulled his eyes away, embarrassed that she had caught him staring at her bottom. "I'm off the clock. I'll drink some wine."

"I thought so."

Out of the corner of his eye he saw her straighten and turn toward him. "Sometimes I work late into the evening. I like to keep a bottle or two here. It helps me relax." If she cared that he had been staring at her backside, it didn't show on her face. In fact, she was smiling coyly at him, as if she was well aware that she had a great ass and wanted him to notice.

She used a Rabbit wine opener to remove the cork and poured the wine into two Bordeaux glasses, handing him one as she returned to her desk. He let the wine breathe in the glass, allowing the complexity of the flavors to come through. Then he inhaled its scent once again before taking a sip and holding it in his mouth for a moment. He could taste the black cherry flavor and ripe tannins.

"Very good wine."

"Cheers," she said, raising her glass.

They drank.

"I have a small wine cellar at home," she said.

"And where is that?"

"I have a loft near here. I can walk to work."

Santana noted that she had used the singular "I." All his years of detecting were finally paying off.

She stared at him over the lip of her wine glass. "Are you ready to share?"

He thought about it. Then he set down his glass, took out his notebook, and recreated the symbol Jack Brody had drawn for him on a sheet of paper. "Ever seen this symbol before?"

She took one look at it and said, "It's a symbol for chaos."

"How do you know?"

"When I was young I had a friend who read fantasy and science fiction novels. He gave me a couple of books written by Michael Moorcock. I'm not a fantasy or science fiction fan, but I remember this particular symbol was used in the stories to represent the struggle between law and chaos. Why do you ask?"

"It was found near where some of the young men drowned."

She nodded as if it made sense. "See, sharing isn't so difficult, is it?"

She was looking at him in a way that made him feel both uncomfortable and aroused. He drank more wine. Then he said, "Any ideas why someone would leave this particular symbol at the sites of the drownings?"

"Are you familiar with the term archetype?"

"You mean like the hero or star-crossed lovers?"

"Those are examples of characters or protagonists from literature," she said. "But in literature there are also archetypal situations like the quest, the initiation, or the loss of innocence. But there are also symbolic archetypes," she continued, "like the cross representing Christianity, or Moorcock's symbol for chaos you drew on the sheet of paper. Symbolic archetypes are found everywhere."

"How come you know so much about this?"

"I was a big fan of Carl Jung in my undergraduate years."

"The psychologist."

She nodded. "I have a minor in psychology. Jung believed symbols are the language of the mind and are connected to each other by the collective unconscious."

"We're all a part of the larger whole."

"Exactly. It's in our DNA. Some of these archetypal images exist in our psyches even before we're born. Others can be found all over the world and throughout history. You become more aware of them in meditation and in dreams."

Santana was reminded of his own dreams and the images that often inhabited them—and how understanding them had helped him solve cases and prolong his life.

"Jung said all of us have a shadow linked to more primitive animal instincts," Jordan continued, "a light and a dark aspect, if you will."

"If someone is murdering young men in the Midwest, maybe he never moved beyond the shadow of his psyche."

"Or never came to grips with it," she said. "We've all been conditioned to fear the darker side of ourselves, to repress it. Jung believed that repression only creates what he called a fog of illusion surrounding the self. We all need a dark side to understand who we really are. I mean, how can you understand courage if you've never experienced fear? How can you understand happiness if you've never experienced sadness?"

Santana was familiar with his darker side, the caged demon that resided inside him, that lived in all of us, according to Jung. He had lost his innocence in the mountainous forest outside the city of Manizales the night he had killed the men who had murdered his mother. Darkness was as much a part of him as light. He knew that in order to control it, he first had to acknowledge it and recognize its power. He understood that to live a true life, to understand the light, he had to have the courage to explore the darkness, to embrace the demon within him.

"You can't defeat the darkness," he said.

"No," Jordan said. "You can't. If you don't understand that, you don't understand human nature."

On the other side of the paper with the chaos symbol, Santana drew a picture of the serpent eating its tail. "You know what this is?" he asked.

"It's an ouroboros. A symbol of immortality, like the Phoenix rising from the ashes. Jung saw it as an archetype. The serpent slays himself and brings himself back to life again. It often represents something that constantly re-creates itself. It also can be considered a symbol for the opposite, like the shadow self. Where did you see it?"

"On a ring someone was wearing."

"Is it important?"

"I don't know," he said.

She gazed at him for a while before she said, "You hungry?"

He nodded.

"We could continue this discussion of Jung and serial killers downstairs while we eat, but why don't I order something and we can eat it right here? That way we won't alarm any restaurant patrons."

Santana had considered asking her again if she would like to have dinner with him, now that he knew she was available. He had been reluctant to extend the invitation because of the risk of forming attachments or relationships. But he was attracted to Jordan Parrish and, he thought, she to him, so he decided to accept her invitation. Besides, having one dinner together certainly didn't represent a relationship or a commitment.

"I could use something to eat," he said. "What did you have in mind?"

She opened a drawer, pulled out a menu, and handed it to him. The menu was from Pracna on Main, a restaurant advertising itself as the oldest restaurant on the oldest street in Minneapolis. Santana had never eaten there.

"I eat at Pracna quite a bit," she said, "and I tip well. They'll send something up if we order."

Santana looked over the menu. "I'll have the twelve-ounce strip steak with sautéed mushrooms, a baked potato with butter and sour cream, and a Caesar salad."

"Good choice. How do you want the steak cooked?"

"Medium."

Jordan Parrish made a phone call and placed the same order for both of them. Then she got up and went to the cabinet and retrieved the open bottle of cabernet. She walked back to his chair, poured some wine in his glass and some in hers, set the bottle on the desktop, and sat down again.

She looked at him awhile before speaking. "Someone once said that figuring out how or why someone becomes a serial killer is like aligning a Rubik's cube."

"That's true."

"Seems the number has increased over the years."

"Mostly since nineteen-fifty," he said. "But it's unclear as to why or how many are operating at any given time."

"I'm guessing there are probably numerous prostitutes, runaways, and other transients that aren't reported missing," she said. "And even when they are, they're not given much attention from media and police departments."

"Everyone deserves the same amount of attention. Their background or what they did or didn't do for a living shouldn't matter."

She raised her glass. "Then you're the exception, John."

"That hasn't been my experience."

"But every police department has unsolved cases of murderers. And sometimes serial killers do stop, at least for long periods of time."

"Any speculation as to why?"

"I remember reading that Larry Ralston, the Ohio serial killer they called the 'Angel of Death,' quit killing for six years while he worked in a morgue."

Santana felt a rush of adrenaline. "Ralston worked in a morgue?"

"Yes. Apparently working with corpses satisfied his need to be close to death. But he's more the exception than the rule.

Some serial killers stop because they commit suicide. Some die of natural causes, some are incarcerated in prison or in mental institutions for other crimes, and some relocate. A few turn themselves in. But I think most start to believe the press releases. The more they kill and get away with it, the easier it'll be. And that's when they get careless and get caught. So I guess the bottom line is there's really not a whole lot of agreement among researchers."

"Except that there's no way to cure a serial killer."

She nodded in agreement. "That's true."

Santana drank more wine.

"Do you live in town, John?" she asked.

"Near the river in St. Croix Beach."

"Sounds like a lovely spot. But a bit of a drive to St. Paul."

"It is. But I like the peace and quiet." *And the isolation,* he thought.

"Not a city guy, huh?"

He didn't want to tell her about his history in Colombia, or that he had chosen his residence because it offered him some security from those intent on doing him harm. An assassin would more easily blend in with crowds and would likely seem less out of place in the busy streets of a city.

"I've got nothing against city living," he said. "Other than I prefer living where there's a little more space."

"Ever been married?"

He shook his head. "You?"

"Once," she said, as a dark cloud drifted momentarily across her eyes. She drank from her glass.

Santana wanted to ask about the marriage, and if she was seeing anyone now, but he didn't want to appear too forward. Yet if he was reading her correctly, she had been sending him signals that she was interested in him. She seemed to know what he was thinking and said, "Finding someone you're compatible with isn't easy."

155

"The vacation you took to St. Maarten wasn't with your boyfriend?"

"It was with two of my girlfriends."

"Oh," he said, feeling suddenly elated.

They sat looking at each other, their eyes locked in an embrace, when Santana heard a knock on the door. Jordan raised her eyes and peered over the top of his head. "Our dinner is here." She picked up her purse and set it on the desktop.

"My treat," Santana said, taking out his wallet.

"Thank you."

He went to the door and returned with a serving tray filled with their dinners, which she asked him to place on a square table near the arched windows. Santana could see the lights of the city and hear the sound of mellow jazz coming from a restaurant below them.

"You do this often?" he asked as he sat down in a chair across from her.

She made eye contact with him and held her gaze. "Not often."

He knew by the tone of her voice and the way she looked at him that inviting him to eat here with her was special, and he was glad.

"Now," she said, "where were we?"

"I was just about to ask you out."

"You were?"

"Yes," he said, "I was."

Before he could continue, his cell phone rang. He wasn't going to answer it until he saw that the call was from the Law Enforcement Center.

"Excuse me," he said. "I have to take this."

She nodded in understanding. He flipped open his phone. "Santana."

"It's Jack Brody. I need your help."

"What's up?"
"I've been arrested for assaulting Ed Kincaid."

Chapter 13

RITA GAMBONI WAS ALONE in her office when Santana arrived.

"Close the door," she said. She motioned him to a lone chair across from her desk. After he sat down, she stared at him without speaking, her blue eyes as hard as ceramic. She was dressed in a black pantsuit, an outfit she rarely wore unless she had an important meeting. "You wanted to see me about the Scott Rafferty investigation."

Santana nodded. "I know it's late, and it looks like you have plans."

She glanced at her watch. "I'm on my way to dinner."

I wish I could have finished mine with Jordan, Santana thought. "Anyone I know?"

"Do you think it's any of your business?" Her tone was more curious than hostile.

"You mean do I *still* think it's any of my business."

"Well, we're not dating anymore, John. And haven't been for quite some time. You were the one who wanted to keep our relationship strictly professional. So when you ask me questions about my personal life, it puts me in a difficult position. I don't know quite how to answer. But if there was someone else sitting in this chair, I doubt very much that you'd be asking about his or her personal life."

"You're right, Rita." He shrugged. "Old habits die hard. I'll try not to cross that line again."

She looked as if she were about to say something and then changed her mind. "So what's so urgent that you needed to see me now?"

"I was meeting with a private investigator at St. Anthony Main when I got a call from a reporter named Jack Brody. The feds have arrested him."

Santana thought Gamboni would ask him about Brody. But instead she said, "Is Sophia's still open?"

He shook his head.

When he and Gamboni were dating, he had taken her to Sophia's, a restaurant in St. Anthony with an extensive wine list, romantic lighting, rosewood tables, heavy velvet drapes, and an intimate dance floor. On weekends the restaurant had featured some of the best jazz in the Midwest. But like many restaurants and small businesses during the recession, it had closed.

"And what were you meeting with this private investigator about?" Gamboni asked.

"Her name is Jordan Parrish."

Gamboni's jaw dropped slightly, and her eyes widened in surprise.

Santana had had no reason to mention that he had been meeting with a female private investigator at St. Anthony Main—no reason other than it might elicit a memory of an earlier time when he and Rita were together. Maybe he was a little angry that she had refused to tell him whom she was having dinner with, and maybe he had wanted to hurt her just a little. He felt disappointed that he had allowed himself to give in to petty jealousy. He shifted gears quickly and gave her some background on Jack Brody, and Brody's arrest for assault.

"Kincaid wouldn't have arrested Brody without cause," she said.

"Come on, Rita. Charging Brody with a federal crime would be payback."

"I don't believe that, John."

"Kincaid set him up."

"According to you."

Santana shook his head. "Brody told me Kincaid swung first."

"Of course he would say that."

Santana waited a few beats before he spoke again. "Kincaid is pressuring you to drop the investigation into Scott Rafferty's death, isn't he?"

Her gaze momentarily slid away from him as she pursed her lips in an attempt to mask her surprise. "What gave you that idea?"

"I talked with Kincaid after he spoke with you."

Gamboni's cheeks flamed at the revelation. "The FBI doesn't run my homicide unit."

"No. But Kincaid can squeeze you pretty hard."

"Why would he want to do that?"

"Because maybe Brody is on to something. Maybe Kincaid doesn't want him to succeed."

"That's not your concern, John."

"It sure as hell is, Rita, especially if he's interfering with my investigation. Why would Kincaid want to do that?"

She shrugged. "I don't know. But I'm not buying your argument about Kincaid trying to stop Brody's search for a serial killer because of some misguided vendetta."

"You've read Rafferty's autopsy report?"

"I have." She tapped a file folder on her desktop with an index finger and fixed him with her gaze again.

"And?" he said.

"And it seems Scott Rafferty accidentally drowned."

"Yes, it does seem that way."

"Meaning what?"

"Meaning I think his death wasn't an accident."

"And what leads you to draw that conclusion?"

"It's not a conclusion at this point, Rita. It's only speculation."

"Okay. So what's pointing you in that direction?"

"I found an empty, broken capsule in Rafferty's apartment. I think it might be propranolol."

"What's propranolol?"

"It restricts adrenaline release when someone is stressed. It's usually taken in a time-released capsule form. But a broken capsule would release too much of the drug into Rafferty's system at one time. An overdose would cause irregular heartbeats, dizziness, fainting, nausea and vomiting. In severe cases it could induce coma, convulsions, and shock."

"You think someone gave propranolol to Rafferty without his knowledge?"

"It might explain why a young Iraq vet suddenly drowns in the Mississippi River in March."

"Maybe Rafferty broke open the capsule and took the drug himself. Maybe he decided to end his own life."

"Then why jump in the river, Rita? The overdose would've killed him."

Gamboni peered at the file on her desk and then at him again. "I don't recall seeing anything about propranolol in Tanabe's report."

"It wasn't mentioned because she wasn't looking for it. I asked her to check again."

"And you learned about this drug from . . .?"

"Scott Rafferty's psychiatrist, Benjamin Roth. But Roth intimated that he had discontinued the prescription."

"Have you asked Tanabe to check the other drowning vics?"

"Not yet."

She sat silently for a while and then looked at her watch. "We need to talk more about this, John, but I have to go."

"Just one other thing."

She let out a sigh. "What?"

"There's a rumor floating around that you might be leaving Homicide."

Gamboni's face paled. "Where did you hear that?"

It had been Pete Romano who had suggested Santana wouldn't have Rita to protect him anymore, but Santana didn't want to burn any bridges with Romano since he would certainly apply for Rita's job if she left. So he would leave him out of it.

"You know how these rumors are, Rita."

"No, I'm afraid I don't."

"Well, *are* you leaving?"

"I have no plans to leave the department," she said. Santana thought her noncommittal answer indicated she was being untruthful. She stood abruptly. "I'm late."

"What about Hank Rafferty?"

"What about him?"

"He's one of ours, Rita. His kid is dead."

Her cheeks flamed again. But this time Santana knew the heat of anger rather than embarrassment had caused it.

"I know that."

"Then we should do everything we can to find out if someone killed Scott Rafferty."

He could see the conflict in her eyes as they darted back and forth. "Damn it, John! Why can't Rafferty's death be a simple case of drowning? Why do you have to make it something it isn't?"

"You know the answer to that question," he said.

She took in some air and let it out slowly. "You really think there's something we might be missing?"

"That's my sense, Rita. Give me some time to see where it leads. If nothing turns up, then we'll write off Rafferty's death as a tragic accident."

"I'll do what I can."

"That's all I've ever asked," he said.

Chapter 14

SANTANA SAW TONY NOVAK the next morning on the steps of the church after Scott Rafferty's Mass.

"I ran the prints yesterday," he said.

"And?"

"The ones I found in the cabin, bomb shelter, and on the shotgun all matched Jeff Tate's prints in the IAFIS database."

Santana had figured the perp had worn gloves, but it was worth the time and effort. *Well, maybe not for Novak.*

"Thanks, Tony."

"Sunday," Novak said. "One week from tomorrow at two o'clock. And bring your new girlfriend. We'd love to meet her."

"Who said she was my girlfriend?"

"Don't be late," he said and headed for his car.

Instead of going to the cemetery, Santana drove to Woodbury, a suburban community just east of St. Paul, where Lyle Cady was holding a seminar in a large conference room at the Sheraton Hotel.

Colorful tri-fold brochures advertising VENTURE TECH were stacked on a long table just outside the double doors to the conference room. Two clean-shaven men with very short blond hair and muscular builds stood on either side of the open conference room door. A nearly identical man stood near the table. He had a cleft chin and a look of challenge in his eyes. He was the man Santana had seen in Monica Vail's St. Thomas office.

They all wore identical black and white herringbone sport coats, starched white shirts, and dark silk ties. Badges clipped to the breast pockets of their coats identified them as VENTURE TECH SECURITY. Santana guessed by their ramrod, spotless appearance that they were ex-military.

As he was about to enter the room, the one near the table stepped in front of him. His security badge identified him as Jess.

"Mind if I search you?" he asked.

The other two guards moved closer, anticipating trouble.

"I'm St. Paul PD," Santana said.

"Gotta make sure," Jess said, his lips pulling back in an empty, emotionless smile.

Santana showed him his gold shield. Jess took a long time looking at it. But he didn't move.

Santana slipped the badge wallet into his pocket and fastened his eyes on him. He had played macho head games before and knew what this one was all about. He was not about to walk around the security guard. He waited.

"Enjoy the seminar, Detective Santana," Jess said at last, breaking into a phony smile as he stepped aside.

Inside the conference room, rows of chairs were filled with what Santana assumed were scientists, researchers, and entrepreneurs, each one hoping that Cady's company would invest in what they believed would be the next medical breakthrough. Santana leaned against a back wall and listened as Cady spoke about his company.

"Venture Tech specializes in venture creation and early-stage investment in medical devices and research technologies," he said. "Our mission is to uncover the groundbreaking technologies that will power tomorrow's leading companies. Then we make those companies viable through public financing or acquisition."

Though Cady was not a large man, he had a surprisingly deep and powerful voice, like that of a commercial pitchman on radio and television. He was dressed in an expensive-looking, navy blue suit and spoke confidently into a wireless, handheld microphone, gesturing with his arms and slowly prowling the room, back and forth, like a caged animal.

"The pace of discovery is rapidly accelerating. Innovative research is providing opportunities to significantly improve both the length and the quality of life. But to be honest, we reject over ninety-five percent of the ideas presented."

Cady paused for a moment and drank from a plastic water bottle he lifted off a round table before speaking again. "As you know, there are a limited number of ways you can meet venture capital firms and other private equity investors outside of referrals, other business contacts, or conferences such as this. Today, you'll have an opportunity to pitch directly to us in face-to-face meetings we call Speed Venturing. Think of it as something akin to speed-dating for capital." A wave of nervous laughter rippled through the room. "You'll have ten minutes to convince my business partners whether they'd like a follow-up meeting to discuss your idea further. You all received a time and room number when you registered. The first pitches begin in fifteen minutes. Good luck to you all."

Santana waited until the audience had dispersed before he walked up to Cady, who was putting his notes into a black leather attaché case. Santana held up his badge and introduced himself.

"What brings you to the seminar, Detective Santana? Interested in some venture capital?" He grinned at his own joke and offered a hand.

Santana shook it. "I'd like to talk to you about Kenneth Vail."

Cady's grin vanished and his brown eyes narrowed with concern. "What kind of detective are you?"

"Homicide."

"Has something happened to Kenneth?"

"No," Santana said. "I'm interested in the research Vail is conducting."

"Then why not talk to him?"

Santana didn't want to acknowledge that he had spoken with Kenneth Vail and that he felt Vail had been evasive. He thought Cady might be more willing to discuss Vail's research, and if he wasn't, Santana had a bargaining chip.

"I'd like to hear your take."

Cady thought it over. "I'm not sure I understand. What does Kenneth's research have to do with homicide?"

"Nothing—as far as I know. But I'd appreciate your time."

Cady looked at his watch, then around the large, empty room. "I'd like to help," he said with a forced smile. "But I'm very busy."

"I understand." *Time to play the chip*, Santana thought. "By the way, do you know Kenneth Vail's wife, Monica?"

Cady's smile suddenly became lopsided and his complexion reddened. "Why, yes. I've met her."

Santana could think of a number of obvious ramifications for Lyle Cady if his business partners and perspective entrepreneurs discovered he was having an affair with Kenneth Vail's wife. He could think of none that would be beneficial for Cady's business. Still, Santana was more interested in Kenneth Vail than Cady's affair. But he would use his knowledge of the affair for leverage if it could help him acquire information. He hoped that merely mentioning Monica Vail's name would rattle Cady and tweak his curiosity. He would want to know what—if anything—Santana knew about his relationship with Monica Vail.

166

Cady glanced at his watch again. "The presentations will take an hour. I suppose I have some time. Why don't we go to the restaurant?"

"Fine."

They found a table in the small restaurant near a flaming gas fireplace. Dark wood furniture and white linen tablecloths gave the room an elegant appearance. A waitress came over, and Cady ordered a cup of black coffee.

"Something for you, Detective?" he asked.

"I'm good." The waitress went away, and Santana took out his notebook and pen. "Let's start with your connection to Kenneth Vail."

"It's pretty straightforward. Vail's research has potential, but it's not at the point where he's able to secure a bank loan or complete a debt offering. In exchange for the risk we assume by investing in his idea, we get a high return on any profits."

"And what's a high return?"

"Generally forty percent or more."

"So what makes Vail's research so valuable that you're willing to take a risk?"

Cady paused, as if he were deciding how much he wanted to share with Santana. "You know anything about the treatment of PTSD, or post-traumatic stress disorder, Detective?"

"I do."

Cady nodded. "Perhaps a man in your position has even experienced it, or knows someone who has."

"Perhaps."

Cady waited awhile and then spoke again. "Well, the idea of manipulating a person's brain chemistry to reduce the impact of a painful memory is not entirely new. There are medications used in behavioral therapy that lessen the emotional impact of traumatic memories in patients suffering from PTSD."

"Like propranolol."

167

Surprise registered on Cady's face. "Yes. But what Vail is working on goes much further. Imagine if there was a drug that could permanently erase a painful memory."

"Sounds like something out of science fiction."

"I'm sure it does, Detective." Long strands of his gelled blond hair fell over his forehead as he emphasized his last point with a forceful nod. "But let me assure you, new scientific advances offer the promise of re-engineering one's brain chemistry. Think for a moment what that would mean for the nearly eight million American adults with post-traumatic stress disorder. Think what it would mean to all those young soldiers returning from Iraq and Afghanistan. What would that discovery be worth in monetary and emotional terms?"

"A lot, I'm sure."

"Exactly."

"Maybe that's why you surround yourself with all this security."

Cady nodded again. "We sometimes deal with government research that could, if it fell into the wrong hands, cause a great deal of damage to the country. I believe it's better to err on the side of caution."

The waitress arrived with the coffee. Santana waited until she had departed before he said, "How long have you known Kenneth Vail?"

"Not long. But I've known of him for quite some time— and of his story."

"What do you mean his *story?*"

"Well, it's something that isn't widely known. I think Kenneth would rather it stayed that way." He offered another forced smile. Apparently, Santana thought, Cady had had plenty of practice.

"I'd like to know what it is."

"Perhaps you should ask Kenneth, Detective Santana."

"I'm asking you."

Cady held the coffee cup in front of his mouth to mask his face. But Santana watched his eyes flit nervously back and forth as he weighed his options—or formulated a lie.

"All right," he said. "Kenneth Vail was sexually abused by an uncle when he was a child. He suffered terrible nightmares for years. He tried drugs and therapy, but nothing worked. The incident was the catalyst for his career in memory research."

"How is it that you know about the sexual abuse?"

Cady sipped some coffee and then let his gaze follow the cup as he set it in the saucer. His eyes remained fixed on the cup as he said, "Kenneth told me."

Santana figured that Monica Vail had probably told Cady, but he let it go.

"Was the uncle ever caught and prosecuted?"

Cady looked at Santana again. "He was, but later died of a heart attack in prison."

Santana was pleased to hear it.

"You haven't asked about *my* background, Detective."

Santana flipped to the relevant page in his notebook. "You're forty-four years old. After graduating from MIT and earning an MBA from the Stanford Graduate School of Business, you became an associate in a Minnesota-based firm that focused on life science and research. You began your venture capital career in the early nineties with money furnished by your father-in-law, who is also a prominent venture capitalist. You and your wife divorced four years ago. You're the father of two daughters."

"I imagine it gives you an advantage," Cady said.

"What does?"

"Knowing things about people."

"Knowledge is power."

"So it is, Detective Santana. So it is."

169

Santana slept late on Sunday morning. After breakfast he sat on the couch in the living room, reading a feature story in the morning paper about Rachel Hardin. Gitana was lying at his feet, soaking up the warmth of the fire burning in the stone fireplace.

The governor had announced that Judge Rachel Hardin would fill the vacant seat on the state's Supreme Court. Her appointment was not unexpected, nor was the blowback. Conservatives lauded her credentials and adherence to what they called "constitutional principles," while liberals denounced her appointment as being strictly political. The arguments were predictable. Governors typically appointed members of their own party and lawyers who shared their general philosophy. Unlike federal judges, the state's judicial appointees were not subjected to a confirmation process in front of the legislative branch, and according to the state constitution, anyone "learned in the law" could be appointed to the Minnesota Supreme Court. Santana figured this definition pretty much left the partisan appointment door wide open.

All Minnesota judges were supposed to be chosen by the electorate, thereby limiting each governor's appointments to vacancies that occurred by death or resignations during a judge's term. But nearly all judges began as gubernatorial appointees and then, observing an unwritten code, retired at a point in their terms when the governor could appoint an "interim" successor, like Rachel Hardin.

Once appointed, justices were almost never defeated for reelection. Some conservatives had launched a campaign to give party designation to each judicial candidate running for election, but Santana wondered if party endorsements and more money pouring into the pockets of party loyalists would finally derail an already polarized judicial system. Open elections with unendorsed judicial candidates at least led to the perception that most judges were impartial and interpreted the law fairly, without any political consideration of the governor who had appointed them.

Though there was no mention of it in the story, Santana recalled Rachel Hardin's reputation as a shy woman when she was in her early twenties who occasionally overcame her reticence with alcohol. Over the next decade, she had carefully and conscientiously constructed a reputation as an extremely ambitious but successful prosecutor, and then as a judge who meted out the stiffest sentences allowed. Because of her good looks and no nonsense reputation, she was a media darling and had garnered accolades among prosecutors and influential members of the police department.

Santana had heard talk around the courthouse that a few years ago, when Rachel Hardin and a colleague at their very conservative law firm were vying to become the next partner, she had purposely leaked that he was gay. Not only had her colleague not been named partner, he had summarily been terminated from his job.

Santana wondered if her marriage to Hank Rafferty had been one of convenience rather than love. The governor was a family values guy and far more likely to appoint a married woman to the state Supreme Court than a single one. Rachel Hardin's marriage to a well-respected cop with a medal of valor reinforced her reputation as a law-and-order judge.

After finishing the article on Rachel Hardin, Santana put down the paper, changed into his running gear, and took Gitana out for a run, hoping to avoid the rain predicted for later in the day. He ran two miles under low gray clouds and into a cool breeze blowing out of the north, his thoughts focused on his sister, Natalia.

He always looked forward to her e-mail messages, which arrived three or four times a week, even if they mostly contained nothing of significance. But each time he read her words on the screen, he felt emptiness in his heart. Natalia was all the family he had, and yet, for her safety, they could not be together.

Santana was reluctant to use the words *never be together*, though in his darkest moments, he honestly believed *never* represented a realistic view of the future. While Natalia continued to insist that she was more than willing to risk her life in order to be close to him, he was unwilling to take the chance. He had already lost his parents in violent and senseless deaths.

When he returned home, he lifted weights and worked out on the heavy and light bags for two hours until his muscles ached and sweat drenched his body. He took a long shower alternating hot and cold water. Then he toweled off, shaved, and dressed in casual clothes. He retrieved Jordan Parrish's business card from his wallet and dialed her home number, which she had written on the back of the card.

She answered on the third ring with a hesitant, "Hello?"

"It's John Santana."

"Oh," she said, her voice suddenly springing to life. "Your name didn't register on my caller ID."

"It wouldn't. I have a private listing."

"Probably a good idea."

"You busy this evening?"

"Are you asking me out?"

"Only if you're not busy," he said.

"What are we doing?"

"Dinner?"

"How about some Colombian food?" she said. "I've never tried it."

"You don't know what you're missing."

Santana picked up Jordan Parrish at six that evening and drove to La Colonia, a small family-owned restaurant on Central Avenue in northeast Minneapolis. The décor was simple—a few paintings of South Americans at work hung on the mostly bare walls—and the ambience consisted of soft Latino music and large families speaking Spanish. But the food from Colombia and Ecuador was excellent. He and Jordan sat in a booth and ordered *empanadas, patacones,* calamari, *chorizos,* rice, and tender slices of sirloin, along with cold bottles of Corona.

"Have you talked with Lyle Cady?" she asked.

"I heard a presentation he gave yesterday to a group of possible investors about his Venture Tech company. I spoke with him after the presentation."

Jordan was about to drink from her bottle of Corona when she paused and looked at him, her bright, shimmering eyes filled with curiosity.

"I didn't mention that Kenneth Vail had hired you," Santana said. "Or that I knew anything about Cady's affair with Monica Vail."

"I didn't say that you did."

"But you thought about it."

She smiled and offered a shrug. "Only for a moment."

Santana raised his bottle in a toast and then drank.

"So what did you two talk about?"

"Memories."

"Yours or his?"

"Neither. We talked about Kenneth Vail's memory research."

"Would you care to explain?"

Santana did. Just as he finished his explanation, a waitress delivered the food.

"This looks wonderful," she said.

"But filling."

She nodded. "There's enough food for a week."

As they ate, Jordan said, "Wouldn't it be something if Vail could erase traumatic memories?"

"Maybe."

"Why just maybe?"

"Because maybe some people would like to retain certain memories."

Jordan finished eating an *empanada* and wiped her mouth with a napkin. "Even traumatic ones?"

"Well," he said, "if our self is made up of experiences and memories, then what are we without them?" He paused and drank some beer before continuing. "And what would happen if we removed specific memories? Would we remain the same, or would we become someone else?"

"But what if we're more than just a collection of memories, John?"

"What do you mean?"

"What about our souls?"

He looked at her without speaking.

"You don't believe we have them, do you, John?"

"Does that bother you?"

"Only if it bothers you. I'm what you might call an agnostic."

"Then we're really not that much different."

"Except for our memories and experiences," she said.

They ate in comfortable silence for a time before Jordan spoke again. "What if you could choose the type of person you wanted to be, John? Say a soldier suffering from PTSD decides that he wants to be a different person than he is at the moment, perhaps the person he was before the traumatic event happened. Who's to say that shouldn't be his choice?"

Santana reflected on the choices he had made throughout his life, the choices that had led him to this moment in time. "Maybe the whole idea of an unalterable self is wrong, Jordan. Maybe we're all simply who we choose to be."

After dinner, Jordan requested a box for the leftovers. Then Santana drove her back to her small condo near St. Anthony Main and accepted her invitation for an after-dinner drink.

Santana took off his tweed sport coat and sat down on the mocha-colored, L-shaped sectional that contrasted nicely with the crème-colored walls, while Jordan put the leftovers in the refrigerator, then slipped out of her coat and brought a bottle of Tempranillo, wine glasses, and an opener into the living room. While Santana opened the wine, she flicked a switch that ignited the gas-burning fireplace. Then she started a CD player with one remote and dimmed the recessed lights in the ceiling and the torchiere-type lights in the corners with a second one.

"Technology," she said with a smile. "How did we ever survive without it?"

Her perfume smelled sweet, caressing him like a soft kiss as she came over and sat down close beside him.

"You like rhythm and blues, John?"

"I like this," he said, pouring them each a glass of wine.

"It's 'Any Love' by Luther Vandross. I enjoy his music. I just wish he were still around to record it." Their fingers touched briefly as he handed her a glass.

As she sat at an angle next to him, her knees brushed against his, and she smiled again.

He liked her smile. "You're not seeing anyone?"

She shook her head. "You?"

"No."

"Why not?"

"You get right to the point," he said.

"Well, you're a very good-looking man. A woman could easily assume you'd be involved with someone."

"I could make the same statement about you."

"Okay," she said—and waited.

He said, "You're a very good-looking woman. A man could easily assume you'd be dating someone. How's that?"

"Close enough. But you haven't answered my question."

"My job keeps me busy."

"That sounds like a poor excuse," she said.

It was. He knew it wasn't the hours that kept him from forming a long-term relationship. Anyone who became a significant part of his life became potential prey for the Cali cartel assassins who hunted him. His reluctance to commit to someone had left him essentially alone, his few significant female relationships as formless and fleeting as shadows.

"Harm seems to come to those who are close to me," he said.

"So you're saying you've had bad luck with relationships?"

"It has nothing to do with luck."

They sat in silence for a time. Then Jordan said, "You haven't told me anything about your family."

He avoided her eyes by drinking some wine. But he could sense her lingering gaze as she waited for details. He didn't want to upset her by withholding conversational information. Yet, even if he trusted her implicitly, Jordan could be made to disclose Natalia's location. Santana knew he would die before giving it up.

"You don't want to tell me about your family," she said.

He looked at her now and could see the hurt in her eyes. "It's not that I don't want to, Jordan. I can't."

"Why?"

"For protection."

"From me?"

"From people who could do great harm. It's better that you don't know."

"Who are these people who are looking for your family?"

Santana figured Jordan was using the term "family" in the broadest sense. But Natalia was Santana's family—at least what he had left of it. He chose not to explain. "People you don't want to know."

"Are they looking for you, too?"

"They've already found me." He drank some wine.

"Why don't you move?"

He looked into her eyes and then let his gaze linger on her face. "And quit my job and change my name? They'll only find me again." He shook his head. "I vowed a long time ago, Jordan, that if they found me I wouldn't run, I wouldn't hide. I'd try and live my life as best I can for as long as I can."

She raised her eyebrows and gave a slow nod, as though she understood. "I carry a gun, John. And I know how to use it."

"Meaning?"

"I'm not your typical date."

He had sensed that from their first meeting, which was one reason he was attracted to her. Still, being good with a gun was no guarantee of safety. In fact, it might lead to overconfidence and a willingness to take risks.

"Your last high-profile case," she said. "The one in the papers. Did that have something to do with your family?"

"Yes." He searched her face and then her eyes, trying to determine if what he had told her or refused to tell her had soured their budding relationship. But he couldn't get a read. "I'll leave now, Jordan, if you want."

She looked at him without expression. "You think you can get rid of me that easily?"

He wasn't quite sure what to make of her statement.

She must have seen the confusion on his face because she broke into a smile. "I don't need to know all the details about your life, John," she said. "At least not yet."

He kept his eyes fixed on hers for a moment longer and then let them wander across the walnut floors to the dining table that sat on a small riser underneath a hanging lamp, and then to the floor-to-ceiling window in a corner behind the table. Through the darkness outside the window, he could see rays of light from lampposts illuminating a dark path along the riverbank. Luther Vandross was singing "Always and Forever" as he looked at Jordan again.

"Why aren't *you* involved with someone?" he asked.

"Good men are hard to find."

"And how would you define good?"

She sipped some wine and thought about it. "I don't have a checklist. And I'm not into dating services. I'm still willing to take my chances in the open market, so to speak. But I believe a good man is honest, trustworthy, and courageous. And I don't mean courageous in just a physical sense. He has to stand for something important, something beyond just himself." She smiled. "And looks help, too."

"What about money?"

"Nice, but not that important."

Santana nodded and waited for her to ask him what he wanted in a woman.

Instead, she said, "I'm not looking for a husband. I tried marriage once, and that was enough. I like my freedom. I like to come and go as I choose without having to answer to someone all the time. But it would be nice to really *be* with someone, if you know what I mean. To be truly committed to someone without all the trappings that marriage brings."

Her hazel eyes were lit with a light so intense he could almost feel the heat. He leaned forward and kissed her gently on the lips, balancing the wine glass in one hand while cupping the back of her head with the other.

She kissed him back.

"That was nice," she said when he broke off the kiss.

"I thought so, too."

Her eyes drifted to the wine glass still in her hand and then came back to his face. "I don't sleep with someone on the first date."

"I wouldn't expect you to."

She held her eyes on his for a long moment before speaking again. "You're not disappointed?"

He shrugged. "Well, maybe a little."

She smiled, and they kissed again—though it lasted much longer this time.

Chapter 15

ON MONDAY MORNING SANTANA CALLED Kimberly Dalton's cell phone and got her voice mail. He then called Regions Hospital and asked to speak to her. When a supervisor told him she wouldn't be coming in, he wondered if she had chosen to spend the day with the Raffertys or with her own family after Saturday's funeral—or perhaps she was home and just wasn't answering her phone.

The thick, wet flakes of snow that were falling as Santana drove to Kimberly Dalton's apartment melted when they hit the windshield and hood of his sedan. But they were falling so heavily that visibility was poor, and lawns and tree branches were coated with a thin layer of white.

As Santana drove down her street, he saw her get out of the passenger side of a black Cadillac Escalade SUV with smoked glass windows. The heavy snowfall prevented him from seeing the license number clearly as the SUV pulled away from the curb. He had no reason to believe the vehicle had been stolen, but he knew that Cadillac Escalade SUVs *were* stolen, broken into, or stripped of parts more often than any other vehicle in the country. Santana pulled into a vacant spot along the curb, got out, and hurried to catch her.

She was standing in front of the outside glass door to the building, reaching into her purse to retrieve her keys, when she whirled to face him, a can of mace in her hand, her bloodshot eyes wide and twitching with anxiety.

Santana halted a few feet from her and held up his badge, his eyes squinting as snowflakes caught in his eyelashes. "It's Detective Santana, Ms. Dalton. Remember?"

She froze momentarily. Then she lowered her shoulders, and the tightness in her face relaxed. "You scared me."

"Sorry. We need to talk."

"About what?"

He gestured toward the sky. "Why don't we go inside?"

She hesitated and then used a key to open the outside door.

Once they were inside her apartment, Santana removed his coat and shoes. He declined her offer of tea and sat on the couch while she brewed a cup and then returned to the living room. "What is it you want to discuss?" she asked, sitting on a cushioned chair opposite him. She tugged at the hem of her emerald green sweater and smoothed a wrinkle in her plaid skirt.

"When we spoke before," Santana said, "you told me you didn't know why your father and Hank Rafferty had broken up their partnership."

Her long dark hair was damp from the snow, and she brushed a strand away from her forehead. "That's right."

"There's nothing you can add to that?"

"No. Ask Hank or my father."

Santana flipped through his notebook. "You and Scott and Jeff Tate were having drinks at Billy's Tavern the last night you saw Scott alive."

She nodded and sipped her tea, holding the teacup between the palms of her hands, as if to keep them warm. Her face looked even more drawn than it had been during his first visit. He wondered if anguish over her boyfriend's death had exacted a toll, or if there was another reason for her change in appearance.

She sniffled as mucus dripped from her nose. "Excuse me," she said, setting the teacup on the coffee table in front of her. "But I've been fighting a cold and need a Kleenex." She stood and quickly left the room.

Santana doubted she had a cold. When she came back and sat down again a few minutes later, he noted that her pupils were dilated, and her eyes were dancing to the beat of the cocaine in her system.

"Did you ever go to Billy's Tavern without Scott?" he asked.

"You mean with girlfriends?"

"Or alone."

She shook her head. "I'm not a big drinker, Detective. And I don't really like the whole bar scene. The only reason I went there was because Scott liked to. Now . . ." she shrugged and left the thought unfinished.

"You're a nurse at Regions Hospital," he said.

"Yes, an RN. Have been for four years."

"What department do you work in?"

"The Heart Center."

"Have you ever had an occasion to give patients a drug called Inderal, Ms. Dalton?"

"Why, yes," she said, breaking eye contact. "We use it to treat high blood pressure. Why do you ask?"

"You work with heart patients. I thought you might be familiar with it."

She looked at him again. "I don't prescribe drugs, Detective Santana."

"No, you just administer them."

Her eyes lost focus, and she seemed momentarily lost in her thoughts, as if she were trying to make sense of his statement. "What are you getting at?"

"You told me before that you and Scott were planning to marry," he said, changing the subject.

"We loved each other very much."

"When I spoke with Jeff Tate, he said Scott wasn't planning on marrying you. That you two had actually broken up."

Her bloodshot eyes quickly gained more focus and intensity. "Why would he say that?"

"I don't know, Ms. Dalton. That's why I'm asking."

"Well, Jeff Tate knew nothing about the relationship Scott and I had," she said, her voice rising in volume.

"How can you be sure?"

She closed her eyes and then opened them again. "Because he wasn't close to Scott like I was."

"What happened to Scott in Iraq that changed him?"

"One of the men Scott was closest to in his platoon was caught out in the open and hit with shrapnel during a firefight. He couldn't move and was calling for help. But the platoon was under heavy fire, and Scott's sergeant had issued orders to stay put, the logic being that Scott was no good to his buddy or the rest of his platoon if he was dead, which made sense."

"Maybe not to Scott."

She nodded. "Maybe not. He believed he could've saved his friend if given the chance. Instead, he had to listen to his cries for help throughout the hour-long battle. When he finally was able to carry his friend to the aid station, it was too late. The incident left Scott feeling very angry. He had to take Ambien to help him sleep, and he wore sunglasses."

"Something wrong with his eyes?"

"The sunglasses hid the tears he shed whenever he thought about the incident, which was most of the time."

"Did he ever share anything else with you about that time in his life?"

She shook her head. "Scott didn't like to talk about his war experiences. They were traumatic. Is that so difficult to understand?"

Actually, Santana understood it all too well. He never talked about his traumatic experiences either. "Did you have an argument with Scott Rafferty the last night you saw him?"

"Did Tate tell you that?"

Santana paged through his notebook until he found the quote he was looking for. "According to Tate, you told Rafferty 'you were going to fix him good.'"

"What does this have to do with Scott's murder?"

"You think he was murdered?"

"Don't you, Detective Santana? I mean, why else would you be coming around asking questions?" She paused for a moment until recognition lit her eyes. "You think I had something to do with Scott's death?"

"I didn't say that."

She stood abruptly and pointed to the door. "Please leave, Detective Santana."

Santana drove out to Biomedical Research to speak with Kenneth Vail. The receptionist at the front desk called Vail and pointed Santana in the direction of the lab in the rear of the building.

Vail, wearing a white lab coat, rose from a stool in front of a workbench on which was an electron microscope and cages holding white mice. Shelves on the wall facing the bench were filled with beakers and test tubes. A functional MRI machine inhabited one corner of the room. In the opposite corner, a door led into a small office with a large glass window. Through the window, Santana could see a computer screen, probably for reading MRI brain scans.

Vail offered his hand as Santana approached. "What can I do for you, Detective Santana?"

"I'd like to talk about your memory research."

Vail cocked his head. "What does my research have to do with Scott Rafferty's death?"

Santana wasn't sure if Vail's research had anything to do with Rafferty's death. But curiosity and instinct had pointed him in this direction. He wanted to see where it might lead.

"I'm just interested in learning more about it."

"I see," Vail said with a slow nod, though the questioning look on his face indicated otherwise.

Based on experience, Santana knew that if he dug into anyone's past, he would unearth a painful memory or two, perhaps even shed some light on unexplored darkness. It was true of his life as well as the lives of those he questioned—those he hunted. He had no desire to inflict pain on the innocent. But he had learned during the course of many investigations that keeping those he questioned off-balance allowed him to direct the conversation and gather information.

"What led to your interest in memory research?" he asked.

Vail's face suddenly creased with pain. A distant look came into his eyes, and he sat down on the stool again, as if the weight of his memories was too much to bear.

"I've just always had an affinity for those who struggle with painful memories," he said, his eyes avoiding Santana's.

Santana nodded but offered no response.

It took a few seconds before Vail escaped the ties that bound him to his past and focused his attention on Santana again. But Vail was looking at him differently now, as though he suspected that his past was written in the notebook the detective had pulled from his coat pocket.

"I imagine you're a man who does his homework," Vail said.

"I like to know something about the people I'm interviewing."

"Perhaps something you can use to extract information."

"Tell me about your research," Santana said, ignoring Vail's statement.

The dark, suspicious look in Vail's eyes slowly vanished, and his eyes once again gleamed with light. "My research involves the nerve circuits in the amygdala, the part of the brain that performs a primary role in the processing and memory of emotional reactions." He gestured toward the mice in cages on the bench. "Perhaps you remember stimulus-response theory from your high school or college days."

Santana nodded.

"Then you know that mice can be easily conditioned with electric shocks to fear certain stimuli, such as a loud tone. Once the conditioning is complete, just playing the tone triggers creation of certain proteins in the fear center, or amygdala, of the mice's brains within a few hours of fear conditioning. These particular proteins peak at twenty-four hours and disappear forty-eight hours later."

"Which means what?" Santana asked.

"It means there's a window of vulnerability before painful memories are solidified, Detective. And because these proteins are unstable, they can be easily removed during the window. I believe the process would be the same in humans."

"You mean if you remove these proteins, you could conceivably erase the memory?"

"Exactly."

"So how would you do that?"

"By creating a drug designed specifically to remove the protein."

"A discovery like that would be worth a lot of money."

"I'm not doing it for the money, Detective."

Santana paused a moment. Then he said, "But from what I understand," *and from what I've experienced,* he thought, "PTSD often develops months or even years after the event. That window of vulnerability you spoke of would be closed."

"That's true. But if you understand PTSD, then you know that certain stimuli can reopen the window."

"Like triggering the memory in mice with a tone."

"Precisely," Vail said. "It's not much different than the genetic brain mapping that has been done. First, you isolate the traumatic memory by having the patient recall the event. Next, you identify the protein responsible for the memory. Finally, you administer a drug to remove the protein from the fear center, thus erasing the memory."

"Isn't there a danger of wiping out someone's entire memory?"

"That didn't happen with mice."

"But mice aren't humans."

"No," Vail said, "they're not. But you can imagine the impact this treatment would have for psychiatry, psychology, and in helping people with a certain type of mental illness that is tied to memory."

Santana could hear the pride in Vail's voice. "Or the memories soldiers often experience due to war."

"Exactly. This country is at a crisis point with many of our returning soldiers. If research doesn't come up with an answer soon, we're going to have hundreds, if not thousands, of traumatized vets on the streets of our cities."

"Haven't we always had veterans from previous wars with PTSD?"

"Of course. But we didn't acknowledge it, because many veterans refused to talk about their experiences. We have more research now, more understanding of the problem, more ways to treat it."

"There must be a few inherent risks, Doctor."

He waved away Santana's statement as if he were shooing away a fly. "Of course there are risks, especially when we're dealing with the brain, or any organ, for that matter. But what if you couldn't sleep because you were haunted by nightmares of combat or some other trauma that you had suffered? Most people would very much like to be able to forget those traumatic memories."

Santana was again reminded of his own painful memories. "I think difficult memories form a part of who we are," he said. "They become part of our character, our identity. We learn from them."

"I wouldn't disagree."

"Some might even suggest that the struggle against bad experiences and memories can make us better people, Dr. Vail. Much like the struggle between good and evil."

"Perhaps," he said, leaning forward. "But let me ask you this, Detective. How bad does a memory have to be before you decide you want to be rid of it?"

"I suppose that would depend on the individual."

"Of course. I would never suggest that you take a patient with PTSD and wipe out all their memories."

"Like what happens with Alzheimer's patients."

"Well, in severe cases of Alzheimer's short term memory disappears, a situation that few would find acceptable. But that's not the result we're looking for. We want to selectively affect the traumatic memories that the patient is suffering from."

"But if we couldn't remember certain events," Santana said, "then perhaps we'd end up repeating the same mistakes."

"That's possible, I suppose."

"And what about the ethical implications of sending soldiers into combat knowing that no matter what they do, they'll have it erased from their minds? They would never have to live with the consequences of their actions. Maybe it's better to consider the answers to these questions before you get too far along, Dr. Vail."

"We need to help those who are scarred and damaged, Detective Santana. This research can't wait."

Santana wondered if Vail was speaking of his own condition. "But even if you manage to have a traumatic event erased, Doctor, others around you still remember it and still remind you of it."

"Having someone remind you of something or tell you about something is not the same as experiencing it first hand, Detective, especially if the event was so traumatic that you can't stop thinking about it, and it haunts your sleep and causes nightmares. You may still find it horrible, but you don't have that searing imagery burned into your mind."

"So who controls what gets erased?"

"I believe that should be up to the individual patient."

"You can be that certain, that precise?"

"Not at this stage of the research. But, hopefully, very soon."

Chapter 16

WHEN SANTANA ARRIVED at his desk that afternoon, David Dalton was waiting for him.

"You're in my chair," Santana said, standing over him.

"And you're still in my daughter's life."

"I'm working a case. Your daughter is part of it." Santana stood close to the chair and directly in front of Dalton, so that the detective had no room to stand up.

Realizing that he had unintentionally given Santana a position of power over him, Dalton rolled the chair backwards and stood. But Santana still had three inches of height on him and used it to his advantage by stepping close to him, forcing Dalton to look up as he spoke.

"My daughter had nothing to do with Scott Rafferty's death."

"I never said she did."

"That's not what Kimberly told me. Why were you asking her about Inderal?"

Santana didn't answer.

"Come on, Santana. What're you after?"

"The truth."

"And you don't care who gets hurt in your pursuit of it."

"Why would your daughter get hurt if she's being honest?"

"Because sometimes the truth has unintended consequences."

"You referring to your daughter or to something else?"

Dalton's eyes met Santana's, but he offered no reply.
"What's going on out here?" Santana and Dalton both
looked in the direction of Rita Gamboni's office. She was stand-
ing in the doorway with her hands on her hips. "Well?" she
said. "Are either of you going to tell me why you're arguing?"
Santana looked at Dalton.
"I was just leaving," he said. He scowled at Santana and
then strode out of the Homicide Unit.
"What was that all about?"
"Nothing, Rita."
"I'll bet." She turned and pushed opened her office door.
"I need to speak to you."
Santana could see Ed Kincaid seated in a chair in front of
Gamboni's desk as he walked toward the office. He suppressed
a smile when he saw the black and blue swelling under Kincaid's left eye.
Kincaid gestured with an open hand at the vacant chair
next to him and grinned, his eyes lit with expectation, like a cat
that had just cornered a mouse. Santana sat down and waited
while Gamboni organized some papers on her desk and then
fixed her intense gaze on his face.
"Agent Kincaid and I have been discussing Jack Brody,"
she said.
Kincaid gave a derisive snicker. "The guy's a drunk and a
has-been. He needs a big story to get back on top. So he con-
cocts a sociopath-on-the-loose scenario to gin up interest. This
isn't the first time the Bureau has looked into these drownings.
They go all the way back to the late nineties. The conspiracy
wing nuts like Brody claim the vics were drugged and tortured
before their bodies were dumped into rivers. But we've found
no evidence in the recovered remains to support the theory that
any of them was tortured."
"Water washes away blood evidence," Gamboni said.
"Sure it does. But we often get fiber evidence."

"What about the chaos symbol found at the sites?" Santana said.

Kincaid shook his head, as though a child had asked the question. "Well, you should be able to figure that out, given your stellar reputation."

"You'd have to prove that the chaos graffiti was painted at or immediately after the time of the killing."

"Hey, Detective. You're brighter than you look."

"Agent Kincaid," Gamboni said in a tone of voice that signaled a warning.

Kincaid raised his hands in gesture of surrender. "I was only having fun with your detective."

"Sure you were," Santana said.

Kincaid glared at Santana. Then a smile quickly reappeared. He looked at Gamboni. "Graffiti was found near a few of the death scenes, not all of them. Forensically, we can't determine the age of the paint. But we believe the graffiti is a recent occurrence."

"So at least in some of the cases, the chaos symbol could've been placed at the time of the crime," Santana said.

"Most of what you've heard, Santana, is urban legend. The whole blogosphere is filled with myths generated by crackpots who bitch about what's wrong with the government and frighten the sheep into believing we're conspiring to take away their guns and individual rights. Lies are repeated until they become fact." Kincaid emphasized the word "fact" with air quotes.

"When citizens can't find easy answers to complex problems like death investigations," he continued, "they resort to the boogieman syndrome, the monster mentality. And it's worse now in a time of uncertainty and fear, when the economy is in the tank and people are struggling financially. The networks and cable channels stoke the fear night after night. Pretty soon people start looking for someone or something outside themselves to blame for their problems and the problems of the country."

Gamboni appeared to be composing her thoughts before she spoke to Santana. "Homicidal drowning *is* pretty rare, John."

"I understand that, Rita."

Kincaid nodded his head in agreement. "It's less than one percent of homicides. And most of those involve parents drowning their own children or a husband drowning his wife. But accidental near-drownings are fairly common, especially with young males. They're more likely to engage in risky behaviors even when they're not drinking. Hell, in some cases, these deaths actually may be suicides. And binge drinking is a strong predictor of actual suicide attempts. Nope," Kincaid said, shaking his head, "these drownings don't fit a serial killer motive. And there's no known serial offender I'm aware of who has ever drowned victims."

"Always could be a first time," Santana said.

"Look, Detective. College students were drowning in the river long before most of these identified cases occurred. And they'll continue as long as students drink to excess."

"Some of these college students weren't drunk."

"Says who?"

"Jack Brody."

Kincaid chuckled to himself. "No matter what evidence is presented, some gullible people aren't going to change their minds. Don't be one of those, Detective. Don't become emotionally invested in the story. You know the risks you take when you over-identify with either the victim or the victim's family. It can cloud your judgment and your ability to remain impartial. You become blind to logic and reason."

"So you're still charging Brody with assault."

"He committed a federal crime."

"And you didn't hit him first?"

"See if you can find a mark on him," Kincaid said.

"There might not be one if you hit him in the gut like he claims."

"You calling me a liar, Santana?"

"I'm telling you I know why you've got it in for Brody."

"Because he assaulted me."

Santana shook his head. "No. You're after him because he wrote a story about FBI agents on the take. And one of those agents was a good friend of yours, Kincaid. Did you plant the coke in Brody's car that cost him his job with the *Times*, or was it one of your agent friends?"

Kincaid's face colored with rage. He started to rise, but Santana was quicker. He stood and purposely stepped on Kincaid's toes, causing the agent to fall backwards into his chair. Kincaid's face was still red as he glared at Santana, but it was caused by embarrassment now. His eyes flicked toward Gamboni. "Can't you control your detective?"

"You provoked him. What did you expect?"

Kincaid looked up at Santana, his knuckles pale as he gripped the arms of the chair.

"Why don't you take a swing at me, Kincaid," Santana said. "See what happens."

"We'll settle this later."

"I look forward to it."

"Oh, cut the macho bullshit, you two," Gamboni said. "Sit down, John!"

Santana sat.

Kincaid rolled his shoulders and adjusted his suit coat. "I'll be in touch, Commander." He stood. "And we'll need to know your decision soon." He left the office, closing the door hard behind him.

Santana wanted to ask Gamboni about Kincaid's last comment, but she spoke first.

"What were you and David Dalton arguing about? And before you respond," she said, holding a palm out in a stopping gesture, "please respect me enough to give me a straight answer."

"All right," he said. "You're aware that Dalton's daughter, Kimberly, was dating Scott Rafferty."

"Yes. Hank and Rachel mentioned the relationship when we met with them following Scott's death."

"Well, I believe Kimberly Dalton is using cocaine, and her supplier is Devante Carter. Carter worked with Scott Rafferty at the Lessard Mortuary."

Gamboni's gaze turned inward. "Devante Carter," she said. "Where have I heard that name before?" She snapped her fingers. "It was two years ago."

"What was?"

"You remember when a banger pulled a gun on Rafferty, and Hank shot and killed him."

"What banger?"

Gamboni thought about it. "The kid's name was Grissom. Montrell Grissom."

"So?"

"Carter testified on Hank's behalf."

"Why would he do that?"

Gamboni shrugged. "I don't know. But you haven't answered my question, John. Why were you and Dalton arguing?"

"Because when I first questioned his daughter about her relationship with Carter, she got upset and told Dalton. He wants me to back off."

"Does he suspect his daughter is using?"

"He says Scott Rafferty was the user. But what he says and what he actually believes may be two different things."

"I see," Gamboni said.

"But I don't."

"What do you mean?"

"It's time for you to respect me, Rita, and give *me* a straight answer. What decision was Kincaid talking about just before he left your office?"

Gamboni's face reddened with embarrassment, and she couldn't meet his eyes.

"Tell me," he said.

She released a heavy sigh. "The chief has offered me the position of commander of the Safe Streets Initiative. I'd be working as a liaison with the FBI."

Santana's heart skipped a beat, even though he had suspected as much. "And you're going to take it?"

Her eyes finally met his. "I haven't decided yet."

"Why?"

"Why what?"

"Why would you want to work with those assholes? What's in it for you?"

"I've always wanted to work with the FBI ever since I took a course at Quantico."

"Who would take your place as Homicide commander?"

"I don't know," she said, peering down at her desktop.

"Don't sell me out, Rita."

She jerked her head up, her eyes a blue flame. "I'm not selling you out."

"You have a conflict of interest. Kincaid wants you to drop the Scott Rafferty investigation because he's worried that Jack Brody might be right, a serial killer might have murdered Rafferty. In turn, Kincaid will put in a good word for you with the feds."

"You think I need a good word, that I couldn't get the job based on my experience and qualifications?"

"I didn't say that."

"Well, that's what I heard."

"I think you'd be excellent, Rita. But you can't sacrifice justice for the sake of a job. You're better than that."

"Don't accuse me of sacrificing justice for my own sake," she said, her voice rising in anger. "And what evidence do you have that Rafferty was murdered by a serial killer—or anyone else for that matter?"

"I'm working on it."

Gamboni rubbed her face with her hands and sat back in the chair. "I want this position, John. I've earned it."

"Haven't I earned your trust?"

"Of course you have."

"Then give me more time. Don't trust Kincaid."

"Bring me something, John. And bring it soon. Otherwise . . ." she shrugged her shoulders.

"How much time do I have?"

"A few days, max."

The voice mail light on Santana's phone was blinking red when he returned to his desk. The message was from Reiko Tanabe. She wanted to meet with him as soon as possible.

"What've you got?" he asked when he sat down in a chair in front of her desk twenty minutes later in the medical examiner's office.

Tanabe held up a file folder. "Scott Rafferty had over a gram of propranolol in his system."

"Meaning?"

"A maintenance dose for hypertension might be one hundred twenty to two hundred forty milligrams a day, or one hundred twenty to two hundred sixty milligrams of sustained release. You wouldn't want to take more than six hundred forty milligrams a day."

"But he wasn't taking it for hypertension."

"Doesn't matter what he was taking the drug for. He had way too much of it in his system."

"Say someone broke open the capsule, Reiko, and then poured it into a drink."

Tanabe opened the file and reviewed it for a moment. Then she adjusted her wire-rimmed glasses and looked at Santana again. "The liver metabolizes the drug. Only a very small amount of it is excreted in urine. Peak plasma concentration generally occurs one to two hours after administration. With a sustained release formulation, the peak plasma concentration occurs seven hours after absorption. But if there was a large dose entering Rafferty's system at one time, the liver couldn't possibly metabolize it fast enough." She pulled a typed sheet out of the folder and looked at it. "The toxic dose is about one gram, although people have died taking less than a gram of propranolol. But generally, a lethal dose is in the neighborhood of six grams."

"So the propranolol didn't kill him?"

"Maybe not. But if he had that much of the drug in his system, it certainly could contribute to his death. Cardiovascular symptoms are the major features of propranolol poisoning. Bradycardia is the commonest symptom and occurs soon after ingestion."

"You mean slowing of the heart rate."

She nodded. "Most resting adult heart rates are between sixty and one hundred beats a minute. Propranolol slows the beat considerably below that rate, which can lead to shock and cardiac arrest within one to two hours of ingestion, particularly if Rafferty was struggling to survive in ice cold water."

"Do me a favor, Reiko. Go back and see if you can find propranolol in the tissue samples you have for Michael Johnson, Thomas Hunter, and Matthew Miller."

Santana returned to the Homicide Unit and sat down at his desk. He stared blankly at the case files for Johnson, Hunter, Miller and the unidentified drowning victim stacked on his desktop, as though he were looking at a difficult equation on an exam. He had read through each of the files carefully and processed what he considered to be the relevant information contained in each. He had interviewed Michael Johnson's parents. He had listened with interest to Jack Brody—and to Jordan Parrish—who both believed that a serial killer was roaming the Midwest, preying on young men who had drunk too much alcohol or had been unknowingly drugged.

Thinking of Jordan Parrish caused his thoughts to drift from the case. He had to force himself to refocus. Instinctively, he knew he was missing something, but he had little time to figure out what it was, since Gamboni had given him only a few days. He had been under pressure before and was used to dealing with it, but this was the first time that he had felt Gamboni no longer had his back. And if she accepted the new position as liaison to the FBI, he was certain he would be the worse for it, no matter whom the chief chose as the next homicide commander.

He was alone in the comfortable afternoon silence of the unit as he closed his eyes and leaned back in his chair, hoping that emptying his mind of all thoughts would allow an idea to bubble to the surface. It took awhile before one came to him.

According to Gamboni, Devante Carter had testified in Hank Rafferty's defense during the Montrell Grissom shooting. Hank Rafferty's partnership with David Dalton had ended shortly afterward. Maybe, Santana thought, the answer he was looking for wasn't in the files on his desk, but in another.

He stood up and headed for the records section. Once there, he signed out the case file on Montrell Grissom and took it back to his desk. As he read through the file, he remembered some of the details of the shooting two years earlier that had created a media frenzy and a week's worth of above-the-fold headlines alleging a police department cover-up. Hank Rafferty had fatally shot sixteen-year-old Montrell Grissom during a foot chase near a high school in St. Paul. Rafferty had said Grissom was selling drugs and had a gun, which was found about two feet from the young man's body. He had been shot five times.

A security camera attached to the roof of the school had videotaped a portion of the chase, but the tape was of poor quality, and the actual shooting had occurred out of camera range. Montrell Grissom's mother had threatened to file a lawsuit against Rafferty and the department, alleging that Rafferty had murdered her son. A grand jury had been convened. A videotape expert hired by Grissom's mother had claimed that the video showed nothing in Grissom's hands, while an expert provided by the SPPD had testified that the video appeared to show that Grissom was carrying something dark in his right hand. But even his testimony was inconclusive as to whether Grissom had been carrying a gun.

Then Devante Carter had come forward and testified that Hank Rafferty had fired in self-defense. Rafferty was cleared of any criminal wrongdoing. An Internal Affairs investigation had found that Rafferty hadn't violated any procedures. He was awarded the Medal of Valor for bravery. Montrell Grissom's mother had abruptly dropped the lawsuit and refused to talk to the press. Santana noted that Wayne Edgell from Internal Affairs had signed off on the report. Santana set the Grissom case file on top of the stack of files on his desk and headed quickly for Edgell's office.

He found the big man with the shaved head and thick, dark mustache sitting behind his cluttered desk. Known as "Edge" because of his quick temper, Wayne Edgell had maintained a reputation as a straight shooter despite his position in IA—a department most cops distrusted and some feared.

Edgell looked up from his paperwork. "What's shakin', Santana?"

"You investigated the Montrell Grissom shooting a couple of years ago."

Edgell narrowed his dark eyes and nodded.

"You interviewed a banger named Devante Carter."

"That's right."

"He claimed he witnessed the shooting."

"You wanna tell me why you're suddenly so interested?"

"Carter has a connection to a current case I'm working."

"So what does your current case have to do with the IA's investigation of the Grissom shooting?"

"Maybe nothing."

"Right," Edgell said. "What's the problem?"

"Devante Carter testified in Hank Rafferty's defense during the grand jury proceedings."

"Uh-huh."

"Didn't you find that a little strange?"

"I thought he was bullshitting us at first. But when we checked all the security tapes, we found Carter was on one of them. We couldn't prove he *didn't* witness the shooting."

"But even if he did witness the shooting, why would he testify in Rafferty's defense?"

"He claimed he wanted to do the right thing."

"Why would a career criminal like Carter suddenly decide to do the right thing?"

Edgell took his time thinking about it. Then he said, "Well, I asked myself that, too, Santana. Particularly since Carter and Grissom were family."

Santana felt his heartbeat accelerate. "Montrell Grissom was related to Devante Carter?"

"Yeah. He was Carter's half-brother."

Chapter 17

AFTER LEAVING EDGELL'S OFFICE, Santana found Hank Rafferty doing squats in the SPPD gym on the fourth floor. Rafferty was dressed in a pair of workout shorts, tattered running shoes, and white socks that hung loose around his ankles. His plain white T-shirt with cut-off sleeves was ringed with sweat. Rafferty gritted his teeth and sucked in a deep breath as he lifted a heavy bar off the squat rack, the large iron weights clanging together as he settled the bar onto his shoulders. Santana noted that Rafferty's arms lacked definition, but his legs were thick and muscled. He waited until Rafferty had completed his set before he sat down on a padded bench beside the squat rack.

"Got a minute, Hank?"

"You have some news about my son's death?"

Santana decided he wouldn't disclose the elevated pro-pranolol level Tanabe had found in Scott Rafferty's liver tissue until he was sure what it meant—or if it meant anything at all.

"Sorry, Hank. I don't."

"Oh," Rafferty said, his voice leaden with disappointment, his face red from exertion. He wiped beads of sweat off his forehead with a small white towel and sat down on a separate padded bench across from Santana.

The large room was the size of a basketball court and was filled with weight-lifting equipment, ellipticals, stationary bikes, and treadmills. But only two other officers were working out, and they were in a far corner, one walking on a treadmill, the other using a bike. Both had iPod buds in their ears. Santana didn't recognize either of them. He felt he could speak freely without interruption and without someone overhearing the conversation.

"I need to talk to you about the Montrell Grissom case."

"That's history, Santana."

"It's not the shooting I'm interested in, Hank."

"Then what?"

"Devante Carter."

Rafferty covered the deepening redness in his complexion by wiping his face with the towel. Then he said, "Why are you interested in Carter?"

"He's involved in a case I'm working."

Rafferty's brown eyes grew large. "You think he had something to do with Scott's death?"

Santana didn't want to reveal too much, but he knew he would have to give Rafferty something. "Carter works at the Lessard Mortuary where your son worked."

Rafferty's eyes were suddenly jittery with thoughts and excitement. "I didn't know that. Scott never mentioned it."

"Did Scott know that Carter had testified in your defense after the Montrell Grissom shooting?"

"Scott was in Iraq during that time. I'm not sure how much he really knew or heard."

"Did you ever talk with him about it?"

Rafferty wiped his face with the towel again to cover his expression and shook his head.

Santana wondered what Rafferty was hiding. "Then maybe it's just a coincidence, Hank."

Rafferty smiled crookedly. "Yeah. That's why you're here asking me about Carter."

"So tell me, why do you think Devante Carter would testify in your defense after you shot and killed his half-brother?"

Rafferty's eyes lost focus, as though he were replaying a video of the shooting on a memory screen inside his mind. "I don't *know* why," he said after a time, though his shifty eyes lacked truthfulness.

Late that afternoon, Santana drove to the Lessard Mortuary to talk to Devante Carter. Santana wanted to ask Carter why he had testified against his half-brother and why he had defended Hank Rafferty, an SPPD detective. But as he followed the driveway to a parking lot behind the mortuary and saw a Cadillac Escalade SUV parked beside an older model red Honda sedan, a second question came to his mind. He figured the Escalade was the same vehicle he had seen in front of Kimberly Dalton's apartment and that it belonged to Carter. He wanted to know what Carter's relationship was with Kimberly Dalton. After lapping the building, he parked under the porte cochere amid plumes of exhaust fumes that lingered in the cold air like lost spirits.

The entry chime pinged as Santana opened the heavy wooden door, but no one came to greet him. He waited a minute more before searching the chapel and the arrangement room where he had first spoken with William Lessard and Carter, but the old mansion was as quiet and empty as an open grave.

A nameplate labeled OFFICE was attached to a closed door in the arrangement room. Santana knocked. When no one responded, he turned the knob and pushed the door open. It was a small office, but expensively furnished with a mahogany desk in the center of the room and bookshelves along one wall. A window on the back wall looked out onto a large evergreen, but it was the painting on the wall to his right that drew Santana's attention. Ominous storm clouds hung over the leafless branches of a silhouetted tree. Jagged mountains to the left of the tree were painted in shades of red, with red smoky clouds hovering over them. It was a beautiful painting, but it had an eerie, apocalyptic theme that was disturbing.

Santana had a strong urge to look through the desk drawers, but he knew if he were caught, it would lead to trouble. So he went downstairs to the lower level and stopped in front of the door marked EMPLOYEES ONLY. It was the same room that Ronald Getz, the ex-con, had been entering on Santana's first visit, but now the door was locked. However, the doors to the traditional crematorium halfway down the hall were open. Santana saw no one when he entered.

A simple wooden casket rested on a set of hydraulic rails that descended just below the floor level, waiting to be wheeled into the furnace. The heat gauge on the computer panel registered a temperature of 632 degrees and climbing. Santana looked around the room once more to make certain he was alone. Then he walked over to the casket and lifted the lid.

The naked body inside it was Jeff Tate's.

His skin had a greenish discoloration on the right lower abdomen, the first sign of putrification, which meant Tate had not been embalmed, and he had probably been dead for at least two days. The coloration would soon spread over the abdomen, chest, and upper thighs. Santana could smell the beginnings of the putrid sulphuric odor from the intestinal gas produced by the breakdown of blood cells. Tate also had a ligature mark around his neck. He had been a big man. Whoever had strangled him had to have been very strong.

Santana closed the coffin lid and went back into the hallway, where he stopped and listened. Silence.

He headed toward the stairs. But when he got to the door marked EMPLOYEES ONLY, he noticed the door was now ajar. He pushed it open and entered.

A man lay on a porcelain embalming table in the center of the 40 x 40 foot room, his arms at his sides. A white sheet covered his body from the waist down. The temperature felt like it was fifty degrees, and the air had a pungent odor that reminded Santana of sour pickles. Fluorescent lights reflected off the white tile that covered the floor and walls. OSHA-mandated signs warning of potential contamination hung on the wall behind a drench shower that could be used in the event of formaldehyde contamination. Shelves attached to the wall behind the shower contained Polyzorb blankets used to clean up dangerous spills and embalming supplies.

Santana walked over to the table and looked down at the man lying there. He was likely in his early sixties. His body had a pinkish hue from the dye in the formaldehyde. His eyes had been posed using caps that kept them shut. A needle injector had set a wire into his maxilla and mandible. Whoever had performed the procedure had made sure that the mouth wasn't closed too tightly so that his lips puckered. The natural body color and the relaxed expression on his face left the impression that he was peacefully sleeping, an effect most funeral directors desired but not all achieved. Still, Santana had seen enough bodies to recognize the complete stillness and the empty expression of death. He no longer believed in a soul, but it was obvious by the man's wax-like appearance that his life force no longer resided in his body.

There were two small incisions on the right side of the man's lower neck where a tube connected to the embalming fluid had been placed into the carotid artery. A third incision had been made just above his navel, where a two-foot long, half-inch diameter needle called a trocar had been placed inside his abdominal and thoracic cavities to remove bodily fluids and inject disinfecting and preservative fluid into the organs. All three incisions had been sutured closed. Santana could see no other marks or wounds on the body indicating how the man had died.

As he scanned an instrument table filled with scalpels, scissors, syringes, and aneurysm hooks to assist in finding and raising arteries and veins, Santana was suddenly struck by the expendability of a body—and by his own sense of mortality. Then, as his eyes shifted to the body on the table again, he felt the hairs on the back of his neck rise. He whirled quickly.

Ronald Getz's large frame loomed in the doorway. Getz was wearing the same outfit he had worn the first time Santana had seen him—a green splatter gown over khaki pants and a blue denim shirt with the sleeves rolled up over his elbows. The white supremacist spider web tattoo was clearly visible on Getz's left forearm.

"What are you doing in here?" His voice was low and threatening.

"I'm looking for Devante Carter."

He stared at Santana without expression. Then he closed the door behind him. "That isn't Carter."

"Do you know who it is?"

He shook his head, his glass eye glimmering under the intense white light. His hawk nose looked larger and his face appeared harder and whiter in contrast to his receding black hair, dark mustache, and goatee.

Santana gestured toward the cremation room down the hall. "Who brought Jeff Tate's body in, and why is he being cremated?"

Getz's gaze shifted briefly toward the door. Then he headed for Santana, his long legs carrying him quickly forward.

Santana popped the strap on his belt holster. The Glock had just cleared leather when Getz clamped his right hand over Santana's in a powerful grip, squeezing it like a vice, until the gun fell uselessly to the floor. Santana tried to pull his hand loose, but Getz grabbed him by the lapels and threw him like a bag of bones against the wall.

Air burst out of Santana's lungs and stars danced in front of his eyes. He shook his head and struggled to his feet, but Getz was on him again. Santana threw a right, aiming for

Getz's solar plexus, but the big man's stomach was corded with muscle, and Santana's fist felt like it had hit a brick wall. Getz grabbed him again and threw him across the room. This time Santana was ready and was able to maintain his balance.

He spotted the Glock lying on the floor near the embalming table. But Getz got to it first and thumbed the release, and the magazine clattered to the floor. Then he ejected the remaining shell from the chamber, the brass arcing away from the gun and landing on the dead man's bare chest. Getz's thin lips twisted into a malevolent smile that was as thin as the edge of a knife. He tossed the empty gun onto the counter behind him.

Santana glanced at the door.

The smile lingered on Getz's face as he pulled a key card from his pocket and held it up. "The door locks automatically. You want out of the room, you need this." He slipped the card into a pocket of his apron. "Come get it."

Santana knew he was physically outmatched. He might be faster than Getz and in better condition, but speed and lung capacity in a confined space were of little use. Getz's lack of peripheral vision in his glass eye was a slight advantage. Still, Santana needed a weapon—and there were plenty of them in the room. Scalpels, scissors, and needles. Problem was, Getz stood between him and the instrument table. Maybe he could outthink Getz, but it was obvious by the grin on the big man's face that he was enjoying the game of cat and mouse. He wouldn't panic and couldn't be reasoned with. The best Santana could do was to avoid him until he could get his hands on a weapon, but that was easier said than done. He figured Getz might be hesitating because he wanted to counterattack, so Santana stood with his back against the cold tile wall and waited. He didn't have to wait long.

Getz ran a hand over the shiny stainless steel instruments on the table, the silvery bracelet on his right wrist flashing in the harsh light, before he bent down and drew a six-inch mili-

tary knife from a sheath clipped to the inside of his right cow-
boy boot. He held the knife in front of his face, peering intently
at it, as though he were examining a priceless jewel.

"You take down a cop, Getz, you're going in for life."

"In a few hours you'll be nothing but ash, Detective. Just
like Tate. Your department won't know what happened to
you."

Santana grabbed a Polyzorb blanket off a shelf.

Getz's deep, hollow laugh echoed in the room, as though
he were standing inside a cave. "A blanket versus a knife. That
seems fair to me." He bent slightly and held the knife down at
his knees. Then he moved cautiously forward, the bright fluorescent lights reflecting off the sharp blade.

Chapter 18

SANTANA COULD SEE THE GLEAM of anticipation in Getz's good eye as the big man jabbed the air with the knife, his thin lips a slash across his face. Santana realized he had to even the odds if he had any chance of surviving. Getz was just too large and too strong—and he had a weapon. The knife would slice open an artery more easily than scissors cut paper.

Keeping his weight balanced as he danced away, Santana dodged the arc of the blade. Getz had a reach advantage, but he was slower and had a bad habit of feinting in one direction before he cut the air with the blade or thrust it forward. Santana remained just out of range, like a boxer avoiding a jab. He used the blanket as a matador would a cape, trying to distract Getz while he moved along the wall behind him. A vicious cut ripped a hole in the blanket. Santana tossed it at Getz, and as he stopped to grab it, Santana ran toward the door and flicked off the light switch, plunging the room into total darkness.

It took a few seconds to slow his thudding heart and the blood rushing in his ears. The spots in front of his eyes would eventually dissolve in the pitch darkness, but even after his eyes adjusted, he would be unable to see anything—as would Getz. Santana felt for the wall to his left and then edged along it, the thick rubber soles on his shoes masking his footsteps. When he reached a corner, he squatted on his haunches and listened. Finally, he could hear Getz breathing softly, and his leather soles scraping lightly against the concrete floor. Santana figured Getz was moving toward the opposite wall. He would use it as a point of reference and would soon make his way to the double doors and the light switch. Santana had only seconds.

From a pocket of his sport coat, he pulled out his mini-Maglite. Holding it toward the floor, he flicked it on, the light forming a small puddle in front of him. Then he lifted the thin beam toward the opposite wall. Getz jerked his head toward the light, his glass eye shining in the beam like a nocturnal animal's. Santana could see that Getz had reached the far corner of the room now and was inching along the wall that held the door. Getz knew—as did Santana— that he had to get to the lights before Santana got to his gun.

Santana turned off the Maglite and moved quickly. Within moments he had reached the counter. He flicked on the flashlight once more to orient himself, letting the beam play across the counter until he spotted his Glock. He scrambled forward, picked up the gun, and shone the light along the floor where Getz had released the magazine—but he couldn't locate it. He drew in a deep breath and focused all his adrenaline-fueled energy on the floor and the beam running across it.

Santana's heart skipped a beat as light suddenly flooded the room. He saw the magazine. In two quick steps he had it in his hand. He slammed it into the butt end of the Glock and racked the slide, turning toward the door and leveling the gun in one swift motion.

The door was open and Getz was gone.

Santana raced across the room and paused at the open doorway. Then he came out fast, checking both directions in case Getz was waiting—but he saw no one. Santana ran down the hallway toward the exit that led to the parking lot in the rear of the building. As he shoved open the door, he heard the sound of tires squealing and a car roaring out of the lot. Both Getz's Honda and Devante Carter's Cadillac Escalade were gone.

Santana called the night watch commander to have an APB sent out immediately on Ronald Getz. Then he alerted forensics, the ME's office, and Rita Gamboni that there was a probable murder victim at the Lessard Mortuary.

While he waited for everyone to arrive, he retrieved his laptop from the Crown Vic and typed a search warrant for Ronald Getz's residence. It was nearly 8:00 p.m. now, and Minnesota law dictated that search warrants could only be served during the hours of 7:00 a.m. to 8:00 p.m. But Santana needed immediate access to Getz's residence. Judges typically waived the requirement if there was a reasonable suspicion that a search was necessary to preserve evidence or to protect public safety. And Santana believed that Getz was an obvious threat. Using his computer to check the courthouse schedule, Santana discovered that Rachel Hardin was the duty judge assigned to after-hour warrants.

When Gamboni arrived at the mortuary, Santana went through everything that had occurred. Then he sped to his office, printed a copy of the warrant, and drove to the courthouse.

Santana pushed open the heavy bronze railing in an empty courtroom and headed for Judge Hardin's chambers. Her office was one of the few that could be accessed directly through a courtroom door. Most judges walking between their chambers and courtrooms had to walk in the open hallways among defendants and their families, a definite security concern.

She was seated behind her desk when Santana knocked on the open office door. She raised her eyebrows and peered over her half-frame reading glasses. "Detective Santana. Come in."

"I need a signature on this search warrant, Judge Hardin."

She held out a hand, and Santana gave her the search warrant before he sat down.

The shelves on the wall-length bookshelf behind her were filled with thick law books and photos of the judge with local celebrities, politicians, and athletes. On one shelf he saw a framed certificate from the National Rifle Association. The other three walls were bare and covered in fabric—no nails allowed—which meant the county would not have to paint the walls each time a different judge moved into the office.

"Mr. Ronald Getz appears to be a dangerous man," she said, her lips pursing slightly as she read the warrant.

"I think he is."

Her eyes hovered over the warrant a moment longer before she removed her glasses and looked at Santana. "While you're here, Detective, I'm wondering if you know anything more about Scott's death."

"I'm in a hurry, Judge Hardin."

"I understand. But just give me your take."

Santana wanted to leave on good terms. "I'm not sure that your stepson's death was an accident or suicide."

"And why is that?"

"I haven't put it all altogether. But I'm working on it."

She sat back in her black leather chair, a bow of her reading glasses hooked in a corner of her mouth, thinking. Then she tossed the glasses on her desktop. "I know you're good at your job, Detective. You've solved a number of high-profile cases."

Santana thanked her for the compliment.

"No need to thank me, Detective. The city, the courts, the citizens all appreciate what you've done and are willing to do to keep us safe."

"I'm not sure I understand what you mean by 'willing to do.'"

"Your willingness to put your life on the line. Your willingness to do what's necessary in times of crisis."

Santana was uncertain if she was referring to those he had killed in the line of duty or those who had nearly killed him—or something else.

"But I'm worried that you might be offering Hank false hope."

"How do you mean?"

She sat forward and clasped her hands together on the desktop as if she were about to pray. "I'm sure you know my husband blames himself for Scott's death. If only he'd been a better father to Scott. If he'd spent more time with him after Scott returned from Iraq. If he'd taken Kimberly Dalton's phone call more seriously."

"You mean when she called and told Hank that Scott was missing."

"Yes."

"It's not unusual for a father to blame himself when his son dies before him, regardless of whose fault it is," Santana said.

"No, it isn't. But what if Scott's death wasn't a suicide or an accident?"

"Then Hank doesn't have to blame himself. He can blame the perpetrator."

"Exactly," she said with a firm nod.

"I'm not continuing the investigation because I want to assuage Hank's guilt, Judge Hardin. I'm continuing to investigate because I believe your stepson might have been the victim of a homicide."

"And what gives you that idea?"

"I'm really not at liberty to discuss my investigation."

She gave him a thin, empty smile. "Of course not. But I don't want Hank to be hurt any more than he already has been. Surely you can understand my concern." She eyed him the way she might a suspect on the witness stand.

Santana nodded but offered no reply.

A long time seemed to pass before Judge Hardin put on her glasses, signed the warrant with a flourish of her pen, and held it out to him.

Santana took it and left before she changed her mind.

It was after nine in the evening when he parked at the curb in front of the small duplex on St. Paul's East Side where Ronald Getz lived. Santana doubted that Getz had returned home after fleeing the mortuary. But he unsnapped the safety strap holding the Glock in his belt holster as he got out of the Crown Vic.

Icy rain pelted his overcoat, silvered the cracks in the sidewalk, and drained off the porch eave like a beaded curtain. An open screen door hanging precariously by two hinges leaned against the plain wood shingles of the Craftsman-style house. A light bulb screwed into a lamp near the front door cast a dim glow over the slatted floorboards of the porch. Santana rang the doorbell for the upper level, not expecting an answer.

A heavyset black woman with thick hands and a wide, flat face opened the front door and flicked on an outside light. She had a cigarette tucked in a corner of her mouth. A plump, sleeping baby nestled against a shoulder. "Help you?"

"I'm looking for Ronald Getz."

She stepped onto the porch, pulling the front door shut behind her. "You in the right place, but Ronnie ain't home," she said, the cigarette bobbing as she spoke. "Don't know where he's at."

"And you are?"

"Cheryl Bryant."

"You own this house?"

"I'm the caretaker. Ronnie rents the upstairs."

"Who owns the house?"

"Bunch of rich white men from the city."

"When did you last see Getz?"

She studied Santana. "You a cop?"

"That obvious, huh?" He showed her his badge wallet.

"I've had some dealings with law enforcement in the past," she said, leaning forward to look at the badge. "And I listen to the news. Seems like Ronnie got hisself in a world of trouble."

"You known him long?"

Her dark brown eyes darted from side to side as she composed a response. "Not long."

"I need to search the upstairs."

She nodded and then appeared to remember something. "You got a warrant?"

Santana offered it to her. "You need to sign it."

She stepped back, as though the paper were toxic. He offered the warrant to her again along with a pen.

She hesitated another moment before taking the pen. "You hold the paper," she said. "I'll hold my baby."

Santana gave her a copy after she signed the warrant. "Do you have a key to Getz's apartment?"

She nodded, went inside, and came back with a key.

"I'm going upstairs now," he said. "I'll leave an inventory of anything I seize." He opened the front door and then turned to face the woman once more. "Getz better not be up there."

Her eyes grew wide. "Far as I know, he ain't."

A sudden gust blew the long, dead ash at the end of her cigarette into the wind, the remains dispersing as quickly as those of a cremated corpse.

Santana drew his Glock from its holster and ascended the stairs sideways, keeping his back to the wall so he could see both the bottom and top. Cheryl Bryant stood in the foyer with her face raised, watching him, the baby still asleep against her shoulder.

He paused at the landing on the second floor and put his ear against the door. No sound. The judge had waived the required "knock and announce" rule. But Santana rapped hard and said, "Police! Open up, Getz."

His voice echoed off the plaster walls in the narrow hallway before it was lost amid the sound of raindrops splattering against the roof. Santana tried the knob but the door was locked. He used the key and waited as the door arced open.

Holding the Glock in a two-handed grip, he stepped into the entryway, where he stood still, listening again.

Nothing.

He conducted a brief search of each room to make sure Getz—or someone else—was not hiding in the apartment. Then he holstered his Glock, gloved up, and returned to the living room. A battered couch, recliner, and coffee table were the only pieces of furniture. He saw no newspapers, magazines or books, and nothing hanging on the walls. The small kitchen off the living room had a round table and two chairs, a gas stove, sink, and refrigerator. Canned goods and box dinners lined the shelves inside the cupboards. The refrigerator contained mostly fruits and vegetables and no meat or poultry. Santana was surprised. He hadn't pictured Getz as a vegetarian.

The walls in the bedroom, like those in the rest of the apartment, were bare. There was a cheap nightstand and a lamp beside the double bed, and a scratched and dented dresser opposite the footboard. Santana looked under the bed and then pulled back the worn bedspread. Underneath it, he saw that the mattress was covered with a plastic liner. Strange, he thought.

He found nothing of significance in the nightstand. Inside a small walk-in closet Getz's clothes had the unmistakable odor of formaldehyde, courtesy of his job, though everything was neatly hung and organized. In a corner behind the clothes, Santana found a Browning Gold 12 gauge shotgun. He figured it was the gun Getz had used on Jeff Tate's dog.

In the bathroom medicine cabinet, he found a prescription solution of Xyrem. He had come across many legal and illegal drugs in his career as a police officer and detective and had acquired an extensive knowledge base. Instinct told him that Xyrem might be important, if for no other reason than he had never heard of it before.

He took out his cell phone and dialed Reiko Tanabe's home number. She answered on the second ring.

"It's Santana, Reiko. Sorry to bother you at home, but I need your help."

"No problem," she said. "I was just reading."

"I need some information about Xyrem."

She paused before replying. "It's a drug specifically designed to treat narcolepsy."

"Really? There aren't many narcoleptics around."

"It is a pretty rare condition, John."

"What can you tell me about it?"

"The general consensus is that genetics, accompanied by an environmental trigger like a virus, may affect brain chemicals and cause narcolepsy. If I remember correctly, narcoleptics lack a chemical in the brain called hypocretin that activates arousal and regulates sleep. I believe researchers are working on developing treatments to supplement hypocretin levels and reduce narcolepsy symptoms."

Santana peered at the bottle he held in his hand. "The directions indicate it has to be taken twice each night."

"That's typical. One dose wouldn't last for an entire night. Generally, the first dose is taken right at bedtime and on an empty stomach. A second dose is taken two and half to four hours later. It works very quickly."

"So whoever was taking it would have to be in bed and ready to sleep for the night."

"Yes. Usually patients set their alarm clocks to make certain that they wake up in time to take the second dose. They have to stick to a regular schedule in order for the medication to be effective. Otherwise, they can become excessively tired throughout the day and sometimes fall asleep, often at inappropriate times and places. Or they can experience very brief sleep episodes in which they continue to function and then awaken with no memory of the activities."

"Any other symptoms?"

"Well, narcoleptics have unique sleep cycles. They enter the REM, or dream, phase of sleep right after falling asleep, whereas most people take about ninety minutes to enter the REM phase. Narcoleptics often experience hallucinations, sleep paralysis, and cataplexy, which is a sudden loss of muscle control. It's a unique symptom of narcolepsy, and in severe cases can cause stiffening of the muscles and total body paralysis."

"Are there any side effects of the medication?"

"Bedwetting."

Suddenly, the plastic liner covering the mattress made sense. And the bracelet Getz wore on his right wrist was a medical bracelet designed to alert others if he fell asleep or was unable to move or speak. Santana wondered if Getz had experienced episodes of cataplexy. If he had no medication with him, he would be in real trouble.

"Thanks, Reiko. Anyone mentions Xyrem again, I'll know what they're talking about."

"Oh, you're familiar with the drug, John."

"I am?"

"Sure. Xyrem is also known as gamma-hydroxybutyrate or GHB."

"The date rape drug?"

"That's right."

Santana thought now that maybe Getz wasn't without his medication. Maybe he always carried some with him. And maybe he had used it on unsuspecting college men in bars.

Chapter 19

EARLY THE NEXT MORNING, Santana obtained a search warrant for the Lessard mortuary and then attended Jeff Tate's autopsy. Toxicology tests had not yet been done, but it seemed apparent from the deep ligature marks around Jeff Tate's neck that he had died from cerebral hypoxia caused by compression, which had occluded the vessels supplying blood to the brain. Because of their location, Santana knew that it took only eleven pounds of pressure to occlude the carotid arteries. Unconsciousness generally occurred in ten seconds. Ronald Getz could have easily accomplished the task, especially if he had surprised Tate.

After the autopsy, Santana drove to the mortuary and had Lessard sign the warrant. Then he searched Lessard's office and the living quarters on the second floor of the funeral home. He found nothing of evidentiary value in the office or in the first four rooms on the second floor. Now, as he gazed out a tall French window in the study at the gray veils of clouds covering the sky and the wind bending the barren tree branches, uneasiness lurked at the edge of his consciousness like shadows in the corners of the room.

He turned away from the window and looked at the red mahogany furniture, the Persian rugs on the hardwood floor, the bookshelves filled with old, thick texts, the brick fireplace with the mahogany surround mantel and intricate scrollwork, and the chaotic, dark oil paintings on the walls.

Closing his eyes, he stood perfectly still, trying to bring clarity to his sensory perceptions that were focused on the whining wind and the rattle of icy raindrops against the windowpane. He shivered as he felt a cool rush of air.

Santana opened his eyes and turned toward the window again, letting his latex-gloved fingers probe the edge of the glass, searching for a crack in the seal—but he found nothing. He stood still once more until he felt the draft again.

He went to the fireplace on the wall to his right and squatted in front of it, thinking that cool air was seeping through an open flue. But when he stuck his head into the firebox and looked up, he was stunned to see no damper, no smoke chamber, and no flue. The fireplace was a fake. He sat back on his haunches and stared at the firebox. Soon he felt the draft again leaking through the edges of the back wall. He leaned in, placed his right hand on the brick, and pushed. The back wall rotated open. Santana removed a mini-Maglite from his pocket and his Glock from its holster before he crawled through the opening.

Once he was through, he stood and let the blade of light from the flashlight cut through the darkness, shining it on the walls until he located a switch and flicked it on. He blinked as his eyes adjusted to the sharp light.

The mahogany paneled room looked like a woman's large walk-in closet. Dresses and pantsuits on hangers hung from wooden rods. A variety of heeled and flat shoes and sandals were neatly arranged on the floor underneath them.

He hadn't listed the hidden closet on the warrant because he hadn't known it existed. A competent defense lawyer might get any evidence found here thrown out of court, even if Santana argued that the room was part of the study. But Santana figured he wouldn't have to alert Lessard—or anyone else—that he had found the secret room, unless he discovered something he considered important. In that case, he thought, he could write another warrant and come back. He turned off the flashlight, holstered his Glock, and began searching.

Inside a set of four built-in drawers, he found jewelry trays and purses. On a shelf above the dresses that ran the length of the closet, he saw wig caps and three long-haired brunette wigs on stands. In a back corner was a dresser and mirror. There were bottles of fingernail polish, makeup, eyeliner, all the cosmetics that a woman would need—or a man pretending to be a woman—but nothing implicating Lessard in a crime.

Later that morning, Santana met with William Lessard in an interview room in the Homicide Unit. He could have interviewed Lessard at the funeral home, but Santana wanted to interview him in an unfamiliar and more uncomfortable environment. Lessard was, once again, impeccably dressed in a dark gray suit and pink tie, his thick black hair perfectly coiffed, his face nearly as white as his starched shirt.

"I appreciate you coming in for an interview, Mr. Lessard."

"I certainly have nothing to hide," he said. "Frankly, I'm appalled by Ronald Getz's actions. I want to do everything I can to help."

Santana nodded and watched him carefully. Lessard's plastic surgery had made it difficult to read his virtually expressionless face. And he gave Santana an uneasy feeling.

"I assume you found nothing incriminating during your search of my office and living quarters this morning," Lessard said.

Santana thought it possible that Lessard had been posing as a woman and then murdering young men, but he had found no trophies, no evidence that Lessard was a serial killer. Whether he was involved in something illegal or unethical was, in Santana's mind, still to be determined.

"Where were you last night, Mr. Lessard?"

He thought for a moment and then leaned back in his chair. "I went to a play at the Guthrie with a friend and then out for a drink."

"What's your friend's name and phone number?"

Lessard told him.

"How long have you owned the mortuary?"

"For the past ten years."

"And before that?"

He regarded Santana for a few seconds before he said, "I was a small business owner."

"You were raised in the Midwest?"

"Pretty much all over. My father was in the service."

"You married?"

He shook his head. "Confirmed bachelor."

"What got you interested in mortuary science?"

"I've always had an interest in science and the human body. It seemed like a natural career choice. You know, Detective Santana, medicine and science depend on the dead."

"So they do," Santana said. He looked at what he had written in his notebook before asking the next question. "Who generally brings the bodies to the mortuary, Mr. Lessard?"

"Ronald Getz was assigned that task after Scott Rafferty's unfortunate death. But I'm hoping to hire additional staff."

"Did Devante Carter ever pick up any bodies?"

"No. Have you spoken with him?"

"He's not answering his phone."

"That's odd."

"Not if he was involved in a crime," Santana said.

"Do you think Devante and Ronald murdered Jeff Tate?"

"We haven't determined that yet."

"Well," Lessard said, "I doubt that I will be hiring any more ex-convicts."

Santana studied him before he said, "You do the embalming?"

"Primarily, yes. But Ronald Getz often assists me."

"Were you aware that he suffers from narcolepsy?"

"Yes. He sometimes complained of tiredness, but he's never fallen asleep during working hours that I'm aware of."

"How much do you know about Getz?"

"Other than his previous trouble with the law, I know that Ronald is not a very bright man. But he's reliable and works hard."

Getz was also big and strong, Santana thought. He had served time for assault and was very capable of strangling Tate to death. But Getz didn't fit the profile of most serial killers. He had narcolepsy, and it had to be treated carefully and monitored regularly by a physician. Loss of muscle function could occur suddenly and without warning, triggered by a high stress situation. Santana found it hard to believe that Getz could be responsible for a large number of murders given this debilitating condition, though he surely would have taken Santana's life without hesitation. Still, Getz had access to GHB, which he—or someone he knew—could have used to drug and murder college students. And Santana had little doubt that Getz had brought Tate's body to the mortuary and was about to cremate him. But why would he kill Tate? And what had Getz—or someone else—been searching for in Tate's cabin?

"So," Santana said, "Getz would do what he was told."

"I believe he would."

"Even if it meant violating the law."

"Well, he's obviously violated it before and again last night."

But, Santana thought, did Getz have something to do with Scott Rafferty's death? Rafferty wasn't strangled and wasn't dead when he went into the river. If Getz had attempted to kill him, it would make sense that he would have strangled him and then cremated the body.

Santana's gaze drifted to Lessard's right hand. He recalled Jordan's description of the ouroboros, the serpent eating its tail, and how it represented the shadow self or the opposite. "That's an interesting ring you're wearing."

Lessard glanced at the ring on his finger, as if he had just realized he was wearing it. "Yes," he said, but offered no further explanation.

The gang landscape in St. Paul cut across all races—from white supremacist groups to Latin Kings to Asian youth gangs —but the shootings and violence had been most intense among the black gangs. The East Side Boys were one of the most violent black street gangs operating in St. Paul. Most recently they had been feuding with the Selby Siders. But the gang landscape in the city was constantly shifting, and new ones regularly appeared like weeds in an untended garden. As a patrolman and as a detective, Santana had dealt with a number of them, most of which had loose, symbolic affiliations with national criminal operations such as the Gangster Disciples or the Crips. He had noted that current members were younger, less organized, and more volatile than in years past.

Santana found Devante Carter slouching against the driver's side door of his Cadillac Escalade parked in a Holiday gas station near Phalen Park. Carter was dressed in a long black raincoat. The two gangbangers hanging with him were dressed in baggy jeans and blue 'do rags. Their T-shirts were emblazoned with the slogan, LET THE BODY COUNT BEGIN. When they saw Santana's Crown Vic pulling into the parking area, they sidled away from Carter in opposite directions.

Santana opened the driver's side window. "I want to talk to you, Devante."

"What fo', man?"

Santana waited.

Carter let out a heavy sigh and shuffled over to the sedan.

"If your PO found out you were associating with known gang members, Devante, your parole could be revoked."

"Hey, I ain't no banger. Can't a man jus' stand somewhere without bein' hassled?"

"Skip the lame ass excuses, Devante, and get in the car."

Carter looked like he was about to object and then thought better of it. He shuffled around the hood of the car and got in the passenger side door, the sweet scent of marijuana wafting in on a cool breeze ahead of him.

"Where you takin' me, Santana?"

"Where we can have a private conversation." He wanted Carter in an uncomfortable environment away from his peer group.

Strings of gray clouds webbed the sky as Santana drove to Lake Phalen, where Carter sat across from him at a small, square picnic table near an empty lifeguard stand and a brick building that served as the concession stand and beach house.

Someone had carved the name SOFIA inside a heart on the wooden tabletop. The name reminded Santana of a case he had investigated in which a little girl had been murdered. It took a moment before he could once again close the compartment in his mind that held all of his dark memories and refocus his attention on the man seated opposite him.

"You work last night, Devante?"

"You already know I did, else you wouldn't be askin' that question."

"So what else do I know?"

"You know Ronald Getz workin', too."

"All right. Then you know I was at the mortuary last night."

"I listen to the news, Santana. Got to keep up on world events, you know."

"I looked for you."

"I probably was up on the second floor."

"Doing what?"

"Mr. Lessard likes me to vacuum the rugs and clean his bathroom."

"But you left early."

Carter nodded. "I had some bidness."

"Uh-huh," Santana said. "You only doing janitorial work at the mortuary, Devante, or are you driving the removal ambulance?"

"Why you askin'?"

"Because I want to know who strangled Jeff Tate and brought his body to the mortuary."

Carter shook his head. "Who Jeff Tate?"

"Answer the question."

"Wasn't me, Santana. I don't pick up dead bodies. They give me the creeps. I jus' the janitor."

"Then who drives the ambulance now?"

"That'd be Getz."

"What do you know about him?"

"Not much. And I don't wanna know. The guy is as creepy as the place."

In a cool breeze blowing off the water, Santana could smell the heavy scent of lake water; old, wet leaves; and the damp, rich earth.

"Where does an ex-con gangbanger who works as a janitor in a funeral home get the money for a Cadillac Escalade?"

"I always been good with finances."

"Have you?"

He nodded and grinned.

"What were you doing with Kimberly Dalton?"

His eyes clouded a moment. "Who dat?"

"She was Scott Rafferty's girlfriend."

Carter ran his tongue across his upper lip. "I don't know what you talkin' about, man."

Santana leaned across the table so that his face was close to Carter's. "Don't bullshit me, Devante. I saw you drop her off at her apartment the other day."

Carter leaned back and raised his hands, palms out. "Hey, Santana, chill out. You the number one jake, man."

"I'm thrilled. Now start talking straight, or I'll have a chat with your PO."

"Okay. So I gave her a ride."

"Where?"

"She into the flake, Santana. But I don't deal no mo'. I gone straight."

"But you know who does deal."

"Sure. I in the bidness once."

"I told you I'd be back if I found out you lied to me about Scott Rafferty," Santana said. "He had cocaine in his system."

"Hey, man. I didn't sell no blow to Rafferty."

"But you sold it to his girlfriend."

"You wrong, man. I jus' took her to a place where she bought it. I can't be responsible for what she done with it. I tole you I wasn't Rafferty's supplier, and I tole the truth. You gotta cut me some slack, Santana."

"I might do that. If you tell me why you testified in Hank Rafferty's defense when he shot your half-brother, Montrell Grissom."

Carter managed to keep his face neutral, but his jaw dropped slightly in surprise. He took a moment to compose himself before responding. "You been busy."

"Always. Now what's the story?"

"You think I popped my own brother?"

"I hadn't considered it. But now that you mention it . . ."

"Montrell was a foo' wid a gun. The cop shot him. Ain't nothin' else I can say."

"You're a gangbanger, Devante."

"Ex-gangbanger."

"Whatever. You sure as hell aren't an upstanding citizen trying to do the right thing."

"That's cold, man."

"You have something on Hank Rafferty, Devante?"

"What you talkin' about?"

"Maybe his partner, David Dalton, too?"

"You crazy, Santana."

"I don't think so. And maybe you had something to do with Scott Rafferty's death? Maybe you've got the hots for his girlfriend?"

Carter stood up. "I'm outta here."

"Think about it, Devante."

"Think about what?"

"The truth."

"Yeah. The truth gonna set me free, Santana."

He turned and shuffled away, his raincoat flapping like dark wings in the wind.

229

Chapter 20

SANTANA USED HIS CELL PHONE to call Kimberly Dalton's apartment.

"What do you want?" she asked.

"I need to talk to you about Devante Carter."

"I don't know any Devante Carter. And I can't talk to you right now. I'm very busy, like I'm sure you are. Busy like in, you know, finding who killed Scott. Was it Devante Carter? Was he the guy that killed my Scott?" She spoke rapidly and in a loud tone.

"I'm coming by."

"I just told you I was really, really busy. You don't listen too well for a guy that's supposed to be a detective, you know what I mean?"

Santana could tell by her elevated speech pattern, the loudness of her voice, and her chatty attitude that she was probably high.

"I'll be there in about fifteen minutes."

He could hear her breathing rapidly, but she made no reply.

"Kimberly?"

She sounded as though she were choking.

Santana hung up and used his flasher to save time as he sped to Kimberly Dalton's apartment. Sunlight cut through the clouds as he raced up the sidewalk and entered the lobby. When she didn't answer the first time he pressed her buzzer,

Christopher Valen

he tried again. Finally, after scanning the names beside each apartment number, he buzzed the landlord. He identified himself and told the man why he needed him to open Kimberly Dalton's apartment door.

"You think she may have overdosed?"

"Exactly. So please hurry."

A sixty-something man with gray, thinning hair that he combed straight back and a chin whiskered with gray stubble met Santana in the hallway near Kimberly Dalton's apartment. He wore a natty green sweater and a pair of wrinkled khakis, and he smelled of cigarette smoke. He knocked twice on Kimberly Dalton's door and then opened it with a key when she didn't answer.

Santana found her slumped over the bathtub and barely conscious. Blood oozed from her nose, and her pupils were dilated. The pulse in her carotid artery indicated that her heart rate was extremely elevated.

"Call 911," he said to the landlord.

"Shouldn't you put her in the shower?"

Santana knew that sudden changes in temperature, like a cold shower, could send Kimberly Dalton into shock. Walking her around was a waste of time, and forcing her to vomit might cause her to suffocate. The best thing he could do while waiting for the paramedics was to keep her comfortable and awake.

"No. Just do what I said. Now."

The landlord hurried into the living room and used the phone while Santana carried her into the bedroom and laid her gently on her side on the unmade bed. He had spotted two open cans of beer on the coffee table in the living room and figured she had created a possibly deadly combination by mixing alcohol with cocaine.

He leaned over her and spoke into her ear. "Kimberly. Can you hear me?"

Her eyelids fluttered. She turned her face toward him, staring with glazed eyes. "Detective," she said, her dry lips forming a little smile.

"I want you to stay awake, Kimberly. Do you understand?"

She nodded her head, but closed her eyes again.

He shook her gently. "Stay awake."

She opened her eyelids and stared at him. "It wasn't my fault."

"I understand."

"No," she said. "You don't. Scott's father is responsible for his death."

"What do you mean?"

Her head lolled and her eyes glazed over.

The paramedics arrived in ten minutes and took her to Regions Hospital. Santana followed in his Crown Vic. On the way, he called the watch commander and asked him to notify David Dalton. He arrived at the hospital a few minutes after Santana. They stood outside the emergency room in a hallway buzzing with activity.

Dalton removed his navy blue watch cap and stuffed it into a pocket of his bomber jacket. Then he put his hands into the pockets of his jeans and leaned against the wall.

"I appreciate what you did."

Santana nodded.

"I wasn't positive she was using," Dalton said. "But I suspected."

"Hard to be sure sometimes. Easy for the parents to get fooled when the daughter lives away from home."

Dalton went quiet for a time, his expression turned inward, as though he were seeking an explanation for his daughter's behavior.

"Kimberly's mother remarried after the divorce and lives in California. She hasn't had much contact with her daughter or with me for the last few years. I'll give her a call once Kimberly is out of the emergency room."

He spoke with the confidence of a man convinced that his daughter would recover, and in a tone that suggested calling his ex-wife was the very last thing on his mind.

They waited in silence until Dalton spoke again. "No need for you to hang around."

Santana wanted to make sure that Kimberly Dalton would recover from the drug overdose. But he also had some questions for David Dalton. He shrugged. "I've got nothing pressing."

Dalton bit his lower lip as his brow wrinkled in thought. "What were you doing at my daughter's apartment?"

"I wanted to talk to her."

"About what?" His tone and body language were neutral and non-aggressive, a far cry from the last time Santana had spoken to him.

"Devante Carter."

Dalton's eyes drifted toward the nurse's station at the end of the long corridor and then came back to Santana. "Is Carter her supplier?"

Santana shook his head. "I don't think so. But he put her in contact with one."

"How do you know?"

"I saw her getting out of his Cadillac Escalade the other day."

Dalton gritted his teeth and his complexion reddened in anger. He pushed himself off the wall as though he was about to go after Carter. Santana figured he would have had a similar reaction had his daughter been in an emergency room. He was about to say something to calm Dalton when the detective placed his hands on his hips and peered down at his running shoes, like a receiver who had just let a pass slip through his fingers. Then he took a deep breath and went quiet again.

A female nurse hurried down the hallway and went through a set of double doors and into the emergency room.

"Before your daughter passed out, she said Scott Rafferty's death was Hank's fault. Any idea what she might've meant by that?"

Dalton looked at Santana without speaking for a while. Finally, he said, "No, I don't."

"Why would she blame Hank for his son's death?"

"What are you getting at, Santana?" Dalton's voice had a slight edge to it now.

"I'm just asking a question."

"No you're not. You're making a judgment, or worse yet, an accusation."

"I'm looking for the truth."

"About what?"

"You told me that sometimes the truth has unintended consequences. I think you were referring to the day Montrell Grissom was shot and killed."

"What the hell does that have to do with my daughter?"

"You tell me."

A young doctor in scrubs came out of the emergency room and walked toward Santana. "You the young woman's father?"

Santana nodded at Dalton.

The doctor looked at Dalton and said, "Your daughter's going to be fine. But we'll keep her here overnight just to make sure. You can come in and see her before we bring her upstairs."

"Thanks," Dalton said with a relieved sigh.

The doctor headed for the emergency room again.

"Looks like you may have saved Kimberly's life, Santana. If so, I guess I owe you for that. But if you want to know what happened to Montrell Grissom, read the report. I don't owe you anything for my daughter's life but a thank you. And you're a real prick if you think I do."

He was standing rigidly now, his hands on his hips, staring at Santana with eyes that were hard and focused.

Santana felt guilty about using Kimberly Dalton's drug overdose to extract answers from her father. But he believed David Dalton was being dishonest with him, and that gave him the right to use any advantage he thought he might have.

"That's not how I look at it."

"Maybe not. But it is what it is, Santana."

Hank Rafferty and Rachel Hardin lived in a renovated Tudor home that had a large chimney, cross gables, and bare brown vines of Boston ivy that clung to the stone cladding walls. Hank met Santana at the door and escorted him to a study in the back of the house. Santana sat down at one end of a dark leather couch. It was just after six in the evening, and the air inside the house smelled of spaghetti sauce. His observation was confirmed when he saw a series of small red dots splattered on Rafferty's white shirt. Rafferty had removed his sport coat and tie but obviously hadn't yet changed clothes after work.

Rafferty sat down in a leather recliner opposite the couch. The shelves on the walnut floor-to-ceiling bookcase behind him were filled with books and photos of Hank and Rachel with friends and together on a boat, and photos of Scott as a younger child with his mother, and later in his Marine uniform.

"Can I get you something, John?"

"No, thanks."

Rafferty gazed in the direction of a small bar in one corner of the room as if he was considering a drink, but he remained in his chair and focused his attention on Santana again.

"I take it this isn't a social call."

"No, it isn't. Is Rachel home?"

Rafferty shook his head. "She had a meeting tonight. Won't be home until after nine." He paused a moment and peered at the fireplace in a corner of the room that was filled with burnt logs and ashes. Then his eyes came back to Santana. "Is this about Scott?"

"It's about you, Hank. You and Montrell Grissom."

Rafferty's eyes narrowed as he leaned slowly forward and placed his elbows on his thick thighs. "Why are you wasting your time with this nonsense, John? It's got nothing to do with Scott's death."

"Maybe not. But Devante Carter worked with your son. There's a connection. I just don't know what it is—yet."

"You told me Carter worked at the mortuary with Scott. But what you didn't tell me is that Scott had cocaine in his system when he died, John."

"You talked to Tanabe."

"Right after our last conservation. And I know Kimberly Dalton has had problems in the past with drugs. I've known it ever since she started dating my son."

"Did Scott tell you that?"

"He said he was trying to help her kick the habit."

"It appears that he didn't have much success."

"What are you getting at?"

"I just came from the hospital. Kimberly Dalton overdosed on coke."

"Jesus. Is she going to be all right?"

"I think so."

"Does her father know?"

Santana nodded. "He's at the hospital with her."

"This is Devante Carter's doing," Hank said, his voice edged with anger, his eyes suddenly flaring with intense light. "He killed my son."

"Why would Carter kill your son?"

"Because I shot his half-brother."

"And yet he testified in support of you. That doesn't make much sense, does it, Hank? Unless . . ."

"Unless what?"

"Unless Carter is blackmailing you."

Rafferty's face went white as he stared silently at Santana.

"Devante Carter had nothing to gain by killing your son, Hank. But he has a whole lot to gain if he has proof that you shot and killed his unarmed brother. Maybe that's why he's driving around in a Cadillac Escalade he couldn't possibly afford."

"Grissom had a gun, John. It's in the report."

"I think it was your throw-down, Hank."

Rafferty's body suddenly stiffened. "Where'd you get a crazy idea like that?"

"What does it matter where I got it if it's the truth?"

Rafferty kept staring, but his eyes had lost focus, as though he was seeing the shooting again in his mind. He sat perfectly still for a while. Then he stood and walked to the bar. "You want a drink?"

"I'm fine."

Rafferty took ice cubes out of an ice bucket on the bar and dropped them into a cocktail glass. He poured three fingers of Johnnie Walker Red Label Scotch and looked at the darkness outside the bay window. He drank half the glass, refilled it with Scotch, and came back to the chair and eased himself into it again, as though he were balancing a heavy weight.

"You want to tell me about it, Hank?"

Rafferty drank another mouthful and set the glass on a coaster on the end table beside him. "I thought he had a gun, John. I really did."

Santana waited.

"I never knew Carter was there that day," Rafferty said at last. "But he took a video on his cell phone. Threatened to go to the media if I didn't keep him supplied with information on the department's gang initiatives. But the information I give him is minimal."

"Is that right?"

Rafferty nodded.

"I recall that the last two times Narco/Vice raided the East Side Boys, they came up empty. But I suppose that had nothing to do with the information you've been giving Carter."

His eyes slid off Santana.

"It's not about how much information you're giving him, Hank. It's that you're giving it to him at all."

"I can take care of Carter."

"What the hell does that mean?"

Rafferty shrugged his heavy shoulders and drank more Scotch.

"Did David Dalton know Carter was blackmailing you?"

"No."

"But Dalton knew Grissom was unarmed, and that you'd used a throw-down."

Rafferty let out a heavy sigh and nodded his head.

"You wiped your prints and made sure Grissom's were on the throw-down. And Dalton covered for you, Hank."

"He was my partner . . . and my friend."

"Not good enough."

Rafferty thought about it. He started to speak and then stopped as if he had trouble forming words. "You've been there, John. You've got maybe a split second to make a decision. And if you make the wrong one, it could cost you your life."

Santana knew Rafferty spoke the truth. "You have another gun besides your department issue, Hank?"

Rafferty's heavy cheeks colored. "You think I'll shoot another unarmed kid and use a throw-down again?"

"I'm just asking if you've got another gun."

"Yeah, I've got one. It's a Walther PPK. But Smith and Wesson recalled the gun because it misfires. I haven't gotten around to returning it."

"Are you paying off Carter?"

He shook his head.

"So in return for giving the East Side Boys information about Narco/Vice that you supply, Hank, Carter must be taking a cut from the money the East Side Boys are making off of drug sales."

He offered no reply.

"Does your wife know that Carter is blackmailing you?"

"God, no! And she can't ever know, John. It could ruin her career."

"You mean if anyone ever found out that she knew and didn't report it."

"Yeah. But this mess isn't her fault. It's mine."

"So what are you going to do about it, Hank?"

Rafferty stared at the melting ice in his glass. Then he picked it up again and finished his Scotch. "I made my decision a long time ago," he said, gazing at Santana. "The question is, what are you going to do about it, John? Are you going to take down two good cops because I made a mistake and shot an unarmed gangbanger? Or are you going to let it ride and find out who killed my son?"

Santana tried to concentrate on the traffic and the headlights spearing the darkness as he drove along the puddled streets of St. Paul. But his thoughts kept returning to his conversation with Hank Rafferty. David Dalton and Hank Rafferty had been involved in a cover-up involving the death of Montrell Grissom. By coming forward with the evidence, Santana could right a wrong. But it would mean destroying the careers of two detectives. It was easy to rationalize the Grissom killing, given that he was a gangbanger and might have gone down in a similar fashion even if Hank hadn't shot him. Still, Santana believed that one life was no less important than another. Yet, as a sixteen-year-old, he had made a conscious decision to avenge his mother's murder. He figured that he was in no position to judge another when it came to life-and-death decisions, especially Rafferty, who, by all indications, had made a tragic mistake.

It was after seven, and Santana was hungry. He thought about calling Jordan and asking if she would like to join him for dinner or a drink, but he dismissed the idea. There was someone else he wanted to see before he headed home, so he stopped at a Subway for a quick roast beef sandwich and Coke. Then he drove to the homeless shelter where Jeff Tate had volunteered.

Santana showed his badge and identified himself to the middle-aged woman behind the counter on the first floor of the brick building on University Avenue.

"I'm Betty," she said, holding out her hand. She was a heavy-set, middle-aged woman who had a quick smile, a no-nonsense grip, and grayish blue eyes that were filled with a bright, welcoming light.

Santana shook her hand. "Nice to meet you, Betty. I'm looking for a veteran that might've known Jeff Tate."

"Has something happened to Mr. Tate?"

Santana told her that Tate was dead, but left out all the details.

Betty blew out a long breath of air. "That's terrible."

Santana could hear empathy in the tone of her voice, but also acceptance, as if she and death had an intimate relationship.

"Is there a vet here that I could talk to?" he asked.

"Do you suspect someone at the shelter had something to do with Mr. Tate's death?"

Santana shook his head. "I'm just looking for a vet who might've known him or had conversations with him."

"Well," she said, looking out at the large room, the round tables nearly filled with exhausted-looking men and women. They wore loose-fitting clothing on their thin bodies and had distant looks in their sad eyes. Very few were making conversation, as though they had no energy for it. "We have a number of veterans of the Vietnam, Iraq, and Afghanistan wars that use the shelter from time to time."

"Someone from the Iraq or Afghanistan conflicts would be best," Santana said.

Betty tapped an index finger against her lips as she scanned the room. "You might want to talk to Paul Munson." She pointed with the same finger in the direction of a bearded, long-haired man in a soiled jean jacket, sitting alone at a table in the far corner of the room. There was a backpack beside his chair and a tattered paperback book in his grimy hands.

Santana thanked her and walked over to the table. "You Paul Munson?"

The man raised his chin and gazed at Santana with dark, wary eyes. "Yeah."

"I wonder if I could talk to you about Jeff Tate."

"I don't know any Jeff Tate."

"Betty says you do."

Munson's gaze slid off Santana and toward Betty, who was still behind the counter, talking on the phone. She caught his gaze and gave a reassuring smile and a wave. As he peered at Santana again, Munson said, "You a friend of Jeff's?"

Santana showed him his badge. "I'm investigating his death."

Munson shook his head and gave a short laugh filled with resignation. "And you think I had something to do with it?"

"Why would I think that?"

"You tell me. You're the detective."

"I'm just looking for information."

"Yeah," he said. "And a suspect."

Behind the thick black beard and underneath the scraggly long hair, Santana could see that Munson was in his late twenties or early thirties. He was still a handsome man, despite the yellow teeth, the wind-burned, weather-beaten face, and the empty eyes that had probably seen more tragedy and death than most men twice his age had seen.

"Mind if I sit down?"

Munson gestured toward a vacant chair on the opposite side of the table. "I suspect it wouldn't matter if I did." He dog-eared the page he was reading and set the paperback on the table.

Santana saw that it was Ernest Hemingway's *A Farewell to Arms*. He pulled out the chair and sat down. "You a Hemingway fan?"

"I started reading him in college before I dropped out my senior year and enlisted."

"What made you decide to enlist?"

"I guess I wanted to know if Hemingway's portrayal of war was accurate." He gave a hollow laugh. "I should've taken him more seriously."

"I remember Hemingway wrote that war is not won by victory."

Munson squinted at Santana as if trying to see him more clearly. "You've read *A Farewell to Arms*?"

Santana nodded.

Munson pointed to the book. "He was right, you know."

"How so?"

"Even if we declare victory and come home, the terrorists won't quit."

"Most likely not," Santana said.

Munson stared at his grimy hands, and his face colored, as though he were embarrassed by what he saw.

"You ever considered going back to college?"

"I'm not in a real good situation right now, Detective. In case you hadn't noticed."

"Things can change."

"I know that. I had a house once, and a wife. Now I've got nothing left."

"Sure you do," Santana said.

Munson peered at Santana for a long moment. "You a vet, Detective?"

Santana shook his head.

"Ever killed anyone?"

Santana nodded.

"Then you know how it is."

Santana knew what killing another human being had meant for him. But he would never presume to know how it was for someone else. "You serve in Iraq?"

"Three tours."

Santana had noticed the nervous tic in the corner of Munson's mouth, as though he were making a half-smile. He saw no outward signs of mental illness, but he knew, based on his own experiences, that the ghosts that haunted men's souls could be buried beneath a stoic façade and strong constitution. Santana figured those same ghosts were at least partially responsible for the fact that a well-spoken, educated man was now living on the streets.

"Were you there the same time as Tate?"

"Pretty much," Munson said. "But I didn't serve with him."

"What can you tell me about Tate?"

"He was a good guy. He knew what we'd gone through over there, and what we needed back here. He did what he could to help."

"You know many of the vets who use the shelter?"

"Some."

"They all share their stories?"

Munson shook his head. "Some don't talk about it at all."

"Is that what you and Tate talked about? The war?"

"Mostly. Nobody prepares you for combat."

"Or what comes after it," Santana said.

Munson nodded. "You have to fight for the right reasons. I've met a lot of Vietnam vets on the streets who were never able to find meaning in what they were asked to do. I think it's the same for vets from Iraq. Once we knew there were no weapons of mass destruction, the less justifiable the motives for combat became."

"And once you start killing for personal reasons, the more guilt you feel."

Munson looked at Santana for a long moment. "For a guy who has never gone to war, Detective, you seem to understand a whole lot about the psychological effects of killing."

Santana certainly did, and a part of him wanted to continue the discussion, as much for his sake as for Munson's. But Santana needed information more than he needed therapy.

"What else did you and Tate talk about?"

He could see a sudden darkness in Munson's eyes, as though a light had been turned off. "Personal stuff."

"Nothing more?"

After a long while, Munson said, "What are you looking for, Detective?"

"An answer as to why Jeff Tate is dead."

"What makes you think I can help you?"

"Maybe you can't or maybe you won't. But you need to know that Tate isn't the only vet who's dead."

Munson's eyes wandered away from Santana's to the book on the table and then came back to Santana's face. "How many?"

"I don't know for sure. But more than Tate."

Munson nodded his head, as if confirming what Santana had said. "All I know is that a few of the vets I used to see don't come here anymore. But that might not mean much. They could've found other shelters or gone to different cities, especially during the winter months when it's cold."

"Did you and Tate talk about those guys?"

"Yeah." Munson took in a breath and let it out slowly. "Look, Detective Santana. You know the suicide rate for vets is incredibly high and seems to be getting worse. These guys that disappeared, they could've killed themselves. Who knows? Most hadn't seen or been in contact with their families for years. No one would miss them. No one would even know they were dead. Still . . ."

"What?"

He shook his head, as though confused by what he was about to say. "A couple of them I knew pretty well. They didn't seem . . . suicidal."

"So you were surprised when they disappeared."

"Yeah."

"Did Tate ever tell you what he thought?"

"He said he was looking into it."

"Did he say how?"

"No."

Santana recalled Tate's ransacked cabin. Someone had been looking for something. He wondered if Munson might know what it was. "Did Tate ever mention a diary or a journal?"

"He said once that he wanted to write a book about the effects of PTSD on war vets and about his own experiences."

"Did he ever show you a manuscript or notes?"

Munson shook his head.

"Did Tate ever mention the name Scott Rafferty in your conversations?"

"Not that I recall."

Santana removed a business card from his wallet and slid it across the table. "If you remember anything else about Tate, give me a call."

Munson looked at the card and then at Santana again. "Doesn't make much sense, does it?"

"What do you mean?"

"Guy like Tate. He puts his life on the line how many times overseas and then comes home and is killed. I can't make much sense of it. I suppose that thought has crossed your mind on occasion given the line of work you're in, Detective."

"It has. It's pointless to try and make any sense of it."

"I know you're right. But it's easier said than done. Still, I imagine it's sort of like a war zone on the streets, what with all the gangs and killing that goes on."

Santana had once heard in an SPPD workshop that a police officer's cumulative trauma over twenty years was similar to what soldiers experienced in fifteen months of combat. "Not exactly like being under enemy fire," he said.

"Maybe not, but whenever you take someone off the street, there's always another to take his place. Just like the terrorists."

"Ever consider getting some help?"

"If you mean therapy, I've thought about it. But I could use a job."

"Not a lot of those available right now. I'll keep my ears open. I hear of something, I'll let you know."

"Thanks. You can leave a message with Betty."

Santana stood.

"You know," Munson said, "even if there isn't any victory in war, there is in your job, Detective. If someone killed Jeff Tate, then I hope you nail the bastard."

Santana was thinking that "nail" might mean kill other than catch when his cell phone rang. It was the watch commander.

"Santana."

"We've got two down, John."

"I caught the last call."

"I know. But one of the vics is Devante Carter. The other is Hank Rafferty."

Chapter 21

FLARES MARKED THE ROADWAY leading to Hank Rafferty's house, light bars on squad cars flashed red against the black sky, and hot white spotlights illuminated the yard.

Devante Carter's body was in the study, where Santana had met with Hank Rafferty just a few hours ago. He was wearing the black raincoat he had worn earlier in the day, and he had been shot twice from close range. A Raven .25 caliber semi-automatic with a wood grip—a "Saturday Night Special" commonly used by gangbangers—lay near Carter's right hand.

Santana looked down at Reiko Tanabe, who was squatting beside Carter's body. "Where's Hank?"

"Regions Hospital," she said.

"He's alive?"

"Barely. He was shot twice and left for dead. But the paramedics got his heart started. He's one tough bastard."

Santana saw Rafferty's Walther PPK lying on the floor near the shell casings. A gun cleaning kit lay on the coffee table.

A female evidence tech was positioning a scale and frame marker for Tony Novak as he shot individual close-ups of each piece of evidence, which would correspond with the item number used on the Evidence Custody sheet. A second tech was kneeling beside Carter's body, bagging the dead man's hands to prevent any gunshot residue from rubbing off.

"I left here around seven this evening," Santana said. "Carter couldn't have been dead long."

"Well, the judge came home just after nine. That makes it easier to determine TOD."

"How do you think it went down, Reiko?"

She thought about it for a moment and peered up at him. "Well, it's hard to say who got off the first shot. And I won't know which shots were the fatal ones until I complete the autopsy on Carter. But even if a shot hits the heart, John, you know a vic can remain conscious for at least ten to fifteen seconds. Plenty of time to get off a second shot."

Tony Novak stopped taking photos and looked at Santana. "I just saw Hank the other day," he said with a disconsolate shake of his head, his expression fixed in disbelief. "He asked if I knew anything more about his son's death."

"Did you say anything about the propranolol capsule?"

Novak nodded sheepishly. "It was his kid, John. I had to tell him the truth."

Tanabe stood up and looked at Novak. "Hank probably talked to you just before his conversation with me. He wanted to see the autopsy report on his son."

"So he knew you'd found propranolol in his son's system," Santana said.

Tanabe faced Santana. "Yeah. He wanted information about the drug."

Under normal circumstances, Santana would have been upset if information about his case had leaked out. But if Scott Rafferty had been his kid and another detective was investigating the cause of death, he, too, would have gone directly to Novak and Tanabe.

"By the way," Tanabe said. "I didn't find any trace of propranolol in the tissue samples from Michael Johnson, Thomas Hunter, or Matthew Miller."

Santana was disappointed, but not surprised. It had been a long shot from the beginning.

He slipped on a pair of latex gloves, knelt beside Devante Carter, and removed a wallet from a back pocket. When he found nothing he deemed important, he placed the wallet in an evidence envelope. A search of Carter's other pockets turned up nothing but the set of car keys for the Cadillac Escalade parked out front. Santana was puzzled. Few people today— and no gangbanger—left their residence without a cell phone.

He stood and picked up Hank's sport coat that was draped over a leather chair. Inside a front pocket he found a Nextel phone typically used by the department. It was turned off. Santana was tempted to check Hank's recent phone calls, but he was concerned about losing data. And he might have to testify in court as to how he had handled the phone. He knew that if he tried to remove the SIM card, a simple static spark could delete the whole card. He wasn't sure if Rafferty used a PIN—most people didn't— but he knew that placing the phone in a special cell phone evidence bag was the best way to preserve data.

"Well, it helps to have at least one phone," Tanabe said. "If Rafferty called Carter, or vice versa, this evening, I can get a closer estimate as to the exact time of death."

"Anyone talk to the judge?" Santana asked after he had bagged and inventoried Carter's wallet and car keys.

Tanabe shook her head. "She went to the hospital."

Santana placed the cell phone in an evidence envelope and gave it to Novak; then he went out the door and drove to Regions Hospital. He wasn't looking forward to speaking with Rachel Hardin, but at least her husband was still alive, unlike Devante Carter. Santana would have to speak to Carter's mother right after his visit to the hospital—and he wasn't looking forward to that visit either.

When he arrived at the waiting area outside the emergency room, Rita Gamboni was sitting in a chair beside a pale Rachel Hardin, whose head was resting against the wall behind her, her eyes seemingly staring at nothing, a white handkerchief in one hand. Huddled in quiet conversation off to their right were Kirk McCall, the Narco/Vice commander, and Tim Branigan, assistant chief and head of the Major Crimes and Investigation Division. They stepped apart when they saw Santana, as if they had been discussing him. Branigan waved him over.

"Any word on Hank's condition?" Santana asked.

Branigan shook his head and spoke softly. "He's still in surgery."

"What do we know about the shooting?" McCall asked.

They walked to the far corner of the room, making sure they were out of hearing range of the judge, before Santana went through it.

"Son-of-a-bitch," McCall said, shaking his head in frustration.

He was a thick-shouldered, squared-jawed man in his early forties. His years as an undercover officer in vice, and now as its commander, had prematurely aged him, as evidenced by the preponderance of gray in his once jet-black hair and the hollowness in his pale blue eyes. But Santana was well aware that McCall was respected by those who worked under him—and those who didn't.

"What the hell was Devante Carter doing at Hank's?" Branigan asked, looking first at Santana and then at McCall.

"You mean besides shooting him?" McCall said, anger evident in his voice.

Santana offered no reply because he didn't have an answer, and neither did Branigan. Instead he said, "How's the judge taking it?"

"Badly," Branigan said. "She's lost her stepson and possibly her husband."

"I still need to speak to her."

Branigan glanced in Rachel Hardin's direction and then his eyes came back to Santana. "Maybe now isn't the best time."

"I need answers if you want to know what happened. And I need them now." He followed Branigan's line of vision as the assistant chief looked at Gamboni, as if seeking permission.

She caught Santana's eye and nodded, knowing intuitively what he wanted. Then she spoke softly to Rachel Hardin, who waved the handkerchief like a white flag of truce, motioning him over.

As Santana walked to her, the judge looked at him with red-rimmed eyes, her chestnut hair splayed against the wall behind her like a fan. She wore little makeup, but Santana could see the tracks of dried tears on her cheeks and the anguish that creased her smooth forehead, as though she were suffering from physical pain.

She lifted her head off the wall. "I would get up, John, but I feel a bit light-headed."

Santana was surprised that she had addressed him by his first name. He couldn't recall another time when she had done so. But death had a way of removing the ranks and titles that often separated individuals in their daily lives, although Santana had no doubt that Rachel Hardin would still use her title—and the power it carried—if it was to her advantage.

"I hope you don't mind, but I need to ask you a few questions," he said.

"I understand."

He took out his notebook and pen. "You arrived home just after nine?"

"Yes. I had a Federalist Society meeting. Then I stopped by my office to pick up a case file I'd left there."

"What time did you leave the meeting?"

251

"Around eight." Her gray eyes were locked on his, as though trying to read his mind. "I have witnesses, Detective."

Santana had no reason to suspect that Rachel Hardin was responsible for the shootings, but he had to establish her alibi. He had hoped she wouldn't take offense at his line of questioning, but she had obviously understood where he was heading. And he understood that her use of "Detective" rather than his first name indicated they were again on more formal terms. He also knew that it would be easy to verify her alibi.

"Besides the bodies, did you notice anything unusual when you entered the study?"

"I never went into the study," she said. "I took one look at the scene and called 911."

Santana thought it was strange that she hadn't at least attempted to verify if her husband was alive or dead. But people reacted in different ways to the sight of a body.

"Did you know Devante Carter?" he asked.

"Was that the man in the study?"

Santana nodded.

"I didn't know him, though I'm familiar with the Grissom case since my husband was involved. But why would Carter try to kill Hank?"

Santana preferred not to go into details until he had everything straight in his mind. But he figured it had something to do with blackmail, and the Montrell Grissom video that Carter had taken with his cell phone.

"I don't know," he said. "But I'm going to find out."

"If there's nothing else, Detective . . ."

"Not at the moment."

Gamboni stood. "I'd like to speak with you, John." She took him gently by the elbow and steered clear of everyone. Once they were alone, she said, "Tell me what you know."

Santana went through it again.

252

When he had finished, she said, "You talk to Carter's parents?"

"It's only his mother. I'm heading over there as soon as I leave the hospital."

"We're short-handed. I'll go with you."

"Just like old times, Rita."

"Not quite," she said.

Santana wasn't positive, but he thought he detected an element of sadness and regret in her half-hearted smile.

"First Rachel's stepson dies and then her husband is shot," Gamboni said with a shake of her head. "How many tragedies can one person have?" She was peering at the darkness outside the passenger window of Santana's Crown Vic as he drove to Devante Carter's house.

"She'll survive."

Gamboni gave him a curious look. "That's harsh, John."

"It wasn't meant to be. I just think the judge will be okay. After all, Scott Rafferty wasn't her son."

"But Hank's her husband."

Santana nodded and left it at that.

They drove in silence before she said, "You're kind of quiet. Are you thinking about Hank?"

It was her last comment at the hospital that he was thinking about—and what the sadness in her smile had indicated. "I was thinking how nice it was that we could take this ride together, Rita, despite the tragic circumstances."

"It's better you didn't go alone," she said, looking out the window again.

He could smell the scent of strawberry shampoo in her hair and see a chain of headlights coming around a bend in the rearview mirror.

"Kind of brings us full circle," he said.

"What do you mean?"

"We started as partners riding together. And here we are again." He felt the weight of her gaze on him now, but he kept his eyes on the road.

"I don't understand."

"You've made up your mind, Rita. You're taking the department's liaison job with the FBI." He listened to the familiar hum of police radio chatter while he waited for her reply.

"I won't lie to you," she said.

"I know."

In his mind's eye he saw Rita in her uniform, sitting beside him in their squad, the two of them just starting their careers. Then he saw her without the uniform, in his arms, and in his bed.

"Does Pete Romano have the inside shot at commander?" he asked, trying to suppress the suddenly vivid memory.

"He'll apply for it."

"Branigan will give it to him."

"You don't know that for sure, John."

Santana did know, but it didn't matter. "I'll miss working with you, Rita."

"I'll be around the building. It's not like I'm leaving town."

"Still," he said.

She reached over and grabbed his free hand. "And I'll miss working with you, John Santana."

Devante Carter's mother, Shanice, lived in a small, two-bedroom apartment in Railroad Island, a heart-shaped area one mile east of downtown St. Paul. Factory closures, falling property values, rising poverty rates, and social instability had transformed the once thriving community. Bounded by railroad tracks to the west and north, and Swede Hollow to the east, many of the 19th century Victorian houses built close together on narrow lots had been divided into multiple rental units, and many of the inhabitants had fled to the suburbs.

"We're very sorry for your loss, Mrs. Carter," Gamboni said after explaining the circumstances surrounding Devante Carter's death.

She and Santana were seated on a dilapidated hide-a-bed facing a cushion chair in which Shanice Carter sat, a pair of soiled denim jeans and chamois shirt covering her rail-thin frame, a small silver cross hanging from the chain around her neck. Though Santana estimated she was no more than forty, her sunken cheeks, disheveled hair, and dark, empty eyes gave her the appearance of a much older woman.

"It's Ms.," she said, straightening up in the chair. "Ms. Carter. And this don't make any sense."

She spoke in a voice that was a hoarse whisper, with a heavy southern accent. Having had previous dealings with her son, Santana knew that she was originally from Mississippi and had done time in Minnesota for prostitution and possession of narcotics.

"Devante done some stupid things in his younger years, and he paid for it. But I know my boy. He ain't no killer," she said. Smoke drifting toward the ceiling from the cigarette she held in one hand mingled with the strong smell of marijuana and mold in the air.

On the end table beside Santana were two framed photos, one of Devante and one of his half-brother, Montrell Grissom. Carter had been a sweet-looking kid, but the childhood photo didn't represent the man Santana knew. A life of crime had hardened Carter's features and robbed him of his youthful innocence. The young man lying dead in Hank Rafferty's study had looked much older than his years.

"Devante had a gun, Ms. Carter," Santana said.

"That don't mean he'd use it. Devante was never a violent child. I guess he needed it for protection."

"From what?"

"The world is filled with evil people, Detective. You should know that."

"Why would someone want to hurt Devante?"

"Because my son done turned his life around and quit the bidness after Montrell was killed."

"You mean the drug business."

"Yes," she said, as though there were no shame in admitting it. "Certain people he know had it in for him."

"Carrying a gun was a violation of his parole, Ms. Carter," Gamboni said.

"So he should be shot dead? Is that what you tellin' me?"

Nothing had changed in her body language, but the whisper that was her voice had become more forceful, like wind before a storm.

Still, Santana had more unpleasant questions. "Did Devante ever mention a cell phone video he had, Ms. Carter?"

Her chapped lips parted, and she quickly looked away, avoiding Santana's gaze. "No. He never said nothin' about no video."

Gamboni glanced at Santana. She had picked up on the non-verbal cue as well. Shanice Carter was lying. He wondered what she was hiding.

"Do you mind if we look in Devante's room?"

"Why?" She glared at him, the sudden intenseness in her dark eyes betraying the non-threatening tone in her voice.

"We're looking for Devante's cell phone."

"He didn't have it with him?"

"Not that we could find."

She sat silently, smoking the last of her cigarette and considering the question. "I don't think so."

"It could help in the investigation," Gamboni said.

"What investigation? You already tole me how you believe my son died. What good would his cell phone do?"

Finding it would save Hank Rafferty's reputation, Santana thought. But he couldn't tell her that. "It would let us know who he spoke to last."

Shanice Carter shook her head. "That don't matter none. What matters is that your police department killed both my boys."

"Do you know why your son went to Detective Rafferty's house?" Santana asked.

"Because the detective asked him to come."

"You know that for certain?"

"Why else would Devante go there?"

"That's what we're trying to establish, Ms. Carter."

"My word ain't good enough for you?"

Santana saw no point in arguing, so he reframed the question. "How do you know Detective Rafferty asked your son to come to his house?"

"Devante told me."

"Did he say why Detective Rafferty wanted to see him?"

She shook her head. "He just said he was goin' and would be back later. But he ain't ever comin' back now, is he, Detective?"

Santana hadn't expected tears from her. She had been used and abused by men all her life and had no doubt seen Devante's premature death—or permanent incarceration—as inevitable, given his criminal history and the environment of parental neglect in which he had lived. The rage simmering inside Shanice Carter was directed at a system that held her at least partially accountable for her poor choices and petty crimes, rather than at a subculture in which drugs, gangs, and violence, particularly against women, was often celebrated. Santana figured she was prepared for the deaths of those around her, as she was no doubt prepared for her own.

"You filed suit against the department over Montrell's death, Ms. Carter."

Gamboni placed a hand on Santana's thigh, a not-so-subtle-warning that he had gone too far.

"And I'm gonna be talkin' to my attorney about Devante's death, too."

"But you dropped the lawsuit, Ms. Carter. How come?"

The question surprised her. A long time seemed to pass before she collected herself and spoke again. "It ain't none of your bidness why I dropped that lawsuit. But you can bet your ass I won't be droppin' this one."

Chapter 22

THE FOLLOWING MORNING, SANTANA MET with Rita Gamboni and Tim Branigan in the AC's office. Santana was surprised at first that Kirk McCall, the Narco/ Vice Commander, was not in attendance. But upon reflection he figured Branigan wanted all the information on the Rafferty/ Carter shooting before deciding how much of it to release—and to whom.

Santana sat next to Gamboni on the black leather couch along the wall opposite Branigan's desk. Branigan sat in one of the two matching leather chairs facing the couch. Monthly copies of *Police Chief Magazine* were neatly arranged on a mahogany coffee table along with a large Caribou Coffee cup.

Besides the ceremonial plaques, awards, and family photos on the office walls, Branigan had a life-sized sculpted raven on the corner of his desk. Santana had heard through the 24/7 departmental rumor mill that Branigan's surname came from a very famous Irish clan and meant the descendent of the son of the raven. But Santana had never asked Branigan about it.

The Irish had dominated St. Paul's business, labor, and politics ever since three Irish soldiers from Fort Snelling had become the first settlers in the city. One of them had also become St. Paul's first murder victim. The AC, having dug very deeply into his Irish roots, prominently displayed the bird along with his family's coat of arms on a wall behind it.

259

"I brought hot chocolate for you, John," Gamboni said, gesturing toward the cup on the coffee table. She sat with her legs crossed, holding a Caribou cup in her hand.

"I want to go over everything before the press conference," Branigan said. "Make sure we're all singing off the same song sheet."

He had the dark hair and eyes associated with the Black Irish and their Iberian ancestors, rather than the stereotypical fair hair, pale skin, and blue or green eyes. Though he wasn't a big man, his well-tailored sport coats, inflated ego, and brimming self-confidence made him seem larger than he was.

"Let's start with you, Detective Santana," he said.

Santana had worked out early in the morning, hoping to clear his mind and inject some energy-producing adrenaline into his bloodstream. While he exercised, he had thought about how the shooting might have gone down, and how Branigan's primary objective would be to protect the department's reputation. And the only way Branigan could do that was to protect Hank Rafferty.

Santana still thought there might be a connection between Scott Rafferty's death and the deaths of the young men whose bodies had been found in the Mississippi. He wasn't sure what the connection was. He could only rely on his instincts—and he had learned long ago to trust them. But Branigan wouldn't be interested in unsubstantiated theories and what Santana's instincts were telling him. So he would offer nothing about the propranolol and cocaine found in Scott Rafferty's system, about Jeff Tate's death, about his encounter with Ronald Getz and what he had found in Getz's apartment, and about Kimberly Dalton's drug habit and her connection to Devante Carter—unless specifically asked.

It was Rita Gamboni who finally broke the stunned silence after Santana finished explaining how Devante Carter had blackmailed Hank Rafferty.

"Well, Hank certainly had a motive, given his anger over Carter's blackmail scheme," she said. "He could've asked Carter to come over and then shot him. Especially if Hank believed that Carter had contributed to, or was directly responsible for, the death of his son."

Santana looked at her. "Killing Carter in his own study is really sloppy, Rita. Too many things could go wrong. Plus, there could be a problem with forensic evidence."

"I agree," Branigan said quickly. "We have no evidence that Hank was the instigator, Rita."

Gamboni looked at Santana. "So maybe Hank had no intention of killing Carter and only did so during an argument, or in self-defense after Carter had shot him. Carter could have requested the meeting or stopped by unexpectedly."

"But if Carter intentionally killed Rafferty, Rita, then he'd lose the hold he had over him. Besides, Carter's mother claims he received a call from Hank."

"Maybe we'll know more after forensics is finished," she said.

Branigan fixed his eyes on Santana. "What about Rafferty's partner, David Dalton? Is he aware of the blackmail scheme?"

Santana had a decision to make, and he didn't have a lot of time to make it—though he had suspected he would be asked the question.

"You'll have to ask Dalton."

"I'm asking you, Detective."

"Hard to keep something like that a secret between partners."

"Perhaps it's the reason they're no longer partners."

"Perhaps."

Branigan's eyes remained fastened on Santana. "I understand your evasiveness, Detective. Normally, I wouldn't appreciate it. But in this case, circumstances are different. My advice to you is to remain evasive."

Santana drank some hot chocolate and set the cup back on the coffee table. Branigan's meaning was clear. He wasn't asking for a response or for an argument. He wanted Santana to keep his mouth shut regarding David Dalton's culpability. Santana wasn't comfortable with it.

"Is there anything else you can tell us, John?" Gamboni asked, possibly fearing that he might confront Branigan about the continued cover-up.

"Something bothers me about the shooting," Santana said.

Branigan spread his hands and let out a sigh. "So let's hear it."

"Hank told me his Walther PPK misfired and that the manufacturer had recalled the gun. I don't know why he would use it to shoot Devante Carter instead of his department-issue Glock."

"Didn't you say his cleaning kit was on the coffee table in the study?"

"I did. But there would be no point in cleaning the gun if it malfunctioned and he planned on returning it."

"Who knows why Hank was cleaning the Walther?" Branigan said. "It's the video on Carter's phone that's the problem. We need to locate that phone. And I mean yesterday."

He leaned forward and rested his forearms on the desktop. "Hank Rafferty was a decorated police officer with a stellar record of performance. If what you're telling us is true and a video of the Montrell Grissom shooting actually exists, it would ruin Hank's reputation and create serious problems for the department—if it ever saw the light of day." Branigan's gaze turned inward as he paused for a moment and considered his options. "I'll speak to Detective Dalton."

Santana knew why Branigan wanted to speak privately with Dalton. Without the cell phone video, there would be no proof that Hank Rafferty had shot an unarmed Montrell Grissom and had planted a throw-down, nor would there be any reason for Carter to blackmail Hank. The responsibility for the two men's deaths could be attributed solely to Carter—a gangbanger who was angry that Hank Rafferty had shot and killed his half-brother—a gangbanger who had murdered Rafferty out of revenge, and had lost his own life in the process. In return for his silence, Dalton would keep his detective shield.

Branigan's gaze shifted to Gamboni. "We're going to tell the press that we're investigating the shooting and have nothing more to say until it's complete."

Gamboni nodded. She and Branigan looked at Santana, their eyes lit with concern.

"It's a tragedy," Branigan said. "But I see no purpose in sullying the reputation of a fine officer like Hank Rafferty. Wouldn't you agree, Detective Santana?"

"Like every investigation, this shouldn't be about reputations. It should be about finding the truth."

"John," Gamboni said, setting her coffee cup on the table and leaning close enough to him that he caught the scent of her perfume. "It's time to step back and let the AC handle this."

"Your commander is offering you good advice, Detective," Branigan said. "I suggest you take it."

Geese flew in a V-formation across a flat gray sky that looked as hard as metal as Santana drove to an upscale neighborhood in Lilydale. He was reflecting on his just-completed meeting with Branigan and Gamboni, recalling that the Greek philosopher Heraclites had once said that a person couldn't step twice into the same stream—that everything changed, and nothing remained still.

Santana's life had drastically changed at the age of sixteen, after his mother's murder. He had become a man with a mission, and eventually, one with a badge. But he refused to allow the deaths and chaos that darkened his everyday life to change who he was now—who he would always be.

Gamboni's suggestion that he step back and let Tim Branigan deal with the fallout that would ensue if the media discovered Hank Rafferty had shot an unarmed Montrell Grissom and planted a throw-down had not dissuaded Santana from his mission, nor had it persuaded him to ignore his instincts. He doubted that Hank would shoot Carter with a Smith and Wesson that could misfire, especially when he had his department-issue Glock handy.

Santana knew that Carter, Tate, Scott Rafferty, William Lessard, Kenneth Vail, and Lyle Cady were all linked in one way or another to Ronald Getz. Santana's mission now was to find out if the men were merely business associates—or if they were involved in something far more sinister.

Kenneth and Monica Vail lived in a brick, one-story, Neo-French style home with a steeply pitched, hipped roof, arched windows extending upward through the cornice line, and a large landscaped yard. Santana walked up to the front door and rang the bell.

"Detective Santana," Monica Vail said as she held open the front door and offered him a wide smile.

"Sorry to drop in on you unannounced like this."

"It's quite all right. But my husband is at his office."

"I'm here to see you, Mrs. Vail. I spoke with your secretary. She said you were at home."

"Yes. I have no classes scheduled on Wednesdays."

She wore tight fitting jeans with open-toed sandals and a turquoise cotton sweater that accentuated her large breasts. She had applied no lipstick or make-up, but she didn't need any.

"It won't take long," Santana said.

Monica Vail smiled again and gestured for him to come in. "Don't worry. We've got plenty of time."

She closed the door, hung his overcoat in the front closet, and walked away without saying a word. When Santana hesitated, she paused and looked back at him expectantly. He followed her down a darkened, carpeted hallway hung with framed modern art into a four-season sunroom with floor-to-ceiling windows and French doors that led to a brick patio.

"Would you like coffee?"

"I'm good, thanks."

"How about a soft drink or juice?"

"I'll take a Coke if you have one," he said, just to be polite.

Monica Vail opened a small refrigerator behind the bar and removed a Coke. "Would you like a glass with ice?"

"No, thanks."

She handed him the Coke. "Please. Make yourself comfortable."

He sat down on a cushioned wicker couch.

She filled a cocktail glass with tomato juice over ice and sat in a matching wicker chair opposite him. "It's nice of you to drop by on a cold, rainy afternoon like this."

"This isn't a social call."

Her eyes darkened momentarily with disappointment.

"I spoke with Lyle Cady last Saturday," Santana said.

Her gaze went quickly to the glass in her hand, as though she suddenly realized she was holding it. She drank and then set it on the glass-topped table in front of her while she composed herself.

"Where?"

Santana popped the tab on the can of Coke. "He was hosting one of his seminars."

"Are you looking for ways to invest your capital, Detective?"

He heard no sarcasm in her voice, nor any warmth. "I'm fascinated by the work your husband is doing."

Her face brightened briefly. "Well, I'm quite fascinated by it, too, Detective. If he's successful, it opens up a whole new world of possibilities for those suffering from traumatic memories."

"Like soldiers."

She nodded, but her face remained expressionless.

"A discovery like that would be worth a lot of money, wouldn't it, Mrs. Vail?"

"I suppose it would be. But that's not why my husband does the research. And please, call me Monica." She offered a bright smile.

"How well do you know Lyle Cady, Mrs. Vail?" Santana asked.

Her smile vanished, and her body suddenly became more erect, her muscles tensing and her eyebrows drawing together in a flash of anger. Santana figured she was accustomed to having her way with men. But he was not deceived or blinded by the wattage of her smile.

"He works with my husband," she said.

"And that's the extent of your relationship?"

She looked at the glass on the table in front of her. Then she picked it up and drank, her eyes never meeting his.

"I know you've been seeing Lyle Cady, Mrs. Vail."

The cocktail glass slipped out of her hand and shattered against the floor, the ice skittering like diamonds across the ceramic tile.

"Dammit," she said, standing abruptly. She went behind the bar and returned with a roll of paper towels, a brush, and a dustpan.

"Can I help you?"

"I've got it," she said brusquely.

She wiped up the liquid, swept up the broken glass, and made herself a fresh drink. Then she sat down again in the chair across from him and lifted her eyes to his.

"What makes you think that I've been seeing Lyle Cady?"

Santana wanted to keep Jordan Parrish out of it if at all possible. Kenneth Vail might confess to his wife at some point that he had hired a private investigator to follow her, but Santana would leave that decision up to him.

"I saw you two together in Fern's Restaurant."

"So is that what homicide detectives do?"

"What do you mean?"

"Investigate the private lives of innocent citizens."

"I go wherever a case takes me."

"You need to clean up your mind, Detective Santana. Just because I had lunch with Lyle Cady doesn't mean I'm sleeping with him. We're just friends."

"You think your husband would see it that way?"

She looked at him for what seemed like a long time before speaking again. "Is that what this visit is about? Blackmail?"

Santana leaned forward. "Despite what you may think, Mrs. Vail, I'm not interested in what you do inside or outside of your marriage. Unless, of course, it relates to my investigation."

"And what does my . . . friendship with Lyle Cady have to do with your case or your department?"

"How much do you know about your husband's research?"

"Why do you want to know?"

"Please answer the question."

"And what will you do if I can't answer?"

"Can't or won't?"

She kept her gaze glued to his as she sipped her drink, her eyes charged with thoughts.

"My husband is a very jealous man."

"I'm not out to destroy your marriage."

She let out a curt laugh. "Then why bring up Lyle Cady in the first place?"

"I need information."

"But you're a homicide detective. Why would you be investigating my husband and Lyle Cady? Certainly you don't think they're involved in someone's murder?"

"Why were you arguing with Cady at the restaurant?"

She sat quickly back in the chair, as though Santana had tried to grab her. "That's none of your business."

"I'm going to keep looking, Mrs. Vail."

"For what?"

He ignored the question. "If you know something about your husband's research, now is the time to tell me."

She finished her tomato juice and held the glass to her mouth for a moment, her lips wet and absent of color from the cold ice. "I don't know any more than you do, Detective Santana."

Santana doubted that very much.

Heading for the LEC after his meeting with Monica Vail, Santana received a phone call from Jack Brody. He was surprised to hear the feds had released the reporter earlier that morning. They met in the lot on Shepard Road, close to where Scott Rafferty's body had been pulled from the river. Brody was dressed in his usual tan trench coat and fedora, and he was smoking a cigarette.

"Turns out there was a witness to the . . . altercation," he said. "She backed up my story that Kincaid hit me first." Brody pointed to his stomach. "Kincaid is in a heap of trouble." He chuckled. "I haven't been in a fist fight since high school. But I got him good, and in more ways than one."

Santana nodded and stood upwind of the cigarette smoke.

The Mississippi had crested, though it was still swollen with water. Sandbags fortified the riverbanks, as if the city were preparing for a siege. A dome of low gray clouds dimmed the afternoon sunlight that was straining to break through, and the bare branches of the oak tree swayed in a cool wind that was heavy with the scent of dirty water.

A gust of wind tugged at Brody's fedora, and he pulled it tighter on his head. "This morning's paper said you're still looking for a guy named Ronald Getz in connection with an assault on a homicide detective and a possible murder."

"That's right."

"You wouldn't be that particular homicide detective, would you?"

"Why are you so interested, Brody?"

"You've been working the serial killer case, haven't you?"

"I'm working Scott Rafferty's case."

"But his death is linked to the serial killer."

"I don't know that for a fact. And the latest vic was found in a funeral home and not in a river. You're looking for college kids who unintentionally drowned, remember?"

"The paper identified the victim as Jeff Tate. How was he killed?"

"Not by drowning. And he was a vet like Scott Rafferty."

"Both of them are still dead, Santana. And Rafferty *did* drown. Getz could've killed Rafferty. He wouldn't waste time figuring out if his victims served in the military. He'd just look for a certain type."

"You're reaching, Brody."

He shook his head. "Look, Santana, our interests are one and the same."

"Are they?"

"We both want to see justice done," he said.

"Justice means finding the right perp."

"Okay. I didn't just get off the banana boat, you know. If Getz isn't a serial killer, then tell me who you think it is."

Santana just looked at him.

"Ah, Jesus." Brody flicked his cigarette into a puddle and turned slightly away from Santana, his gaze fixed on something on the opposite bank. Santana followed Brody's gaze and saw a large bald eagle perched at the end of a high tree limb on the opposite bank, searching for prey.

"I did some thinking while I spent time in federal custody," Brody said. "I believe I've got enough material for a book. One of the big six New York publishers is interested."

"Congratulations."

"This is a big story, Santana."

"So go ahead and write your book."

He turned and faced Santana again, his hands hidden in the pockets of his trench coat, his eyes intense and focused. "I was thinking I should maybe wait till you catch the serial killer. But if the killer is Getz, he's already in the wind and you won't find him. And maybe another college kid or war vet will go missing somewhere and his body will turn up in a river. That's not the ending I planned to write."

"In Homicide we deal with facts, Brody, not fiction."

"I get that. My whole career was about finding the truth."

"Then maybe you should wait till you know for certain what's true and what isn't."

Brody spread his hands. "Look at me, Santana. Do I look like a guy who can wait around for his next big break?"

Santana could think of nothing positive, so he offered no response.

"Great," Brody said with a frustrated sigh. "You could've at least had the courtesy to disagree with me."

Santana considered Brody to be one of a vanishing breed of journalists, someone who actually was interested in the truth, and he respected that. Still, he was disappointed at the reporter's insistence that Getz was a serial killer. Santana wondered if Brody, in his quest for the big story—and the obvious fame and money that would follow—was willing to frame the truth to fit his version of the facts.

Brody lit another cigarette and then smoked for a time, his brow knit in concentration. "If this whole story goes south, Santana, my career is over."

"I'm not your agent."

"No, but I thought we had established a relationship of sorts, an understanding."

"Perhaps you thought wrong."

"Perhaps I did." Brody turned abruptly and strode away, tossing his cigarette angrily into the wind.

Back at his desk late that afternoon, Santana received an e-mail from Katherine Bailey, the forensic anthropologist. She had attached a digital photo of the facial reconstruction she had completed on the unidentified man pulled from the Mississippi two months ago.

Activating his computer, Santana clicked on the link for a website entitled, "Let's Bring Them Home." The website contained hundreds of thumbnail-sized photos, listed alphabetically by last name, of unsolved and suspected deaths, missing adults, and unidentified persons whose bodies or remains had been found.

Based on the digital photo, Santana was searching for a man in his mid-to-late-twenties. He knew he was swimming against the tide, because he had no information beyond the man's facial features and the U.S. Air Force ring that had been found on his finger. He hoped it would be enough.

Using the dropdown menu, he accessed the missing persons section. Many of the photos in the unidentified section were actually drawings made by sketch artists, or photos of reconstructed skulls done by forensic facial artists and anthropologists like Katherine Bailey. If he couldn't find a photo in the missing persons section that matched the face of the man he was searching for, he would upload the digital photo he had received into the unidentified section and hope that someone would eventually recognize it.

He poured a cup of hot chocolate from his thermos and began scanning the pages quickly, his mind instantly eliminating any photo that wasn't a match. He had just about given up hope by the time he reached the letter "W." But there he was. Greg Ward.

Santana clicked on the photo to access more detailed information.

A resident of Minneapolis, Ward was twenty-seven at the time of his disappearance. He was last seen in the vicinity of his home. The Minneapolis PD was the investigative agency.

Santana wrote down the case number and phone number and then dialed.

An MPD detective named Harrison answered. Santana identified himself and told Harrison why he was calling.

"I got the photo from Bailey, but I haven't had a chance to search the database," Harrison said. "You're sure it's Ward?"

"I will be once his wife identifies the body. You have an address and phone number?"

Harrison gave it to him. Santana promised to keep him informed.

Chapter 23

THE NEXT MORNING, SANTANA DROVE to Jennifer Ward's modest, wood-frame house in south Minneapolis. He rang the doorbell and waited until an attractive woman with brunette hair pulled back in a ponytail opened the door.

"Mrs. Ward?"

"Yes?"

Santana showed her his badge and ID. "I wonder if I could talk to you for a few minutes about a case I'm working."

Her eyes widened and her complexion paled. She grabbed the doorknob with one hand as though she needed support.

"Does this have something to do with Greg?"

"I believe so."

"You've found him?"

"If I could come in."

She hesitated, sensing, perhaps, that letting the detective enter her home would forever change the course of her life. Then she backed away from the door and pointed him toward a cushioned chair near a fireplace, where the ashes from a recent fire still glowed red.

"Could I get you something, Detective Santana?"

"I'm fine. Thanks."

"I could hang up your overcoat."

"I'll keep it with me if you don't mind."

She smiled thinly and stood in front him with her hands clasped tightly together, the shirttails of her flannel shirt hanging over her jeans. Her brown eyes would not meet his face.

Instead they darted toward the newspaper on the couch, toward her loafers on the floor in front of it, then to the photos on the mantel of two young girls and their uniformed father, Greg Ward.

"Your kids in school?"

She nodded and said, "Maybe I'll pour some coffee for myself. You sure you don't want any, Detective?"

"I'm sure," he said.

"Coffee's good on a cold spring day, don't you think?" Her lean body had begun to shake, and tears had welled in her eyes.

Santana stepped toward her. She backed away as though he were a threat and held up a palm in a stopping gesture. "You stay where you are," she said in a voice filled with anguish. "You just stay where you are, Detective."

He waited.

"I'm going to get a cup of coffee and then we'll talk. Okay?"

"Okay," he said.

"You can tell me what you want and then you can leave and everything will be just as it was before you came to my door. Do you understand?" Tears ran down her cheeks and her voice and nose were clogged with mucus.

"I understand."

She gave a firm nod, turned, and headed unsteadily toward what he assumed was the kitchen.

He was already moving toward her when her legs gave out. He caught her in his arms before she hit the wood floor and held her as she cried, her face pressed against his chest, her arms wrapped tightly around his waist, as though she could bring her husband back if she just squeezed Santana hard enough.

Later, after he had gotten her a cup of coffee and a box of Kleenex, he took off his overcoat and put another birch log on the fire, the flames rising quickly from the hot embers.

"I've been so cold for so long, Detective Santana." She held the digital photo he had given her in both hands, a wool blanket draped over her shoulders, and looked at him sitting across from her, her eyes bloodshot from crying. "It's like I've had this . . . emptiness inside me."

Santana peered at his notebook and gave her a moment. "Do you know why your husband disappeared?"

"The war," she said. "Or at least the memories of it."

"Your husband was in combat?"

"Greg never personally fired a shot. Never fought in battle."

"I'm afraid I don't understand."

"Not many do," she said. She drank some coffee and gathered her thoughts. "You see, Greg wanted to fly F-16s when he joined the service, but he was too nearsighted. So he became a military policeman. When the Air Force ran out of pilots for their expanding Predator drone program, Greg jumped at the chance. He went through a nine-month training program for officers from non-flying backgrounds at Creech Air Force base, an hour's drive outside of Las Vegas."

"You were both living in Nevada?"

"Yes."

"When did you move here?"

"Two years ago, after Greg left the Air Force. My family lives just outside the cities. I wanted to be closer to them, and the job climate was much better here than in Nevada."

"What about your husband's family?"

"Greg's mother died of cancer a few years ago. His father left when Greg was in his teens. He has no brothers or sisters."

"How long have you been married?"

"Ten years. Right out of high school. We had the two girls in our second and third years of marriage. Things were going so well." Her gaze drifted to the photos on the mantel, as though she were recalling pleasant memories of the past.

"Why did your husband leave the service?"

She set her coffee cup and the photo on the coffee table, slipped a cigarette out of a package of Camels on the coffee table, and lit it with a match. "Two reasons," she said, blowing a cloud of smoke upward. "Even though he considered himself a pilot, most of the actual fighter pilots didn't. They thought what he did was nothing different than a kid playing a video game."

"And that bothered your husband."

"Of course. The Air Force couldn't decide if drone pilots should wear the same wings as traditional pilots, or if they qualified for extra flight pay. Hell, they couldn't decide if they should even be called pilots. But Greg knew that drones saved soldiers' lives."

"You said there were two reasons why your husband left the service."

Jennifer Ward inhaled another lung-full of smoke and blew it out slowly.

Santana waited.

"One of his drone strikes killed a number of women and children. Greg never got over it. He wasn't like the other drone pilots."

"How do you mean?"

"They're so removed from the effects of the war, from the decisions they make. In a way, it *is* like a video game. They sit in a room in Nevada and drop bombs or missiles on targets, and then drive home for dinner. Wars shouldn't be fought like that."

"Because it makes killing easier," Santana said.

She nodded. "Too easy. A man in your position, if you fire your gun and kill someone, there is no distance. You're in the moment. You see and experience what you've done, like soldiers in past wars."

Santana thought that pilots in most wars rarely experienced the trauma of the foot soldier because they had distance. But he understood Jennifer Ward's point. "So even though your husband had considerable distance from the damage he'd inflicted, it still affected him psychologically."

"It should have," she said. "But not to the extent that it did."

"He just walked out?"

"He left a note for me."

Santana could hear the bitterness together with the sadness in her voice. "Had he ever disappeared before?"

"No. And that was a problem when I first contacted the police department. They told me if Greg was acting of his own free will, no police report could be made."

"Did he say why he left?"

She thought for a moment before responding. "Greg felt that he should be punished for his actions."

"How so?"

"He didn't believe he should have a family when those he killed had lost theirs."

"Did you ever feel you were in danger?"

She shook her head and crushed out the cigarette in an ashtray on the coffee table. "Greg wasn't a danger to us, only to himself."

"He was suicidal?"

She nodded again. "It's the reason I was finally able to get his photo and name in the national database of missing persons. But the police said they weren't going to actively search for him unless there was some evidence of foul play." She looked expectantly at Santana.

"The autopsy report listed death by drowning, Mrs. Ward."

She shivered and pulled the blanket tighter around her shoulders.

"Did your husband abuse alcohol or drugs?"

"Never," she said. "At least while we were together."

"Did your husband ever contact you after he disappeared?"

"Occasionally."

"What did he say?"

She shook her head and exhaled a breath of air. "That he missed me and the kids."

"He never sought counseling?"

"Not at first. But the last time I heard from him, he said he may have found help."

"What kind of help?"

"I don't know. He said he'd spoken with someone at a homeless shelter."

"Here in town?"

"In St. Paul."

"Did your husband mention the name of the person he'd spoken to?"

Her eyes narrowed as she focused her thoughts. "I believe his name was Jeff."

"Jeff Tate?"

"Yes," she said. "Jeff Tate."

Chapter 24

SANTANA HADN'T KNOWN WHAT he was looking for the first time he searched Tate's bomb shelter. But Paul Munson had mentioned that Tate had planned to write a book about the effects of PTSD on war vets. And Jennifer Ward had said that after talking with Tate, her husband had spoken of finding *help* for his PTSD symptoms. Santana wondered now if Tate had, in fact, been writing a book about PTSD.

After typing a warrant and having a judge sign it, Santana drove out to Jeff Tate's cabin and searched the bomb shelter again. When he reached the end of it, he still had found no manuscript, no diary, no journal, nothing that might explain why the cabin had been ransacked—or account for Tate's murder.

But as Santana stepped toward the ladder near the emergency exit hatch, he felt the floor give slightly under his feet. He stepped off the rug underneath his feet and picked it up. Then he took out his mini-Maglite and flicked on the beam. Immediately, he could see that he was standing on a three-foot square panel that had been cut out of the floorboards. He used a screwdriver he found on one of the shelves to pry it up. Hidden underneath was a small floor safe.

Santana called a locksmith named Jimmy Healy. While he waited for Healy, he called Jordan and left a message on her office phone that he might be late for their date, but he would pick her up at her office, as they had planned.

Forty-five minutes later, a short, wiry man clothed in a flannel shirt, bib overalls, and Minnesota Twins cap worn backwards on his small head got out of his van carrying a large toolbox. "Haven't seen you in awhile, Detective," Healy said. He had a permanent squint, as though he were staring at a bright light.

"Haven't needed your skill set for a while, Jimmy."

Healy was an odd combination of excess energy and Zen stillness, a trait he called upon whenever he opened a safe. He had done time two decades ago for burglary, but had turned his life around, gotten a college degree, and now ran a successful small company.

"How's business?" Santana asked.

"Real steady despite the lousy economy. Lotta paranoid people locking up their valuables. Figure they're safe." He laughed.

"That a pun, Jimmy?"

"Sure was. You know, Santana, you're one of the few cops I've met who would get that."

He glanced at the cabin. "Safe inside?"

Santana shook his head. "This way." He led Healy to the camouflaged hatch on the bomb shelter and opened it.

"Holy shit! I didn't think people were still building these things after the Cold War ended. Someone must think Armageddon is just around the corner."

He followed Santana down the ladder, holding the toolbox in one hand, and then to the floor safe in the last section of the shelter.

"It's a standard group two lock," Healy said, staring down at the safe. "Simplest way to attack it is to drill into the lock module through the front. I've got a database of safe diagrams and precise drilling points on the laptop in my van. But most modern commercial safes use the same mechanical locks."

"Does this safe have a relock device?"

"Uh-huh. Most safes and vaults on the market nowadays have one. Got to be careful, though. We don't know if there's anything hazardous in the safe. And if the relock senses an attack, it prevents the door bolts from moving even after the lock bolt is retracted. High temperatures can trigger certain relocks, so I don't want to use a torch."

Healy set his toolbox on the floor beside him, got down on his knees, and set the dial on the safe at zero.

"The lever is near the dial position ninety-seven," he said, looking up at Santana. "So I need to drill a hole about an inch from the center of the spindle. That'll give me a good view of the top of the wheel pack with my borescope."

"So you can decode the combination and open the safe."

He nodded. "Once I can see the lock, I can manipulate the dial to align the lock gates. Then the fence falls and the bolt is disengaged."

Healy opened his toolbox and removed a portable magnetic drill rig, which he attached to the front of the safe. The rig allowed him to maintain control of the pressure and depth of the drill. Then he attached a tungsten carbide bit to his drill that was designed to cut through the hardplate surrounding the locking mechanism.

"How long will it take, Jimmy?"

"Not long," he said.

It took less than thirty minutes.

Once the door was opened, Healy stepped back and let Santana remove a leather-bound journal that was wrapped in plastic. Santana wasn't sure what was written inside it, but he suspected that whatever it was, it had cost Jeff Tate his life.

The last rays flamed the horizon as the sun sank below the soot-colored clouds, the light gradually fading as Santana punched in the code on the keypad outside Jordan Parrish's office door and went in. He left the lights off and walked to one of the three arched windows along the stone wall behind her desk. He stood in the shadows at the edge of city light spilling through the glass and peered at the darkening sky, his thoughts swinging like a pendulum from Jordan to the case and to Jordan once again.

In the empty silence of the room, he was struck by a deep sense of loneliness. He had made a choice to live his life alone, but in contemplative moments such as these, he questioned the soundness of his decision.

Then he recalled the dream he'd had of Jordan surrounded by sharks, and he was overcome with a feeling of dread. He had learned long ago never to dismiss the images he saw in his dreams, and he would make no exception now, especially when the dream involved her.

He walked to her desk and sat in her chair, the vague scent of lavender and jasmine from her floral perfume triggering the memory of her lips pressed warmly against his.

His gaze drifted to her desk calendar. He smiled when he saw that Jordan had drawn a small heart next to his name in the box for today's date. He wondered if she had drawn it subconsciously or purposefully, knowing he was coming to her office and would probably see it. Regardless of her motivation, being the astute detective that he was, he considered it a very positive sign.

Santana was off the clock, but he wanted to read Jeff Tate's journal before leaving it in one of the after-hours evidence storage lockers at the LEC. He glanced at his watch, wondering how late Jordan would be. Then he leaned back in the chair and began reading.

Tate had written about his own wartime experiences in the first third of the journal, including an account of how he had won a Bronze Star for rescuing a wounded comrade. Santana could sense the pride in his accomplishments and his unwavering faith in the cause and in his own combat skills. Tate had returned to civilian life believing that he had not just physically survived the trauma of war, but he had survived it emotionally and psychologically as well.

There was a three-month gap in the journal before the nightmares and paranoia began.

Tate had considered counseling, but soon decided that he alone could deal with the demon that now haunted his soul. Building the bomb shelter had given him a clear purpose once again and had refocused his attention and thoughts. But nothing could assuage the guilt he felt. It wasn't until he met Scott Rafferty—and they began sharing their war stories—that Tate's nightmares decreased somewhat in both intensity and occurrence. He started volunteering at the homeless shelter and recording the stories of others who suffered from PTSD. It was there that he first heard rumors about a new miracle drug that could erase all the dark memories.

Could it have been propranolol, the drug that Benjamin Roth had used to treat Scott Rafferty? Santana wondered. But if the miracle drug had been propranolol, wouldn't Rafferty have told Tate that he was taking it? Unless Rafferty was embarrassed to admit that he had sought counseling.

Santana could find no mention of propranolol. What he did find on the following pages, however, shocked him.

Then his cell phone rang. He thought at first that it might be Jordan, but he didn't recognize the number.

"Santana."

"You have to do something," Monica Vail said, her voice strained, as though a wire were wrapped tightly around her neck.

"What's wrong?"

"Kenneth told me he hired a private investigator to follow me. He knows about my relationship with Lyle Cady."

"I don't know how I can help you, Mrs. Vail."

"It's not me you need to help, Detective Santana. It's Lyle. Kenneth is meeting him at his lab this evening. He's going to confront him with the evidence. And he took his gun."

Santana sat up. "Your husband owns a gun?"

"Yes."

He was about to tell her to call 911 when his gaze fell on the desk calendar. What he saw sent an icy chill through him, as though the hand of death had reached out and touched him.

The name of the client Jordan was meeting was Kenneth Vail, and she was meeting him at his lab. Jordan would be walking right into a potentially dangerous situation—one already charged with dynamite—one in which the flame had already been lit.

"I'm on my way," he said.

Chapter 25

NIGHT GRIPPED THE LANDSCAPE, and dense fog clotted along the lowlands, choking off the city lights, as Santana sped toward Kenneth Vail's lab, his heart beating hard, the Crown Vic's emergency flasher pulsing into the darkness like blood spurting from an arterial wound. Santana dialed Jordan's cell phone, but got her voice mail. He left a message to call him immediately. Then he phoned dispatch and requested that a squad be sent to the lab.

A patrol car was parked in the lot near a Lexus when Santana arrived, the officer seated behind the wheel, his head lolling to the side, the blood-spattered, driver's side window spider-webbed from a bullet that had pierced the glass and cored out the back of his head. There was no sign of Jordan's van.

Santana felt for a pulse and called for additional backup. Seeing a fellow officer brutally murdered drove a spike of anger through his heart, but he had to keep his emotions in check. Charging angrily into the building could get him killed, too. He removed his tie and overcoat, changed his sport coat for a raid jacket, and drew a deep breath—and his Glock.

The main entrance door was unlocked, the lobby lights dim, as were those in the hallway leading to Vail's lab. Santana moved swiftly down the hall, legs slightly bent, eyes and senses alert. When he reached it, he stopped and pressed his back against the wall. Holding his Glock with both hands, the barrel pointing at the ceiling, he peered around the door jamb. The bright lights and white walls stabbed his eyes like sharp blades. He blinked twice till his vision adjusted.

Lyle Cady lay on the lab floor, his head turned toward the door, his eyes closed, a small black Ruger LC9 in his right hand.

Sitting in the far right corner of the room with his back against the wall was the blond security guard named Jess who had confronted Santana at Cady's presentation. His chin was resting on his blood-spattered shirt, and the palms of his hands were open on his thighs, as if he were begging for forgiveness.

Cady moaned, and Santana holstered his Glock, stepped into the room, and squatted beside him. There was a small patch of blood on Cady's head, where he had apparently been struck, but Santana saw no bullet wound and felt a strong pulse on the carotid artery.

He slipped on a pair of latex gloves, removed the Ruger from Cady's hand, and engaged the thumb safety on the left side of the frame, locking both the slide and trigger from movement. Then he placed the Ruger on the floor out of Cady's reach.

"Cady," Santana said, slapping him lightly on the cheek.

A few seconds passed before he blinked his eyes and mumbled, "What happened?"

"Why don't you tell me?"

Cady seemed momentarily confused by the question. "I don't know. I came here to meet Kenneth. I think someone struck me from behind. The next thing I remember is seeing you."

"That your gun?"

He followed Santana's gaze to the Ruger and then nodded. "Monica gave it to me."

"Why would she do that?"

"For protection."

"From whom?"

"Her husband."

"Can you sit up?"

"I think so." He grabbed Santana's hand and pulled himself up into a sitting position. "I've got a lump on my head," he said, gently touching the wound with the tips of his fingers. "Guess someone did hit me."

"Who shot the security guard?"

"What security guard?"

"The one named Jess." Santana turned toward the security guard—who was now standing in the corner of the room, pointing a Sig Sauer in his left hand directly at Santana.

"Surprise," Jess said, baring his teeth in a cold smile.

Santana stared at Jess's blood-soaked shirt, trying to make sense of the situation.

"Stage blood looks real, doesn't it?" Jess said. "Almost fooled me." He laughed and motioned with the gun. "Stand up. Both of you."

Cady grabbed Santana's forearm. "What's going on?"

"Do as he says," Santana said, helping him up.

Jess motioned again with the Sig Sauer. "Take your Glock out of your holster, Santana, and put it on the counter. Then back away."

"What are you doing, Jess?" Cady said. "You work for Venture Tech."

"Not anymore."

"He's a mercenary working for the highest bidder," Santana said.

Jess shook his head. "Those of us in the business prefer the term 'professional military contractor.'" He motioned with the Sig Sauer again. "The Glock."

Santana placed his gun on the counter and stripped off his latex gloves. Then he stepped back a few paces.

Cady looked at Santana with eyes that were wide with panic. "Is he going to kill me?"

"I'm not going to kill you," Jess said. "Santana is."

Cady jerked his head toward Jess. "What?"

287

Jess walked calmly to the counter, holstered his gun, picked up Santana's Glock, and shot Cady in the chest. "Nice weapon. But I prefer the Sig." He set the Glock on the counter again and picked up the Ruger off the floor. "Step this way, Detective."

"I don't think so."

He shrugged. "I can shoot you where you stand."

"You do that, Jess, and you're going to have to move the bodies around. And I won't have any gunshot residue on my hands. Forensics is going to figure out Cady and I didn't shoot each other."

"Maybe," he said. "But maybe not. In either case, you'll be dead."

Jess aimed the Ruger at Santana's chest and pulled the trigger—but nothing happened.

"Surprise," Santana said.

Had Jess been right-handed, he could have quickly switched off the safety with his right thumb and probably gotten off a fatal shot. But the location of the safety on the Ruger was a problem for a left-hander. The extra seconds were all Santana needed.

He led with his head as he tackled Jess like a linebacker sacking a quarterback. The impact shattered the cartilage in Jess's nose with a loud crunch and sent the Ruger flying. Santana kept his arms wrapped tightly around Jess's waist and his weight balanced as he lifted him off his feet and drove him backwards, slamming him hard against the wall. The back of Jess's head bounced off it, and his breath rushed out of him in a squealing gasp.

Santana released his hold and pulled the Sig Sauer out of Jess's shoulder holster as the security guard slid down the wall and rolled onto his side, dazed, struggling for air, *real* blood pouring from his nostrils.

Two uniforms entered the room, their guns drawn. "Drop your weapon!"

Santana set the Sig Sauer on the counter. "I'm a cop," he said. "Homicide."

"You got ID?"

Santana showed them his badge wallet. "Call the paramedics. And cuff the one near the wall."

He knelt beside Cady, who was breathing rapidly, creating a sucking sound as air entered and then was exhaled from the open wound in his chest. In the sharp light, Santana could see the familiar terror in Cady's eyes that comes from knowing that you're dying, and that this life may be all there is.

Cady opened his mouth to speak, but he couldn't seem to form the words. Blood leaked over his bottom lip and ran down his chin. Santana's ears were ringing, and even if Cady had spoken at that moment, he wasn't sure he would have heard what he said.

"What are you trying to say?"

Cady stared silently at him.

One of the uniforms squatted beside Santana. "You shoot him?"

Before Santana could reply, Cady grabbed the officer's hand and shook his head. "Jess shot me."

"He's the one you just cuffed," Santana said. "Jess shot him with my Glock."

"What?"

"I'll explain it to the OIS team later," he said, peering down at Cady. "Was there a woman here earlier?"

He nodded.

"Jordan Parrish?"

Cady took hold of Santana's coat and pulled him closer. "It has to be at Tate's," he said. "Go now."

His jaw fell open, his face suddenly slackened, and blood drained from his complexion. Then he lost his grip and exhaled a final breath.

"It has to be at Tate's. Go now."

Santana figured Cady was referring to Tate's journal.

He stood and retrieved his Glock. It was department policy to collect a gun that had been fired, even if he had not pulled the trigger. A range gun would be given to him while the investigation continued, but he wasn't about to wait for the Officer Involved Shooting team to arrive. He would no doubt find himself in hot water for leaving the scene, but it wouldn't be the first time he had been in trouble with the department—or, he hoped, the last.

Chapter 26

AS SANTANA APPROACHED THE OPEN GATE fronting the muddy driveway leading to Jeff Tate's cabin, he killed his headlights. The silver coating on a broken lock hanging from the hasp shone in the moonlight that he used to guide him along the puddled, pot-holed road. He drove until he spotted what appeared to be a Jeep Wrangler parked in the clearing in front of Tate's cabin. He braked and shut off the Crown Vic's engine.

He was staring at the cabin about thirty yards in the distance, wondering what had happened to Jordan Parrish, when a round blew out the Crown Vic's front and back windshields, spraying glass across the front seat. The shooter let off two more rounds that thudded into the engine block, but Santana was already rolling out the driver's side door onto the ground, his Glock held firmly in his right hand, his Maglite in his left. He got to his feet and ran toward the woods, parallel to the cabin, tree branches slapping wetly against his clothing, the muddy ground squishing under his shoes, his heart pounding with adrenaline.

He felt the heat of a bullet pass close to his head, heard the crack of a rifle and the sound of shredding leaves, and felt the sting of wood splinters against his cheek as bark blew off the tree just ahead of him. He veered right and then left again, zig-zagging, as the forest and darkness grew thicker. His brain screamed at him to run faster. But colliding with a tree or heavy branch could knock him unconscious and leave him vulnerable, so he slowed to a jog and worked his way toward the south end of the lot, where he hunkered down in a stand of birch trees, the white trunks glistening like bone in the pale moonlight, his heavy breathing fogging the cool blackness surrounding him.

In the light haloing the sky above the cabin, he could see lights burning in the windows of the A-frame, which he estimated to be about fifty yards in the distance. He had no idea who was shooting at him and if there was more than one perp. He needed reinforcements. But when he reached for his cell phone in a jacket pocket, he realized he had left it on the front seat of the Crown Vic after his last futile attempt to contact Jordan. He had no idea where she was or if she was in immediate danger, and he felt a sudden emptiness in his chest. Still, he had seen no sign of her van at Vail's lab, and that gave him hope. Maybe she was safe. Maybe she was alive.

Santana waited five minutes before he spotted dark shapes at the edge of the forest straight ahead. There were two of them—probably the other Venture Tech security guards.

One held what looked like a Bushmaster AR-15 semiautomatic rifle at port arms. Santana could tell by the flash suppressor on the barrel. The other had what appeared to be a shotgun. Santana couldn't be sure—until he heard the pump slide back as a shell was jacked into the chamber. It was a distinctive sound, a sound like nothing else.

The two men fanned out, as professionals would, making it tougher for Santana to take them at the same time. He had to make a decision and make it soon before he was outflanked and pinned down between them. He had a nearly full clip in his Glock 23, minus the round Jess had fired, which gave him eleven rounds in the magazine, plus one in the chamber—more than enough ammunition to accomplish his task, if he avoided a senseless firefight. The security guard to his right, the one with the shotgun, would have to get close for the kill. He was the most vulnerable. Santana came up into a crouch and moved off to his right.

Using the moonlight to guide him, he covered thirty yards in an easterly direction, through thick undergrowth, before turning north toward his Crown Vic and the man with the shotgun. He was tempted to use his Maglite, but he knew the beam would make him an easy target, so he slipped it into a jacket pocket.

The shooters might be thinking he would head for the river a quarter mile away, where he would make a stand. If he attempted to cross in the swiftly moving current or swim downstream, he, like the young college men who had drowned in the Mississippi, was unlikely to survive, even though he was a strong swimmer.

He paused beside the trunk of a tree at the edge of a small clearing and tried to get a fix on the security guard with the shotgun. He had planned to get behind the man, but he had lost sight of him once the two men made the tree line.

A dark cloud slid across the moon, and thick raindrops began falling. The rain was cold and stung his face and hands. He could hear nothing besides the raindrops, but the men with the guns would have the same problem. Santana wiped the rain from his eyes and waited, hoping to catch a break.

It came minutes later when the downpour abruptly ended. The moon broke free of the clouds, casting a ghostly light that once again illuminated the small clearing. The man with the shotgun came cautiously through an opening between a stand of trees, the barrel pointed slightly toward the ground, his head moving from left to right.

Santana heard a squish and a sucking sound, as though a boot had been pulled out of mud. Branches moved and leaves rustled as they scraped against fabric. A twig snapped like a small bone.

Santana waited, trying to contain his emotions, his Glock ready. The air was dead calm. When the security guard passed by him, Santana stood up, pointed the gun at the man's back, and said, "St. Paul PD. Drop your weapon and put your hands on your head."

The man stopped in the faintly lit clearing and stood perfectly still, at a forty-five degree angle slightly to Santana's left. He wore a hooded black poncho and utility rain boots. He had pulled the hood off his head, and Santana could see that he had short blond hair cut close to the scalp—military style. Santana wondered if he had a Kevlar vest under the poncho.

"Do it now," he said. "Or you'll die where you stand."

The man shook his head slowly, as though he thought he still had a chance. Or more likely, it was an acknowledgement that he had made a tactical mistake and was now resigned to his fate.

Santana wanted both men alive. That way he could play one against the other when he questioned them—and maybe force one to talk by getting Pete Canfield, the Ramsey County attorney, to offer a deal.

"Drop your weapon," he said again.

"I had nothing to do with whatever happened at the lab, and neither did Ray."

"You work security for Venture Tech?"

"Yeah."

"Ray the guy with the AR-15?"

"Yeah."

"So who are you?"

"Billy."

"Okay, Billy. I've told you twice to drop your weapon. I'm not going to tell you again."

"Look, we're just doing our job."

"Cady's dead."

"I had nothing to do with that."

"I guess you had nothing to do with protecting him either."

"I fucked up."

"Then don't fuck up again."

A long moment of silence ensued before the security guard spoke again. "I'm not going to jail."

"You might not have to if you cooperate."

"Like how?"

"Like telling me what you're doing out here."

Billy whirled and swung the barrel of the shotgun toward Santana.

Santana fired two shots that caught Billy in the chest. He pitched forward, his finger still wrapped around the trigger, a shot exploding from the shotgun barrel into the soft ground as he went down.

Then silence.

Santana's ears rang with the echoes of gunshots that cascaded through the forest like the cries of a wounded animal. He moved quickly through the cloud of gunsmoke fogging the air above the body, knowing the shots had been heard and that Ray would soon be coming with his AR-15.

He rolled Billy on his back and unzipped the poncho. He had guessed right. Billy was wearing a Kevlar vest. A quick check for a pulse told Santana the guard was unconscious, not dead. Inside Billy's pockets, Santana found a Sig Sauer P226 and a four-battery flashlight. The gun was designed for the U.S. Army and carried by Navy SEALs.

He stripped off Billy's poncho and rolled him back on his stomach, so that his face would be hidden. He took off his raid jacket and laid it over Billy. The SPPD logo on the back would be visible. In the dim light, Ray would be hard pressed to tell that it was his partner and not Santana, at least until he got real close.

Santana was certain now that all three men were professionals with military backgrounds and training. Yet, despite their training—or perhaps because of it—Billy and Jess had underestimated him. Maybe Ray was better than the two of them. Santana couldn't be sure. But the sound of the Glock was much different than that of a shotgun, and Billy had fired the last shot as he fell. Ray might let down his guard, figuring his partner had killed Santana.

Santana retrieved the Maglite from a pocket of the raid jacket, slid the Sig Sauer in the waistband of his pants next to his right kidney, and put on the poncho. He and Billy were about the same size, and the poncho fit him well. He slipped his Glock in the empty right pocket, the Maglite in the left. Then he picked up the Remington pump action 12-guage and racked a fresh shell into the chamber.

Chapter 27

SANTANA TOOK A SERIES of deep breaths to slow his racing heart. He pulled up the hood on the poncho as he stood over Billy's body, holding the shotgun at port arms. All he could do was wait, and waiting, when placed in a position of the hunter or the hunted, was difficult. His emotions were in overdrive, and his brain urged him to act.

Time passed slowly. The ringing in his ears faded like an echo. He wondered if Ray had left the property—though he must have fled on foot because Santana would have heard the Jeep's engine. Then he heard footsteps tromping through the underbrush. Ray was heading directly toward him.

He came into the clearing ten yards in front of Santana with his hood pulled back, carrying the AR-15 in a ready position. When he saw what he thought was Santana lying on the ground, he lowered the barrel of his gun—as Santana had hoped he would.

"You got the bastard," he said.

Santana leveled the shotgun at Ray's stomach. "Drop your weapon."

Ray stopped.

Santana couldn't see Ray's eyes clearly, but he imagined what the man was thinking. "You raise that weapon, I'll cut you in half."

"Son of a bitch."

"I've been called worse," Santana said. "Don't make the same mistake your partner did."

"You kill Billy?"

"No. But I could have."

Ray thought about his limited options for a moment longer. Then he dove to his right and pulled the AR-15's trigger.

The night erupted in semi-automatic gunfire that rolled across the woods like cracks of thunder. Ray had firepower on his side, but he fired wildly as he fell to the ground, making no attempt at accuracy, figuring he might get lucky if he just opened up.

Bullets ripped through the branches and leaves above Santana's head and thudded into tree trunks, but he was on the move, the shotgun gripped in his hands, his arms held high and out in front of him to prevent the damp branches from whipping across his face. He had run less than twenty yards when the gunfire abruptly ceased.

Unlike in Hollywood movies, where actors fired endless rounds without reloading, the standard capacity AR-15 magazine held just thirty rounds, and emptying it on full-auto took seconds, not minutes. Forty, sixty, and even one hundred capacity magazines were available, but Santana doubted Ray was that well armed, given the usually mundane tasks required of Venture Tech security guards. Ray might not have more than one extra magazine with him—or none at all.

The wet underbrush was strong with the smell of rain as Santana slashed through the woods like a running back through a field of tacklers, heading for the bomb shelter at the edge of the clearing near the cabin, knowing that it might be his one and only chance, that any return fire would give away his position and make him a sitting duck.

Pale moonlight lit the forest like a dim bulb, but there was enough light to locate the camouflaged escape hatch. Winded and breathing deeply, Santana opened it, climbed partway down the ladder, and held the hatch slightly open with the end of the shotgun barrel so that he could see the woods.

Ray ran past him thirty seconds later and then stopped abruptly just beyond the edge of the forest and five yards north of the hatch. Figuring Ray's ears, like his, would still be ringing from the gunfire, Santana pushed open the hatch and climbed out of the shelter. Ray's back was to him, but in his mind's eye, Santana saw Ray turning toward him, the barrel of the rifle level on Santana's chest, a smirk on his face as he pressed the trigger.

Taking the Maglite out of a pocket, Santana flicked it on and tossed it over Ray's head, hoping the distraction would draw his fire and give him the advantage he needed.

When it landed on the ground ten yards in front of Ray—the beam illuminating a tree trunk on the opposite side of the clearing—Ray fired a quick burst, then stopped.

Santana moved up behind him and pressed the shotgun barrel hard against the back of his skull. "Drop it."

Ray didn't hesitate this time.

Santana grabbed him by the collar and backed him into the forest beside a pine tree. "Lie on your face with your arms around the trunk," he said.

After Ray complied, Santana cuffed him. Standing over Ray, Santana said, "I'll ask you the same question I asked Billy. What are you doing out here?"

"Fuck you."

"Suit yourself."

"You just gonna leave me out here?"

"For now."

Tate's cabin was twenty yards directly behind Santana. As he turned toward it, he saw a silhouette pass by a window. He knelt beside Ray and studied the log structure, watching as a trail of gray smoke snaked its way out of the stack on the roof.

"Who's in the cabin, Ray?"

"Fuck you."

"You've got to work on your vocabulary. It's rather limited."

"Hey!" Ray yelled. "I'm . . ."

Santana cracked him in the skull with the butt end of the shotgun, and he went silent.

The best plan was to retrieve his cell phone from the Crown Vic and wait for backup, Santana thought. But he knew he couldn't. He had to know if Jordan was inside the cabin. He took another minute to formulate a rough plan before he circled to his left. The ringing in his ears had cleared, and he heard his own footsteps on the twigs beneath his feet now. He kept moving along a path that smelled of pine needles and burning firewood until he could see both the front and back doors.

When he saw that Jordan's van was parked behind the cabin, it sent a shiver through him. He wasn't sure what to make of it. Was she being held against her will? Was she dead and had Ray and Billy stolen her van? Or was it something more sinister, something he had missed?

He took a deep breath and let it out slowly. Then he sprinted out of the woods and into the clearing until he reached the back of the cabin, where he knelt beneath a window. His sweat felt cool and damp on his skin, and his breath clouded white against the darkness.

Once his breathing slowed, he raised his head and looked through the window, but a shade had been drawn. He could see only light along its edges. If Jordan was inside the cabin, she might be in trouble. Doing nothing wasn't an option.

Santana duck-walked under the window to the edge of the back door that was pockmarked with holes from a previous shotgun blast. He stood and kicked in the door. It banged against an inside wall as he charged into the room with the shotgun's stock against his shoulder.

He saw Jordan tied to a wooden chair, her cheeks red and bruised, her mouth covered with duct tape. Ronald Getz loomed over her, his hands covered with leather gloves.

Getz lunged for a 9mm on the kitchen table, but Santana moved forward and hit him hard in the temple with the butt end of the shotgun. Getz went down with a heavy thud, his breath rushing out of him like air from a deflated balloon.

Santana couldn't understand what Jordan was saying behind the tape over her mouth. He set the shotgun on the table and used the six-inch knife in the sheath clipped to Getz's boot to cut the twine holding her wrists to the chair.

"Are you all right?" he asked, removing the duct tape from her mouth.

"Behind you," she said.

Santana spun and reached for the Glock in his right pocket, but it was too late. Monica Vail stood at the bottom of the stairs, pointing a snub-nosed .38 Special at him. Kenneth Vail stood beside her.

"You are a persistent man, Detective Santana. I'll give you that," Monica Vail said. A nervous smile creased her face, and her eyes glowed with excitement. "Lose the knife and the gun. And use two fingers."

Santana set the knife on the table. Then he picked the Glock out of his pocket with his thumb and index finger and set it beside the shotgun on the table.

"Anything in your other pocket?"

Santana slipped out of the poncho and tossed it on the table. "See for yourself."

Monica Vail had been careless in assuming his Glock was the only gun he had. Jordan, who was still seated slightly behind him and to his left, would certainly see the Sig Sauer nestled in the waistband near his right kidney. He wanted Jordan to see it. What he didn't know for certain was whether or not she would go for it—or whether he wanted her to. He was reluctant to force her to take a life, even though not doing so might mean she would lose her own. If Jordan killed Monica Vail, she would carry that burden with her the remainder of her life.

"The security guards?" Monica Vail said, cocking her head.

"They won't be coming to help you."

"My, you are quite the optimist, Detective." She wiggled the revolver in her hand. "I have all the help I need."

"This has gone far enough, Monica," Kenneth Vail said, beads of sweat dotting his brow. Looking as though he were about to be sick, he jammed his hands into his pockets and then pulled them out again, as if he didn't know what to do with them.

"Let me handle this, Kenneth."

"Please, Monica. Give the gun to Detective Santana."

She kept her eyes locked on Santana, as if she hadn't heard her husband. But her gun hand was no longer steady, and a thin sheen of sweat had formed on her face.

"Why Jordan?" Santana asked.

"I spotted her following Lyle. I wanted to find out what she knew."

"Knew about what?" Jordan said. "I have no idea what you're talking about. How many times do I have to tell you? Your husband hired me to find out if you were having an affair. That's all."

Santana was relieved to hear the strength in Jordan's voice. If she was afraid, she wasn't showing it.

"Kenneth Vail was using human subjects in his memory experiments," he said. "Primarily homeless soldiers suffering from PTSD. Some of those experiments caused the vets to lose substantial portions of their memory."

Monica Vail gave a little start, as if pushed by an unseen hand. "Who told you that?"

"No one. I found Jeff Tate's journal, the one you've been searching for since you had Getz kill him."

Kenneth Vail's eyes widened with shock. "My God! Killed?"

"Your wife was afraid Tate would tell the world what you were doing," Santana said. "You would have been disgraced."

"My husband is a brilliant scientist," Monica Vail said. "What he's discovered has the potential to change the world for victims of PTSD."

"Maybe," Santana said. "But you were worried that if he found out you were having an affair with Lyle Cady, he'd file for divorce. You stood to lose a lot of money."

Vail looked at his wife. "I love you, Monica. I would never divorce you. I thought if I could prove to Cady that I knew about your affair and threatened to take my research elsewhere, he . . ." Vail ended the sentence with a meek shrug.

"Your wife didn't know that," Santana said. "She wanted Cady to help her get rid of Jordan. Cady refused. They argued about it at Fern's Restaurant. When she thought I was getting too close to the truth, she set up Cady and me."

"Set up?"

"Cady's dead."

Kenneth Vail wavered for a moment. "Oh, no," he said, and lowered himself into a wooden chair near the stairs.

Monica Vail's breathing was rapid now. "It doesn't matter."

"I think it does," Santana said. "Without Cady, you have no financing."

"There'll be plenty of venture capitalists interested in my husband's work."

"Then how are you going to explain all of this?"

She gestured with the gun barrel. "Ronald Getz," she said. "You killed him. He killed you and the private investigator." She spoke rapidly, the words running together.

"But you still won't have the journal."

"Once all of this is settled, the journal will be returned."

"You better hope no one in the department takes the time to read it. And that Jess doesn't spill his guts when questioned."

She swallowed hard and raised the revolver slightly so that it was pointing directly at the center of his chest.

Ordering someone shot and killed was much different than pulling the trigger yourself. Santana could see the panic in her eyes now, and the pulse in her neck increased. He imagined her throat was dry, her mind filled with sudden doubts. Still, his heart thudded against his rib cage with adrenaline-laced energy, and blood rushed in his eardrums.

Kenneth Vail, still seated in a chair beside her, put a hand on her arm. "Stop, Monica. Give me the gun. It's over." He spoke quietly, but with strength. "No more killing, please."

As she turned slightly to look at her husband, Santana reached for his Glock on the table.

But Jordan was quicker. She slid the Sig Sauer out of his waistband, brought the gun out from behind him, and fired, just as Monica Vail swung the .38 toward Santana.

The force of the bullet striking her abdomen knocked her back a step. For a fraction of a second, there was a stunned look in her eyes, as though she couldn't believe that fate had destroyed all her carefully laid plans. Then Jordan fired again.

Kenneth Vail let out an anguished moan. He stood and reached for his wife, but she slipped through his arms and went down, the light slowly fading from her eyes like the dying flame of a candle.

Chapter 28

SANTANA WAS SEATED across the table from Kenneth Vail in an interview room in the Homicide Unit.

"You didn't know?" Santana said.

Vail shook his head slowly and gazed at Santana with eyes that were as empty as a freshly dug grave. "I was using human subjects, yes. But I tested the drug on myself first. I've had no side effects, and my nightmares have substantially diminished."

"And because the drug apparently worked on you, it's going to work on everyone?"

"That was my hope."

"You needed more than hope, Dr. Vail."

Vail looked down as his white shirt, which was spattered with the blood of his dead wife. "I never ordered anyone killed and cremated."

"Was William Lessard involved?"

He shrugged his shoulders. "Not to my knowledge."

"How many vets did you give the drug to?"

He raised his chin. "Only a handful. But they all volunteered. None of them were forced to try it."

"How did they know you were looking for volunteers?"

"Jeff Tate brought them to the lab."

Santana hadn't seen any mention of that in the journal, but Jennifer Ward had said that Tate had offered her husband *help*.

"And did you use the drug on Tate?"

Vail nodded. "It seemed to be working."

"And how did Tate find out you were experimenting on vets?"

"Scott Rafferty told him."

"Was Rafferty one of your subjects?"

"No. I learned of Rafferty's PTSD while he was working at the mortuary, but he thought he was getting satisfactory results through more traditional methods. He told me about Tate, and we talked. Tate agreed to be a test subject. The drug seemed to help him—for a while. Then his symptoms returned."

"Only worse."

"Unfortunately, yes."

"How did you know Tate had a journal?"

"I required all the participants to keep journals detailing their reactions, sleep patterns, dreams, and so forth. All of them were supposed to return for follow-up and monitoring to judge their progress."

Santana wondered if Tate had hidden his journal in his safe when his fellow participants had started disappearing or turning up dead. "And that's what you were doing in his cabin. Looking for a journal while you had a woman beaten."

He spread his hands and shook his head slowly. "I never agreed to that."

"Were Greg Ward and Michael Johnson two of your test subjects?"

He nodded.

"But the drug didn't work on them."

"No."

"What about Mark Conroy?"

"He was one of Monica's students and had terrible nightmares after he fell in the river. She asked him if he'd like to volunteer to test my drug."

"But it didn't work on him either."

"Regrettably. But the tests gave me hope that I was close to a breakthrough."

"And how are the deaths of Greg Ward, Michael Johnson and Jeff Tate not your responsibility?"

He looked down at the floor. "I know what I was attempting was risky, Detective Santana."

"More than risky. Try unlawful and unethical."

He lifted his head. "I understand. But without some kind of cure, many vets will take their own lives, or the lives of others. They're human IEDs just waiting for something or someone to set them off."

"Three men are dead, Dr. Vail, because you were treating them like lab rats."

"I told you. I never ordered anyone killed."

"Maybe you didn't," Santana said. "Maybe your wife did. But it appears your experiments led to their deaths."

Santana was placed on a three-day administrative leave, per department policy, while IA completed their interviews and investigation. Whenever a weapon was discharged, the SPPD classified it as a critical incident. His Glock had been taken away from him in the privacy of the station, and he was given another used at the range. The confiscated gun would be held in the evidence room for seven years.

He spent considerable time with his case notes, typing his reports and trying to answer questions that still lingered like dark memories. The rest of the time he thought about Jordan. She had assured him that she was fine and had returned to work. Santana wondered if it was too soon.

The last night of his leave, Santana took her to dinner at the Downtowner Woodfire Grill on West Seventh Street in St. Paul. They sat at a table near the fireplace, listening to a jazz trio playing softly in the background as they shared a bottle of McGuigan Shiraz with their New York strip steaks.

"You don't need to keep asking me if I'm all right, John. I'm fine. Really."

"Your steak okay? You haven't eaten much."

"It's good. I'm just not that hungry."

He noted that the light in her pretty hazel eyes appeared eclipsed by a lingering darkness. "You saved our lives, Jordan."

"That's a good thing."

"Yes, it is," he said.

She stared at her hands resting on the tabletop, as though they belonged to someone else, and then at Santana again. He knew what she was feeling. What he didn't know was what she would feel tomorrow and for the rest of her life.

"Why did she do it?"

"You mean Monica Vail?"

Jordan nodded.

"Money, power."

"Is it really that simple?"

He could hear an undercurrent of frustration and anger in Jordan's voice. "In my experience, yes. It's a rare murderer who thinks they won't get away with it."

"If she just didn't—"

"She *did*, Jordan. You had no choice. You have to remember that. Always."

She looked at him in silence, then at the candlelight reflecting in her wine glass.

"Any leads on the serial killer?" she asked. "Or is that just another urban myth?"

He was relieved to hear that her thoughts had shifted from the shooting, though he knew it was only temporary. "I'm not sure there really is one."

"You think William Lessard could be another serial killer like Larry Ralston, the Angel of Death? They both worked around bodies. Ralston in a morgue, Lessard in a funeral home."

"Right now we've got nothing on him."

"Does Lessard have a record?"

"Not that I could find."

"What about Ronald Getz?"

"I doubt he's a serial killer. But he's going down for mur-dering Jeff Tate. I don't know if we can get him for killing Michael Johnson and Greg Ward. My guess is he drugged them with GHB and threw them in the river to make it look like they drowned."

"Like the college kids."

Santana nodded and poured more wine into his glass. Jor-dan declined his offer of a refill.

"Did Getz kill Scott Rafferty, too?" she asked.

"That one still bothers me. Rafferty never volunteered for Vail's experiment. Plus, he had significant amounts of propran-olol in his system. His death just doesn't fit."

The next morning, Santana was summoned to the office of Assistant Chief Tim Branigan. Rita Gamboni was there as well. Branigan was seated behind his desk, Santana and Gamboni in two chairs in front of it. Since they were sitting in chairs instead of on the couch, as they had been the last time they had met with Branigan, Santana knew this meeting would be more for-mal in nature—and far more stressful.

Before Branigan could launch into the meeting's purpose, Santana told them what he had learned about Kenneth and Monica Vail and how it had all gone down.

When he finished, Branigan said, "This whole case is FUBAR. Do you know what I'm talking about, Detective?"

"Fucked up beyond all recognition."

"Exactly."

"How exactly?"

Branigan looked at him as if he thought Santana was kid-ding. "Well, for one thing, we've got the wife of a prominent professor and researcher shot dead, along with the head of one of the largest venture capital firms in the state—or country, for that matter."

"Cady was murdered by one of his own security guards. And Monica Vail was about to murder Jordan Parrish and me."

"Have you considered how this might have turned out, Detective, if you had called for backup instead of acting alone?"

"I called for backup at the lab."

"But not at the cabin."

"There wasn't time. Jordan Parrish was in danger."

"At least she's a former Minneapolis police officer," Gamboni said.

Branigan's gaze shifted her way. "I fail to see how that's relevant, Commander."

"She's had training. She knew what to do given the situation. And she acted appropriately."

Santana gave Gamboni a nod, appreciative, as always, of her support.

"Is anyone talking?" Branigan asked.

"Thankfully, yes," she said. "Kenneth Vail. His attorney is trying to cut a deal with the Ramsey County Attorney's Office. I haven't spoken to Pete Canfield yet, but I suspect I'll be hearing from him soon if a plea can be worked out. Ronald Getz is trying to work out a deal as well. And each of the security guards is pointing a finger at the others."

Santana was relieved to hear that Gamboni had been involved in the plea bargains.

"It's a shame a man like Vail, someone who could do so much good, got way ahead of himself," she said. "He should never have used vets as subjects."

"Vail was on the right track, Rita. But in order to treat the PTSD symptoms, soldiers had to relive their traumatic experiences. Once those windows into the past were opened, the experimental drug couldn't always close them again."

"And their nightmares became unbearable."

"Yes. So Monica Vail convinced Getz to drug Michael Johnson and Greg Ward and toss their bodies in the river. But Jeff Tate put up a struggle and Getz strangled him and decided to cremate his body."

"William Lessard had to know about it," she said.

"He may well have, Rita. But there are no records of it and no one has implicated him."

Gamboni turned in her chair slightly so she could look directly at Santana. "One question I still have, John. Do you think Scott Rafferty, like Jeff Tate, was murdered?"

"Tate never implicated Getz in the death of Scott Rafferty. And Rafferty never was one of Vail's test subjects."

"But he knew about the testing and told Tate."

"Yes. But I don't believe Scott Rafferty knew that it was turning out badly," Santana said. "His death still bothers me."

"He got drunk and drowned," Branigan said. "End of story."

"Why did he have such a high dosage of propranolol in his system?"

"He was taking the drug for his PTSD."

"His psychiatrist had taken him off it."

"Maybe he had some left and took it."

"That's a possibility."

Santana saw a glimmer of satisfaction in Branigan's smile.

"There's one other issue that needs to be discussed, Detective. Commander Gamboni has informed me that your conversation with Devante Carter's mother did not go smoothly."

"She's a little upset because she believes both her sons were murdered by police officers."

"Are you being sarcastic, Detective? Because sarcasm has no place in this discussion."

"I'm just stating a fact. She's hiring an attorney and looking into Carter's death just as she did when her son Montrell was killed."

Branigan shook his head in frustration. "That's all we need."

"My guess is she knows about the video Devante took of the shooting. I think he convinced her to drop her lawsuit."

"Because he was blackmailing Detective Rafferty?"

"Yes. But now that Carter's dead, and at the hands of Rafferty, I don't think she's going to remain quiet."

"You think she has Carter's cell phone?"

"She could have. But that would mean that Carter left home without it, an unlikely scenario."

"Maybe she made a copy of the video," Gamboni said. "In case something happened to Carter. You know, like an insurance policy."

"Don't even suggest that," Branigan said.

"Well, we've got to consider the possibility."

"If she took the video to the press, it would be a public relations disaster for the department. I can't let that happen on my watch," Branigan said. "You've got to locate that phone, Detective Santana. And the sooner the better."

Chapter 29

KIMBERLY DALTON CALLED SANTANA as he was leaving the station and asked him to meet her at the Caribou Coffee on Grand Avenue near Dale in St. Paul. When he arrived and saw her seated at a table, he noted that she had some color in her cheeks and had added a pound or two to her thin frame. The weight had filled out her face some, and she had a healthy, girl-next-door-look.

"You look good," Santana said with a smile.

She blushed and drank from the cup of tea she had ordered. "My father thinks so, too."

"How's he doing?"

"He's upset about Hank Rafferty. Is Hank going to live?"

"I hope so. But he's still in a coma."

She nodded and looked out a window at the sunlight brightening the patio and glinting off the hoods of the cars parked in the lot. Then her eyes drifted back to Santana again. "I never thanked you for saving my life. I'm in out patient drug rehab now and I'm doing much better."

"I'm pleased to hear it."

She stayed silent for a while, as if she didn't know what to say next.

"I want to ask you about Devante Carter," Santana said.

Her face registered no surprise. "It's all right."

"Was he your dealer?"

She shook her head. "But he put me in touch with one."

"You met Carter through Scott."

"Yes. They worked together at the funeral home."

"Was Scott using?"

"When he first came back from overseas. But after he began seeing Dr. Roth, he pretty much quit." She lowered her gaze. "I had more trouble quitting. It's one of the reasons Scott broke up with me." She raised her chin. "I wasn't totally honest with you before, Detective Santana. Scott and I had no plans to marry."

"I understand," he said. "But the medical examiner found traces of cocaine in Scott's system, so he must've been using again."

She gave a little nod.

A question had lingered for a long time at the edge of Santana's awareness. "There's something else I've wanted to ask you," he said.

"About what?"

"The day the paramedics took you to the hospital, you told me that Scott's father was responsible for his death. What did you mean by that?"

She closed her eyes and opened them again, but offered no response.

"Kimberly?"

"Yes?"

"Tell me what you meant."

"I was drugged," she said with a little laugh. "I didn't know what I was saying."

"I believe you did."

She hooked a few strands of her long, dark hair behind an ear and smiled shyly. "I'm indebted to you, Detective Santana."

"Don't answer my question because you feel you owe me something, Kimberly, because you don't. Answer it because it's the right thing to do."

She sucked in some air and exhaled slowly. "Well, about a week before Scott disappeared, he told me that Devante Carter had a video of his father."

Santana's heartbeat kicked up a notch. He leaned forward. "The video of the Montrell Grissom shooting?"

"Yes."

"How did Scott find out about it?"

"Carter told him."

"Why would he do that?"

"You have to understand, Detective Santana, Scott was always bragging about his father being a cop. He used to say that he wanted to be one when he got out of the service. I think Carter wanted to hurt Scott because Hank killed his brother."

"What did Scott do?"

"He asked his father about it."

"What happened?'

"Hank denied it. He said Carter had just made up a story. Then Carter showed Scott the video."

"Is that why Scott and Hank were estranged?"

"Yes. It's probably why Scott had cocaine in his system when he died."

And maybe why Hank hadn't taken Kimberly seriously when she had called and told him Scott was missing, Santana thought. "So Scott went back to Hank and confronted him with the evidence."

She shook her head. "He went to Rachel."

"Judge Hardin knew about the video?"

"Uh-huh. Scott told her she needed to convince Hank to resign, or he'd go to the press."

"Did Hank know that Scott had told her?"

"I don't think so. I pleaded with him not to tell her, but Scott wouldn't listen."

"Why didn't you want Scott to tell Judge Hardin?"

"Oh, she had her own problems, what with her therapy and all."

"Do you know why she was seeing a psychiatrist?"

"Anxiety. She was petrified of getting up in front of people."

Santana could feel the heat from a sudden rush of adrenaline coursing through his bloodstream. "Do you know if she was taking any medication?"

"I believe so. But I don't know what it was."

"How come you didn't tell me this before?"

She blushed. "My father was Hank's partner. If it came out that he knew Hank had shot an unarmed Montrell Grissom and then helped cover it up, he would've lost his job."

"So why tell me all of this now? Your father could still lose his job."

"One of the ways I'm hoping to stay clean is by being honest. I think I started using heavily because I believed by not telling anyone this I was in some way responsible for Scott's death. And because, as you said, Detective Santana, it's the right thing to do."

"Have you spoken with your father about this?"

She nodded. "I think he'll do the right thing, too."

Santana finished his hot chocolate and paged through his notes. "I've got one more question."

"Okay," she said, hesitantly.

"When I was in Hank's study, I noticed a photo of Hank and Rachel on a boat. Would you know where that photo was taken?"

"Probably at the Windward Marina. Hank and Rachel bought one after they got married. Scott and I would take it out once in awhile."

"I thought Scott was afraid of water?"

"Oh, he was. He'd always wear a life preserver, and we never went far from shore. Mostly we'd just sit on the deck while the boat was tethered to the dock."

Santana nodded and added a new entry to his notebook. As he wrote, he recalled the dream of him sitting on the deck of a boat. When he looked up, Kimberly Dalton was staring at him.

"I have a question, too," she said. "But I'm afraid to ask it."

"Don't be."

She drank some tea and then settled her hands on the table. "Do you think Hank killed Scott?"

"No," Santana said. "But I have a pretty good idea who did."

A layer of thin gray clouds diffused the March sunlight, and a cold wind blew out of the north as Santana spotted Shanice Carter stumbling along a sidewalk near her apartment, a tattered jacket her only protection against the elements.

He pulled to the curb and opened the passenger side window. "Get in, Ms. Carter."

She nearly lost her balance as she stopped abruptly beside a four-foot cyclone fence encircling a small front yard, the gate hanging precariously on the fence by one hinge, like a broken limb.

"What you want?"

"I need to talk to you."

She straightened up, adjusted the hem of her jacket, and made her way carefully toward the sedan, as though she were walking on thin ice. "My son's funeral is tomorrow," she said, placing her hands on the roof of the car and leaning in the window. "I'm busy." Her breath reeked of alcohol.

"We can do this now, or at the station later. Your choice."

"You ain't much for sympathy, are you, Detective?"

"I'm truly sorry about your loss. But I need answers."

"And you think I have 'em?"

"That's what I intend to find out."

She hesitated a few seconds longer before opening the car door and sliding in.

Santana left the window open slightly and turned up the heat. "I want to ask you about Devante's cell phone again, Ms. Carter."

"We already talked about that."

"I think you know more than you're telling me."

She stared at him, her eyes without focus, but offered no reply.

"You saw the video of Montrell's shooting, didn't you?"

"If you're askin' me about it, then you seen it, too."

He shook his head. "I haven't. But I know it exists."

"Detective Rafferty murdered Montrell. And he murdered Devante, too. He goin' to answer for his sins."

"I'd question the use of the word 'murder,' Ms. Carter. And a jury might as well. But I'm not here to debate the circumstances of your sons' deaths. I want to know what happened to Devante's cell phone, and if you have a copy of the video."

"And why the hell would I tell you anything?" she said, her voice rising above a whisper. "You a police officer. Your department is coverin' up the deaths of my two sons. You just tryin' to protect your friend's reputation. You could care less 'bout my boys."

"I can see why you would believe that, Ms. Carter. But I'm on your side."

"Ha," she said. "That's a laugh. Since when are the police on the side of a black man accused of tryin' to kill a white police officer?"

Santana was reluctant to discuss the doubts that were swirling around him like a cold March wind. But he knew disclosure might be the only way to gain her trust. "I don't believe Devante shot Detective Rafferty, Ms. Carter. And I don't believe Rafferty killed Devante."

Her blurry eyes were large as she stared at him. "You just sayin' that so I help you."

"I'm saying it because I believe it's the truth."

She regarded him warily. "You askin' me to trust you like you different than all the rest."

"The rest being the police."

She nodded.

"I'm asking you to trust me because I want the truth, whatever it is."

"And whoever it hurts?"

"Yes."

She looked at him a long moment without replying, her glazed eyes trying to focus, her forehead wrinkled in concentration.

"Why don't you tell me about it," he said.

Chapter 30

THE CONTROLLED ACCESS GATE leading into the Windward Marina near downtown St. Paul was open, allowing Santana entrance into a small, dirt-covered lot in front of the sales office and store. As he got out of the Crown Vic, he could see empty slips, a long gas dock, and a large service and storage warehouse.

Inside the store, aisles of racks were filled with marine batteries, spark plugs, cleaning supplies, bilge pumps, life vests, tubes, line, anchors, oars, motor oil, and other mechanical fluids. A heavy-set man behind a counter wore a red Windward Marina sweatshirt and had long dark hair and a beard.

Santana introduced himself and showed him his badge wallet.

"I take it you're not looking to purchase a boat or rent a slip, Detective. Otherwise, you wouldn't have shown me your badge." He smiled good-naturedly.

Santana nodded. "I'd like you to tell me about your security."

"Is there a problem?"

"Not with the marina. Something else."

"Well, we've got someone on site twenty-four-seven," he said. "The place is well-lighted and fenced in. And you need a code to open the gate."

"Any video surveillance?"

He shook his head. "Too expensive."

Santana was disappointed. He thought for a moment. "Could someone come here after hours?"

"Sure, as long as they knew the entry code."

"Would security log them in?"

"Definitely."

"I need to see your March log," Santana said.

The young African American doctor standing beside Hank Rafferty's bed at Regions Hospital said, "He hasn't been awake long."

"Has he said anything?" Santana asked.

The doctor, whose nameplate identified him as Dr. Abasi, shook his head. "It's a small miracle he's even alive. But his vital signs are good."

"Has his wife been notified?"

"A call was just placed. How did you know he'd come out of his coma?"

"I didn't. I just stopped by to see if his wife was here."

"Well, she was here about thirty minutes ago, but she left before her husband awoke. She'll be here again shortly, I presume." Abasi looked at the chart on the clipboard in his hand and made a few notes. "You shouldn't stay long. Mr. Rafferty needs rest."

"I just want to ask him a couple of questions."

"Make it brief," Abasi said and left the room.

Santana figured he didn't have much time. He looked down at Hank, whose red eyes were focused on his. An intravenous line hooked on an IV pole fed antibiotics into a vein in his left arm, and a nasal cannula blew oxygen into his nose. "Can you speak, Hank?"

He lifted his left arm slightly and said, "Water," in a raspy voice.

Santana flagged down a nurse in the hallway, who retrieved an insulated covered mug with a straw. She helped

Hank sip the water and then set the cup on an overbed table beside a lipstick-stained Styrofoam coffee cup.

As the nurse picked up the coffee cup, Santana said, "Excuse me. Do you know who that cup belongs to?"

She peered at the cup and then at him, a curious expression on her face. "I believe it belongs to Mr. Rafferty's wife. She was drinking coffee when she was here earlier."

"I'll take the cup if you don't mind."

The nurse shrugged and handed it to him.

Santana waited until she departed before he put the cup in his sport coat pocket and spoke again. "Who shot you, Hank?"

Rafferty looked at him silently and then turned his head away.

"It was Rachel, wasn't it? She knew about the video. She knew if it went public, she could kiss her state Supreme Court appointment and her career good-bye. She killed Carter with your Walther, and then shot you with his Raven."

"Let it go, John," he said, his eyes staring blankly at the ceiling.

"I can't do that, Hank."

He turned his face toward Santana. "It doesn't matter now, John. No one has to know."

"We'd know, Hank. And we'd know it wasn't just Carter she killed."

Rafferty squeezed his eyes shut, as though he were trying to block out a painful memory. Santana wondered if he had lapsed into a coma again. When he finally opened his eyes again he said, "It can't be true."

"But you know it is, Hank. You knew right after Tanabe told you she'd found propranolol in Scott's system. Rachel was taking the drug for her anxiety. She picked up Scott at Billy's Tavern the night he disappeared and took him to his apartment. Then she slipped him an overdose of propranolol, drove him to your boat at the Windward Marina, and pushed him into the river. Scott and Rachel's names were listed on the marina log."

"But Scott was taking propranolol."

"No, Hank. His psychiatrist had quit prescribing it. You knew that."

"Oh, Jesus," Rafferty said as tears flooded his eyes.

"You confronted Rachel the night she shot you, Hank. She denied killing Scott. But then she had you contact Devante Carter and had him come over, because she wanted his cell phone and the video."

"What's going on?"

Santana turned and saw Rachel Hardin hurry into the room.

She rushed to the opposite side of the bed and held Hank's hand in hers. "Thank God," she said. "You're awake."

Hank's eyes remained locked on hers, but he kept silent.

Rachel looked across the bed at Santana. "Has he spoken?"

"Not a word."

"How long have you been here?"

"Just arrived."

Her gray eyes were swimming with doubts. "Well, thank you for coming by, John. I know Hank appreciates it. And so do I."

"I thought I'd hang around awhile."

"No need," she said with a false smile. "I'll look after him now."

"Like you looked after him before?"

She cocked her head. "I don't know what you mean."

"Sure you do, Rachel."

She let go of Hank's hand and stepped back from the bed, a flash of outrage reddening her face. "It's Judge Hardin to you, Detective Santana."

"I don't think so. At least, not for long."

"What in world are you talking about?"

"Two murders and an attempted third."

"What?"

"You're going down, Rachel."

"You're crazy," she said.

"No he's not," Hank said, seizing her by the wrist.

"Hank," she said, trying to pull away. "You can talk."

"Yes, Rachel," he said. "And I will."

Epilogue

THE MOON WAS FULL AND YELLOW as it rose slowly above the horizon and settled in a space between dark clouds, leaving a wide strip of light reflecting off the smooth surface of the Caribbean Sea. Santana watched from a bedroom window of a villa overlooking Simpson Bay on the island of St. Maarten. In the distance, he could see the city spangled with lights and yachts anchored in the bay, their hulls glowing like fluorescent fish. He stood silently in the shadowed darkness, listening to waves rolling onto the mile-long curve of white sand beach, the scent of salt water heavy in the warm breeze.

A Ramsey County grand jury had returned an indictment against Rachel Hardin in the murders of Devante Carter and Scott Rafferty and in the attempted murder of her husband, Hank. The fingerprint found on the broken capsule of propranolol had matched hers, as well as the type of lipstick found on the wine glass in Scott Rafferty's apartment and the lipstick found on the coffee cup in Hank's hospital room. A Windward Marina security guard had testified that Rachel had been with Scott Rafferty around the time of his disappearance. Ballistic tests had determined that the bullet that had killed Devante Carter had come from Hank Rafferty's Walther PPK found at the scene. The two bullets taken out of Hank Rafferty had come from Carter's gun.

Santana was confident that the preponderance of circum-
stantial evidence, together with Hank's testimony that Rachel
had, in fact, shot and killed Devante Carter and attempted to
kill him, would send her away for a long stretch. The governor
had already named her replacement to fill the vacancy on the
state Supreme Court.

Shanice Carter and her lawyer were in private negotiations
with the SPPD regarding the wrongful death of her son,
Montrell Grissom. She had agreed to turn over her copy of the
video of the shooting to the department in exchange for a
considerable cash payout and a signed confidentiality agreement. Devante Carter's cell phone had not been recovered. Santana suspected that Rachel Hardin had destroyed it.

Hank Rafferty had taken a permanent disability leave from
the force. David Dalton had been given a suspension and a
demotion in rank after admitting his part in the cover-up. By
working out a deal with Shanice Carter, Assistant Chief Tim
Branigan had managed to protect the department's reputation
while quietly dealing with Rafferty and Dalton.

Ronald Getz's DNA was matched with skin and blood
found under Tate's fingernails. He was indicted on a first-
degree murder charge for strangling Tate.

Jess, the security guard, was also indicted on a first-degree
murder charge in the death of Lyle Cady and for attempting to
murder Santana. Both Ray and Billy, the other security guards,
faced attempted murder charges.

Kenneth Vail was charged with third-degree murder for
indirectly causing the deaths of Michael Johnson, Mark Conroy,
and Greg Ward.

William Lessard had put his funeral home up for sale and
had moved away.

Jack Brody was planning to write a book about Kenneth
Vail's failed attempt at finding a drug to cure PTSD. It wasn't
the book he had wanted to write, but with all the vets returning

from Iraq, and PTSD in the headlines, he believed it had Holly-wood written all over it.

"And in your spare time you'll keep looking for a serial killer," Santana had said to him.

"Yeah. I'll keep looking. It doesn't make any sense that Ronald Getz would leave chaos symbols near the drowning sites."

"Unless Monica Vail wanted everyone to think a serial killer was responsible for murdering the vets."

"I don't buy it," Brody said.

"I didn't think you would. But no one can prove when the symbols were painted, or if they're just graffiti."

"You're not real helpful, Santana."

"You have anyone in mind?"

"I thought I'd start with William Lessard."

The department had held a party for Rita Gamboni at Alary's. Though Santana knew he would see her in the building on occasion, he also knew that things would change with Pete Romano's appointment as Homicide commander. Santana would no longer have Rita watching his back. But it was more than that. They had been through much together, as partners, lovers, and friends. Santana would always have feelings for her—and she for him.

When he heard Jordan stir, Santana turned away from the villa window, pushing thoughts of the case and the department out of his head as he went to the double bed, where she lay sleeping.

He crawled in beside her. "Bad dream?"

"Not too bad," she said, kissing him gently on the lips.

He lay facing her on the pillow, his eyes studying her in the pale light. "Not this time," he said.

"You think I should see a therapist about the nightmares?"

He wasn't sure if Jordan's nightmares would continue or if they would get worse over time. All he knew was that whatever way she chose to deal with her memories, he would support her.

"Only if you want to," he said.

"You never sought therapy."

"No," he said. "But that's just me."

"Are you ever going to tell me what caused the darkness you see in your dreams?"

"I don't know."

"Because you think my not knowing will keep me safe?"

"*Safer*," he said. "I can't guarantee your safety anymore than you can guarantee mine, though you did a heck of a job in Tate's cabin."

"I can try."

"Me, too."

She looked at him silently for a moment. "Maybe if I knew more about your past, it would help me understand you—help me understand my own dreams."

"Maybe," he said.

She brushed a hair off her forehead and then rested the palm of her hand on his cheek.

"Even if science develops a pill or drug that can erase painful memories, like Kenneth Vail attempted to do, you wouldn't take it, would you, John?"

"I don't think so."

"Because it's important for you to remember."

"Yes."

"And by changing or removing your memories, you wouldn't be who you are today."

"I don't think so."

"Well, I like who you are, John Santana. I wouldn't change a thing."

She smiled and kissed him again and then rested her head against his chest.

Santana felt the heat from her body as he listened to the rhythm of the waves and the sound of her soft breaths, till she finally fell asleep in his arms.

He wished for a moment that he could remain here forever, that he could somehow separate himself from the violent world in which he worked and lived, separate himself from his past. But he knew it was a false hope, like the false dawn of early morning. Because wherever he went, the dark memories that haunted his nights would go with him. And maybe that wasn't such a bad thing, he thought. Maybe we are all damaged in some way. Maybe that is the price we pay for being human.

Acknowledgments

On the personal side, the author would like to thank Abby Davis, Linda Donaldson, Lorrie Holmgren, Peg Wangensteen, and Jenifer LeClair for their friendship and for reading and editing the manuscript. Also, I want to thank Debbie Erickson from the Office of the County Manager and Commander Ty Sheridan of the Ramsey County Sheriff's Department for the wonderful tour of the Ramsey County Court House and holding cells, and to Judge Teresa Warner for taking the time to speak to me about the District Court.

As always I want to express my thanks and appreciation to my wife, Martha, for her love and support, and for helping and encouraging me to create the character of John Santana.

On the literary side, I owe many thanks to my editor, Jennifer Adkins, for her careful reading and attention to detail.

Lastly, it is true that many college students have drowned in Midwest lakes and rivers over the last decade, though the FBI and local police and sheriff departments continue to insist that these deaths are due to excessive use of alcohol rather than a serial killer. It is also true that neuroscientists are working to develop a pill that will erase painful memories. Researchers at the University of Montreal are using the drug metyrapone to reduce the brain's ability to re-record the negative emotions associated with painful memories. Metyrapone significantly decreases the levels of cortisol, a stress hormone that is involved in memory recall.

Researchers at Johns Hopkins are working to erase traumatic memories from the mind by removing certain proteins from the amygdala, as the fictional Dr. Kenneth Vail attempted in *Bone Shadows*. Other cutting-edge research is taking place in facilities throughout the world.

And so I leave readers with a question. If you were suffering from PTSD like John Santana and the soldiers in the novel, should you be allowed to take a pill that would permanently erase painful memories, knowing that it might alter your personality? You may not have to answer that question now. But given the amount and pace of current research, it appears that you, and we as a society, will have to answer that ethical question soon.

An Invitation to Reading Groups/Book Clubs

I would like to extend an invitation to reading groups/ book clubs across the country. Invite me to your group and I'll be happy to participate in your discussion. I'm available to join your discussion either in person or via the telephone. (Reading groups should have a speakerphone.) You can arrange a date and time by e-mailing me at cjvalen@comcast.net. I look forward to hearing from you.